TENURE

TENURE

A NOVEL

RICHARD LEVINE

SUNSTONE
PRESS

SANTA FE

Cover by Jeff Babcock

Sunstone books may be purchased for educational, business, or sales promotional use. For information please write: Special Markets Department, Sunstone Press, P.O. Box 2321, Santa Fe, New Mexico 87504-2321.

Library of Congress Cataloging-in-Publication Data:
Levine, Richard, 1932–
    Tenure: a novel / Richard Levine.—1st ed.
        p. cm.
    ISBN: 0-86534-350-0 —   ISBN: 0-86534-351-9 (pbk.)
    1. College teachers—Tenure—Fiction.   2. Universities and colleges—Fiction.
3. Atlantic Coast (U.S.)—Fiction.   I. Title.

PS3612. E83 T46 2002
813'.6—dc   2002021669

Published in SUNSTONE PRESS
Post Office Box 2321
Santa Fe, NM 87504-2321 / USA
(505) 988-4418 / *orders only* (800) 243-5644
FAX (505) 988-1025
www.sunstonepress.com

FOR
FELICE

FOR
BRUCE

" The bird would cease and be as other birds
But that he knows in singing not to sing.
The question that he frames in all but words
Is what to make of a diminished thing."

—Robert Frost, "The Oven Bird"

ONE

Billy Mann sat at his desk, ready to start another day, another week, another month on his journey to his tenure meeting. Doomsday, he whispered, and tried to look confident. In a few minutes his office hours would begin, students lining up to talk about their first long paper in his course.

On the drive to campus that morning, Billy thought about all the things he'd rather be doing. Halloween decorations were already up. The air breathed of pompoms and the smack of footballs snared by sure-handed wide receivers. It was only a few days before the arch enemies from up north invaded Hellman Stadium. Billy stopped at a red light and looked at the skeletons hanging from an almost barren maple in front of the Alpha house. It's going to be an early winter, his old neighbor told him each time they met at the curb when they brought out the rubbish. Just watch the squirrels. Their cheeks are bulging with nuts. Yes sir, an early winter.

A couple of young fraternity men in V-necked sweaters threw a ball to each other. They blew jet streams of warm breath onto their hands before every toss. Each fell back a few paces after an imagined snap from the center. Every pass was for the ballgame, the whole enchilada, the trip to the Rose Bowl. Each throw was a winner. Why not, Billy thought, why should those elitist brats be any different? He had his own fantasies. And wasn't he heroic in each victory? Why shouldn't Assistant Professor Billy

Mann throw the winning touchdown pass in the last seconds of the crucial game? Why not indeed? He had day-dreamed of far lesser victories, or at least lesser to the blond guy who pumped both arms toward the heavens in ostentatious joy while he shouted "touchdown, touchdown." Just like the fucking pros. No grace or decency anymore, even on the playing field. Damn millionaires dancing for their adoring fans. The other fraternity man was bending down to brush the fresh grass clippings from his cordovan loafers when the light changed and Billy responded to the horn-blower behind him. Probably a New Yorker, he thought, as his Honda jerked forward. Next time he'd take Sally's advice and get automatic transmission. Okay, okay, hold your horses. Don't get into a sweat over a few lousy seconds. He lit a cigarette. God-damn jerk. Billy was relieved when the horn-blower turned left at the next corner.

One of those simple anonymous pleasures of the road. The color receded below his collar. Another shit who wouldn't understand the stuff of my dreamings. Like my students. They, too, would throw their arms to the heavens on Saturday and give high fives all around when their ape-man running back broke through the enemy line to score for the blue and white. Bullshit. Billy ground out the cigarette in the car's poorly placed ashtray. Don't the Japs smoke? An environmentalist, he would never throw a butt out the window. More than once, he had blown his horn at morons who did just that. Not once did the criminals comprehend the sound. Usually they waved, assuming, Billy thought, that he was a friend tooting a greeting. Dumb shits. They wouldn't understand either.

He smiled at he entered the campus and one of his favorite fantasies floated over him. The jacket of his first book hung before his admiring gaze. He had often imagined the title and his name on a handsome green and gold background of an autumn grove. Always uneasy that he resembled Little Chandler at that delirious moment, he quickly moved beyond the richly imprinted dust jacket to the text itself. Jet black words on luscious, heavy cream pages. Words and words, paragraphs and paragraphs, chapters and chapters. All brilliant. And all of them thought brilliant by the best of his colleagues at the most prestigious universities in the country. Billy flushed in the euphoria of that dream. Not only would it produce tenure and promotion, but invitations to lecture and offers of handsome positions elsewhere.

He pulled his car into the parking lot behind his building. But those frat boys wouldn't waste a high-five on a book about the pastoral tradition in English poetry. No Rose Bowl for that one. He lit another cigarette. But his step would be lightened by that book. How his colleagues in the department would respond so differently after all those glowing reviews. Secretly envying him, as he had quietly envied so many of them for so long, they would mask their malice with warm-sounding congratulations. Some might have actually read the reviews. Slapping his back, they'd talk a little too loudly about how old Jones at Harvard loved the book and wasn't old Smith's last paragraph particularly flattering. One or two of the farts might have actually read the book. Their praise would invariably be undercut by piddling quarrels with some inconsequential footnote. Just to show him they read the thing and found him wanting as they examined the book oh so critically and smartly. Screw them. Silent malice was much better.

But the greatest fantasy pleasure was reserved for the new demeanor of the departmental graybeards. Especially the ones who always winced when he offered a current colloquialism at a meeting, or when he tossed an appropriate expletive into his commentary about some matter no one in his right mind should be interested in discussing in the first place. Only in the groves of academe do they bend their minds out of shape over such crap. But he loved the new body language after some of their fellow ancients wrote so approvingly about the work of the young Turk who not only talked cogently about the fucking curriculum, but, worse, smoked cigarettes. Unfiltered ones to boot. He'd never understand why the hell those septuagenarians had to worry about second-hand smoke. This was a regular refrain he'd chant to Sally after an afternoon listening to them bemoan the fate of humane learning. Only a silver bullet could kill them anyway. And to watch them eat at the faculty club. It made him sick. No butter, low fat salad dressing, diet bread. Jesus, do they let themselves enjoy anything?

Billy walked among the cars in the faculty parking lot. He adjusted his tie and checked his zipper as he approached a group of undergraduate students who stood with placards and distributed flyers to the few passersby who would take them. "Wipe Out Elitism." "Free Parking Lots For All." "Classism Sucks!" Another group of geniuses. What social conscience, Billy thought as he smiled sympathetically in their direction. He recognized one of them as a student in his Brit Lit class. Billy returned the wave and took a left onto the cracked flagstone path to the humanities building. The president was still looking for a rich donor who would give his name to the hideous structure for a mere million or two. He was sure precious little would go to any of the departments in that citadel of western culture. What the hell does President Richard Maxwell care about literature.

The building's interior was even cooler than the October weather outside. The nameless home of the humanities was always a refrigerator in the winter and a furnace in the humid summer. Its faux Georgian exterior contrasted with the pale green tiled walls of the fluorescent lighted halls. Looks like a gigantic shit-house, a visiting poet had once said as he walked toward the converted classroom pretentiously called the Creativity Center. There the poorly paid poet gave a reading to a paltry group of students. Faculty rarely showed up for readings unless they were inextricably involved in the program or wanted to be seen in the presence of an unquestionably major figure. All of them taught literature, of course, but they were not comfortable with living writers. They really feel like the second-class citizens they are, Billy said to anyone within earshot whenever he entered the room. Old Matthew Arnold understood the role we critics play. He'd nod wisely to the few students. An important role, but a secondary one. As long as you understand that, you'll never be too frustrated. Billy liked endorsing his views with references to great figures of the literary tradition. And not just to students. When he had an audience, in the faculty lounge or at a departmental meeting, he enjoyed quoting someone like Arnold to his colleagues who believed their work was far more important than the writers they wrote about.

But it was in the Creativity Center that he had his best audiences. He'd wave his hand in the direction of the picture gallery of long dead writers that lined one wall of the barracks-like room. Each was the stuff of a colleague's dissertation that earned the scholar a union card to teach literature. And some were actually more avant garde in their day than the writers who now show up here. But they can't draw our lit lovers from their cozy homes for a lousy hour. They probably don't want to miss Archie Bunker on the tube or down another bourbon before they reel away to sleep. And what do they dream about, I'd like to know. Billy always managed to attract one or two young undergraduate writers to listen to his indictment of their professors. He would warm to his subject, partly because he loved to act; partly because he actually believed the catalog of vices he dispensed; mostly, perhaps, because he knew the targets of his mock venom were not present and were unlikely to ever hear of Assistant Professor Mann's performances.

What do you think they dream about, these mentors of yours? Billy loved asking that question. He'd offer his practiced lascivious wink to his audience. He'd nod wisely in the direction of the bright looking young man, insinuatingly at a delicate young woman. Sally hated his rehearsals of these encounters. So, my young charges, what do you think Professor Allison dreams about? Chaucer and pilgrims and Canterbury? Is that the dream of a medieval scholar? Or might his imagination, set free by sleep, clothe him in a suit of armor and have him slay the dragon? Or does he show up in Guinevere's bedroom where she extends her beautiful arms in his direction? And does he suffer fear as the dragon's enormous nostrils spit fire and acrid smoke at him? Does he practice safe sex with the beauteous Lady G? Billy would always laugh rather than expect answers from the embarrassed, titillated students. He enjoyed the realization that his comments would be repeated to other students before the night was over. He wished he could overhear those conversations. The performance always concluded with pats on the young man's leg and the young woman's shoulder.

It was a large literature department and Billy hadn't yet been to enough readings to skewer all his colleagues. He would spare no one. His plan was to offer himself as the last professor to come under his humorous scrutiny before he started again with the alphabetically first of the full professors. But there was a way to go. Poor Allison was only the second associate professor to get the Mann treatment. If the Creativity Center's budget weren't augmented and more writers brought in each year, he calculated he might be a full professor himself before he had to lambaste Billy Mann.

Would he have the courage to joke about his dreams which, after all, he would not have to invent. Would he tell the bright young man and the delicate young woman about the lustrous dust jacket, the glowing reviews, the Rose Bowl clinching touchdown pass? Perhaps that last. Yes, the last. That one they would understand best. He saw them throw high fives at each other. Then they'll probably fuck. He'd think of that encounter while the dreary introduction of the writer droned on. Spent and naked, the young man and woman throw their arms to the ceiling. Touchdown.

Billy stopped at his mail box in the main office. Two secretaries were typing manuscripts. The receptionist smiled at him. "There's fresh coffee in the lounge. Made it only a few minutes ago. And one of your students called," she handed him a pink while-you-were-out slip, "said he had car trouble and can't keep his appointment." Billy glanced at the name. Fucking twit's missed every conference. He nodded thanks and collected his mail. Book catalogs and announcements from university presses interested him only because he wanted to see what the competition was up to. They also allowed him to imagine his dust jacket and name on one of those full-page ads reserved for important books. Generally, he dismissed the work being hawked in the catalogs. Their brief descriptions were enough to tell him that the books were unimportant or faddish silliness. His gaze always fixated on an announcement of a publication by someone he knew, especially one who had been in graduate school with him. Those were the real enemies of his well-being. Their names in print lacerated his psyche. He was certainly smarter than they, and yet their books were published and his was still in progress. Even elephants have shorter gestation periods than you, Sally sometimes commented bitterly when Billy railed against his former classmates. They were soon to have honest-to-God reviews while his were still mere figments of his imagination. And he was more articulate than they. Better groomed and dressed. Better liked by his students. Even though he had not seen those losers for years, he believed these things to be true.

Billy leafed through his mail as he walked the lavatory hall to his office. He threw his briefcase on a chair and closed the door. Carefully untacking a signed poster of the Beatles, he examined himself in the now revealed large mirror. He smiled at the reflection of a ruggedly handsome college professor. Too bad he found Marlboros too strong. He tried a nonchalant wave. He bent forward to explore the spaces between his near perfect white teeth, lest there be even the smallest remnant of breakfast caught in one of the almost invisible crevices. Nothing must taint his winning smile which he reserved for students and members of the tenure committee. Today was a brown day. Your Ronald Reagan color, Sally said as he left the house. A muted brown tweed jacket over a beige denim shirt open at the collar, corduroy slacks just a shade lighter than the jacket, tan desert boots, sporty Eddie Bauer thick ribbed brown socks. Billy's black hair, fashionably long, was full around the temples of his silver framed aviator glasses. It was always cut so it fell perfectly. He sometimes thought he spent as much money at the barbershop as his next door colleague did at the bookstore. He toyed with the idea of a discreet earring, but a nagging fear of being thought gay kept him from that. I can't remember which ear used to be the code. Even athletes wear them now. But, who knows, there might be others out there whose perceptions of earrings were frozen in a time past. And those cretins might be important to him. Even though he liked the idea of a discreet gold post, he had decided it wasn't worth the risk. Not yet. Not until he had his tenure. Not until he was invincible.

The neighbor was also standing for tenure this year, and Billy wished some terrible malady would befall him. He hadn't yet decided on the precise disease which would wither his adversary, but there was still time to create an appropriately solicitous hospital visit for a forthcoming imaginative scenario. He had already created bits of the drama in which he'd play the sympathetic teammate to the dying Lou Gehrig. It was delicious.

In the uncomfortable real universe where he was not the author of the script, however, the unanswered question remained. Would the department recommend two assistant professors for tenure in the same year? This question haunted Billy. If only one were to be awarded the prize of a guaranteed lifetime of teaching and writing, would it be Billy or Honest Abe?

Abraham Smith looked into Billy's office and smiled. "How's it going?" He sounded as though he really cared about the answer to the greeting he offered every morning.

Billy responded with his nonchalant wave. "Couldn't be better, Abe."

"Glad to hear it. Talk later. Got a bunch of kids coming in."

Billy lit a cigarette and shook his head in disgust. Always the same fucking words. Always those sentences without subjects. He mimicked. Talk later. Got a bunch of kids coming in. He flicked his ash with an expert snap into his large ashtray whose white ceramic interior depicted diseased lungs. Sally's parents had given him this monstrosity for his last birthday. Real subtle people, his in-laws. He could always count on his mother-in-law to turn in an oh-my-God-he's-going-to-smoke performance whenever he took out a cigarette. Then her chest-clasping, sighing search for their one frigging ashtray. Of course she knew exactly where it was, but she had to go through her dippy routine. When she finally located the thing, an old transparent green glass candy dish with three short stubby legs that every woman of her own mother's generation collected, she'd place it next to her son-in-law as if she were delivering a bag of shit. She screwed up her nose and turned to her husband, long-suffering Harry, and mentioned some acquaintance who had recently packed it in because of cigarette smoking. It didn't matter what the actual cause of death was, smoking was the culprit. An auto accident, suicide, falling under a lawn mower, being struck by falling frozen crap from an airliner, they were all the same. In Hazel's eulogy, the victims were all done in by cigarettes.

Looking at her back, Billy wanted to burn her ass with his lighter. But it was one of those child-proof jobs that never lit on the first try. Damn kids. Life is controlled by the brats of the world. More than once he had thrown a new bottle of aspirins at the bathroom wall after fruitless minutes of trying to line up the two tiny triangles. He never had finger dexterity, but those bottles had been created by a monster. He sympathized with the arthritics of the world. So Hazel would turn around to see Billy, lighter in hand, bent down behind her. Only God knows what perversions her warped mind would conjure up. And then she'd certainly look at her daughter and start her god-damned chest clasping and sighing. If she thought he tried to burn his mother-in-law's ass, imagine what he must do to her darling Sally.

So Billy merely nodded at the green glass, grateful that he had something in which to deposit his ashes. He took a deep breath of smoke and blew it in the direction of the lamenting mother-in-law who continued her account of a local woman who was mugged and raped only last week. And we know why, don't we, whispered Billy to Sally. Sometimes he couldn't resist playing Hazel's game, especially at breakfast in her house. Sipping his coffee and longing for the best cigarette of the day, but stopped by the knowledge that no one ever smoked at Hazel's table, he would gratuitously continue a conversation that had never existed. Yes, I do think we've finally uncovered the reasons for the Nazi atrocities in the concentration camps and the Japanese torture of so many millions. The huns and the nips smoked cigarettes. Hitler and Hirohito were chain smokers, don't you know.

Billy emptied the ashtray into a tissue which he would later wet and discard in the men's room, opened the office window, and activated a Glade air freshener kept behind a photo of Sally at the left corner of his desk. The Georgian shit house, after all, boasted a smoke-free environment. Replacing the Beatles poster, he was ready to admit students to his carefully prepared presence.

Abraham Smith, still healthy despite his neighbor's imaginative voodoo, dropped his ancient green canvas bag on his desk and glanced at his appointment book. There was time for a cup of coffee before the first conference. Abraham, who disliked the nickname Abe, enjoyed morning conversation in the faculty lounge. He was fond of his colleagues and except for their penchant for gossip, he looked forward to the coffee and professional talk that set him up for the day in the same way that a very dry martini with Eleanor prepared him for an evening at home. Abraham knew full well that he romanticized both daily events, but they gave him an added sense of warmth and security that were important ingredients in the rhythms of his well-ordered life. His lectures, too, held their place in the routinized existence he cherished. They were meticulously crafted. Abraham disliked the notion of winging it in class, the sort of master-of-ceremonies, stand-up comic approach favored by some members of the department. Either they're lazy or they just want to be popular entertainers, he'd complain over his martini. But even about teaching, which he cherished equally with his scholarship, his complaints only glanced in the direction of the nasty or the vindictive. In the words of his closest friends, Abraham Smith was simply a nice guy. Even his two children thought of their father in those terms. Rushing inexorably toward adolescence and away from devotion to home and parents, Teddy and Ann held fast to both. It was not an easy feat for youngsters surrounded by friends who were already scornfully deriding their parents. But some of those suddenly old-looking kids thought well of Abraham. Teddy and Ann were lucky to have such a neat dad.

Abraham entered the faculty lounge. Another ugly room that had been renovated from a barren classroom to something approaching the task force's notions of what a faculty gathering place in an old British university should look like. Leaded glass windows of an amber hue had been installed as a gift to the department from a retiring dean who had once been a professor of literature. There had been a few dollars remaining in his contingency budget and no longer fearing the slings and arrows of the scientists, he allocated them to his former department. Admittedly old Dean Wallace had left town for a semester's leave in England, his reward for subservient service to the university's president, before the announcement of his gift of leaded windows was made public. But the funds had been allocated and the renovation of the faculty lounge had begun. Chairman Walter Henry had immediately convened a task force, a term he preferred to the more common committee, to create a proper lounge. It was, of course, to carry the name of its benefactor. And the faculty lounge task force had done a rather decent job. They managed to inveigle a few gifts from alumni who had not gone into teaching; they organized book sales; they badgered President Maxwell to the point of his distraction until he kicked in enough to purchase several overstuffed easy chairs, sofas, and a few heavily ornamented iron lamps with faux Tiffany shades. Bookcases were appropriated from the library and paintings were permanently borrowed from the university art gallery. A handsome silver coffee service disappeared from the provost's office between the time the former occupant of that position retired and his successor was named. Eyes were sometimes raised at literature department receptions, but the elegant service remained in Wallace Lounge. Even the dark green tiled floor, some bureaucrat's idea of an impressive contrast to the pale green walls, was covered by three large oriental rugs which Mrs. Henry had donated after the death of a distant wealthy aunt.

Abraham smiled in the direction of two elderly professors seated in twin red velvet wing back chairs. They sipped coffee and spoke quietly to one another, their morning newspapers spread on their laps. As Abraham poured coffee from the 30-cup urn, the good silver service being reserved for those special occasions to which Provost Lansing was not invited, he nodded at his surroundings. Even on sunny days the amber windows prevented the room from becoming too bright. The soft light was exactly right. This room should be different. Like the interior of a great cathedral, it should envelop its occupants with a sense of difference. It should offer a contrast with the workaday world which surrounded Wallace Lounge.

Abraham thought the room was so special that he was disappointed when students were invited to join their faculty for the department's annual Christmas party. It was inappropriate for students drinking punch from paper cups and dropping fruitcake crumbs on the ancient rugs. Abraham thought it bordered on the sacrilegious to ever have students in the room at all. In each of his few years at the university he had suggested that the Creativity Center would be a more spacious room for the party. It was larger than the lounge to be sure, but Abraham's recommendation had little to do with the comfort of the party-goers. A small irritant, but one of the few times that Abraham Smith dissembled at department meetings.

He joined two young women instructors who had waved him to their corner.

"Good morning, comrades," Abraham smiled as he lowered himself into his favorite easy chair. He placed his cup on an old mahogany table that had once belonged to Eleanor's parents. Conspicuously out of place in their starkly contemporary living room with its angular white leather couch, Eames chairs, Scandinavian abstract geometric rug, large framed reproductions of two Mark Rothkos, and an original Roy Lichtenstein which Eleanor could not resist bidding for at an auction in New York. It was a room which had taken Abraham a long time to get used to, but which now he loved as much as his wife did. The more he looked at the living room's straight lines and clean whiteness, the more its linearity spoke to order and regularity.

The only other pieces of Eleanor's family home to survive were in his study. A brooding dark desk and credenza, both fronted with carved oriental-looking reliefs, which he had admired when Eleanor's parents were still living, were saved from the estate sale. The mahogany table was spared only because Eleanor thought it was perfect for the dreadful Wallace Lounge, the love of whose ambience she did not share with her husband. She was glad only that she didn't have to visit that room very often. "It gives me the willies. I think it's more appropriate for an academic mortuary than for guys like you who teach something as living as American literature."

"Your chair, as usual," said a leggy Joan Eastland. "What are you going to do when that antique wears out, Abraham?" She laughed affectionately.

"Did Robert Frost ever write about his favorite chair?" asked the other woman, Helen Abrams, making reference to the subject of the book Abraham was writing.

Not yet having completed their dissertations, Joan and Helen were instructors. They would receive battle-field promotions to assistant professor when their doctorates were finally awarded. Abraham liked them both.

"So what's the news from the front?" asked Joan. She adjusted her black leather mini skirt. Joan was the hippy member of the young group of the department, our hope for the future as Walter Henry referred to them. Joan was asking about the tenure and promotion task force's meeting of the previous Friday. "How many of you guys will they promote this year?"

"They're only two of you, for Christ's sake. What's the big deal? Walter had to appoint a task force to decide if the department can stand two promotions in one year? God, it's stupid." The older faculty had decided that Helen was their stereotypical New Yorker and, therefore, they accepted her brashness as a genetic fact over which she had no control. In reality, Helen was from Tenafly, New Jersey. "They figure all Jewish dames in this racket must come from New York. Who cares? New York, New Jersey. Abrams, Abromovitz. It's all the same to them." But Helen felt deeply about the image that had been foisted upon her. That she attempted to embellish it in public was more play-acting defense than natural proclivity. "And if they decide on only one, whatever their stillborn reasoning, it's got to be you."

"Billy Mann? No way," added Joan. "If they only knew the way that conniver talked about them, they'd fire him rather than promote him."

Abraham knew these two were squarely in his corner. He also knew they were mere instructors who were fighting for their own places in the department. "If only they could vote," Eleanor had said more than once as they cleaned up after a dinner party where Joan and Helen had joined other good friends at the Smith table.

Walter Henry was pouring coffee into a mug bearing the words "numero uno," a gift from Billy Mann at the last Christmas party. He looked around the sparsely occupied room, wondering which of the two groups he would join. He decided on the future of the department and greeted the old-timers on his way to the mahogany table which he admired. "And how are the youngsters today?" He sat down in an uncomfortable straight back chair that he hoped would ease the pain in his lower back. "Have a good weekend?" It was more than a rhetorical question since he reported everything, even unimportant conversations, to Margaret each evening. The power behind the throne, Maggie Henry stored information like a CIA operative. You never know what might be significant or when.

An organizer of people and events, she was a firm believer in conspiracies. Whether it was the assassination of JFK or imminent plans to overthrow her husband, she was ever mindful of possible gatherings of dark clouds on brilliantly clear summer days. Life, like the weather, she often reminded Walter, is changeable. Maggie always carried a folding umbrella in her large handbag. And you better do the same, she urged her husband and children. And I speak literally as well as metaphorically. The familiar movements of her handsome face and athletically trim body punctuated her advice when the twin boys went off to high-school at seven and Walter to the university at eight. Alone at the kitchen table after her men left, Maggie would compose her list of activities for the day. She believed in careful planning.

Helen smiled as she studied her chairman's crooked face. "Had a great time," she lied. Helen had spent the weekend cleaning her one-bedroom apartment and bemoaning the lack of eligible men in the small college town. She would never tell that to Walter for fear that Maggie might act the match-maker. She dreaded the need to please the chair's wife as she feared the man Mrs. Henry might think an appropriate match for the New Yorker. She pondered Walter's gray eyes to see if he believed her. Those eyes were the best feature of a countenance otherwise thrown together in a haphazard way by some drunken genetic engineer. As handsome as Maggie was, her husband's claim to fame was not his face. Luckily for them, the twins had inherited their mother's features. They certainly must be the best-looking sixteen year-olds at University High.

Having been born late in the Henrys' marriage, they were treated like princes come to save a failing dynasty. And Maggie insisted that her three men look like royalty. This morning Helen admired the expensive tailoring of Walter's gorgeous pale blue, soft wool jacket, complemented by a striped blue and white shirt and a tie that looked like the pattern of a Tiffany window. He dressed so well one rarely noticed how really homely the chairman was.

"Wonderful. I sometimes think it isn't easy for single women in this town. And how about you, Joannie?"

She hated the diminutives Walter used with members of the future of the department. Helen was spared only because he couldn't come up with one for her. "Did you break some young guy's heart?" He winked at Abraham who colored slightly. Walter was not a smarmy man. Rather, he often said or did things he thought appropriately hip for an older man attempting to make younger folks feel comfortable in his presence. He wanted to be with it in the company of his junior colleagues. James and Jeremy groaned when they heard their father's recitations at dinner. Oh, Dad, you didn't really say that, did you? They'd have laughed out loud if their mother hadn't been at the table, but they remained straight-faced in her presence rather than risk the lecture about well-bred young men's behavior. That sort of behavior might be expected at Helen Abrams' dinner table, but certainly not at ours. They knew the routines by heart. At night they'd sometimes mimic their parents in the security of their suite, as Maggie called the rooms she had created for the princes.

The wall between two bedrooms had been taken down and the boys had a two-room suite. A bedroom with twin beds and a study with matching desks and easy chairs. Jeremy and James also had their own bathroom. Young men need their privacy, Maggie had told the architect when they sat at the kitchen table planning the renovation. Walter had suggested a separate entrance for use when the boys became active young men, but Maggie thought the suggestion beneath consideration. She assured the architect and Walter that her boys would be different. Both men smiled inwardly.

Joan counted the fingers on her right hand. "Let's see if I can remember them all." As she bent down each finger, she thought of the men she had actually encountered since last Friday. There was the mechanic who checked her anti-freeze, the kid who bagged her groceries at the market, her landlord who had held up his leaf rake in greeting, and the long distance telephone operator. She knew she was stretching on that fourth since he had been only a voice at the other end of her inquiry. But given this town's meager possibilities, what difference could that addition make in her pathetic inventory. It was a bad joke anyway. "Yes, Walter, only four broken hearts this weekend." Helen always lamented that most of the best looking single men back east were homosexual. Joan would settle for a gay companion after two years locked in the greeting-card pretty college town she now called home. Anyone to share a dinner with, go to the movies, have a beer after class. As long as he didn't teach at the university. She longed for talk that didn't center on things academic. Her last fling, two dinners and one bedroom disaster, was with an assistant dean who kept talking about class size and space utilization. That is, before he apologized for not being able to get it up. The pressures of higher administration, you know. She smiled at the memory of having to comfort a nearly weeping, boring factotum because his pecker wouldn't respond to her charms. She had said all those stupid things she had heard in bad movies. Joan had been ashamed of herself when she reported the incident to Helen. "At least he's a man," her friend had said after listening to the story of his bashful tool. "And he's not half-bad looking. You could probably cultivate him and train his dick."

"Not a bad weekend's work," laughed Walter. "I noticed the list of suicides in the police report this morning. Four young men dying for un-requited love." He slapped Abraham's thigh. "Puts you in mind of your bachelor days, doesn't it?" The chair thought he was in good form. Abraham changed the subject. "What did you decide at your meeting Friday?" He asked the question as casually as he could, but he had wanted the answer so badly, he nearly called the chair at home on Saturday. He almost wished he hadn't given up smoking, for it would have been the perfect time to light a cigarette as off-handedly as Bogart always did. What better way to show his lack of concern than to light up and blow a perfect smoke ring.

"I was going to discuss that with you and Billy this morning. But since you brought it up." He glanced at the two instructors. "Nothing confidential you understand. I'll be announcing the decision to the whole department anyway." He sipped his coffee. Perhaps he, too, would have liked a cigarette. "The task force on personnel decided we can promote only one person this year."

Helen interrupted. "But why? Why only one when there may be at least a couple who should be considered?" She wanted to tell him she thought they were all idiots, but her job and her friend's future throttled her tongue.

"Oh, we'll certainly consider every qualified candidate. But we'll rec-ommend only one for tenure and promotion."

"Why?" Helen asked again. This time her voice betrayed a hint of anger.

"Because one is the number we decided on."

"That's an answer, Walter, not a reason." Helen used the tone she reserved for students who rephrased her questions rather than answer them. "What's the logic of the committee's decision?" She knew that word would rankle the chairman.

"Well, Professor Abrams," Helen's tone had not gone unheeded, "in the opinion of the task force, the department should not grow at a rate of more than one new associate professor per year." Walter made a mental note to rehearse Helen's insubordination to Maggie. That report alone would enliven the cocktail hour. His wife particularly enjoyed skewering Helen Abrams.

"But Walter, you still haven't answered Helen's question." Joan spoke quietly and calmly.

"Well, I think I have." Walter stood up. "I'm sorry some women aren't satisfied with my response." He was about to leave when he added, "someday you'll appreciate the collective wisdom of senior faculty, especially when they convene in a task force mode." He was about to sit down again, but thought better of it. "Someday you two will finish your degrees and you'll be happy with them when they promote you to assistant professors."

"But that's an automatic promotion," said Helen. "At least that's what you said when you hired us. Why would a task force," she preferred not to irritate him again, "be formed to consider something that's pro forma?"

Walter smiled as he backed away. "You'll learn that nothing's automatic in this life." He thought of his wife's umbrella. "Things can change. Like the weather." He paused, realizing that battlefield promotions were indeed automatic. "Of course I'm not suggesting that there'll be any difficulties in your cases. But it's best to carry an umbrella, even on a beautiful summer day."

The chairman paused for a few moments to chat quietly with the two old professors. They all laughed.

"I wonder what the farts were chortling about?" Helen looked at Abraham. "Well, you certainly entered the fray, didn't you?" She shook her head. "Sometimes I worry about you, my friend. You acted like you didn't even care about the stupid decision." She lit a long mentholated cigarette. "It's only your frigging career they're talking about." She blew a bluish-white stream in the direction of the old professors. "I bet they're immune even to second-hand smoke." Helen screwed up her eyes and ground out the half-smoked cigarette. "This clearly wasn't one of the fifty percent I enjoy." She nodded in the direction of her senior colleagues. "Don't you wonder if they'll ever retire?"

"What, and deprive the youngsters of their wisdom. And think of their students who would be denied the nap time they look forward to when those scintillating dons lecture," added Joan. "Can you imagine sitting in their classes. Rosenthal droning on about John Dryden."

"I don't believe any one actually reads that stuff except under duress."

"Or Willoughby telling them about watermarks and proper bibliographic methodology."

"Another winning subject," Helen piped in again. "I'd love to get a peek at their lecture notes. I bet they're as yellow as Ben Rosenthal's complexion."

"Or Calvin's teeth."

"Okay, ladies. You're speaking of your elders, if not your betters." Abraham held up his hand. "Did you really expect me to challenge Walter's news about the decision? What good would that have done? He'd only report it to them."

"After he reported to dear old Maggie," said Helen, lighting another Virginia Slim.

"And then there'd be at least one strike against me when they had to determine which one of us to recommend."

"Maybe true," said Joan, "but you can bet your bottom dollar that Billy Mann wouldn't have let the chair off the hook so easily. Oh yes, dear Billy boy would have challenged the decision and ingratiated himself with Walter at the same time."

"He's a master of self-serving bullshit." A light stream of smoke floated in the air above her gesturing hand. "I still squirm whenever I think of the mealy-mouthed toast he made last Christmas."

"With a paper cup of kool-aid no less. . ."

"when he presented Walter with that mug. . . "

"which he said he and Sally had to order from Chicago."

"I don't know how she can stand living with that four-flusher." Another puff of smoke wafted to the ceiling of Wallace Lounge. "I'm surprised they haven't added a Michelangelo-lookalike up there."

"And it was the only gift delivered at the holiday party." Joan, too, worried about Abraham's flaccidity in the face of the campaign Billy had already mounted as much in his own service as against his major challenger. Nice guys usually finish last in this business. Abraham's reluctance to blow his own horn, never mind take on Billy Mann, was a subject both women had frequently discussed with Eleanor. Abraham's wife was not unaware of her husband's public diffidence, but always she assured his friends that he was a lot tougher than he appeared.

The Russian Coffee House was always crowded. Eleanor stood by the front door, looking for Joan and Helen. She smiled and nodded at the waving hands from a corner window table. The place was a favorite with university types, but not many students could afford the steep prices the émigré owner got away with. No one thought the Russian Coffee House would survive, but here it was into its third successful year. The proprietor was the father of two faculty members, brothers who joined the university in the same year and were now distinguished professors of physics and music. Igor was mentioned as a future Nobel Laureate and Nicholas was conductor of the university symphony orchestra and a well-known composer. When they were awarded tenure, the brothers brought their parents and sister to the United States and the three of them ran the coffee house. Dressed in costumes that reminded Helen of Cossacks or walk-ons in a Moussorgsky opera, Boris and Ivana rushed around the busy shop while Natasha, better versed in the operation of the computerized cash register, sat on a high stool behind the counter. She wore a white blouse brightly embroidered around the square neckline with happy flowers of blue, green, and yellow. The Petrovs had decorated the coffee house with shiny copper samovars, red mini-blinds, a red ceiling, and black and white tiled floor. The chairs glistened in their black enamel and surrounded red glass-topped tables. During the day the stereo delivered Russian music, while a trio of ethnic-looking musicians entertained from a back corner each evening after five. Boris had decided to add a light supper fare only a year ago and was now thinking of a full dinner menu.

"Everything but pictures of Yeltsin," said Eleanor who had been one of the early doubters.

"Or of Clinton and the drunk laughing themselves silly at that embarrassing press conference," added Helen who had little sympathy for anything Russian. The best she could say was that next to the Poles, even Russians looked good. "But I must admit the coffees are delicious and the cakes are really terrific."

"They better be at four bucks a throw," said Joan as she pointed toward the strudel on her plate. "Sorry, Eleanor, but I couldn't wait. I was famished after three classes and a department meeting where we had to listen to Billy give a report on the future of the department."

"You do know, don't you, Walter made him the chair of the task force?" In this company Helen freely let loose her distaste for that appointment. "That shit-heel's interested only in the future of Billy Mann."

"But he gave one great performance today. I have to give him credit for that," said Joan, "even though I agree with Helen." She stabbed the last piece of strudel with her fork. Only flakes of pastry surrounded by powdered sugar remained on her black and red plate. "He scored big points with the old boys today." Before the words were out of her mouth, she was sorry she said that. Joan colored and pushed the crumbs into a small pile that covered the gold embossing at the center of her plate.

"Trying to obliterate the family crest, toots?" Helen said lamely, trying to rescue her friend from having to apologize.

"Oh, don't be so protective of my feelings." Eleanor waved their embarrassment away. "You know we do talk about Billy and this whole tenure thing." She smiled and reached for Helen's cigarettes. Eleanor smoked only occasionally. "I've told you before that Ab and I are not oblivious to what's going on." Only she and a few friends called him that. She lit her cigarette and gazed into the burning match. "He's able to take care of himself. Honest, girls, Ab is not the pushover some of his colleagues think he is." She inhaled deeply as much more addicted smokers do. "And if Billy Mann thinks he's dealing with some easy prey, he's in for one big surprise."

"So what's the strategy?" asked Helen. "When does Honest Abe roll out the heavy artillery?"

"You'll see soon enough. All I can say now is that his armored division is on the move as we speak." Even if she didn't believe her own words, she laughed the laugh of the cat that swallowed the canary. "Now let's have some girl talk."

Joan and Helen knew Eleanor well enough to know she was lying. Rather than call her on it, they followed her lead. Helen believed she was among the world's greatest protectors of husbands.

The chairman's office was the one great exception to the building's architectural mediocrity. Walter's predecessor, who had served the department for fifteen years, had been in on the planning of the humanities building and he had fought successfully to insure a chair's office that would befit a king. Walter sat on a caramel brown soft leather chair behind a teak executive desk. That desk itself had produced gasps of astonishment in the purchasing office when the invoice arrived from Maurice Vallency in New York. It was to be only the first gasp from the accountants. The former chair had gone on a shopping spree in the Big Apple and had spared no expense in selecting furnishings for his new office. The conference table, couch, and easy chairs had all come from fashionable shops. If the clerks had not read his university credit card with care, they would have assumed their client represented the CEO of a Fortune 500 company. Even the delicate drapes that flanked the picture windows were pricey. A soft beige color, they complemented the sea of earth tones that greeted visitors to the office. The former chair had even made sure the wall of glass that ran the length of the office faced the central mall and offered a splendid view of the criss-crossed, red-bricked paths that moved through grass and around grand old trees to the library. The chair's space had originally been allocated to two classrooms, but the architects yielded to the professor and reconfigured the plans to produce the best chairman's office on campus. Not even the president could boast a better view.

Alone in his inner sanctum, with an hour of peace before the next task force was to occupy the teak and leather chairs encircling the conference table, Walter swiveled his chair to the glass wall. He sipped coffee from the infamous numero uno mug and nodded appreciatively at the golden-leaf covered grassy mall. Small clusters of sweat-shirted students sat on and around benches which lined the walkways. Like his boys, they didn't mind the brisk air and cold ground. He used to do the same thing years ago before his lower back went out. Luckier than the twins, he hadn't been reminded daily of the tornado that could come sweeping out of the blue west, ready to destroy their J. Press clothes, if not their very beings. Walter enjoyed looking at the students whose vignettes seemed so happy and carefree. Still innocent undergraduates able to take pleasure in the slightest pressure of a friend's hand or the songs of the birds not yet ready to head south. Graduate students were already well on their egocentric, humorless journey to facultyhood. God, but they so soon lose the ability to laugh.

Walter carefully placed his mug on the tile coaster displaying a portrait of his meal ticket, old Will Shakespeare. The tile had been a birthday present from Maggie's parents. Even though they never thought a professor quite adequate for their Margaret, they were pleased at least that he was a teacher of the great bard. They surely had in mind for their only daughter a husband of greater substance. A diplomat perhaps; at least a professional whose status and income in modern America were more substantial than a college professor's. Nevertheless, they remain rather happy in the fact that their son-in-law was a department chairman and had published three scholarly books which they displayed prominently in their handsome old house. But most pleasing to the Tafts was the gift of grandsons.

Not related to the great conservative political family, John and Millicent Taft did not discourage those who assumed they were. Of their three children, only Margaret had followed the biblical injunction to be fruitful and multiply. There was no hope that her brothers would continue the family line. Robert and Howard, their names more than coincidental, would not sire offspring. One had agreed to a vasectomy to satisfy his wife's career; the other, about whom the parents rarely spoke, was gay or, as Millicent preferred to say, was still looking for the right girl. Of their daughter-in-law they boasted, even if in private they lamented her barrenness. But Rebecca was a leading Washington attorney and a major consultant to the Republican Party. Robert could have done worse.

A lawyer also, he labored for a minor government agency, filing briefs against polluters of the environment which his parents thought a more fitting position for a rotund, balding liberal. But they were a good looking couple whom the elders enjoyed showing off to their friends. John invariably kept the two in animated conversation on the front lawn whenever the tall, trim couple returned from their morning jog. He liked to believe his neighbors envied the good health Robert and Becky exuded. If only there were a little Taft to run with them, his own sweat shirt stained with the exertion of a long run on a warm spring morning. That would make the ideal tableau for his friends to admire. It would be perfect. Especially when John thought of the neighbors' paunchy sons and their unattractive wives. But at least there were the two handsome attorneys from D.C. to keep on the lawn on their infrequent visits.

Howard's move to New York had added insult to injury. Even though the Tafts were not thrilled with their son's desire to open an art gallery, at least his first one had been on a discreetly gentrified corner in Philadelphia. A waste of his Harvard MBA, they thought, but he was engaged in a form of business, even if it could never lead to a senior executive position in some prestigious old firm. And they had been impressed by the smartness of Howard's gallery of early Americana and by his growing distinguished clientele. The chaste sign, The Taft Gallery, in deep purple letters on a white background, over the converted red brick townhouse surprised Millicent. She had expected something overstated, even flamboyant. But all that hob-nobbing with the gentry changed when Howard took up with Max. He sold the shop and moved to New York. The Tafts had to acknowledge that Maxwell's pedigree was more impressive than their own, but his tastes were suspicious.

Fellow students in graduate school, Howard and Max renewed their friendship in the city of brotherly love. Max had abandoned a frustrating career as a painter and was looking toward a new venture as a gallery impresario. Weary of the dull routine of his own gallery, Howard was ready to join Max in something new. Their combined capital was substantial and they decided to join forces in New York. They also became lovers.

The Taft Gallery of Philadelphia became the Morris-Taft in Soho. The space was huge. Three large, high ceilinged, white rooms lit by spots and custom designed Swedish fixtures which more than one customer wished to purchase. In the rear of the building Howard and Max built a massive vaulted glass room that housed a large Venetian fountain, live trees, and what *The New York Times* called "a spectacular sculpture garden." As with everything else in the Morris-Taft, the sculpture was aggressively avant garde and very expensive. Catering to the rich and, by intention, to the sophisticated New York gay community, the two men frequently displayed works which were shocking to sensibilities such as those of Howard's parents.

John and Millicent were on hand for the grand opening. Having arrived at their hotel in early evening, they had barely enough time to shower and dress before joining their son and Max for dinner at one of the city's trendiest restaurants. They were impressed by the extravagance of Howard's solicitude. In advance of their arrival, he had ordered the dishes his parents relished most. They never had an opportunity to peruse the menu or wine list, but the champagne did not blur Millicent's vision as she peeked at the check which arrived at her son's place. When he opened the rich leather case that held the bill, only her good breeding held a gasp in check. Later that evening in their suite at the Plaza, courtesy of Morris-Taft, she whispered, "over seven hundred dollars for four people." She repeated the figure twice more before they retired.

The next morning was an early breakfast at Howard and Max's apartment which they had built above the gallery. The architect had done a brilliant job, even if John thought the place looked like the home of the two fairies in *La Cage aux Folles*. Like the gallery below, the apartment was white. Even the furniture and carpeting were white. John wondered if he should remove his shoes. The only color in the converted loft appeared in the art. Brilliant shades of primary colors greeted visitors as they left the elevator which opened to the foyer. A painting of four nude male bathers lolling on a shady knoll by a lake, one of them waving to two others lying on a wooden raft surrounded by the blue-green of the water. The acrylic work was very large and no guest could ignore it. At least their organs aren't erect was the first thought that crossed John's mind as he gently pushed Millicent into the living area. But if the painting's subjects were not in a state of excitement, some of the artistic subjects downstairs were in various states of obvious arousal. After juice, croissants, and coffee, it was time to view the Morris-Taft in advance of the noon grand opening. John half expected the swishy black housekeeper to sing some damn operatic aria as he cleared the table.

"You're not going to wear that, are you?" Millicent asked. She rolled her eyes in the direction of her husband.

"Of course, Mother," Howard laughed. "Style's half the game in this business."

"And in this town," added Max.

"But really, Howard. You look like an extra in an Arabian Nights movie." Millicent touched the gauzy white fabric. "I used to wrap you and your brother in material like that on Halloween. Or dress your wounds. But clothing. . . ."

"That outfit was designed by a friend for the opening," said Max.

"With friends like that. . . " John began the cliché.

"Please, folks, let's not ruin this day of all days." Howard gathered the yards of fabric around his waist and tied it all together with a red silk sash.

"Well, that's a bit better. It looks less like a dress that way." Millicent suddenly felt naked in her black pin-striped suit. To think that this morning she almost felt daring when she put on the large broach she had received the previous Christmas from Howard. Never having had the courage to wear that bejewelled snake at home, she thought it couldn't be too garish for New York City.

"At least Max is wearing man's clothes," said John. He pointed to the three piece business suit the partner wore. A tasteful blue and red tie complemented the dark blue suit. "Even a white shirt." John was about to suggest something about the sexual roles the two entrepreneurs must assume. He thought better when his son again warned about ruining the day. He recalled the quarrels of so many other meetings. His wife, in particular, invariably found serious shortcomings in either the dress or behavior of her wayward son.

As they left the elevator and entered the gallery, Millicent leaned on John's shoulder. "I could weep,' she whispered. "All those people will see Howard looking like the androgynous freaks we saw in Morocco." The mother shook her head sadly.

"Let's not start that again, Millie. Not even your psychiatrist buddy thinks we did anything wrong." John tried to laugh. "Two out of three's not bad."

"Please dear. Robert is not what I'd call a success."

"Well, maybe he'd be one if that harridan ever decided to give him his balls back." The Tafts were less than kind to their children's partners whenever they whispered to each other about the successes of the family.

"And please don't use that language. It's bad enough we're here surrounded by those things." She nodded in the direction of a painting of a reclining nude male.

"Be grateful it's not of Howard."

"Oh God. Do you really think. . . "

"Well, that one sure looks like him." John pointed to a life size bronze sculpture of a man holding his crossed hands over his private parts.

"That is Howard," said Max. "A new work by a terrific young Hispanic sculptor. He goes by the name of Omega. You'll meet him later. We hope to sell a good number of his works, and very quickly. There are more in the garden, but this is the most discreet. You know Howard."

Millicent wasn't sure she did. She looked at her discreet son in swaddling clothes making a final check of the caterer's tables.

Walter gazed at the cheap tile. He sighed as he thought of the upcoming weekend visit from his in-laws. John was a devoted football fan and a graduate of the upstate university's graduate business school. Oh God, he'll be wearing that red blazer and stupid beanie again. And he'll want the twins in the same outfit, the ones he raves about as they help him load the station wagon for their tailgate lunch before the game. Walter had no interest in athletics and went to this game only on the alternate years that it was played at Hellman Stadium. But he would not wear a blue blazer or wave a blue and white pompom to counter the red and white one that Millicent shook every time John rose to his feet to applaud his team's prowess. She knew nothing about the game after almost forty five years with John. However, she seemed to enjoy the ambiance of the event. It made her feel like one of the prols. For a couple of days a year, my mother-in-law cons herself into believing she's common folk. As if sitting next to them on a beautiful autumn afternoon, waving her silly pompom, and actually joining the cheer-leaders in their inane shouts make her simpatico for a few hours. It's better than writing a check to one of my charities, she once said. And a lot cheaper, Walter would add. The boys, however sophisticated he thought they were, actually enjoyed the outing with their grandparents. Walter knew that on the Saturday following the invasion of the Tafts, they would ask to go to another game. Come on, Dad, be a sport. Mother said she'd pack us a lunch. Maybe some of your students will see you there. Wouldn't they be impressed to see the Shakespeare scholar cheering for the team.

The in-laws were subversive. And they were victorious. For at least once a season after the visit, Walter would break down and take his sons to Hellman. How he longed for heavy rain or a sudden freeze or, best of all, an early blizzard. Then he could play the disappointed fan to the hilt. But the weather always held and Walter would eat lunch in the vast parking lot, sit on the cold concrete bench of the stadium, and watch twenty two men knock each other down. It was always a very long afternoon. Yet he was invariably surprised by how much James and Jeremy knew about the game and how familiar they were with the names and numbers of the blue shirted home team. He couldn't name a single player. They're all recruited from some steel mill town or inner city ghetto. They don't take my courses. Walter tried to account for his lack of interest by this tactic. He was not a racist by any means, but the boys' yearly bristling at their father's annual defense of his ignorance bothered him. You know what I mean, he lamely defended himself. Each year Walter promised himself never to utter those words again, but each year he said the same thing and each year Jeremy and James scolded him.

Now the passage of the seasons again brought the Tafts to town for the great game. Maggie was excited on the morning of her parents' arrival. The guest room was ready, invitations had gone out in plenty of time for the Sunday cocktail party, a turkey was ready for the oven. Maggie always served a Thanksgiving dinner on the night John and Millicent arrived. Not only did her father love turkey, but the Tafts spent alternate holidays with their married children. Because the big game fell so close to Thanksgiving, they went to Robert's Washington townhouse in those years to celebrate what John, in his cliché ridden small talk, called turkey day. I don't know how that man can be such a lion on Wall Street when he sounds like the winner of some cliché contest. No wonder he doesn't like Shakespeare. At least Howard's flying in for the weekend. Maggie's surprise for early turkey day. Walter smiled at the prospect of that surprise. He liked Howard. There'll be someone to talk to about something interesting.

Between analyzing last year's football game and carping about Robert and his barren successful wife, John monopolized the Friday night dinner. At least most of the Henrys' friends had never met Howard. With rave reviews in the *Times*, the Morris-Taft had quickly become a well-known and trendy gallery. Howard will be sought out by the cocktail party guests. Walter enjoyed hosting a celebrity. His old buddy, Ken Elliott-Cox, was right about fame by osmosis.

But there was the personnel task force meeting to attend before Walter could make it an early Friday and head home to help Maggie prepare for the visit.

Maybe pancreatic cancer, Billy thought. He doodled on a desk pad. The word that kept repeating itself in a variety of calligraphic forms was *sympathy*. Yes, that's a pretty good one. Fast and incurable. A sudden onset of symptoms, the terrible diagnosis, the terminal hospital stay. Sympathy. I'll visit often. Every day? No, a little too much. Christ, how many times has Honest Abe been to my house? Or I to his? A couple of times a week sounds about right. But I'll make sure Sally visits Eleanor. And she'll bring a casserole or a pie to help lighten the burden. I mean they've got to eat. A hearty casserole's just the right touch. That's sympathy in capital letters. He continued to doodle.

The late afternoon sun, filtering through the mini-blinds, cast horizontal lines on the yellow legal pad. Billy bit on the end of his Mont Blanc pen. I'll suggest to the task force that they promote Abe. He laughed. What a magnanimous gesture. Give tenure to a dying man. They'll love good old sympathetic Billy Mann for that grand generous touch. And they can still promote me too and not break their fucking rule. They'll still have only one new associate professor next year. He stretched his arms over his head. It's been a long week. Pancreatic cancer. Sounds right. Billy tore the sheet of doodles into small pieces and placed them in his jacket pocket. Never discard in the office anything that might be incriminating. He had asked the department for a shredder more than once.

Arriving home, Billy was in high spirits. He waved to the old codger who lived next door. "How are the squirrels today?" he shouted over the high hedge that separated their almost identical tract homes. "Their cheeks heavy with winter storage?" Stupid old shit.

The neighbor returned the wave and continued raking green-gold leaves.

Billy looked at his own lawn, in need of the same labor. To hell with it, I've got more important things to do. Besides, it'd be good for Sally's figure to get out in the yard more often.

He bounded up the three steps to the front door. "I'm home, Sal." He dropped his briefcase by the hall table and caught a quick glance of his flushed face in the mirror. He noticed a bouquet of purple mums that hadn't been there that morning when he had spent more time at the mirror before starting his drive to campus. "What's up with the flowers?" he asked.

Sally walked from the kitchen. "Have you already forgotten that we're having the Willoughbys and Rosenthals to dinner?" She kissed Billy on the cheek. "How can you forget two important members of the promotion committee?" She went to the bar. "It's part of your master plan. It wasn't my idea." She poured two glasses of red wine. "If it were up to me, I'd never have those boring men over here." She handed Billy an ornate cut-glass goblet. "I've also asked that new young couple, the Chases. Just to reduce the average age of the guest list to something over ninety-five."

Billy was not upset by the prospect of another young couple. Peter Chase was in his first year in the department and posed no threat to Billy's strategies to gain tenure. And he knew Peter admired his performances at meetings. The earnest young man had told Billy that on several occasions. Probably preparing the soil for his own promotion quest, even though it was several years away. "Fine," Billy said as he lowered himself into his man's chair to the right of the fireplace. He loved that large burgundy leather easy chair. It exuded stolid, old-monied comfort. Although the Manns were not wealthy, they could afford to live beyond the limits of his assistant professorial salary. Billy's father was generous to a fault when it came to his favorite son. Owner of a small furniture factory in New Hampshire, he kept his academic son on the payroll as a "cultural consultant" as his accountant reported to the IRS each year. In return, Billy filed an annual report to the company in which he described British furniture tastes in previous centuries. Actually, he enjoyed writing those reports and over the years he'd become a minor expert on English interior decoration. He even got two published articles on the subject. Billy the Renaissance Mann his father called him. He toyed with the idea of a book on the subject. Perhaps British writers and their furniture. Why not? Topics of far less importance were finding publishers every day. In his research he noted particularly striking pictures that might be suitable for the dust jacket of that book.

"Fine, the Chases seem like a nice couple." He held his glass up to Sally. "Had a terrific day," he toasted. Thoughts of pancreatic cancer floated happily through his mind. Make a wonderful screen saver, he laughed to himself "What's Peter's wife's name?"

"Alice. Don't you remember the conversation you had with her just last week at the Henrys? You said you were impressed with her."

"Sure, sure. Just forgot her name. She's a hell of a lot clearer than her husband." Peter Chase had been appointed in deference to the growing move to popular culture courses in literature departments. Even though Billy thought their proponents were intellectual lightweights, he had spoken enthusiastically in favor of Peter's candidacy. Hell, he could always count the house. And at least Chase wasn't one of those pseudo-scholars who make bogus careers writing about Madonna and Mick Jagger. Peter's doctoral dissertation studied the motion picture and American politics. Those were subjects Billy enjoyed. "We won't have to talk about Dryden and water marks all night."

"Do you think our other guests ever go to the movies?" Sally laughed. "Calvin and Dorothy don't even own a television set. I think they spend their evenings listening to an old gramophone." She filled their wine glasses. "At least Ben and Joyce love the way we've decorated the house."

"Why not? Their place looks a lot like ours." Billy waved his hand as though he were a guide on a home tour. "It's a beautiful room."

"Thanks to your dad."

And it was a tasteful room, even if surprisingly traditional for an assistant professor who toyed with the idea of a discreet earring and thought of himself as being on the cutting edge of university politics. The oversized floral upholstered furniture, the rich toned oriental rug, heavy gilt framed paintings of English country scenes all suggested a former time and older people. The only room in the house that spoke to a contemporary taste was the kitchen. Sally had wanted a bright airy look. The skylight she had fought to have installed still bothered Billy, but he had come to appreciate it, on gray days at least. He still felt somewhat embarrassed by the look of that room which he called cheap motel modern. He preferred to have his breakfast in the dining room. His chair backed on the arched door to the kitchen so that he could survey the dark solidity of the dining room without having to look at the jarring contrast of the kitchen. The heavy dining room furniture comforted him. Even the massive hutch which contained his late mother's expensive, gold embossed dinner service gave him pleasure. Sally hated that dining room. Often they ate their morning meal in separate rooms.

"So what time do the festivities begin?" Billy stretched his legs out onto the intricately patterned blue and red rug. Thoughts of book jackets, touchdown passes, and pancreatic cancer occupied his imagination as he yawned and closed his eyes.

"Oh no you don't, professor. There's too much to do and not enough time before they get here." Sally slapped Billy's thigh. "Better shower now so you can help get things ready." She consulted a list on the hall table. "But I'll make it easy on you. Set the table and get the bar ready and then you can relax." Billy enjoyed preparing the dining room for dinner parties. Selecting the cloth and napkins from his mother's large store of linen, arranging the plates and silverware, deciding on an appropriate centerpiece were all activities his research fostered an interest in. Generally he eschewed the more contemporary dinnerware he and Sally themselves had purchased over the years. Except for a guest list peopled by young faculty or graduate students, he much preferred his mother's china and crystal. He was particularly partial to the heavy, ornate sterling silverware instead of the sleek Dansk flatware he once thought so handsome. Over the years his preferences had changed dramatically. Once upon a time he disliked the complex patterns of his mother's taste. The simpler the better. But now he enjoyed even the feel of heavy platters and silver pitchers with carved handles and vine covered short legs. And a drink simply tasted better in a cut-glass goblet. He liked holding his glass to the sun and turning it to capture the light's refractions. He planned to write something on the esthetics of drinking. Can you imagine drinking wine from a dixie cup? he often asked Sally as he held his glass to the sunlight. She was happy that he actually enjoyed polishing the silver to a high shine and handwashing the crystal which he would not trust to the dishwasher. He even seemed to like getting into the many crevices of each piece of silverware before inspecting it and placing it in its own crimson cloth bag.

"Okay, okay, I'll hit the shower and be down in plenty of time for my chores. Did you say the show starts at seven?"

"Yes, and you know the old folks will be here on the button." Sally was moving toward the kitchen. "And don't dawdle up there. This isn't academy award night. You won't have to worry yourself about what to wear. Calvin wears the same thing all the time, and Ben really doesn't care about *Gentlemen's Quarterly*. Peter will probably show up in jeans."

"At least the women might show some style," Billy said. He grabbed his briefcase and started upstairs.

Sally's advice notwithstanding, Billy dressed with care. Striking a balance between the older faculty who were important to him and the Chases whom he wanted to impress with his tasteful hipness, he had stood before his open closet and pondered the many choices. Clad only in a white terry bath towel, Billy shivered as he fingered a number of items. He shook his head this way and that as he considered his options. Here there was no need to conceal a mirror behind a Beatles poster. He looked into its full length and held up several outfits before deciding on Ralph Lauren dark blue wide-wale corduroy pants, a Calvin Klein pale blue denim shirt, and a hand tooled leather vest he had bought in Mexico. The blue and yellow design on the vest was picked up by the argyle socks which were sheathed in dark brown loafers. Billy was partial to argyle socks. Before leaving the bedroom, he considered an ascot which Sally had given him the previous Christmas, but he thought it might be too continental for this evening. He'd save it for the visiting Irish poet next month. He gently touched his left ear lobe and tried to imagine a gold earring. One day perhaps, he thought.

"Well, don't you look great." Sally kissed Billy on the cheek and pointed to the loin of pork she was readying for the oven. "Gorgeous, isn't it?"

"With pepper sauce?"

"But of course." She kissed him again and turned him toward the dining room. "Now go to work."

Sally loved Billy. She was his constant supporter, if at times his harshest critic. Although it had taken him years to accept her criticism, he had never been able to completely overcome anger and hurt. That she was often right simply made Billy angrier. Whether it was a critique of something he wrote or a post-mortem of a dinner party conversation, Sally's comments were meant only to help her husband. For all her silly modernity, her notions of a wife's role were as old fashioned as her mother-in-law's dining room. Whatever Billy wanted, she provided. Only Billy's decision to delay having children darkened Sally's otherwise pleasant life. Between Billy's salary and his father's generosity, she did not have to work. That, too, pleased her. Although she had been certified to teach, Sally had disliked her two year sentence in a high school classroom. She discovered that she didn't like the kids any better than their parents or the school administrators. The golden promises of her undergraduate training had turned to brass when she left university theory and entered public school reality. Now she gave herself to volunteering at the local hospital, serving meals at a homeless shelter, and acting as secretary of the newcomers club. She had become an active member of the community which was what she enjoyed and Billy figured couldn't hurt his position at the university. Sally was the seemingly bright young faculty wife. The older women of the department held her up as a role model whenever they talked to new arrivals.

"Had coffee with Joan and Helen this afternoon," Eleanor began the dinner conversation. Abraham stared over his pea soup as if he were examining the molding around the kitchen window. His soup was untouched.

Eleanor winked at the children and tried again. "I shot the president and the provost at the Russian Coffee House this afternoon."

"That's nice." Ab moved his spoon through the soup. "Did you have a good time?"

"Sure Dad," Teddy laughed. "Annie and I bailed her out of jail with our allowance money."

"What jail?" Ab asked, suddenly concerned. "What happened?" He looked at Eleanor. "What's this about jail?"

"Forget it Ab. You weren't listening to a word I said." She touched his arm. "Everything's fine. Teddy was just joking."

"You were daydreaming again, Dad," said Ann.

Ab tasted the soup. "Delicious. As usual." He offered a half smile.

"Oh no, you don't get off the hook that easily." Eleanor crossed her arms over the white reindeer of her blue sweater. "What's been eating you for the last couple of days? You've wandered around this house like a zombie."

Ab shot a glance at the children.

"You can talk in front of them. They're old enough to know what's bothering you." Eleanor nodded at Teddy and Ann. "They do live here, you know." Her look told them to remain quiet.

"Billy Mann is clobbering me." He pushed the soup bowl away. "Are you satisfied now? So you know what's been upsetting me. Billy's miles ahead of me in that damned race for tenure." Ab took off his glasses and rubbed his eyes. "And I don't seem to have the legs to catch him." He looked down, embarrassed at his confession in front of the children. "Can we please talk about this later."

He left the table and went into the den. Over Jim Lehrer's soft drawl Abraham heard the quiet small talk from the kitchen as his family went on with dinner. He tried to concentrate on the regional editors' responses to Lehrer's question about the last presidential election and the upcoming congressional races. Who gives a damn, he thought. Clinton, Dole. Dole, Clinton. I couldn't get excited. I just held my nose and voted for Clinton. That presidential campaign struck Ab as a quirky metaphor for his own dilemma. Maybe the task force can't see any real differences between Billy and me. Or maybe they've bought into his campaign the same way so many Americans did with the two presidential candidates. Maybe they believe the line that Billy has been offering at every opportunity. He shook his head. No, they've got to be more perceptive than that. They must be just as tired as I was with ten million more jobs or a fifteen percent tax cut. The evil of television is that we got to hear their speeches every night. He almost laughed. Except for the change of location, the words were always the same. But maybe the task force is just as unconcerned about character and ethics as the general population. Can't they see through Billy Mann? Don't they care?

Eleanor was already in bed when Ab came upstairs. "Can I welcome you back to the land of the living?" She let her book drop to her chest and reached her arms toward her husband. "How about a little relaxation to lift your spirits?"

Abraham nodded his head. When he returned from the bathroom, he was wearing the nightshirt the kids had given him. "Best Dad" was imprinted within a bright yellow sun. "At least Billy can't wear this badge," Ab said as he pointed to the logo.

"Nor can he beat you down there either." Eleanor nodded her head in the direction of the tent in the white cotton night shirt.

"Do you speak from your vast experience?" Ab laughed. "Or is that the sort of contest sweet little Sally arranges for all you faculty wives at Newcomers?"

"But of course. We all bring in Polaroids and notarized measurements."

"And what about all those single women and . . . "

"Oh they can enter also. Joan's supermarket young man was very impressive."

"And our stable of gay colleagues?"

"Peter Chase for instance?"

"That's just a rumor, you know." Ab wagged his finger in a schoolmarmish scolding motion. "Besides he's married."

"Come on, professor. You know better than that. We've known more than a few who swing both ways."

"Are you still on Walter Henry's case?" Ab was unhappy with Eleanor's insistence that the chair had eyes for young men. "Besides, Maggie would cut it off if it were true."

"Someday we'll see who's right." Eleanor and her coffee companions had discussed that very subject earlier in the day. Joan agreed with Ab, but Helen admitted that she had sometimes thought the same thing about homely Walter. All three had laughed like teen-agers as they developed a variety of obscene scenarios. Their favorites, of course, featured Walter and Maggie or, and here the game turned nasty, Walter and Billy. "Meanwhile, come over here. And take off that night shirt."

Ab stood naked by Eleanor's side of the bed. "You've got the best body in the department. By a mile." She sat up and kissed the tip of Ab's penis. "And there's not a jock on the football team that can beat the iron in that pecker." Her right hand gently caressed Ab. He closed his eyes. Her grip tightened. Her hand moved in a smooth rhythmic motion.

"Why don't I get into bed?"

"Why don't we just continue what we're doing." She stopped her movements. "Isn't this a perfect way to relax?"

"But I'll mess you up."

"Mess? I love to see you come."

Ab closed his eyes again. He began moving against her hand's motion.

"And I love to hear your breathing quicken. And that little catch in your throat just before, and the slight buckling of your knees."

There was no turning back now.

Abraham slept soundly. The subject of Billy Mann was not discussed that night.

Walter stood at the bar. He was preparing drinks for his in-laws. A very dry martini for Millicent and vodka on the rocks for John. Although they had not retired yet, Walter thought they fit the syndrome. They drink like fishes, he grumbled to Maggie. And both of them smoke like chimneys. Why did he always fall back on clichés when he spoke of the Tafts. He, the scholar, who berated students for such locutions. Maybe it's because you want to make dad feel at home was Maggie's familiar response.

The two couples sat in facing love seats in front of the fireplace. The boys hadn't returned yet from junior varsity football practice.

"I think it's wonderful that James and Jeremy are on the team," said Millicent. She was almost finished with her second martini.

"It's only J.V.," said John. "They're big enough for the varsity. Why aren't they mixing it up with the real team?" He directed the question to Walter. "Don't they have the right stuff?"

"Oh Dad," Maggie answered, "don't get on them when they come in. They're doing the best they can."

"What sort of athletes were Howard and Robert?" Walter asked, knowing that neither of the Taft boys had made their father proud on any playing field. He smiled into his bourbon.

"One of the great disappointments of my life." John handed his empty glass to Walter. "They didn't even want to play." He shook his head in an exaggerated show of unhappiness. "Can you imagine that. The sons of a second team All American center, and they weren't even interested in trying out for the team."

Walter mouthed his father-in-law's lament to himself. As always, Maggie would ask him why he always goaded her father about that issue. As always, Walter would say it made him feel a little better to see the old blowhard do his wounded parent routine.

"But, dear, the boys have succeeded in other ways," Millicent said. "In their own ways, they're very successful."

"Sure. Very successful." John took a long pull on his vodka. "One of them works in a basement office of a crummy building. A petty bureaucrat who can't even father a baby. . . ."

"Not fair, Dad," Maggie interrupted, "it's Becky who doesn't want children."

"So is Robert a real husband or not? He ought to assert his manhood." John lit an unfiltered Camel. "And the other one's a fairy."

"Please, John," Millicent protested.

"Okay, Millie, call it anything you like. But Howard's a fag." He waved his hand in the direction of the younger couple. "You wouldn't believe the get-up he wore at the opening of that queer gallery he and Max run."

Walter worried about the surprise visit Maggie had arranged. Howard's plane had landed thirty minutes earlier. He's probably in a cab right now. Still, he was anxious for Howard to arrive. He was, after all, the only member of Maggie's family he actually enjoyed being with.

Maggie prayed her brother would be wearing something nice and normal.

"Please, Dad, none of this talk when the boys get here."

"All right. All right. But they should be alerted to all those predators out there."

Millicent held up her hand. "Hush, now, John. Maggie's right."

John grimaced. "I'll never know why they call themselves gay. I don't see anything gay about their lives." He touched his wife's arm. "Did you ever think of Howard as being gay?" He finished his vodka. "Seems morose to me."

Beverly Berlin pranced out of her library office. She was late for a meeting with Mitchell Murdoch. Carrying her trademark open briefcase bursting with documents and books, she believed the abundance of her case demonstrated the importance of her position in the profession. She was in the habit of arriving at meetings after they had been called to order, breathlessly offering her apologies. "I have so many goodies on my plate after all." As though no others had anything of real importance to keep them from being prompt, she rustled through her bag to locate the papers appropriate for the session, and whispered in her breathless way that she'd have to leave early because of pressing meetings with publishers' representatives or foundation officers. Her acolytes in the feminist studies group admired their guru's energy as much as they worshipped her significant presence. Nor did Beverly ever miss an opportunity to confide in her followers. And her confidences invariably increased the luster of her self-proclaimed growing brilliance. She was indeed a worthy leader. Surely worthy of being the next full professor in the literature department.

Having written her doctoral dissertation on the poetry of Emily Dickinson, Beverly Berlin had experienced the frustrations of conventional scholarship after eight university presses turned down the book. Of necessity, she returned to Miss Emily and mined the Amherst Belle for the few precious metals her study contained. Fortunately, a few brief notes and several queries, including two author's requests for assistance in the *Times Book Review*, were enough to land her a beginning position at a second-rate state college. She knew she would not stay long. Her fortunes changed with her new-found focus on the depiction of women in comic strips. As Berlin wrote in her resume, she became the profession's premiere expert on the subject. That there were no others tilling in her field made no difference to her customary rhetorical excess. Facts never did. But soon, in a profession gone rancid, she achieved a reputation. She began to pour out studies of Blondie, Betty Boop, and Olive Oyl, her historical work, and, later on, their contemporary sisters as they suffered daily abuse in the funny pages. After a landmark study of Mary Worth, offers came to her; she chose this department; and she bid farewell to the boonies. Beverly's current project, an extension of her earlier groundbreaking work, a term repeated four times in her resume, dealt with the television members of the Beverly Berlin sorority. Her research house looked like Sears' appliance department. There were television sets and VCRs everywhere. An enormous TV dish, the blight of her neighborhood, sat on the roof, looking like a brooding black sentry standing guard at the gates of modern scholarship. Cable television would not do. This scholar must have state-of-the-art access to the scores of programs that went into her research. She must know if there were demographic differences she might explore in future groundbreaking studies. Were victims perceived differently in Des Moines than in Chicago, in the suburbs than in the cities, in rural America than in the urban centers? The possibilities were unlimited: age differences, education level, income, vocational choices. Were there correlations between viewing preferences and racial strife, marital discord, political decisions? Her future brimmed with studies. The university agreed with the professor's high estimate of her work and supplied her with research assistants who spent their allocated hours watching videos and noting on their yellow legal pads themes, character development, and plot manipulations that coincided with those on the large red posters Beverly had positioned over each television receiver. Two granting agencies had underwritten the project, thus insuring daily trays of donuts and danish by the coffee makers and bountiful sandwich choices in the refrigerator. Beverly's assistants never went hungry as they watched hour after hour, noting their findings on pads. They had been assured they were at the cutting critical edge of cultural studies as they sat transfixed, staring at the screens, what their professor referred to as the carriers of modern texts. The house's soft cacophony was the music of grants, salary increases, conference invitations, and, soon, the professorship. Next year perhaps; surely the year after.

The Berlin industry was in full swing when Beverly decided the time was ripe for a meeting with Mitchell Murdoch, the one man in the department whose reputation she envied. It was time for the womens studies group to ally itself with the literary theorists. The goal was nothing less than control of the department. Its future must belong to them. Her initial agenda was to block tenure for both Billy Mann and Abraham Smith. The new associate professorship must remain vacant until the right candidate could be attracted from the outside. A feminist committed to womens studies and literary theory. A woman who could be counted on to vote for the interests of both groups. An empire builder himself, Mitchell Murdoch could not refuse.

At first, Beverly considered a dinner meeting at her home. But that posed problems. Would she invite Murdoch's wife and then excuse herself and the literary theorist after dessert, leaving Isobel to the hospitality of her Martin? Sweet nebbish that he was, what would a real estate salesman have to say to a former research biochemist? The Murdochs already had a house. They'd only be bored by Martin's talk of the real estate market. And her Martin's strength was not small talk. All he knew of the university was that his wife was a major player there. He did follow the athletic teams, but Beverly doubted sports was one of Isobel's passions. No, dinner was out for now. Perhaps after the alliance had been forged, celebratory cocktails and dinner for the two groups. A far better idea. And Martin was very good at large parties. He loved tending bar and dispensing drinks along with inside information about the town's property values. He attributed two sales to previous parties his beloved Beverly had given. Yes, a party later. For the present, a professional meeting in Mitchell's office. No food; all business.

Both she and Murdoch had research offices in the library in addition to their small departmental offices. Mitchell's space was grand. When Yale offered him a job, a real plum for someone who had studied there with Derrida and Miller, the president opened his purse to keep the star here. Mitchell had cut himself one sweet deal. So sweet that it was the talk of the following MLA convention. So sweet that Beverly took careful notes so that when her big offer came, she'd have a model for her negotiations. After all, neither of them wanted to move. But the trick was to finesse the administration. Make them believe you're willing to go. Beverly remembered her dissertation director's advice: never use an offer unless you're willing to accept it. And it was good advice. She could think of more than one colleague who stood before the chair with egg on their faces when he shook their hands and hoped they'd be happy in Madison or Urbana or wherever. The point was that they didn't want to leave, but they didn't play the game right. She'd been an astute student. When her time came, she'd master the board.

Murdoch actually had an outer office with a half-time secretary. He had finagled a suite with outside windows in a library building that resembled a medieval fortress. That the associate librarian had to be demoted to inside rooms didn't upset the theorist's plans. He had his demands, and the university would meet them or else. He told the president that librarians were a dime a dozen. He, Mitchell Murdoch, was far more expensive. Yale knew it. He hoped President Richard Maxwell knew it too.

One look at the computer print-outs on Trish's desk showed Beverly the extent of Murdoch's operation. Expert at reading upside-down, she was impressed by the headings: research assistants, travel account, library budget, telephone and fax, released teaching time, summer stipend. There were others hidden beneath the pile. Beverly was about to push the top ones aside when Trish returned to her office.

"Hi, Beverly. Haven't seen you since the seminar." She kissed the professor on the cheek. She had taken Beverly's course, "The Deconstruction of Mary Worth." Trish Martin had been a graduate student in the department until she ran into a bad case of writer's block on her dissertation. Now splitting her time between Murdoch and queer studies, she had put together full-time work.

Rumors had her in bed with Mitchell. Beverly had told Martin that there was a long line of attractive young women who were alleged to have shared his bed. "Lots of hanky panky at your university," was his customary response whenever Beverly reported the latest gossip to her husband while he prepared dinner.

Trish was a striking young woman. Probably in her early thirties. Red hair like Maureen O'Hara's and a figure to match. Divorced and the mother of a retarded son, she needed work and, from all reports, was in line for the administrative assistant's position when either queer studies or literary theory gained department status. That Mitchell was pushing for that bothered Beverly. She'd much prefer his clout on her side in the literature department.

"He'll be free in a minute. Coffee?"

"Thanks. I have to get the taste of Walter's instant junk out of my mouth."

"He's still serving Sanka over there?"

"What else. You know the old guard actually petitioned for that stuff." Beverly lit a cigarillo.

"It probably keeps them awake, if not alert, for their late morning classes. Thank God old Bullock puts on the real stuff after she finishes with Walter's mail."

The buzzer sounded on Trish's desk. "Yes, she's here." Trish laughed. "Right. The long black cigarette." She nodded toward the inner office.

Mitchell Murdoch did not stand when Beverly entered. He waved her to a black leather easy chair to the right of his desk, rather than to the uncomfortable stiff-backed university-issue chair that faced his desk. Obviously reserved for students. "So what's up, Bev?" He looked at her over his gray half glasses.

She always felt Mitchell was amused by her, that he didn't really take her or her work seriously. She imagined sardonic laughter played behind those beautiful blue eyes that captivated students as much as his brilliance did. From where she sat, she could see Mitchell was wearing his usual blue jeans and boots. She tried to relax.

"I want to talk about the future of the department." She leaned forward to flick her ash as much as to suggest the conspiratorial strategy she was about to present. "I want us to take over the joint." She laughed a bit too self-consciously.

"Well, now, Professor Berlin, that's an interesting subject. A real interesting subject." He leaned back and placed his hands behind his head. As always, Beverly was struck by how handsome he was. Not that she ever wanted to stand in line at his bed. Her appreciation was esthetic rather than sensual. Sex was among the least important ingredients in her otherwise richly furnished life. She knew her Martin was loyal and was more than satisfied with an occasional roll in the hay, his term for an activity she was perfectly willing to endure to keep him happy. Take one for the team or lay back for the empire floated through her mind whenever she allowed him to grunt and groan above her. Small price to pay for good meals and a beautiful house. She cringed when she thought in those terms. They reminded her too much of the grin-and-bear-it advice her conventional mother had once given her in a rare confidential moment. Beverly had liberated herself from that bourgeois homestead long ago.

An hour later Beverly's thin, birdlike frame preened as she nodded to Trish and left the office. Once outside the library building, she stopped under the portal and gazed at a campus transformed into her university. Her meeting with Mitchell had gone better than she could have hoped for. Not only did he agree to an alliance between his theory and her womens studies, but he was enthusiastic about her notion of a new appointment instead of a promotion for Mann or Smith. And as she was about to leave, Mitchell had walked her to the door, touched her arm, and promised that he'd present her name for promotion to the personnel task force that very week. She lit a cigarillo and inhaled deeply. I didn't even raise the subject. He did. She smiled at a passing student. She wanted to shout. Mitchell Murdoch approves of my work. Mitchell Murdoch wants me to be promoted to full professor. Beverly felt like skipping along the flagstone path to the humanities building.

After Millicent hushed John's verbal assault on Howard, the twins arrived home and the cocktail hour proceeded in an almost civilized manner. John turned his attention to the boys' football practice. He did not mention their junior varsity status. Walter's headache improved slightly. Maggie looked for the right time to announce the imminent arrival of her brother. Please Daddy, she prayed, don't say anything in front of the boys. Please, Howie, look like one of us tonight. Don't give Dad any more ammunition. She called her mother into the kitchen.

"So, boys, what've you got to say to your old grandfather?"

"How're you doing, Gramps?" Jeremy asked as he hugged John and kissed him on the cheek. "Ready for the big game?"

"Dad got us seats on the fifty yard line," said James.

"Pulled strings, did you, Walter?" He winked at the twins. "Bet he doesn't even know the difference between the fifty yard line and the end zone." He held out an empty glass once again. "Shakespeare didn't write much about football. Isn't that right, Walter? I guess the old bard wasn't much into sports."

Jeremy took his grandfather's glass. "I can fix the drink, Dad."

Embarrassed by John's laughter at his father's expense, James made a spitting motion to Jeremy.

"Don't forget to add that special ingredient to Gramp's drink." Both boys laughed. Before John could comment, the women returned from the kitchen. "Dear," Millicent began, "Maggie has arranged a wonderful surprise for us."

"Sweet potatoes with marshmallows?"

"No, no. She'd never forget that." Millicent was uncommonly nervous, especially when she saw John sipping from a fresh drink. "Howard's joining us for the weekend."

John looked at her blankly. "Howard's coming all the way out here for a football game?" He laughed. "How about that, boys. Your uncle's now a football fan." He winked at the room again. "Probably likes to watch all those young studs running around the field." His laughter was interrupted by the doorbell.

Maggie rushed to the door. She hugged her brother. "Welcome, welcome." She hugged him again. "You look great."

At least one of Maggie's prayers had been answered. Howard looked like the quintessential fraternity man. A navy cashmere v-neck sweater, open collared white shirt, chinos, mountain boots. No swaddling clothes. He looked terrific.

Howard dropped his luggage by the front door. He carried a Bloomingdale's shopping bag into the living room. Gifts for all.

Walter greeted Howard warmly. They embraced. "Great to see you, Howie." His headache was gone.

The boys followed their father's lead and hugged their uncle. Maggie wondered for only a moment what perverse thoughts her father was having as he watched all this male bonding. Please, Daddy, don't say anything.

As Walter carved the turkey on the sideboard, Millicent asked Howard about the gallery. "Great. The Morris-Taft is the hit of the season. Mother, you wouldn't believe the business were doing." He drank from his wine glass. "And the reviews have been sensational." He touched his mother's arm. "Moving from Philadelphia was the best thing I ever did."

"When can we visit you?" asked Jeremy.

"How about Christmas vacation?" added James. "You'd meet us at the airport, wouldn't you?" James took a small sip from his wine.

This was the first dinner that the parents had allowed their sons to imbibe. They felt particularly adult when Walter asked them, just as they had heard him ask others for years, that thrillingly grown-up question: red or white? The twins' eyes met in a silent smile. They had been nipping on the sly for a couple of years. And not just from their folks' open wine bottles. Jeremy had grown fond of his grandfather's vodka. After several unpleasant attempts, James had begun to share Walter's preference for bourbon. They were both thought of as sophisticated by their friends who still swilled down beer whenever they were at unchaperoned parties. Walter and Maggie would be shocked by the number of times the boys had helped each other to bed. They were in training for the college years ahead.

"They're too young to go to New York alone," said John. Blurred visions of the sculpture garden at the Morris-Taft clouded his imagination as he chose between the wine glass and the vodka he had brought to the table. That darkie, dressed in a maid's outfit, gave the grandfather a slight tremor. "Too young by far."

"I'd love to have you visit," said Howard. "What do you say, Maggie. This Christmas in New York. The boys would love it." He looked at his mother. "You know we've got plenty of room at the apartment."

"Please, Mom," both boys pleaded.

"We'll see," said Walter.

"Come on, Dad, that always means no."

"Maybe we'll all go," said Maggie. "I'd love to see the gallery." She nodded to Walter. "And we haven't been to New York in ages."

John was mollified. "That sounds like a much more sensible idea.

And you can all stay at a hotel." He drank wine. "Still have those statues," he accented that word as though he were uttering a curse, "in that greenhouse of yours?"

"A whole new show." Ignoring his father's tone, Howard remained animated. "We sold every one of Omega's pieces. Can you believe that? Every work you saw at the opening is gone." He waved his hands at the table. "I even posed for one of the sculptures."

"You?" Walter asked.

"You bet. I was thrilled when Omega asked me to model."

"Yea, I saw that work of art." John tried to sound sarcastic.

"It was beautiful," Millicent cut in. "And very tasteful."

"At least he covered his nuts."

Oh God, thought Walter, we haven't even had our entree and he's almost in the bag. He grimaced as he butchered the last of the turkey in order to get it to the table as quickly as possible. Maybe food will counter the booze in his system. He brought the platter to the head of the table. Bypassing the customary formalities, Walter heaped gargantuan portions of turkey, yams, creamed spinach, and glazed carrots onto his father-in-law's plate. Only Christ knows what he'll be like by dessert. He hand delivered the overflowing plate to John. "Bon appetit," he said and then returned to the formalities of serving his other guests. He rolled his eyes at Maggie. She nodded in return.

"Walter," said Howard, "I'd love to have your advice about a show Max and I have been thinking about."

"Must be about football." John guffawed. Food and alcohol were having their way with him. John had been lulled into a blessedly quiet state for the past fifteen minutes. "You two he-men going to huddle on the fifty-yard line?" He looked around the table for approval of his joke.

"Sure," said Walter, also ignoring John, "what's your idea?"

"Shakespeare. An entire show about Shakespeare. Multi-media. You'd be amazed by how much art plays off his works."

"Shakespeare in the buff?" John tried again. "Maybe the professor there," he pointed his fork at Walter, "can pose for your Omega." His eyes closed for a moment. "Then we'd see what kind of stuff our son-in-law is made of, wouldn't we, Millie?"

"Eat your food, John." There was a threat in Millicent's tone.

Even in his boozey state, John was cowed. He colored slightly and looked down at his plate. "But Millie, he gave me too much food."

"Eat." She turned her attention to Howard. Her tone changed. "That sounds like a splendid idea." She stood up and went to the sideboard. "I love this crisp skin. Oh, I know its no good for me, but I do love it." She kissed Howard on the top of his head. "I think Walter's advice will be very helpful." She looked at the twins. "Do you two know how much your father knows about Shakespeare? Your grandfather and I keep his books on our coffee table at home." Maggie was grateful for her mother's taking charge of the conversation.

"And tomorrow, boys, your grandfather will be as good as new. Don't you worry about a thing. He'll eat like a horse at your tailgate party and he'll cheer with the best of them when the good guys score a touchdown." She nodded toward her husband. "Jet lag always affects him this way."

Neither boy mentioned that their grandparents had arrived in their new Mercedes. Walter was excited by Howard's request for his assistance. He remained the only member of Maggie's family with whom he felt a bond. He looked forward to the two of them retiring to Walter's study.

"I bet you voted for the draft dodger, didn't you, Walter?" John's voice was thick, his words slurred.

At least he's trying to change the subject, Maggie thought.

"At least he screws women," John laughed. Maggie groaned.

"No politics tonight," Millicent interrupted. She avoided looking at her grandsons. "Perhaps tomorrow. When our heads are clear and we're not so tired." She smiled at the boys. "Did I tell you your grandfather is chairman of the county Republican campaign committee?"

The political discussion was at an end.

As soon as Peter Chase made eye contact with Walter at his MLA interview, he knew his chances for the appointment had increased.

Although there had been nothing more than that momentary locked gaze, Peter knew there was a connection between him and the chair that he might one day exploit. As he selected his clothes for dinner at the Manns, indeed as he spent as much time as his host was expending at the same time, he wondered if Walter would be there. In his first few months in the department, Peter had not had the opportunity to display his talents. In an earlier time, Peter Chase would have been called a cock tease. He enjoyed the game, the pursuit, the parry and thrusts, even more than the conquest itself. And there had been many conquests. Men and women. His swimmer's body, green eyes, long blond hair tied in a pony tail, actor's good looks, a Brad Pitt lookalike, coupled with an easy smile and a considerable intellect had made him a darling of the academy. Since his freshman year in high school in Los Angeles, Peter had been a player. In the dozen years that had passed since he had bedded both the male diving coach and the female Latin teacher, Peter had become an expert.

Alice, pregnant with their first child, appeared completely oblivious of his double life. But Alice had made her own special accommodation for her own reasons.

Peter was only slightly disappointed that the chair was not at dinner. Not because he harbored any desire for Walter, but, rather, because he had not been to a social event with him since the start of school. Yes, there had been the traditional opening of the year party hosted by the Henrys, but that was a crowd scene where one simply put in face time. Alice had heard that Maggie noted the absences with considerable unhappiness. If one wanted a subsequent invitation to her home and wanted to avoid Madam Chair's disapproval which could be costly, one made sure to attend the opening party. And the food was always good and the drinks plentiful. In addition to creating the lavish office, Walter's predecessor had established a slush fund for chairmanly entertaining which had become a permanent item in the department's annual budget. Hidden under the broad heading of "miscellaneous administrative expenses," the fund allowed Walter and Margaret Henry to be exceedingly generous hosts.

But the Henrys were not at Billy Mann's house. Just as well, thought Peter, who found Billy one of the most attractive men in the department. But, Peter concluded early, Billy was straight. Nevertheless, he could enjoy his style and wanted his company as well as his approval. He also would have liked Mitchell Murdoch's support, but that was fraught with complications.

Just the week before, he had been at the Murdoch home for cocktails which turned out to be a recruitment party. Peter and Joan Eastland were the objects of the attention of Murdoch and Beverly Berlin.

"Your thesis interests me very much," Beverly had said as she handed

Peter a drink. Her eyes never stopped scouting the room as she spoke to him, but his active involvement in womens studies was her goal. "The chapter you call sirens of the silent screen would make a wonderful talk at one of our colloquia." She touched his arm gently and quickly looked around the large living room as if she feared someone might overhear the forthcoming confidence. "We really want as many sympathetic men as possible in our womens studies group." She gestured in the direction of their host. "Mitchell is one of our strongest supporters."

As if the scene had been scripted and rehearsed, Murdoch took his place at Peter's side as soon as Beverly carried a cheese tray over to Joan. His pitch was the same as the nervous, thin woman's, except in behalf of the literary theory group. Clearly, they were in the same camp. And just as clearly, their perceived enemies were the so-called traditional members of the department.

"You understand, of course, they just don't understand us." Mitchell smiled without looking into the young man's eyes. He seemed tentative. Perhaps even embarrassed, if Mitchell Murdoch could ever be truly embarrassed. "Even worse, they don't like what we do." Peter pulled away almost imperceptively from Mitchell's light touch on his arm. The older man smiled knowingly. "Imagine that. They don't like what they don't understand." Mitchell, too, examined his room before continuing. "But, of course, you know the situation. Fresh from your graduate years at Duke, you're familiar with the deep tensions that exist in the profession. Surely from the seminar you took with me if from no other source." Mitchell thought better of rehearsing his widely anthologized essay on the subject of the profession, a word his voice elevated to sacred heights. It was one of the few reverential terms in his usually easy and fluid style. Murdoch was a grand conversationalist. Witty and urbane, deliciously coarse at appropriate moments, his speech was far different from the tortured prose of his professional writing.

Peter had, of course, read Mitchell's celebrated piece on the state of the profession. More than one professor at Duke had called his attention to it. His dissertation advisor had urged him to take that essay to heart when he learned of Peter's appointment. "Murdoch is at the critical forefront," he had said. "And if I were in your shoes, I'd want to latch on to him." The advisor pushed his fingers into Peter's chest three hurtful times.

"That man's at the head of our class." His fingers attacked again. "Yes, sir, Chase, you could do a lot worse than latching on to him." It was a locution Peter never fully understood, but he nodded in understanding. He also folded his arms over his vulnerable ribs.

And that was the cocktail party at the Murdochs. No commitment asked for; no promises made. But Beverly and Mitchell had done their jobs so well that he and Joan Eastland left the house feeling they had been honored to have been invited.

"She asked me to call her Bev." Peter sounded like a schoolboy, almost willing to forget the darker side of his association with the great Mitchell Murdoch. "And Bev told me to stop by her library office any time."

"At least the fresh air is clearing my head," Joan responded with much less enthusiasm. They stood by her car. "I wonder how much of all that," she shot a thumb over her shoulder in the direction of the house, "was a con."

Peter did not say anything further and they separated.

Sally greeted Peter and Alice warmly. As they walked into the living room, Peter glanced into the dining room to count the place settings. They were the last of the eight.

When he took a glass of white wine from Billy, Peter looked around the room. He was disappointed. Expensive, tasteful contemporary is what he had figured Billy for. But this? It looked as ancient as the old foursome already seated on the ugly furniture. He didn't look forward to a lively evening. "Don't forget to get a headache as soon as you can," he whispered to Alice.

At least the food was good. Sally was also the chair of the dinner exchange which allowed newcomers to partake of their senior colleagues' fare as well as see their homes. After all, one of the most frequent topics of conversation among men as well as women was the size, price, location, art work, and furnishings of colleagues' homes. As if there were a correlation between square feet and scholarly accomplishment. Cars were way down on the list of popular conversation. Most of them drove Japanese compacts anyway. There were a few notable exceptions, of course. Mitchell Murdoch drove a red Jaguar that made him feel like Inspector Morse, and Beverly Berlin surprised even herself when she bought a bright yellow Porsche. "Your father's insurance money sure burned a hole in your pocket,"

Marty had said when she dragged him to the dealer. Walter Henry longed for a Miata, but Maggie kept rejecting the idea. He saw himself wheeling around town in that little convertible, white aviator's scarf blowing in the wind, dark glasses, tartan plaid cap, leather bomber jacket. He longed for that vision, but he yielded to his wife's choice of the more practical Volvo station wagon.

"So, where did you find a house?" Ben Rosenthal asked Alice. They had met only briefly at the chair's opening party.

"Oh, we're renting in Oak Estates."

"It's lovely there," said Joyce Rosenthal, trying to be kind about one of the town's older subdivisions. It was there that most divorced faculty men ended up. Small homes built shortly after the second world war, a mini Levittown. 'Don't you own a couple of houses there, Calvin?" Joyce asked the water mark expert.

"Three, to be exact," Calvin answered.

"And we're in the process of getting a fourth," said Dorothy Willoughby.

"Have to think of our old age," Calvin laughed.

Old age, thought Billy. What the hell do you think you're in now. Fucking dinosaur. "Becoming a regular Donald Trump." He tried to sound friendly. You'll never get inside this house once I get tenure. He smiled. Or at least not until Sally and I run the chair's opening of the year party. If he had been alone in his great easy chair by the fire, a drink in his hand, his shoes thrown off, Billy would have entered another of his favorite fantasies, Chairman Mann. He had often imagined himself in that grand office. Except he would have his name added to the chair's letterhead. Yes, he thought, perhaps in a heavy Gothic script.

"Billy, wake up," Sally quietly interrupted his reverie. "We're ready to go to the dining room. Get them seated and pour some wine into your grotesque goblets."

If the living room disappointed Peter, the dining room depressed him completely. He was glad only that he didn't have to see it in the daylight when it must be positively gloomy. The Munsters, he thought, would find this room creepy. Billy's mother's furniture overwhelmed the space. Peter imagined it sucked the very air out of its few empty spots. When he pulled his chair back in order to sit down, he had to squeeze his lean frame between the chair and the table. He backed the mammoth hutch that held the mates to the heavy wine glass he lifted to his lips. Oak Estates looked better every minute. He glanced around the large table at his dining companions. They seemed pleased with everything. And why not? Their houses, too, must reek of the past. But dapper Billy Mann? Peter couldn't figure it out.

"What beautiful dishes," Alice exclaimed as she held her dinner plate to the light of the chandelier. The bulbs of the crystal fixture created a translucent garden of intricate flowers. She turned the plate over. "I just knew they were Rosenthal." She smiled at Sally. "I love them."

"Compliment him." she nodded at Billy. "They belonged to his mother." She placed soup bowls and matching liners on the dinner plates. "My tastes run to simpler things. The master there has written several articles on stuff even uglier than all this." She waved her free hand in the air, trying to embrace the entire room. Even about the ambiance she disliked, Sally's voice exuded a good-natured resignation. Billy was not the only performance artist in the family. "The kitchen is where I drew the line," she laughed.

Peter immediately liked Sally. He made a note to look into her kitchen before the end of the evening.

"Oh, you're being unkind," said Ben. "I think this is a wonderful room."

"It makes us think of home," added Joyce as she tasted the soup. "Delicious, dear, simply delicious.

"What is it?" asked Calvin. The flat interrogatory tone was pure Calvin. His voice rarely changed volume or pitch. More than one colleague and student had been driven into a state of torpor by it.

If it was a frigging watermark, you'd know. Billy poured more wine into Willoughby's glass. On top of it all, he drinks like a fish. Glad I'm not serving the good stuff. He had told Sally earlier that he wouldn't waste expensive wine on these ancients.

"You must have bought this Chateau Villandry at Wong's Wine Shop last week," Dorothy Willoughby said as she pointed to the bottle. "We bought a case for everyday drinking. A good buy."

Billy colored slightly.

"I still don't know what Chinamen are doing in the wine business,"

Calvin said. "Never thought they drank anything but tea." He pointed to the soup, still wanting an answer to his earlier question. "Dorothy and I were in China last year. Between semesters, you know. We generally take an alumni tour every winter." He poured more wine. "Hated the food. Their tea, by the way, was terrible. And we didn't have wine once." He held up his spoon to accentuate a point. "When you get there, let me tell you, never eat their breakfasts. Terrible stuff. All that gelatinous junk. Yes sir, be sure to spend a few extra bucks and have breakfast at one of the fancy American hotels. We finally took breakfast at the Hilton. Never mind that all meals were included in the price of the tour. But lunches and dinners were all right. We sure would have loved to see a Denny's on the corner, though, for breakfast. And for a cup of decent coffee."

Peter wondered if he was listening to the conversational high point of the evening. Even with the good aromas escaping from the kitchen, he awaited Alice's announcement of a headache. But one glance at his wife's animated face as she talked with Joyce Rosenthal told him she was far from a migraine.

"Reminds me of the time we took one of those tours to Africa," Ben began.

Billy had to change the topic. He interrupted. "The soup, Calvin, is cream of broccoli. But with Sally's secret ingredients added." He smiled and continued. "But enough talk of food." He was pleased to note Peter's grateful look. "What's new on the task force front?" Billy ventured into the evening's mine field. *Might as well get them talking about the fucking reason I invited them in the first place. Let them earn their meal.*

Ben's normal high color heightened. He suffered from hypertension, another subject he enjoyed discoursing about. *What the hell he's got high blood pressure for I'll never know.* Billy feared any mention of medical topics. Between Calvin and Ben, every disease common to old men was a subject of great interest and anecdotal tedium. *I hope my question doesn't give him a stroke. At least not here.* Ben looked at Billy and then at Peter. "Do you think we ought to bore the others with shop talk? Especially in this charming place." Ben clearly didn't want to discuss tenure.

Bore the others? Christ, it'd be the only interesting thing we've talked about yet. A hell of a lot better than your procardia and lozol. Billy remembered a previous dinner party where Ben talked for an eternity about the clinical differences between procardia and procardia dx. He thought he was going to scream that night.

"You wouldn't bore us," Sally said sweetly. "After all, Ben, we're all members of one big family."

Billy beamed at his wife's perfect words.

"One happy family with Walter and Maggie as its parents."

"Oh God," Billy muttered, "she's going to over-do her happy family bit." He stifled a groan. The first time he had heard that routine was before he met Hazel and Harry. He remembered it well. Some fucking happy family. Can't even smoke. He had been about to excuse himself and have a quick cigarette in the TV room when Calvin started talking about Chinese cuisine, but he feared it was too early in the evening to leave the podium. There was conducting to do. Please, Sally, don't embroider that family shit. You started great. Don't screw up now.

Sally caught the look in Billy's eye. "Anyway, Ben, it is a family." She laughed. "Sometimes a dysfunctional one, but we're a family nonetheless."

"Especially when the wayward children throw their tantrums and demand attention," Billy sneered. He knew where the two older men stood regarding people like Murdoch and Berlin. He hoped Peter also signed onto the anti group, but as a new member of the department, neither his voice nor his vote was yet needed by Billy. He'd talk to him quietly before the evening was over and ask him to treat as confidential any talk about theory and womens studies. "What did you think of the number Beverly and Mitch tried today?" Billy knew neither was on the personnel task force and he doubted either would have voted for him anyway.

Ben was happy the topic had unexpectedly moved from questions of tenure. He folded his hands over his fat stomach and was about to join the attack when Sally placed the entree before him. Ben looked down with pleasurable anticipation.

"Ben, it looks like a dish you adore," said Joyce. "If I'm not mistaken, that's Sally's lemon pepper sauce." She turned to Alice. "You'll have to join the dinner exchange she chairs," nodding toward Sally. "This amazing young dynamo has gotten even some of us old crones cooking again." She put her nose down to the dinner plate. "Just enjoy the aroma. I made this dish for Ben and he went wild."

I'd love to see that one go wild, thought Billy. The old goat probably inhaled the meal before the biddy had a chance to sit down.

"And it's her recipe that surely carried the day at that meeting." Joyce was one of Sally's favorites among the older women of the department. Ignoring Billy's guffaws whenever she mentioned anyone over fifty, she believed Joyce was a wonderful woman. "Give her a break, Billy. She's smart and nice. And she likes us." Professor Mann remained unconvinced. He rarely felt comfortable in the company of people whose facial expressions made clear their distaste for the language he enjoyed sprinkling into his conversations. And most of them were so piously politically correct. Don't they know the best jokes are ethnic. And who the hell are they to challenge his liberal credentials anyway? Fuck them. If they're obtuse enough to think he's anti-black or anti-Semitic simply because of some of the stories he loves to tell, then they're the ones who have no sense of humor. They just can't separate a joke from real social or political commitment. He didn't like to be constantly on guard lest he offend some old jerk.

It was bad enough at the university where women walked around with those frigging long antennae sticking out of their heads. Damned thought police just waiting to misinterpret whatever he said. Yet he, too, had changed some of his habits. Never again would he close his office door during a student conference. All I need is for one of them to scream sexual harassment charges against me. The open door at least cut the odds a little. You were never safe, of course. He'd get a chill whenever he thought of the charge brought against Calvin Willoughby. Of all people, Calvin.

A disgruntled doctoral candidate had reported that gray bore to the academic judiciary. Claimed he had tried to fondle her in the midst of a conference about her documentation methodology. Only a dinosaur like that would even have a conference about a footnote. All the poor fuck says he did was bend over her chair to point out the errors of her documentation form. Miss Militant insisted he touched her breast. Poor Calvin. I actually felt sorry for him.

The big dyke who chaired that sexual harassment star chamber had peered over her heavy black rimmed glasses at a trembling Willoughby. Billy, a witness since his office was across the hall from Calvin's, had sat in the front row of the conference room, watching the proceedings.

"And was your office door open during your interview with Miss Carstairs?"

"No, it was closed." Calvin's thin voice shook.

"And why, pray tell, do you lock your door when you interview female students?"

Walter responded for his client. The chair was acting as Calvin's attorney. "Professor Willoughby said the door was not open. He did not say it was locked. Nor have you established that he closed the office door only when conferring with females."

Billy was pleased by Walter's statement. The chair spoke confidently. It occurred to Billy that Walter seemed always to be on the side of due process. He just may be a decent guy.

The committee chair glowered at Walter. She stuck her glasses on top of her head. *The bitch thinks she's William Kunstler.* She offered the room a tight, thin smile. "You're quite right, Professor Henry. We haven't yet established the defendant's m.o." *Believing she also sounded like Kunstler, sure as shit looks like him,* she nodded smartly in the direction of the witnesses for the prosecution. Beverly Berlin, acting as a friend of the plaintiff, sat among the coven. She smiled broadly and whispered to the young woman sitting next to her. Billy recognized the other witch as Mitchell Murdoch's secretary. Trish something-or-other who had given him a hard time in a seminar during his first year at the university. *"Why were there no women poets and writers of color on his syllabus?"* Billy wanted to slug both of them.

"Tell me, professor," the lessie purred like a giant lioness waiting for her prey to come into range, "why do you close your door when innocent young students cross the threshold, assuming they're entering the security of a senior faculty member's office?" She ran her stubby fingers through her short butch haircut. *Probably cuts her own hair with a man's barbering set from K-Mart.* She looked up to the ceiling and smiled as she awaited Calvin's response. *I bet she's got a dildo motoring under that pair of dungarees.* She tapped her black workboots rhythmically on the green tiled floor. *The cunt's dressed like she's ready to bale hay.* Billy ran his hand along the good cut of his sport jacket.

Calvin glanced at Walter. The chair motioned for him to speak the words they had rehearsed. "I am a respected authority on bibliographic methodology, not on judicial proceedings. However, as an admittedly lay person in such matters, I must take exception to your insinuations. Indeed, I insist that my objection to these proceedings be made part of the official transcript which I assume is being compiled." Calvin licked his white coated lips. He tried to smile at Walter. "Furthermore, I do not intend to participate any further in this charade of judicial process." He pointed his trembling finger at his inquisitor. "I will also make my displeasure with your manner and words known to the university president and to my lawyer."

The interrogator began to respond, but Calvin stood up. "I don't want to hear another word from you." He gathered his few papers and carefully placed them in his old briefcase. "I find your manner offensive, madam, and I had better be quiet now lest I tell you exactly what I think of you and your evil cohorts." He glowered at Beverly Berlin. "You have demonstrated precious little respect for either rank or decency." He looked at Beverly again. "And I will not forget this affront to professional conduct." He lifted his briefcase. "Good day to you all." His anguish was not apparent as he walked from the room.

Good for you, Calvin. This'll be the high point of your career as far as I'm concerned. Billy was about to cast a withering smile at Beverly. He turned to her, but was disappointed at the sight of her and her compatriots hugging and congratulating their prosecuting attorney. They think they won. Can you believe it? Those bastards can pervert anything to their advantage. Billy left the room with Walter.

Dinner conversation continued to focus on Sally's culinary skills. Billy was happy that Alice Chase participated with obvious interest.

"Did any of you watch Meet the Press last Sunday?" Billy tried to move the conversation. Except for an abortive try by Peter, there were no takers. Peter's words were drowned out by loud and enthusiastic talk about favorite sauces for pork. During a pregnant pause Billy tried again. "I think Honest Abe Smith's the only one who thought Newt Gingrich made sense."

"Is Abraham a Republican?" asked Ben. His tone and raised eyebrows suggested that no young, serious academic could possibly be a Republican.

"No, of course he isn't," said Sally. "He was simply offering his reading of the interview itself. Isn't that right, Billy?"

For a moment Billy wondered if a lie might not do himself some good here. Surely, the Rosenthals were Democrats. Weren't all eastern Jewish intellectuals Democrats, after all? If he were sure that the Willoughbys weren't staunch supporters of the GOP, he would have quarreled with Sally's comment. But it wasn't worth the risk. "Sure, honey, you're right."

"And what's wrong with saying a good word about a Republican?" asked Dorothy. Her once beautiful face revealed not a trace of humor or irony. Her blue eyes went from person to person, awaiting a response to her challenge. "Calvin and I have voted Republican since the first Eisenhower-Stevenson race." She smiled. Even though she fell into that age group Billy disliked, he was taken by the beauty of her smile. He looked at her closely for the very first time. She must have been a looker. Even now, her long white hair was lovely. Held tight in the back by an Indian clasp, it fell midway down her back. Dorothy was fond of wearing clothes and jewelry that reflected her southwestern background. Sally had earlier admired the silver and turquoise squash blossom necklace that looked so good against her black turtleneck. Billy envied Dorothy her vest. His own paled in comparison with the intricate Indian beadwork that adorned hers. It must have cost old Calvin a bundle.

Billy sipped his wine and thanked God for smiling on him that evening. Christ, if I had shot off my mouth about Abe and the Republicans, who knows what Willoughby would have thought. Probably throw his vote to a fellow Gingrich lover.

"There's something too precious about self-congratulatory liberals," Dorothy continued. "But I'm no longer cowed by their arrogance. Arrogance like that of the Clintons. They think they have all the right answers. They simply suffer the rest of us."

"Now, Dorothy, don't get wound up." Calvin advised gently.

"I am not getting wound up." Dorothy smoothed her necklace against the material of her blouse. "I am simply making a point. I shall not be ashamed to announce my political affiliation."

"But surely, you must admit there are factions in your party that are pretty shameful." Peter finally had a chance to enter the conversation.

"Of course there are, young man." Dorothy smiled benignly. She had a terrible time remembering names. "But aren't there in every institution?"

"But more crazies find a home in the Republican party," said Peter. Alice feared he was spoiling for a fight.

"I used to think the very same thing when I was your age," Calvin said. His words sounded more combative than he had wished. "What I mean is that when I was a young man, I truly believed I had cornered the market on the true and the just." He tried to sound conciliatory. "And the most liberal wing of the democratic party represented to me that truth and justice."

"And did the party change?" asked Ben. "I still think the left wing of the party is our best hope." It was clear these two had debated the question many times.

"Of course the party changed," said Dorothy. "More importantly, we changed." She chose her words carefully. "Please don't think me as arrogant as Hillary Clinton, but Calvin and I grew up. We came to distrust politicians. Oh yes, in many ways we remain political junkies, but we really loathe politics." She paused. "I think we'd probably be Libertarians if we could convince ourselves that we weren't merely indulging ourselves and wasting our votes. So we vote Republican. Not because we're devoted to any particular candidate. Only because we think the Republicans are less interested in interfering with the lives of individual citizens than are the Democrats."

"It's really as simple as that," added Calvin.

"But too many Americans need the help of government," said Ben.

"Now you're in danger of riding your hobby horse," said Joyce, "and of elevating your blood pressure." She tried to laugh the subject away. "Why don't you talk about something less contentious. Like Billy's earlier question about the task force."

Less contentious to you, lady. Not to me. I'd trade both Clintons for my tenure. Christ, I'd vote for Buchanan, for Jesse Helms, for that asshole Sharpton if it would guarantee my promotion.

Abraham entered the seminar room and took his seat at the head of the table. Really two university issued utility tables pushed together to form a long rectangle around which sat the ten members of a seminar on the poetry of Robert Frost. Who better to teach such a class than Abraham Smith? Who in the department loved the subject as much as he did? Why, then, did the instructor enter the weekly meeting with such a heavy heart? And on the sort of late autumn day that Frost loved. The mid-afternoon sun shone on the remaining maple leaves, painting them a soft orange, highlighting the last color of the season. The day was pleasantly warm, casting Abraham's mind back to the mild summer now past while reminding him of the fleeting fall moments before winter would blast its way across the campus.

No, it had not been the changing seasons that slowed his step as he approached the seminar room. Nor was it the barrenness of the room. Just as Abraham believed the Wallace Lounge was a special place, so he wished for a seminar room that befit advanced literary studies. His own graduate classes had been held in carpeted, wood-paneled seminar rooms. Handsome decorative brass sconces graced those walls. And paintings and drapes. His present room replicated the rest of the humanities building. He shook his head at the green tiled walls, the chalkboard, the contrasting green tiled floor, the mini-blinds that failed to operate properly. His love of the symmetrical was assaulted as he looked at three different rectangles of broken blinds and dirty glass. He had given up trying to force the blinds into something approaching symmetry. Not even the chairs matched. He looked at the graffiti and messages scratched onto the table top. Janitors had failed in their half-hearted attempts to erase the art work bored students had engraved. A copulating couple, "education sucks," a heart containing the words "eat shit." The last, at least, interested Abraham each time he placed his books and papers at his place. The critic in him wondered about the incongruity of the italicized words so carefully inscribed within a universal symbol of romantic love. Was the author suffering unrequited love; had he been jilted; was he an ironist? Someone had tried unsuccessfully to enliven the room with a few travel posters. Adjacent to the chalkboard, student-oriented offers were scotch-taped to the wall. Little cardboard containers held postage free cards for subscriptions to magazines, applications for Visa cards, Kaplan GRE study courses, the Peace Corps, home pregnancy tests, study abroad opportunities. Worlds beyond the small compass of the campus beckoned from each colorfully designed container of post cards.

But the reason for Abraham's sigh of resignation had nothing to do with the unpleasant ambiance of the seminar room. Rather, it was the class that sat around the pushed-together tables. Only mid-way through the semester, Abraham was already counting the meetings before Christmas break and freedom from these graduate students. Thank God he still enjoyed the undergraduates he met three times a week.

He knew it was only bad luck that had given him this group. He knew he mustn't take it personally. But he did. What had he done to deserve them? Worse, what had Robert Frost ever done to have his work man-handled, lacerated, yes, murdered by so smug a bunch of critical butchers? Abraham had the misfortune, which he complained about each Tuesday night to his family, to have attracted a class filled with followers of Mitchell Murdoch and Beverly Berlin. Seven of the ten faces awaiting his opening remarks belonged to disciples of literary theory and womens studies. He had come to hate them. Each week, Abraham had six days to read the reports they would present at the following seminar meeting. Each week he put off until the last possible moment his examination of their mutilations of the poetry. Each Monday he would retire to his study and groan. Poor Robert Frost.

Abraham decided to begin this day with a student report rather than a discussion of the assigned poetry. He asked one of the holy three, those who tried to understand the work rather than force it into some alien context, to read his paper. Even though it was a good report, Abraham's attention remained fixed on the dream he had the night before.

He and Eleanor were at a chamber concert at Saint Peter's chapel. A small, beautiful neo-Gothic room with magnificent acoustics. He was fond of chamber music and had series tickets since his first year in town. He enjoyed the total experience. The intimacy of the chapel, the seats that were his for every performance, the joy shared with the other hundred or so members of the audience, the dozen lit candles at the front of the church, the vaulted altar with an ornately carved silver cross at its apex, the statuary which lined the walls on each side of the audience, the beatific Virgin to the right of the musicians, the softly lit Jesus, arms outstretched, at the center of the ivory paneled altarpiece. It was perfect.

Suddenly, in the midst of a slow, stately second movement of a Beethoven quartet, Abraham heard the locks of the chapel's doors crack shut. The four musicians and their instruments froze in the process of their bowing. The Virgin rose from her base and hovered over the astonished audience. Bright orange flames engulfed the altar. Though frightened, no one was able to speak or move. The flames neither damaged the altar nor gave off smoke. The Virgin spoke. "Do not fear. No harm will come to you." She smiled. Abraham was comforted. He felt a peace he had never before experienced. He wanted to thank her, but he could not speak. The Virgin floated toward Jesus and gently touched one of his outstretched arms. Having given life to her son, she returned to her pedestal. The flames subsided and Jesus left his place at the center of the altar. He lowered himself to the floor and stood at the priest's lectern. He raised one arm, the posture of blessing. The audience discovered it could stand. Without any instruction, each person took the hands of those on either side. Christ spoke. "I have come to bless you, my faithful servants." Abraham had never imagined himself to be devout. Christ floated just above the audience. He touched each person's head as he moved from the front of the chapel to the rear and then back again to the priest's podium. Abraham wanted to ask Eleanor if her head felt as warm as his own. He joined the others as the audience got to its knees.

"I have created this moment in order to make manifest to you the existence of a living and loving God." His voice resonated like that of a great actor. The role of a lifetime, Abraham thought. The chapel thrilled with the quiet power of that voice. Christ's eyes glowed. "Having borne witness, you will go forward to carry to the multitudes, each in your own way, the promise of my words." His smile was healing. "And your reward will be the granting of your deepest desires. Those will come to pass in the days ahead. And you will know, because you do know, which of those desires are worthy of coming to fruition." He returned to his place.

Abraham heard the locks slide back to their open positions The musicians resumed at precisely the point where their motions had been frozen. He looked around the room to see if he had been the only one to experience the fantasy, the experience. He saw that everyone looked as he did. They were all smiling and nodding their heads in affirmation.

The concert ended. But instead of filing out of the chapel as was customary, the audience lingered. Strangers hugged one another. "Bless you, brother. God be with you, sister." Abraham and Eleanor embraced.

"Professor?" asked the student at the conclusion of his report. "Professor Smith? Are you all right?" Even the unregenerate among the theorists looked concerned as they turned their chairs toward the silent instructor.

Abraham was lost in contemplation. He had only a few minutes to tell Eleanor about it that morning. The kids had overslept and Eleanor was running late for her breakfast treats discussion and demonstration with Sally Mann's eating group. It was a meeting she particularly wanted to attend. Breakfast was Abraham's favorite meal. "No way will I give her something to prattle about with the biddies," Eleanor said as she rushed about the kitchen. "I'll be all sweetness and light." She drank her coffee while walking toward the front door. "Over my dead body would I let anyone know that Billy's gotten to me."

Abraham stood in the middle of the kitchen, trying to tell her about his dream. Teddy and Ann raced to force down their toast and eggs, gather their books, and put the finishing touches on their attire, all the while shouting the time to each other.

"Yes, Ab, it sounds very interesting, but not now, please." Eleanor made a last check of the children, kissed Abraham on the cheek, and was out the door. "Talk tonight, honey."

She waved as she backed the car out of the driveway.

Abraham was suddenly alone at the kitchen table. The room was quiet. He poured a cup of coffee and nibbled at the food left by his frantic children. He cleared the table and loaded the dishes into the washer. He sponged off the place mats. He took Alexander, their old lab, for his walk. He dressed and packed his green bag. But the dream would not be denied. What did it mean? What would Eleanor think it meant?

"Professor?"

Abraham shook his head and re-focussed his attention. "A good report, Roger." He smiled at the angular, homely young man who had just completed his reading of "Out, out." Fortunately, Abraham had read the paper only the day before and remembered it very well. Roger had stayed with the poem and had examined it pointedly and intelligently. One of the sane members of the seminar, Roger Cohen was a favorite of Abraham's. This was the second time Roger was in a Smith course. He was also Abraham's teaching mentee. They had visited each other's classes and met frequently to discuss pedagogy and the profession. Abraham had been delighted when at the past year's commencement ceremonies Roger had been named the best teaching assistant. He and Eleanor had run a celebratory dinner for Roger and his girl friend, Emily, about whom the professor had heard so much when their conferences strayed from pedagogy to personal matters. She was a little beauty from Thailand. Eleanor liked them both, even though she giggled about what they must look like when they did the nasty. He so tall; she so petite, Eleanor's lovely term for a shrimp.

"Any comments?" Abraham's usual request after a report. He dreaded the missles which would, of course, be launched against Roger's reading of the poem. It was much too clear and far too coherent to go unchallenged. If for no other reason, Roger's use of language was an affront to the disciples of Murdoch and Berlin. His style was a pleasing blend of critical sophistication and charming prose. This could not be allowed to succeed. Certainly not by the disciples. Our common English tongue would never do. They were committed to a language not within the range of the uninformed, the untutored, the uninitiated. After all, as Mitchell was fond of saying, if the average lay person, even the well educated lay person, were able to read our stuff as easily, say, as they read novels, where would that leave us? What would that do to our claim to professionalism? He generally drew on his pipe at this point or tapped a cigarette on his silver case. Do you think for a moment that physicists would allow such easy entree into the fruits of their research? Do you really think doctors are happy when patients actually know something about their medical problems?

Abraham looked around the table. He waited for the onslaught. Murdoch's words angered him. The wider the audience, the better was his credo. Privileged language indeed. It was nothing but posturing bullshit. Probably the only thing he and Billy Mann agreed on.

"I'm concerned about the literality of Roger's reading," a swaggering voice began the discussion.

"Literality?" Abraham chuckled and stared at Murdoch's confident clone. "What exactly do you mean, Michael?"

A short bearded young man, Michael was Abraham's mortal foe. Arrogant and smart, he had been led down Murdoch's garden path to professional preferment. He never laughed. The closest he came was a crooked sneering smile when he challenged opposing viewpoints. That Murdoch had nominated that surly sycophant for the teaching assistant award fueled Abraham's disdain for the great theorist. More than once he had wondered if either the master or the disciple enjoyed literature. Did sour Michael enjoy anything? Earnest to the point of monomania, the instructor thought, Michael was not one for bantering conversation. Worse, he wrote a turgid prose that he believed was important. Everything his crowd did was thought important. Their inflated notions of their work made them seem preposterous to Abraham. And in some crazy way, they believed they were at the forefront of political and social change as well as of the profession of humane letters. Nothing humane about them. And their politics was centered on old-fashioned Marxism. Defunct except in the minds and classrooms of these new soldiers who liked to think their dreadful, unintelligible essays and classrooms were akin to revolutionary barricades. They were the red army liberating the fields of academe from the reactionary white forces.

"Well, professor," Michael made the title sound like a curse, "Cohen reads the poem as if it meant what it seems to mean." Taking aim at the remaining members of the Romanoff family, the bearded one continued. "Even though there's a corpus of traditional literary criticism that obviously valorizes the sort of interpretation Cohen offered, there are newer, more exciting ways of approaching texts." He almost smiled as he made eye contact with his accomplices. "One might even suggest that the poet's own name speaks to the new and dynamic criticism I'm referring to."

"How's that?" Abraham asked.

"Well, sir," another curse, "think of the many connotative meanings of the word, frost." He looked away as though his thrust had pierced the professor's heart.

"Now they're explicating writers' names." Roger laughed.

"You can laugh all you want," said Clara Little. "But you're in Mitchell's seminar. You heard him last week talking about the paper he's writing on the unconscious symbolic values of names." Clara was angry. A tall, dark haired woman, she was the handsome alter ego of Michael. "It's simple. But like most great ideas, no one thought of it before."

"Before Murdoch did," said Tim Cooper, one of Berlin's television monitors. He turned to Abraham. "Frost is cold and the product of winter. The death of the year."

"So?" asked Roger.

"What do you mean, so?" Michael's sneer returned. "It means that new, fresh, spring like, if you will, interpretations are required to breathe life into Robert Frost's poetry."

"Sure," shouted a second of the saints, Audrey Connors. "Authors' names are the keys to understanding their work." She waved her hand in disgust. "I know you guys even hand out this crap to your kids in freshman comp. They have enough trouble putting three coherent words to-gether and you subject them to this." She shook her head and folded her arms across her chest. "Give me a break." She spoke to Abraham. "I dropped the great Murdoch's course after that last meeting they're so proud about." Audrey was getting more agitated. "You wouldn't believe his spiel. Oscar Wilde was wildly innovative and C. P. Snow wrote in the winter of a novelistic tradition."

"Then he began stretching. Thomas Hardy loved the hardy peasant. And Anthony Trollope. Well, you can imagine." Roger pumped both arms into the air. "I can't wait until he does his number on Browning and Snodgrass."

Michael stood up. "You can laugh all you want, Roger. The point is that Mitchell's work is groundbreaking. Not the kind of moribund stuff." He checked himself before offending Professor Smith and jeopardizing his straight A average. "The kind of moribund stuff he's struggling against."

Having read Michael's paper on the same poem Roger had so sensi-bly discussed, Abraham elected to cut the class short rather than endure Michael's reading. His head was now throbbing. The dream and the semi-nar had been too much for one day.

He fled from the room and sought refuge in the Wallace Lounge. The amber windows had the desired effect. Abraham sat in his favorite chair and set his face to the pale light of the late afternoon sun as it filtered through the glass. He breathed deeply. God, they make it hard to take them seriously. He folded his arms across his chest and closed his eyes. Images of the dream crowded his mind. Spread the good word to the likes of them? It seemed like a hopeless enterprise.

"Getting a little shut-eye before the trek home, Abe?" Billy Mann broke into Abraham's reverie. He was standing by the coffee maker. "Want a cup for the road?"

The two men sat in facing chairs, drinking coffee and avoiding eye contact. Billy thought of pancreatic cancer. Abraham toyed with the idea of mentioning his adversary's dirty tricks.

Billy pulled his chair closer to Abraham, even though they were alone in the room. He put his coffee on the table Walter liked. He touched Abraham's knee. "We have to talk, you know."

Here it comes. Finally, an admission.

But forgiveness was not on Billy's mind. "I assume you've heard about Murdoch and Berlin's plot?"

Walter Henry was very careful. Whenever the longings became too great, he'd drive to a roadhouse thirty miles from town. He first read about The Hideaway in the personals column of *The Journal,* a weekly alternative newspaper that emulated its better known cousins, *The Free Press* and *The Village Voice.* He brought it home every Wednesday, ostensibly for its good movie reviews. Maggie enjoyed the fine arts calendar. The boys claimed it had the best sports coverage in town. But it was the personals pages that Walter poured over in the privacy of his study. A man of no actual gay experience, he was titillated by the anonymous writers under "men seeking men"; he wondered what the masseurs looked like and what their services included under "complete massage" and "body rub"; he sometimes considered calling one of the numerous telephone sex lines, all featuring photos of handsome young men in bulging briefs; he wanted to visit some of the bars and clubs that had such enticing advertisements. Invariably, Walter was aroused by the personals. Invariably, his heat was attacked by the chilling fear of discovery. What would he do if he did answer an ad and the man at the other end was not discreet or if he was a serial killer or if he was diseased. The papers were filled with such stories. He shuddered in relief whenever he read them. What if he did visit a massage parlor and was recognized by another patron? What if the handsome hustler at the other end of the sex line was one of his kinkier students earning a few extra bucks? What if he went to one of those clubs and everyone there knew him? One of his recurring nightmares.

He woke up in a panic one night when that dream first entered his unconscious. All those masseurs and men-seeking-men authors and sex-line operators had thrown him a surprise birthday party at some subterranean club. Leather and chains and old, painted queens. And in the center of them all, Walter Henry being feted. A birthday cake with lit cocks instead of candles. "Blow them. Blow them. Blow them out." The hordes of perspiring, semi-nude men chanted and laughed. It was a scene from an Isherwood novel or Brecht fantasy. And suddenly there appeared a photographer from *The Journal.* Flash bulbs. Fear. The front page picture the following Wednesday. "Chairman Walter Henry celebrates his birthday surrounded by his friends."

The warmth of unfulfilled desire was gone. Walter's reading of the personals would end with him in a cold sweat. His shame would be unbearable. Maggie, the boys, his career. All destroyed. And his in-laws. God, what a hideous field day John would have. Only Howard would understand. Could he ever face his wife again, his sons, his colleagues, his students?

But Walter did visit The Hideaway. Perhaps it was the restaurant's logo, "a family place, and so much more," that made him feel it would be a safe place to try.

He dressed carefully that morning. No expensive suit, no shirt and tie, nothing that might set him apart from the others. But how would those others be dressed? What does "a family place, and so much more" look like? Would there actually be families there? Enjoying lunch while "so much more" went on around them? Or might "family" mean something altogether different? Was it a code word that the initiated understood and the neophyte chair did not?

Walter decided to visit at lunch. It seemed an innocuous time, a safe time. He told Maggie he was going to a rare book store which was also in Winchester. He wore jeans, a blue denim shirt, sneakers. Maggie knew the store was dusty. She was not at all suspicious when he left the house. "Have fun with your old books."

When Walter pulled into the parking lot, he was surprised by the number of cars already there at 11:30 in the morning. He sat in the car for a few moments and looked around. The building looked like hundreds of other roadside restaurants one finds on highways across the country. Well-kept plantings in the front, a large blue awning with the place's name printed in white, double glass doors bearing the small labels of credit card companies, newspaper machines, public telephones. As Walter left his car he scanned the parking lot, looking for university parking decals on rear bumpers. He didn't notice any in the rows he passed.

Once seated at a window table, water, menu, and bread basket delivered by a pretty young waitress, he examined the menu and the restaurant. Both struck him as quite ordinary. Could the ad have been misplaced in the paper or was The Hideaway simply what it seemed to be, a pleasant roadside restaurant? Walter ordered a tuna sandwich and coffee.

There were more men than women, more parties of one or two than families, but it was midweek. Children were, of course, in school.

Walter thought a good-looking man was staring at him. He looked down at his food. My imagination. He looked up. The man smiled at him. Walter blushed and felt foolish. He returned a smile that looked more like a pained grimace. He continued to eat. Was he really staring at me? Walter was nervous, but excited. He enjoyed the security of his cover. After all, he was only having lunch before his date with rare books. He had committed himself to nothing but a tuna sandwich and coffee. He smiled more confidently.

The other man left his table and paid his bill at the desk. Walter watched him. He took a couple of mints from a pink glass bowl on the counter. He gently touched one of the roses in a vase next to the cash register, obviously checking to see if it were real or cloth. He lit a cigarette and walked toward Walter's table. Walter's heart beat furiously. The pulse in his head was throbbing. His palms were damp. What would he say?

"Mind if I join you for a minute?" The stranger had an easy warm smile. His voice was cultured. "I hope you don't mind this." He pointed to his cigarette.

Walter's voice trembled just a bit. The same nervousness it evinced at the first class meeting of every semester. And just as in the classroom, it quickly regained its customary confidence. "Not at all." He motioned to the chair opposite his own.

"Haven't we met before?" the stranger asked, putting his cigarette out in the ashtray. He reached his hand across the table. "Dennis," he said.

"Walter." They shook hands. The chair was immediately worried about having used his real name. "I don't think we've met." He tried to sound friendly. He took in Dennis without being too obvious. An attractive man, perhaps thirty-five, clean shaven, business suit, striped shirt, tie, neatly cut brown hair, a firm handshake, well-cared for nails, slim fingers, a wedding band.

"Your first time here?" Dennis asked.

"As a matter of fact, it is. Passed the place a hundred times, but I've never stopped before."

"And what brought you in this time?" Dennis smiled and lit another cigarette. "As you've discovered," nodding at the half eaten sandwich, "the food isn't the great appeal of The Hideaway." He looked at Walter, trying to glean something from their eye contact.

Walter looked down. He was flooded with conflicting emotions. Fear and desire. "Oh, I'm not finished yet." He lifted his sandwich. Again, he felt foolish. Like a young high-schooler fluffing his lines when the class beauty finally talks to him. He thought of James and Jeremy. His cheeks were hot. He knew they must be scarlet.

"That's all right, Walter." Dennis spoke softly and gently. "We've all been there." He gambled that his impressions were correct. "I've got a family too."

Walter felt he could trust this man, but his fears were not easily overcome. "But, really, Dennis, I'm here only for lunch." He stammered. "I'm going to spend some time at the Book Barn. The antiquarian book store in town." He wanted to say that he wasn't "that way," but he didn't want to end this meeting.

"Perhaps I spoke out of turn," Dennis said, sure that he had not. 'If so, I'm sorry." He put out the cigarette and stood up.

Walter looked up imploringly. "Please. . . ."

Dennis sat down. "Walter, there's nothing to worry about. Secrets are safe here." He motioned the waitress for a cup of coffee. "Kelly has kept this place as a safe haven for us married men for years. He's got the same problem, you know." He remained silent while the waitress served his coffee. "You see, Walter, it really is a family restaurant. There's no steamy back room or cheap hustlers hounding the bar." He laughed. "There's no bar. About the hardest thing Kelly serves is root beer."

"But the ad. . . ."

"Oh, *The Journal*. Kelly tried that a few years ago when business was slow and his libido high. Says he was curious to see what kind of clientele it would bring in." He gestured toward the rest of the place. "You can see. Guys who want the bar life didn't want this. But a few curious men," he lowered his voice and dared, "a few curious gay and bi men came in. Usually older, certainly cautious. Anyway, they continue to come. Fewer gays with each issue of the paper. But a steady stream of people like me and Kelly there." He waved to a sport-jacketed portly man of about sixty who had joined the cashier behind the desk. "And you?"

"I honestly don't know what I want," Walter answered. He looked down again.

Dennis stood up. "Well, Walter, I hope you find out some day." He touched Walter's shoulder as he moved away. "Good luck to you."

Walter watched Dennis. He spoke with Kelly for a few minutes. He took another mint. He checked his pager and made a telephone call. He moved toward the door and then stopped as though he had forgotten something. He walked to the rear of the restaurant, twice looking back at Walter before he entered the men's room.

Had Walter misunderstood again? How many times had he thought handsome men had given him a sign, only to have discovered that it was his desire rather than their interest that led to the false interpretation. How many times had he stood at a urinal, staring straight ahead, urging his penis to grow just enough to gain the interest of the man standing next to him. Heart throbbing, waiting for some sign, mortified by a scoff or disappointed by silence. Far worse, he thought, the few times he had dared use the tea houses on his own campus. Those bathrooms that attracted the queers, the homos, the fairies that fascinated Walter. He had never done anything in those tea houses but read the scribbled requests and responses on the walls. Each time, he stood there scared. Each time, he left feeling dirty. But The Hideaway was not on campus and Dennis was not a student or undercover cop or photographer for *The Journal*. He made his way to the rest room. His legs trembled.

Dennis stood before the white porcelain urinal. He smiled at Walter. "The pause that refreshes," he said.

There was a bank of five urinals. Walter stood next to Dennis. They were alone in the room. Dennis backed up a step or two. Walter realized it was to give him a better view, to let him see that Dennis had been awaiting his arrival.

They did not touch each other. Neither man said anything until they were finished.

Outside the restaurant, they shook hands.

"Can I have your phone number?" Walter asked, emboldened by their mutual experience.

Dennis smiled. "Perhaps later." He touched Walter's shoulder again, but this time the grip was firmer and it lasted longer. A thrill went through the chair's body. "We'll see each other again. I know we will."

"But when?" asked Walter. He knew he sounded like a high-schooler. He feared that he'd never see him again.

"Lunch next week? Same place, same time? I'll be here." Dennis walked to the parking lot. He waved as he got into his car. Walter made a note of the MD license plate on the Lincoln Continental.

"Well, I don't see why we have to import someone when we have talented assistant professors right here in our own department," Ben Rosenthal said.

"And it's a lot cheaper to promote one of the boys we've already got than to recruit some fancy dan on the make." Jack Williams didn't look up from his pornographic doodling. "At least Billy Mann, creep that he is, would add some spicy language to this group of," he laughed derisively, "oh so distinguished professors of literature." Because Williams did love books and attended every reading in the Creativity Center, he was familiar with Billy Mann's roasting of their colleagues. "I need some reinforcements in these antiseptic trenches." He put the finishing touch on a copulating couple. "I'm tired of being the only one trying to get a rise out of you guys." He held up his creation. Jack enjoyed irritating his fellow professors. "Now that's a hell of a better use of time than debating the merits of hiring some jerk who'll come here and teach another section of queer studies." He turned the page of his pad and immediately started another drawing.

Walter cleared his throat and looked away. Although the two men truly liked each other, Jack Williams was the only member of the department who intimidated the chair. Walter feared his quick acerbic tongue which regularly skewered some pompous professor or another. Secretly, Walter agreed with most of Jack's irritations, but he frowned on his colleague's language as he did on his heavy drinking. Maggie couldn't stand Jack Williams. He was allowed in the Henry home only when the entire department was invited. She didn't care how important a critic and writer he had once been. To her, he was a trying bore.

The discussion had been going on for the better part of the meeting. The personnel task force sat around the teak table in the chair's office.

"But the only reason for our request is to make this a stronger department," said Beverly Berlin. "An even stronger department," added Mitchell Murdoch, a better diplomat than his ally.

"Yes, of course," Beverly cooed. "And Mitchell and I do appreciate this opportunity to meet with the personnel task force."

Walter looked at his watch. "I know some of you have classes at eleven so let's try to wrap this up in the next fifteen minutes." He looked at Beverly. "I'm always happy to convene the group whenever colleagues make a request such as yours, but you know we've already decided to promote one assistant professor this year. And, frankly, I don't think the dean would look kindly on a request for an additional tenured position."

"Walter, perhaps we haven't made ourselves clear," Beverly touched the chair's arm. "What were suggesting involves only one position."

Walter looked confused.

Mitchell took the ball from Beverly. He knew she could push this group only so far. He was a full professor and she was looking forward to her own promotion which would have to be recommended by this very personnel task force. "That's right, Walter. We want to bring in an associate professor from the outside instead of promoting one of our own assistant professors." He looked at the six men and one woman who composed the voting members. "And please understand. We have nothing against Mann or Smith. They're both fine young scholars. But," he smiled, "they're not going anywhere."

"Who the hell would want any of us?" Jack seemed half in the bag. And it wasn't even noon, thought Walter.

"As far as I know, both of them are happy here," Beverly said, ignoring Jack. "And let's face it, the world isn't beating a path to their doors. Neither of them has finished his book. . . "

"And we're sure both books will be splendid," Mutdoch interrupted.

"Even if both works will be," she paused, "somewhat traditional. We want to bring in someone more on the cutting edge."

"Someone who watches videos instead of reading books?" The question sounded like the discharge of a shotgun in the quiet room. The speaker frowned at her colleagues and raised her eyebrows in the direction of Beverly. Wilma Crouse sat with her hands folded on the table. Her note pad was blank. The youngest full professor in the history of the department, Wilma was openly scornful of Beverly's work. A head taller than Beverly, Wilma was a beautiful thirty-five year old and had already published three books of criticism and a volume of poetry that won the Wesleyan Young Poets Award the year before. The academic world was beating a path to her door, but Walter had little difficulty matching outside offers. The university wanted to keep this one.

"You give it to them, kid." Jack threw a warm, if smarmy smile in the direction of Wilma Crouse. Having decided long ago that he was brilliant and really sweet under that crusty veneer, even if too vulgar at times, Wilma dismissed him with a good-natured wave of her hand.

Beverly bit her lip. This bitch isn't going to make me lose my temper. She'd known for a long time that Wilma would be the sure negative vote when she stood for promotion. She also knew that the affirmative action committee had badgered the department to promote another woman to full. And Beverly knew she was the only female associate professor ready to be promoted. Even better, the president had kept pouring money into her projects. A social scientist, he understood little of the work done by literature professors. But he could count publications and grants. On a purely quantitative scale, Beverly was important. Who cares what Wilma Crouse thought. She wasn't the only one with administrative endorsement. Beverly nodded at Wilma. "Oh, Willie," she forced a friendly laugh, "we know there isn't another person of any consequence in my field." She smiled at the men. "No, we're talking about someone who reads books." She looked at Walter. "Only books. Not the texts of electronic communication as well as books." She reminded the others that she did both.

"Well, I'm not convinced we really want another theorist or feminist in this department. Even if we were fortunate enough to get both in one package." Wilma returned Beverly's nod. "I certainly don't mean this personally, but my position is that we need more people who actually work with real literary texts." She nodded again. "Even if such an enterprise is considered somewhat traditional by some." Wilma's own work was traditional to the core. All three of her books dealt with canonical British novelists. No flashy questionable contexts. No interpretations that vitiated the works as products of their time and place. No deconstruction or postmodernism for her. "Whatever those words actually mean," she was in the habit of scolding her seminar students whenever they introduced the critical terminology she argued was hostile to literary understanding. The farthest Willie Crouse moved from the text under her scrutiny was to its historical matrix, a term which was included in the title of her first book. Whether or not Beverly or Mitchell approved of her work, they knew she was a superstar in the profession. She was also very smart. This was not a person to take lightly or to offend. And Willie took offense easily.

"Do you have any names for us to consider?" asked Calvin Willoughby. He looked up from his loose-leaf binder which contained careful notes of the meeting. For years Calvin had served as secretary to the personnel task force. "It would be helpful to have some names to consider."

"As a matter of fact, we do." Mitchell passed batches of stapled sheets around the table. "Here are six people we feel strongly about. They're all at good universities now. And believe me, they're all going to go places.

"As long as they're far from here," Williams snorted. He was working on a very small man with an enormous phallus.

"We've included a substantial amount of information about each of them," said Beverly. "We've spoken with senior colleagues in each instance, and we've been assured that these are very strong candidates indeed."

"You mean you've suggested there's a position here?" asked Wilma.

"That is, of course, the prerogative of this task force," Calvin scolded.

Mitchell held up his hand. "Only preliminary inquiries. Don't worry, Calvin, we didn't go beyond that."

Beverly cooed once again. "We would never violate the mandate of this group." Her smiling face ingratiated itself on every member but one.

Walter called for an adjournment. He thanked the task force and its guests.

Mitchell and Beverly left the chair's suite, sure they had planted the first seed. Their next stop would be the dean's office. Then the president's. Their campaign had just begun.

After their departure, Jack Williams held up his drawing. "What do you think, gang? Is this Murdoch or Berlin?" He was the only one who laughed.

Helen Abrams loved politics. Ever since childhood, she had been surrounded by political discourse. Her parents moved in a circle of political activists who seemed always involved in some crusade or another. Even as a small child, Helen accompanied them to meetings and rallies, handed out leaflets, helped prepare refreshments for supporters of this candidate or that referendum. When she got older, she manned the telephone to urge people to follow her folks' lead. The house seemed always filled with pols and workers as it was filled with political magazines and periodicals. Only after she left home for college did disillusionment set in. The more her studies focussed on dispassionate analysis, the farther her positions veered from partisan commitment. The more carefully she examined politicians, the more she came to dislike them. Will Rogers was right, she had once said to her father. All they're interested in is getting reelected.

He looked up from stacks of mailers, lists of voters in their precinct, and piles of bumper strips. "What kind of crap are those professors handing you." He held up a poster. "This is a good man." He pointed to the photo of Walter Mondale. "What do you want? Another four years of the actor." He made a face. "He wasn't even a good actor, that Reagan."

Helen had no heart to challenge her dear father. She didn't tell him she thought both of them were bums. Nor did she want to open the wounds of a former terrible argument. She had once lamented her parents' movement from belief in real principles to this, what her father claimed was practical politics. "I'm tired of beating my head against a brick wall. Yeah, sure, ideals are terrific. Especially in that ivory tower of yours. But it'd be nice to win one for a change."

Her mother nodded in agreement. "We know all about the greatest good and equality for all and social causes you haven't even studied yet. But we also learned that if we ever get to them, if the country ever gets to them, it'll be by baby steps."

"Right. Little steps, not some leap into the golden future." Her father kissed her forehead. "And, believe me, even if Mondale's steps are small ones, they at least go forward. Not backwards like the actor's." He went back to stuffing envelopes.

Helen realized she had skipped the stage her parents still inhabited. They were probably right now sitting in the den she knew so well, posters of some candidate or other on the bridge table, stuffed envelopes ready to mail, lists of voters to be contacted, coffee and danish on the table by the television set. Mr. Abrams was addicted to CNN Headline News. He'd watch it for hours. "You never know when something's going to break. You never know when the polls might change. And when something happens, you think the commercial stations are going to interrupt some stupid program to tell us. No sir. Only CNN lets you know when it happens." The *it* was the magical word Helen grew up with. Almost never within a discernible context, it was always only moments away. In her father's world, *it* shared the spotlight with *they*. Whenever there was trouble in the neighborhood or in the world, he would invoke *they* and *them*.

"But dad, who are they?'

"What do mean, who are they?" He'd look at his precocious daughter in exasperation. "Someday, maybe, you'll understand." He'd smile indulgently. "Someday, little Helen, you'll know that they are them. Someday, when you go to college and make us all proud of you, you'll know."

She wondered if he was that clear when he dealt with his customers in the drug store. How did he explain the prescriptions he filled every day? Did he dismiss all those sick people with "they know what they're doing. Trust them. This'll take care of them. And don't forget, without the medicine it could happen."

Helen Abrams was thinking of her folks as she awaited the start of the meeting.

The small basement room in the student union was only half full. Maybe twenty people. She was the only faculty member in the midst of mostly students and a couple of townies. It was the monthly meeting of the local chapter of Citizens for Campus Freedom.

If politicians were all self-serving pricks, her numerous memberships gave her some small hope for positive change. Her wallet bulged with membership cards: ACLU (even though she would never forgive them for Skokie), ADA (even though no one seemed to know it still existed), Habitat for Humanity (even though she couldn't stand Jimmy Carter), Common Cause (even though she despised their surveys in those oversized envelopes), The Urban League (even though she hated Jesse Jackson, Al Sharpton, and most other self-appointed black leaders), NOW (even though she thought most of them were dykes with all their sex is rape bullshit), Anti Defamation League (even though she wished they wouldn't wear yarmulkes, but they're right on the money about that bastard Farakhan), Sierra Club (even though she thought most of them were self-righteous prigs and they didn't smoke). Helen was not easy to please.

As always she tried to look like a professor for the monthly CFCF meeting. No jeans or sweatshirt even if the meeting fell on one of her non-teaching days. Her buddy, Joan, looked good in anything, but Helen knew she had to work at reaching something even remotely approaching attractiveness. God, she hated models. What a profession. Those airheads making all that money just because they were lucky enough to be born beautiful. It's a real meritocray we live in. Those bimbos sign their checks with an x, but peckers all over videoland swell with desire when those broads follow their tits onto the screen. Go figure, as her father was fond of saying. Helen unbuttoned her navy blazer and leaned back in the uncomfortable chair as the chapter president called the meeting to order.

"I'm happy to see you here tonight." The young man smiled at the sparse group. "You know what they say about few in number, don't you?"

Oh, God, it's *they* again.

"Some of our members are still on the picket line, but I'm sure they'll be here soon." The president wasn't much of a public speaker, but he raised his voice to announce the fruits of the picketing. "And we won't let up until all campus parking lots are free to all motorists." He held up a fisted right hand. A few people applauded.

Helen had been opposed to this latest crusade. She particularly disliked the poster that proclaimed "classism sucks." In reality, she had come to believe that classism was not a half-bad thing. More importantly, she had presented real problems that plagued the campus and which were more important than access to parking lots. But the neo-Marxists (could they define the term?) urged a fight against elitism (another poster she disliked). But Helen had kept her temper in check. She wanted to scream against those scruffy potheads who thought they were creating a better society with their raised fists and open access to parking lots. But she did not. As faculty advisor to the CFCF, she knew the group would eventually fight a fight worthy of its mandate. Walter's sly comment that her promotion might not be automatic, as promised, seemed a worthy cause. As was the issue of female representation at the upper faculty ranks. Even if such a crusade might help that dreadful Beverly Berlin, it was still worth a rally and a few posters. If these kids don't get their consciousness raised, then the organization which she helped found when she was in graduate school had failed. She'd bide her time until her forces could be sent into a worthy battle. They like to think they got a New York radical Jew. Okay, boychicks. I'll give you a New York radical Jew. And I don't mean stuffing envelopes and handing out posters of slick Willie.

Eleanor thought the Wallace Lounge actually looked inviting. The undergraduate student society had made the dreary room look festive. Red and green streamers hung from the amber windows; large paper balls decorated with Santa Claus, reindeer, and the names of faculty members hung from the faux beams; a perfectly shaped Christmas tree, glistening with tinsel and gleaming with little blinking colored bulbs, stood in the center of the room; recorded carols filled the lounge. Gold and silver banners on the walls proclaimed Merry Christmas and Happy New Year. A blue and white Happy Chanukah had been bootlegged in by Helen Abrams for the pleasure of the other eastern radicals. Tables imported from seminar rooms lined the front wall of the room. Sally's food group had made unattractive university furniture look appealing. Covered with green cloths and red napkins, they held egg nog, mulled wine, fruit punch and assortments of holiday cookies. The room smelled good. Eleanor was impressed. The party would go on all afternoon so students and faculty could partake of holiday cheer regardless of their class schedules. The brief formal program was scheduled for four o'clock.

Faculty spouses were expected to attend at least that portion of the party. Everyone would gather in a large circle around the tree and the chair would distribute gifts to the folks who actually ran the place: two administrative assistants, four secretaries, and a handful of work-study students. Each year Eleanor was mildly curious to see what presents the holiday task force came up with. After all, they had the annual tariff to play with: a hundred bucks from full professors, fifty from associates, and twenty-five from assistants and instructors. A healthy hunk of change, she said at breakfast. Only the part-timers were forgiven the gift tax. Those poorly paid adjunct faculty who labored in the freshman composition trenches along with graduate student teaching assistants were invited to the holiday party, but along with their grad student colleagues, the academic gypsies were guests of the full-time faculty. Noblesse oblige indeed, Eleanor snorted to herself when Walter made a big deal of welcoming them. He always made it sound as if they were free-loaders. Have you ever noticed, she would say to whoever was standing next to her, that all our Marxists who claim such devotion to the downtrodden masses never even blink about the plight of those part-timers. I bet they don't even know their names.

"But they know the names of every frigging corrupt dictator in every dissolute African country," Jack Williams once said in agreement. Eleanor had to admit she had a warm spot for him, his vulgarity and groping notwithstanding. She had set him straight on the latter account. She still wanted to have him to dinner, but she hadn't yet found the nerve or right mix of guests to risk the adventure. It'll be a disaster was Abraham's only comment whenever she broached the possibility. But now with that strange alliance between her husband and Billy, maybe she could kill more than a couple of birds with a single dinner party.

Abraham found her in the crowded room. He kissed her on the cheek. "So, what have I been lucky enough to miss?" He looked around his favorite room with distaste.

"Don't be so obvious, Ab. They'll think you're Scrooge."

"Just look at the place." He smiled broadly. "Is this better?"

"A little too obvious. You don't have to look like Howdy Doody."

"Even the windows are covered." He bent down to pick up a discarded red napkin. "They'll ruin the lounge." He looked at his watch. "I wish Walter would get it over with before all those stupid candles burn the place down."

"Stop being such a fuss-budget," Joan Eastland said. She embraced Eleanor. "I almost wish they would move the damn party to the Creativity Center." She squeezed Abraham's arm. "It might keep this guy from having a stroke."

"And just before the semester break," added Helen Abrams who joined the group. "Next to summer recess, the best time of the year." Most academics would agree. The best campus was an empty campus. No classes, no meetings, and, best of all, no students. You didn't have to worry about wearing the same outfit on consecutive teaching days. Jeans and sweaters were perfect. Your office was a place you could work in without interruption. The library was free of the bustle and noise of students honing the art of plagiarism. The grounds looked their best during recess. The campus became a well-maintained estate for scholars. For weeks on end they could pursue their quest for professional preferment. It was a lovely time.

Walter cleared his throat. He clapped his hands. The noise level did not abate. Someone flicked the overhead lights on and off several times. Walter was grateful. He smiled toward the crowd around the light switch. He cleared his throat again. Maggie handed him his Santa's hat. The twins had vowed never to attend another department Christmas party if their father wore the full costume again. He yielded, but James and Jeremy didn't show up anyway. It's just too gruesome, they maintained.

"Speech, speech," a few cruel people shouted.

Walter colored. "Only a few words. Only a few, and then you can return to your merrymaking."

Abraham wanted to add, "but only until five. And then it's good riddance until commencement." A couple of faculty members escorted, rather pushed, the honorees to a cleared space in front of the chair. Sycophants took pictures. The first flashbulb ignited memories of Walter's nightmare birthday party. He smiled them away. "Ladies and gentlemen, here before me are the people who do all the work around here." Applause. "I want to thank them and wish them every happiness for the holiday season. As tokens of our appreciation, my wife, Margaret, will distribute gifts from a grateful department." Applause as Maggie did her first lady's duty. Walter held up his hand. "These good people have asked that we break with traditional practice and not have the presents opened now." He held up his hand to silence the mock groans. "I know we'd all like to see the gifts, but we really don't want to embarrass anybody, now, do we?" He smiled manfully in the face of a chorus of "yes we do, yes we do." He shook hands with some and gave chaste kisses on the cheeks to others. "Now," he shouted, "enjoy the rest of the afternoon. And to you all, a very merry Christmas." He removed his red and white hat and shook it in the air. The small bells tinkled.

"For this he gets twenty per cent added to his salary?" Helen asked. "He couldn't just say have a happy holiday season?" She sipped her punch. "I could use something stronger than this. You'd think the great defender of equal rights could remember we live in a pluralistic society."

"Fucking-A," said Jack as he poured from his flask into her red plastic glass. He also laid his hand on Helen's ass. "Happy Chanukah, kiddo," he said and kissed her on the forehead. There was something so genuine in his voice and look that Helen responded with a kiss on his cheek.

She removed his hand. "Merry Christmas, Jack."

Williams staggered away to try his luck with others.

"You know, I actually like him," said Eleanor. On the spot she made a decision. She invited Joan and Helen to a dinner party she was going to give in honor of the publication of Jack Williams' new book. "I'll have to check on the exact date the book comes out."

Abraham looked on and shook his head. "Now you've gone and done it." He laughed. "And who else do you plan to invite to the disaster?" He pointed around the room. "Why not the chair and," he offered a mirthless smile, "my new ally, Billy?"

Eleanor nodded her head. "Okay, you're on." She scanned the room. "And why not the video queen and her real estate tycoon?" She continued to look around. "We'll make it a buffet. How about the great theorist and," pointing to the door, "Willie. She's come in just in time to get an invitation. And that new young couple. The guy who writes about the movies.

"Peter Chase."

"Right, why not?'

"And the old timers?"

"I happen to like Joyce and Dorothy."

Abraham shrugged. "We're going for broke anyway." He winked at Joan. "You can bring the alka seltzer. It's going to be a hell of an evening."

Helen grasped Eleanor's arm. "Are you serious, Ellie? Are you really going to put all those people in the same room at the same time? You better have a doctor on call."

"Or at least a referee," said Abraham.

"Well, I could invite the kids' new doctor. We discovered this terrific guy in Winchester who specializes in adolescents. He's opened a second office right here, just a couple of blocks from the main entrance to the campus."

"One civilian in the midst of all those academics?" Helen wondered if he'd be out of place.

"Why? He and his wife wouldn't be the only non-teachers there. Look at me for instance." She pondered for a moment. "But I'll think about that one."

Wilma Crouse leaned back in her office chair. She shook her fist at the front page of *The Journal*. I'm glad my parents aren't here to see it. Looking back at her from the desk was a two column photograph of herself. At least it's a good picture. She smiled ruefully. "Black, Female, and Brilliant" headlined the article about Professor Wilma Crouse. That should teach me to give interviews. It'll never change. Why can't the article just be about a faculty member at the university? Gender's bad enough, but race too?

She poured a cup of tea and sat down in an easy chair. She looked out at the empty campus. Heavy gray snow clouds were lumbering in from the west. It was a classic winter sky. She pulled her heavy cardigan tighter around her.

The green-shaded desk lamp illuminated the newspaper. The only light in the rapidly darkening room made Wilma feel comfortable. The same security she felt as a child when her mother read to her on late wintry afternoons. They sat close to each other on the living room couch, under the single lamp her mother turned on. It's more cozy this way, isn't it, Willie? They'd sit together until her father came home.

Tears filled Wilma's eyes. She wept for the lost past and the unfair present. *The Journal* was only the most recent instance of what she had encountered throughout her entire academic life. Why can't they just treat me like anyone else? When she graduated from Newton High School with a perfect A record, some wondered aloud about the breaks surely given to one of the few blacks in that superior school. That she was valedictorian made little difference. Her admission to Wellesley produced the same cruel insinuations. She remembered her freshman advisor asking which scholarship she had been awarded. Or that so-called liberal history professor's asking her in front of an entire class what it was like moving from the inner city to a town like Wellesley. That he thought his pony tail and Farm Workers pin entitled him to be kind to a poor black girl suddenly thrown in with so many rich kids was no excuse. She was still too shy to say aloud what she thought. I live in Newton, only a few miles from this very campus. My father is a physician and my mother has an M.A. in library science. We have two cars and a summer house on Cape Cod. My family was perfectly capable of paying the outrageous tuition at this college. But I won a competitive academic scholarship. Do you hear? Competitive. Academic. Neither your silly badge nor your pony tail nor your designer jeans entitles you to be so patronizing. That history professor was only the first in a line of self-proclaimed, self-serving, smug so-called radicals who made her distrust the liberal beliefs she had brought to college.

Things were no different when she started her graduate work at Harvard. She knew people wondered which affirmative action program got her into the Ph.D. program. And the very assumptions that drove the Wellesley history professor powered her new classmates and faculty in Cambridge. Her major research interests must be in black studies and womens studies. What else? Her desire to specialize in nineteenth and twentieth century British novelists brought smiles to her doctoral committee.

"Seriously, Miss Crouse, what do you intend to carve out for your area of special interest?" Old Professor Cummings continued to smile at her and his two colleagues. "No, no. The modern British novel is not for you." He placed his folded hands over her record, open on the table before him. "We must think of your career after all."

The youngest member of her committee, himself a specialist in the very period she claimed as hers, spoke quietly. "You are aware of the job market out there, Miss Crouse?" She was grateful that he did not smile. Professor Katz continued. "No offense meant, but your gender and your race coupled with a Ph.D. from this university will make you a hot property."

"They'll swamp you at MLA," said a portly eighteenth century scholar. "I dare say, you may have a boatload of offers before the convention." He smiled. "It's all in the packaging."

Katz broke in. "I think what Doctor Murphy means is that the hiring committees will assume, rightly or wrongly, that you'd be prepared to teach black and womens area courses."

"Then I'll have to contradict their expectations." Her voice betrayed her nervousness. "I certainly don't mean any disrespect to any of you. But I've wanted to study the British novel ever since I was in junior high school." Her voice calmed. "That seems so long ago, but it's true. Ever since my mother and I read together, I've loved those writers."

"Tell us more," said Professor Katz. His demeanor convinced her that he was really interested. She was so used to condescension.

"My father's a doctor and his dream was that I'd follow in his footsteps. You see, I'm an only child. It took time, but I was able to bring him around. Can't I do the same with this committee?" Wilma looked down. "I've lived with other people's assumptions and expectations for so long."

She recounted some of her experiences at Newton High, at Wellesley, at Harvard. "Why is it so difficult for people to accept my interests for what they are? I have nothing against womens studies or black programs."

"Nothing?" Katz raised an eyebrow.

"Well, not much anyway." They smiled at each other. "They're not for me. I want something more rigorous. And even though it sounds scandalous to many of my classmates, I see nothing wrong in studying so-called canonical writers."

"My, you are a rebel." Katz laughed. "Has our distinguished visiting professor, Mitchell Murdoch, heard your blasphemy?"

"I take his course next semester." She gave Katz, whom she decided she liked, a coy smile. "It should be interesting."

The meeting concluded with the committee recommendation that Miss Crouse's specialty would be the British novel and her dissertation chairman would be Oliver Katz.

God, I wish Oliver were here now. I need a shoulder to cry on. Wilma stood up and stretched. It had been a long day of polishing her talk for the MLA meetings in New York. She'd be flying out the next morning. Her first MLA paper since the year they did swamp her with offers. She turned on the overhead light. And they yakked about my promotion to full professor too. Packing her briefcase, making sure her lecture, airline tickets, and hotel reservation were where they should be, she realized she was excited about the convention. Wilma loved New York at Christmas. She knew her paper was good. And dinner with Oliver and Becky Katz would cap the trip. She touched a finger to her lips and then to the framed photo of her parents with whom she'd spend the new year. Things could be a lot worse.

She walked along the brick path to the parking garage. The snow flakes looked beautiful as they fell around the orange sodium lights that lined the walk. She was eager to look at the store windows on Fifth Avenue, the tree at Rockefeller Center, and Saint Patrick's all decked out for the holiday.

TWO

The campus community was exhilarated. It had snowed every day during the last week of the semester break and now the sun shone brightly on the pristine white academic enclave. Under a brilliant cloudless blue sky, students and faculty strode confidently along the plowed walkways on this first day of spring semester.

Things would improve this term. Grades would be higher, professors more interesting, dates more plentiful. So said the paying members of the community. Students would be smarter, classes more interesting, publications more plentiful. So said the paid members of the community. All was confidence. And why not? asked Walter Henry as he enjoyed the spectacle from his wall of glass. It's a Norman Rockwell come to life. He sipped coffee from his Shakespeare mug and almost laughed out loud, his pleasure was so great. He loved the texture of the world below him. From his crow's nest, he nodded approvingly at the colors and shapes making their way toward the un-named humanities building. Little Pippa might have been right. He mouthed, "God's in His heaven and all's right with the world." There were the colors of the rainbow moving in living kaleidoscopic wonder. The semester would be a good one. For starters, no annual football game and no in-laws. His sons would have been surprised and perhaps a little worried if they had seen Walter throw both hands into the air. Touchdown!

The chairman saw Billy Mann and Abraham Smith in conversation, walking together toward the building. Now, if that's not a harbinger of the fifteen weeks to come, what is? If those two can march together, can departmental harmony be far behind? He closed his eyes for a moment and imagined a blissful semester. A sober Jack Williams. A conciliatory Mitchell Murdoch. A total blackout of Beverly Berlin's video screens. No outside offers to Wilma Crouse. Walter sat at his desk. He turned his rolodex to Dennis' name, carefully coded under The Book Barn. And lovely visits to The Hideaway. Perhaps more. Who knows? The terrible birthday dream no longer haunted him.

His relationship with Dennis had brought a quiet calm to Walter. He was now enchanted by the prospect of his new friend moving to town. The local practice had gone so well that Dennis was house-hunting in Walter's very neighborhood. The schools were better than in Winchester and Dennis' three children would be much better off. The cultural offerings of the university attracted his wife, Norma. Ever since Dennis had mentioned a possible move, Walter had fantasized about inviting Dennis and Norma to dinner, becoming neighborly, trading visits, hoping Maggie and Norma would become friends. Nice people, the Collins couple, he imagined Maggie saying. He would learn something about professional football which Dennis followed with passionate interest. Surely the boys could give him a crash course. He remembered his ignorance when Dennis talked of his favorite team, the Broncos. For all the tea in China he could not have said what city those Broncos came from. Walter did not believe he had ever heard of the Broncos. He had heard of the Yankees and the Bulls, but who hadn't? Neither played football, of course, but Walter could at least nod about those teams. He knew their cities too. Even the games they played. But he knew little of Michael Jordan or Bernie Williams. He had heard Jeremy and James talk of them, but which played which sport or for which city, he knew nothing.

Now he needed a quick study. Even John would be impressed. Well, maybe not John. Walter had begun to read the sports pages. He memorized the standings. He started to watch Sunday afternoon games. He mimicked Martin Crane, the father on *Frasier* and bought beer and pork rinds. He offered Ballantines to the twins. He hung on every sage comment they made during the course of the games. He became fond of the Buffalo Bills after he read of Marv Levy's academic background. A historian, no less. The twins were delighted with their father's newfound interest. Margaret shook her head in wonder. She couldn't understand Walter's desire to watch football rather than attend the Sunday chamber music series at the university. Male menopause, she concluded. Pork rinds and beer? Really, Walter. Where did you ever develop a taste for them? She confided in Joyce Rosenthal. Ben loved sports.

A knock on the office door interrupted the chair's bliss. Mary Bullock, the secretary to four consecutive chairs, whispered to Walter. The dean was in the outer office. She screwed up her nose. She had seen deans come and go. This one she did not care for. The Irishman doesn't have an appointment, she continued to whisper. Shall I send him away? Mary despised the Irish.

Walter stood to greet Patrick Donovan. A man who had planned on becoming a Jesuit, he was never to be trusted. Born and bred in Boston, he affected all things Irish. Even his slight brogue was a cultivated thing. And that silly tweed hat he always wore. More than once Mary had said she wanted to cut off that little red ball that perched on the top and replace it with a bomb. Then, when that mackerel snapper put on his dumb hat, kaboom. After that, we can have a search for a real dean. Whenever the chair's secretary invoked the first person plural, she clearly meant the president, the provost, the board of trustees, and Mary Bullock. You know, she was fond of saying, I've been in this department longer than most of them.

"Good morning, Patrick," said Walter, extending his hand. "What brings you to my neck of the woods? And on the first day of classes. I'd guess you've got a million things to do."

"Now, now, Walter, what could be more important than a lovely chat with the estimable chair of this distinguished department?" Donovan chuckled. "You know my fondness for the glories of the mother tongue." He selected a handsome chair. He ran his hand along the am, obviously enjoying the feel of the supple leather. "In my four years at the university I haven't been able to convince the powers that be to furnish my office with such beautiful things." He waved his hands in an attempt to embrace the chair's surroundings. "I'll never know how Wallace did it."

"Money wasn't so tight in his days," Walter said softly. He was always uncomfortable when the dean admired the office. Mary was convinced that one day the Irishman would requisition everything in her suite. She'd come in on a Monday morning and it would all be gone. In her bad dreams of such a calamity, she chained herself to her gorgeous teak desk which Dean Wallace had let her pick out herself. It was one of her prized possessions. At least once a day, she could be seen polishing her handsome office furniture. Just let them try, she muttered as she sprayed Pledge onto the glistening wood. Just let them try. Damned Irishman.

The dean lit his pipe. He never asked if smoke might bother anyone. Walter opened a drawer and slid an ashtray toward his guest. Patrick dropped his spent match in the glass ashtray, blew a cloud of aromatic smoke into the room, and looked out the window as if he were deep in thought. "You know, Walter," his brogue seemed particularly thick this morning, "I've been thinking about the future of the university." He blew another cloud. "And I can't imagine a great university without a great literature department."

"We surely agree about that, Patrick." Walter tried not to look apprehensive. When a dean says he's been thinking about your department, you have to wonder how broad the ax stroke will be. "And what do you have in mind?" Walter wanted to sound casual.

"Well, to tell you the truth, I don't believe we've paid enough attention to the cutting edge specialities of your profession." He savored each syllable of specialities.

"Oh?" Walter knew immediately that Murdoch and Berlin had had a successful discussion with the dean. Those two had easy entree to the higher reaches of the administration. From President Maxwell down to Patrick Donovan, every one of them was a scientist, genuine or social. What they all had in common was their ignorance of literature, but they all could count publications and add up grant money. They even applauded the length of Calvin Willoughby's bibliography. Now, Walter had nothing against Calvin or the work he did. But those pages of citations were primarily insignificant notes about bibliographic methodology. Walter had been around long enough to know that a brief note about an unimportant matter took up exactly the same space on a resume as a magisterial book on a truly significant question. But if all one could do was count items, one could not make qualitative judgments. And these administrators were quantifiers.

More than once, Walter had been forced to write lengthy memoranda to explain the importance of colleagues' work when their bibliographies looked sparse next to Calvin's. He had written more than one about Wilma Crouse to insure the counter offers which kept her here. But the memos were not nearly as impressive to those entrusted with the future of American higher education as the offers from universities they admired. Who cares about the praise of other English teachers? They all scratch each others' backs anyway. But bona fide offers from great universities must mean that Professor Crouse was worth holding onto. Patrick Donovan had never read a single word Wilma had written, but he praised her effusively whenever he had the opportunity. His staff prepared enough notes so that he actually sounded conversant with their work as he stood before an audience and heaped praise on this or that member of the literature faculty. He never took questions about the scholarship of his faculty.

"Yes, Walter, I do believe we need to inject some new blood into your department." He turned his face from the window and stared directly into the chair's eyes. Walter looked away. Patrick smiled. "As a matter of fact, I've husbanded a few extra dollars which I'd be happy to put at your disposal. To insure a healthy transfusion, you understand." The dean drew on his pipe, pleased that he had continued the imagery.

"And just what do you mean by the cutting edge of the profession?"

"Oh, my dear lad," Patrick laughed, "I'd never presume to tell you what's what in your business." His heavy gray eyebrows rose in mock surprise. "No, no, Walter, that's for your people to decide." The dean stood up and went to the window. "All I can suggest is that you appoint a search committee," he smiled a cold smile, almost a smirk, "a task force, I believe that's the term you prefer, to bring to me the names of the best people in the country." He turned away from the view Walter admired. "But not too expensive, mind you. Not too dear." He put his hand on Walter's shoulder. "Perhaps an associate professorship for a start. An attractive offer to some smart young person ready for promotion elsewhere. Yes, that sounds about right." He quietly slapped his hands together as if that good idea had just come to him. "And with the money we'd save by not promoting one of your own assistant professors and the few dollars I can spare, I do believe we could put together an attractive package. Yes indeed, a very attractive offer."

Walter was angry, but his voice remained controlled and low. "Our personnel task force has already recommended that we promote one of our own this year." He stood up. It was his turn to look out the window. His back was to the dean. "We have two particularly talented young assistant professors whom we must consider for promotion. Right here in our own department, Patrick."

"They'll wait. As far as I know, neither one's been flooded with offers. And I don't think Mann or Smith exactly fits the job description I have in mind."

The dean had been well briefed by Mitchell and Beverly. "Again, Patrick, what would that job description look like?"

Donovan was becoming irritated. Apparently the chair was not properly grateful for the offer which the dean had delivered in person. "Why do you look at a gift horse with so little enthusiasm?"

The horse is an apt image, Walter thought, but in his version of events, it was more Trojan than gift. "And do you have any recommendations about who should chair such a search?"

"As a matter of fact, I've given that some thought also." The dean joined Walter at the window. "Beautiful sight that, isn't it?" He re-lit his pipe. "I think Murdoch would give great luster to a national search. Wouldn't you agree? The president and I think display ads in the *Times* and *Chronicle* with Mitchell's name perhaps in bold print would be terribly impressive. Not too large, but ads in discreet good taste can only enhance the effect. Yes indeed, very impressive."

Walter saw this was clearly not a request. Christ, he's already cleared the search with his boss. Probably has a draft of the advertisement in his pocket. "I assume you'd also like to have Beverly Berlin in on the search?" He knew it was a rhetorical question.

"Another splendid suggestion," the dean said, as if the entire search was now Walter's idea. "I agree. Your most visible people should be involved." The dean looked at his watch. "I must run." He tapped his pipe over the ashtray and placed it into his shoulder bag. "Opening of the semester lunch with the trustees today." As he moved to the door, the dean added, "They'll be delighted to hear the literature department is moving into the future in high gear." He waved and departed.

Walter remained at the window. The scene was less thrilling now. He had been a wimp and now he would have to pay the price. What would he say to the personnel task force and to the two assistant professors?

"Well, he looked happy," said Mary as she placed the morning mail on the chair's desk. "We better count the silverware." She arranged various letters and memos in neat piles. Most bore yellow post-its carrying her remarks and suggestions. She glanced at the chair's back. "Are you all right, Walter? That scheming man didn't upset you, did he?" She looked concerned. "Can I get you a cup of coffee?"

"No, Mary, nothing." Walter told her everything that transpired in his meeting with Donovan. "Terrible," she frowned. "That terrible man. You remember, Walter, I thought both Billy and Abraham should be promoted this year. Your personnel bunch made a lousy decision about only one promotion. But now, I don't know how you can tell the department no one will be promoted." She asked him again if he'd like coffee. "You better be careful. Those awful people are eager to take over." Mary touched Walter's arm and returned to her office. She reached into the bottom drawer of her desk for the Pledge.

The blissful prospects now dashed, Walter stretched out on his couch. He covered his eyes to block the sun streaming in through the windows that had given him such a pleasant view only minutes before the dean's visit. He groaned. Who needs this miserable job? The extra money, the office, the prestige all seemed shallow. Not even the fact that the chairmanship was the only honor his in-laws thought worthy of their daughter. To hell with John Taft. Walter groaned again at the sound of his intercom. "Don't forget the lunch meeting you scheduled with your personnel group. They'll be expecting you at the faculty club in ten minutes." Mary's professional voice suggested that she wasn't alone. "And, Walter, Billy and Abraham want a minute of your time."

The two assistant professors were sitting in the secretary's office when the chair emerged from his own. He tried to sound cheerful. "So, what can I do for you two on this gorgeous day?" He was putting on his olive green duffle coat as he spoke. "Mary must have told you I've got a lunch meeting at the faculty club." He checked his briefcase. "Why don't you walk with me."

"Can we see you later this afternoon?" asked Billy. "It's important."

Walter looked at Mary who was already consulting her calendar.

"Three is good," she said without looking up.

"Then three it is," the chair said. "I'll see you then."

"Why's he so happy?" Billy asked Mary. "I saw the dean walk down the corridor. A visit from that bastard couldn't have been good news."

Mary frowned at Billy's language, but it was a mock frown at best. Actually, she enjoyed his blunt words almost as much as she did Jack Williams'. Jack was her favorite. Of course she was aware of his problems, but she knew she could always trust his judgment. And Jack was fond of her. They went back a long way. It was not uncommon to see the two of them huddled in her office, trading confidences and laughing at his colleagues. Jack had the line on every one of them. On cold winter afternoons, when the building was quiet, Mary would make tea for the two of them. She drank hers straight; Jack added medicinal spirits to his. She hated cigarette smoke, but she always had the ashtray handy when Williams sat down for a heart to heart. And if the truth were known, those two compatriots offered advice and counsel to each other about their most personal problems. The years had created an intimacy between them that no one could really comprehend, although many enjoyed speculating. In the groves of academe, rumors and rumor mongering are year round sports. Gossip was the coin of the realm.

Bare of holiday decorations, the faculty club once again looked impressively chaste. Once the president's residence, the brick Tudor building had the great advantage of location. It was an easy walk from virtually every academic building that occupied the campus' central core.

Walter adjusted his tie and checked his zipper after he hung up his coat in the unattended cloak room. Professors were compulsive about checking flies and always going to the men's room before entering their classrooms. An observant reporter of academic habits might be led to the conclusion that the seat of learning was below rather than above the waist.

The task force had already assembled. They appeared to be a convivial bunch as they chatted and smiled at each other. Jack and Wilma were drinking beer from heavy glass mugs which bore the university logo. Calvin was waiting for his tea to steep the appropriate five minutes. He had bored more than one luncheon table about the differences among teas. He knew more about that beverage than any sane person would want to hear. Walter was pleased that they had taken one of the round tables by the window that overlooked the gardens. Even though it was winter and nothing was blooming, he could at least look out at the sculpture court whenever conversation lagged or became unbearingly boring. He had become expert at thinking about other things while appearing to be considering the subject that held the table's attention. More and more, the topic of Walter's inner attention was professional football.

He had developed nonsense words to help him remember the names of the teams and the places they represented. He couldn't understand why some teams used the names of cities, some states, and even an entire geographical region. Why weren't they the Boston or Massachusetts Patriots? And why were the Giants from New York when they played in New Jersey? And whoever decided that some eastern teams were in reality western? Dennis had laughed at these questions. Forget about it, Walter. Just enjoy the game. Who cares that a Carolina team is called western or that the Giants play in the Meadowlands? Look at the mess of geography the NCAA gets into every basketball playoff time. Walter had gone directly to the twins. What in God's name is the NCAA?

After ordering the day's special, sliced chicken breast over an arugula salad, and tasting a good California chardonnay, the chair delivered the dean's encyclical.

Peter Chase lay stretched out on the living room couch. Struggling with an impenetrable study of film noire, he continually sighed at the density of the argument and the writer's invocation of a gratuitously technical vocabulary. When he did actually penetrate the damn thing, the commentary was banal. Why did I ever assign this to my seminar, he sighed. The author's standing in the so-called avant garde of film studies had prompted Peter to add a touch of continental élan to the reading list. He didn't want his doctoral students to think he wasn't with it. But he hated the book and everything it represented in contemporary academic criticism. Fucking fraud, he muttered and closed it. He wanted to punch the smiling arrogant face of the author which covered the entire back of the dust jacket. I wonder if that bastard ever enjoyed a movie.

But more than the book bothered Peter this morning. Alice had been out all night. Ever since their graduate days at Duke, Peter knew Alice had been involved with Mitchell Murdoch during the theorist's year as a visiting professor. Then and now, she didn't seem to mind that she was only one of many charms on that cocksman's key chain. But this was the first time since North Carolina she had spent the entire night. Doing what and where, he wondered. His concern was bred more by worry about her wellbeing than jealousy. Theirs was what in earlier days was called an open marriage. They never talked about their extra-marital activities. They carried on as though there weren't any. Peter and Alice kept open secrets from each other. He never talked about Murdoch except in professional terms. Nor was Peter surprised when he learned that Mitchell had urged the recruitment committee to hire him. Why not? They could get a good young scholar and he could get a dependable fuck. Alice had urged him to take this job. And even in a lousy job market, Peter had garnered four good offers.

Yet Peter and Alice loved each other very much. They knew many of their friends and colleagues, especially the older ones, could never understand the depth of their devotion to each other in the light of their quirky marriage. They enjoyed each other's company; their sex life together was satisfying; they appeared to be a perfect young couple. Long ago they had decided to keep the openness of their relationship secret rather than try to explain it.

Peter had readied the kitchen table for breakfast. Not one of his teaching days, he had plenty of time. The coffee was on, English muffins were in the toaster, grapefruits had been sectioned, eggs were ready to scramble. Peter was pouring a cup when he heard the front door open. He was prepared for that inevitable moment of embarrassment. He heard Alice open the closet door to hang up her coat. He imagined her stopping at the hall mirror to check her face and put on a smile. He pushed down the lever on the toaster oven and turned on the cook top burner.

"Peter, I'm home." Alice entered the kitchen. She hugged Peter and kissed him on the cheek. "The house husband at work," she laughed. "I'm famished." It was the perfect line for a nasty rejoinder. Instead, Peter waved her to the table.

"Start on the grapefruit. The eggs will be ready in a minute." He wore an apron bearing a picture of James Cagney pushing a grapefruit into the face of an actress famous for that scene. Alice always tried to buy him presents related to the movies.

"I see you've been reading at that book again." She looked up from her grapefruit. "Why not just delete it from your list? All it does is make you angry."

"I read another chapter this morning." Peter held his nose. "I'd like to kill that guy." He spooned scrambled eggs onto matching plates. A large sunflower dominated the centers of the white surface, surrounded by a brilliant blue band. On the way to the table, Peter put the muffins into a small wicker basket. He poured coffee into a matching sunflower mug for Alice. He placed a white dish towel over his arm and affected a French accent. "Would Madame care for anything else?"

"At least the French can still cook," Alice said, "even if their literateurs are a bunch of schmucks."

They ate breakfast, happy that the embarrassment had passed. Peter didn't ask where Alice had spent the night. She behaved as though she had spent the night in her own home with her husband. Each wondered how curious the other was.

"So what do you do now?" asked Helen Abrams.

"Maybe kill a few of them," Abraham answered with a weak smile.

"Why not?" Joan Eastland muttered, her mouth full of cinnamon and raisin coffee cake. "You should really try this," she pointed to her plate. "This is one of the Petrovs' specialties." She addressed those words to Billy Mann. This was his first visit to the Russian Coffee House.

Helen had never dreamed she'd be sharing a table with Billy. Yet there were the four of them sitting in the crowded room. Classes over for the day, she and Joan had been sharing their day's events when Abraham and Billy entered the restaurant. Both women did double takes. The men joined them.

"The news from the front is pretty grim today," Abraham tried to sound like Walter Cronkite. He told Helen and Joan about the meeting with Walter.

"That sanctimonious bastard with the fake brogue told our dear chair to jump, and all he could do was ask how high." Billy turned the old joke on the chairman. "Can you imagine the balls of that man? A few words and departmental decisions go right out the window. And we're kaput."

"What would you have done?" Helen asked, still not impressed with

Abraham's new friend. "Me?" Billy smiled. After all, in his dreams of a future chairmanship, he had played a number of war games. "My dear Helen, I'd have told him to take a flying leap."

"And if he refused?" asked Joan.

"I'd be in the president's office in a flash."

"But he already had the president in his pocket," said Abraham.

"Okay, let's assume he wasn't just bullshitting Walter about that. If that were actually the case, I'd carry the issue of departmental autonomy to the floor of the academic senate."

"And you think those people would give a damn?" Helen had dealt with that body about CFCF issues. "Most of those so-called senators are only interested in across-the-board salary increases. They're the sweethearts who vote against merit increases every year." She flipped her hand under her chin. "That's what I think of those losers." She leaned forward. "There isn't a decent publication or a teaching award in the group. They're apparatcheks. Factotums for the bloodless union we're forced to belong to. I'll tell you, the last thing to energize most of them was Vietnam protests. Life stopped for them with the end of those good old days when they could urge students to do things they themselves would never dare do."

"Come on, Helen, you weren't even here then." Abraham laughed. "Where were you? In kindergarten?"

"Very funny. I wasn't at Fort Sumter either, but I know the rebels had to be beaten. The same way I know that heroes like our senators re-acted the same way all over the country. No, Abraham, I didn't have to be here to know their kind."

"All right," said Billy, "then I'd carry the battle to the press. If you're right about the courage of our colleagues, I'm sure you'd agree that the glare of public opinion is something the dean and his administrative gang want to avoid at any price."

"Public opinion?" Helen snorted. "Get off it, Billy. Do you really think the public gives a damn about a struggle between a literature depart-ment and a dean?" She waved his statement away. "A losing football sea-son. That's what the public cares about. Higher taxes to pay for lazy pro-fessors. That they care about. But a couple of disappointed assistant pro-fessors? Forget it."

"She's got a point," said Joan. "I hate to admit it, but it's only an illusion to think we really matter to all those good folks who pay our wages."

"Fine," said Billy. "Let's assume you're correct again. I'd get to network news. I've got an old buddy who's a big shot at ABC."

Helen shook her head. "You're unbelievable. Now you think Ted Koppel's going to do a Nightline on us? Or Peter Jennings' going to give it a closing feature on the evening news?" She motioned to a Cossack for more coffee. "I can see it now. David Brinkley asks about the literature department and a dean." She laughed. "And Cokie, Sam, and George spend ten minutes on Sunday morning defending Henry, Smith, and Mann against the machinations of the IRA. Sure, Billy. Big time news at ABC." She winked at Joan.

"Laugh all you want. I rather think George Will, at least, would be interested in the case. He might even write it up in his end paper in *Newsweek*."

"And Beverly Berlin's going to win the Pulitzer Prize, Jack Williams' gong on the wagon, and Mitchell Murdoch's pecker's going to fall off"

"And Walter Henry's going to get a spine," Billy laughed for the first time. "So I was carried away. But the issue is an important one." He finally took a forkful of his coffee cake. He held his fork up to Joan. "This is good."

"At least you showed us you can laugh." Helen's tone softened.

Richard Maxwell awaited the start of the meeting with his cabinet. A political scientist by trade, he liked the sound of the word cabinet. Always imagining the stakes to be greater than they actually were, the president liked to think the national press awaited his presence in the conference room after important cabinet meetings. A tall handsome man, Maxwell had been president for six years. He had brought to the campus a sense of style unknown in previous presidents. Even Maxwell's detractors, which numbered virtually everyone in the humanities and others of even modest intellectual interest, admitted that their leader knew how to dress. But that was about as much as they would concede to a man they thought outgoing, personable, and shallow. Maxwell himself judged his faculty more on their style than their substance. For him, appearance was far more impressive than scholarly accomplishment, which, in fact, bored him.

Like Bill Clinton, Richard Maxwell had decided early in his career that he would become a president. Not as early as the nation's president, but at the start of his graduate work, Maxwell knew where his academic career would lead him. Also like Clinton, he liked people and eagerly sought their admiration. He was a natural fund-raiser. He enjoyed telling people what they wanted to hear. So President Maxwell could enthusiastically tell a union delegation at eleven in the morning that he favored a hefty salary increase, and with equal enthusiasm tell the board of trustees at two in the afternoon that he would vigorously oppose any increase in the personnel budget. And at eleven and two, he may well have believed what he said to each of his approving audiences.

The president had a perfect pedigree for search committees to admire. Andover Academy, Amherst College, and the University of Chicago; a doctoral dissertation turned into a popular trade book on the history of presidents' illnesses and their effects on public policy; a charming wife with an advanced degree in philosophy; three picture-perfect sons. His physician parents, a surgeon and an oncologist, had hoped that Richard would have followed in their footsteps as his pediatrician brother and psychiatrist sister had, but they at least had the satisfaction of having suggested his dissertation subject to him. His dedication to them could not do justice to the assistance the parents had given to the son.

The book, his first and last, had made Richard Maxwell a popular figure on talk shows during its ten week run on the best seller list. He was a natural on television. Charming, affable, and winningly articulate as long as the conversations were centered on his book, at least one network toyed with the idea of making him a political consultant. But Maxwell suffered a terrible moment from which his TV dreams could never recover. Appearing on a panel hosted by Bill Moyers, Maxwell suggested a possible link between politicians' attire and their ideological commitments. With infinite tact, Moyers tried to save Maxwell from the barbed comments of Robert Novak and Sam Donaldson, but the day was lost. In a halting rear guard action, the successful author counter-attacked his attackers. Novak's funereal dark suits surely suggested a moribund political philosophy. As for Donaldson, just look at the windsor knot of his tie. Maxwell offered a lame laugh. Clearly a throwback to a past time Sam longed to recover. Even the polite Moyers smiled. Curiously, a fair number of letter writers thought Maxwell was on to something interesting. He received five invitations to lecture on the subject at universities. Still smarting, he declined them all. He later learned his remarks had spawned three doctoral dissertations. At least in the academy he was still respected. Maxwell concluded that television commentary was not for minds as fertile as his. The book's success over, the author returned to his teaching post at Columbia and planned his campaign to climb the administrative ladder.

With the aid of his wife's considerable fortune, the Maxwells' fashionable East Side apartment became a place for academics, foundation officers, and philanthropists to be seen. They were marvelous hosts who loved to entertain. Not surprisingly, one of their most distinguished guests threw Richard's name into the hiring hoppers for deanships at Southern Methodist and Georgetown. He was offered both positions. Washington was inviting, even if he might run into Novak and Donaldson. And Richard's devotion to the rituals of his high Anglican upbringing struck him as closer to Georgetown's ethic than Southern Methodist's. Of course, he knew little about the Texas university, but he did recall his grandmother's admonition about low Protestant sects. The old lady clearly meant all sects other than their own. The Maxwells moved to the nation's capital. He worked hard and quickly became a popular dean. From Georgetown, the climb to the apex of the administrative hierarchy was a swift one. Four years in Washington were followed by a three year stint as provost at Minnesota and then the call to a presidency six years ago. Adversaries were sure his successes were largely due to the brevity of his tenure at each place. It takes more than a few years to sort out appearance from reality.

Politically, Richard Maxwell was true to his family's conservative values, but he was a registered independent. Once he had decided that university administration was for him, he dropped his affiliation with the Republican Party. He would tread the middle of the road. Every two years, the Maxwells contributed equal amounts to both parties. In a grand show of devotion to the grandeur of the American political system, Richard Maxwell had thrown open the president's home for receptions for both Bill Clinton and Bob Dole when they spoke at the university. He thanked God that the awful little man from Texas did not grace his campus. And Ralph Nader had to be satisfied with whatever those green people could come up with. Maxwell had issued an open letter to the campus in which he explained his impartial commitment to those candidates who stood a chance of election to the highest office in the land. He was delighted when the presidential debate commission reached the same conclusion.

The town's alternate newspaper, surely in the hands of pinkos, attacked him. A front page article in *The Journal* lampooned Maxwell with a lengthy satire about the attire of the presidential candidates and their ideological commitments. That front page was not dry-mounted to join the numerous other self-aggrandizing framed items on the wall of the president's private office. Like a physician, Richard Maxwell displayed his college diplomas. But there was much more. The wall carried a handsomely framed dust jacket of the book, a full page ad from the *Times*, two particularly glowing reviews, letters of offer from Columbia, Georgetown, and Minnesota, photos of Maxwell doing various presidential things, commendations from university support groups, a photo of the ill-fated TV panel. During rare moments of self doubt, the president gained sustenance from that wall. His desk was reserved for a picture gallery of Barbara and the boys. He stood with his back to his wall of praise and awaited his cabinet. The sun illuminated him as a spotlight might. He practiced a few poses for the imaginary photographers. He ran through his repertoire of smiles. He reached the sympathetic half smile reserved for widows of newly departed faculty when the provost entered the office. Maxwell interrupted his practice session. "Good morning, Oscar," he said in a flat matter of fact tone. He had inherited Oscar Winter Lansing. For the life of him he couldn't figure out how that man had survived so long as the university's chief academic officer.

The president was not the only administrator who marveled at Lansing's longevity. But not Oscar. He continued in a job he did not particularly relish out of his deep sense of Christian duty. A shy, diffident physicist, oxymoronic as that may sound, he had a range of interests that often astonished strangers and continued to befuddle friends. He managed to reconcile his beliefs in extra-terrestrials, remote viewing, and Art Bell with his near fundamentalist Christianity. Although not interested in national politics, he did admire Jimmy Carter enormously. Lansing, too, taught Sunday school, eschewed spirits of every kind, and was given to high sounding moral commentary. If the provost had passions beyond the university, they were for gardening and bird watching. He and his wife made several trips a year to watch birds migrating, returning, molting, nesting.

The dean was the first to make light of the word the provost's initials spelled. OWL. Perfect, Patrick Donovan chortled whenever his brogue was put to use to belittle Lansing. Which meant the dean chortled frequently. Patrick Donovan saw himself as the great mover in the intellectual and academic vacuum he perceived at the top of the university's hierarchy. It would be, it must be Patrick Donovan alone who could chart the course.

The provost nodded his greeting and took his customary chair to the right of the president. He sat alone at the conference table, laying out his papers and awaiting the start of the meeting.

Three other deans arrived. Graduate School, Undergraduate Studies, and Adult Education poured cups of coffee, and took their places at the table. Only the dean of the college was missing. Patrick Donovan was partial to the grand entrance.

President Maxwell took his seat at the head of the table and surveyed his cabinet while he, too, arranged a few sheets of yellow lined paper. Graduate School was wearing a gray sweater over brown corduroy trousers. Maxwell shook his head. Undergraduate Studies looked like he was a pall bearer at a pauper's funeral. That same frayed black sport jacket. Not even the hospital thrift shop would accept that thing. And a shirt that was probably once a five dollar special at Sears with a drab tie that the clerk undoubtedly threw in for nothing, and gray plaid pants that must represent a long abandoned clan. Maxwell ground his teeth. Only Adult Education had tried to emulate the president's style. Maxwell thought well of his future and of his nicely tailored suit. And he had a slight British accent too. He smiled at Adult Education. Then there was the provost. Maxwell could never fault Oscar Lansing's attire. This bothered him. The provost should dress badly if he were to fit Maxwell's sartorial paradigm. But long before the president had arrived on campus, Oscar was as careful about his clothing as he was about everything else. He kept a neat desk, ran an orderly office which always contained fresh flowers as well as fresh coffee for those so inclined, and bought tasteful if not expensive suits. He always wore suits to the university. And long sleeved shirts even on the dog days of August. A confirmed gardener whose advice was sought by many friends, Oscar was sensitive to color combinations. In a word, he dressed well. The president was frustrated. His low opinion of his provost collided with his grudging admiration for the man's pleasing appearance. At least Novak and Donaldson weren't there to offer Oscar as a challenge to the paradigm. Every rule has its exception. Maxwell glanced at the provost's blue herringbone jacket. Looks good. And the tie was beautiful. Even those old fashioned leather elbow patches that Oscar was partial to looked good on him. "Curious," muttered the president as though he were commenting on a document before him. "Shall we begin, gentlemen."

The door opened and Dean Donovan made his entrance. "So sorry to be late," he said with a shake of his full head of hair. "My plate is full this week." His tone made it clear that he was the only administrator who worked for a living. He unzipped his shoulder bag and removed several manila folders, far more than were necessary for a month of meetings. He lit his pipe and nodded in the direction of the president as if giving him permission to continue. Donovan used a half empty styrofoam coffee container for an ashtray.

Richard Maxwell disliked smoking, but he did not want to upset the dean. Donovan was the only member of the cabinet he was uneasy with. He had often tried to analyze his response to the dean, but the simple fact was that he feared Patrick. He didn't like him. He certainly didn't trust him. But he realized the dean was capable of stirring up trouble. As often as he tried to count the house, Maxwell was just as often unsure of the votes in the university senate if those sloppy looking teachers had to choose between him and the dean. He was not willing to suffer a public relations debacle. He knew the glee with which *The Journal* would report such a humiliation. So Patrick Donovan, who sensed the president's dilemma, got what he wanted.

"I think the most pressing problem today is Dean Donovan's request for additional funds for recruitment." Maxwell shuffled through his papers. "You've all received copies of his memo." He held up the five page document. "A most compelling argument, Patrick." He nodded at the dean. "Yes, most eloquent. But we wouldn't expect any less from our Gaelic wordsmith, would we?" Maxwell smiled.

"I thank you for those kind words, Richard." The dean tried to look slightly embarrassed. He, too, had a repertoire.

"The request, of course, should have come to my office," Oscar Lansing said. "All funding requests come to the provost. Not directly to the president." He removed a small red booklet from his briefcase. "Perhaps the dean of the college of arts and science has lost his copy of this university's protocols and guidelines." He slid the slight volume in the direction of the dean. "I have an extra." One of Oscar's great strengths and a major reason for the faith faculty placed in him was his absolute adherence to established procedures. He could be trusted to be scrupulous and honest.

"Oh, that little book." Patrick waved it away. "Yes, yes, Oscar, I know it well. I read it every night." He laughed and slid it back toward the provost. "But there are times when procedures must be bypassed, or, shall I say, overcome. The red tape of all those protocols impedes swift action." He looked at the president. "And the ability to act swiftly is a mark of genuine leadership." He blew smoke in the direction of the provost. "Rules, my dear Oscar, are meant to be bent to the needs of the moment." He folded his hands as if in prayer.

That posture of prayer had offended the provost on more than one occasion. Hypocrite was what Oscar thought as he pushed the book back to Patrick. "Perhaps you could use another copy. Yours must surely be threadbare by now." Oscar did not smile.

Undergraduate Studies laughed. Patrick scowled. The president preferred not to look at him. "I thought it was funny," said the pall bearer. "Besides, Oscar's right. The request should have gone to him."

"Well, it didn't," Patrick snapped. "As a matter of fact, Richard agreed that the extra dollars are necessary. We've got to build the college into a research facility of the first rank if we're ever going to put ourselves on the map." He re-lit his pipe. "Surely, you understand that," he directed his comment to Graduate School. Why that man is dean of the graduate school I'll never know, he thought. Published a bad book thirty years ago and has sat on his fat duff ever since. After the provost, he'll be the first one I'll get rid of when I sit in Richard's chair. Patrick was sure that Maxwell was on the lookout for a more prestigious presidency. He looked forward to writing a glowing letter of recommendation for him. Fat duff's days were numbered. "Indeed, the president himself made several marvelous suggestions for the ads I plan to run in the *Chronicle* and *Times*." Patrick blew smoke again at the provost.

"Ads?" asked Oscar. "Advertisements now emanate from the dean's office?" He stared at Patrick's still folded hands. "They are the responsibility of departments," he spoke slowly but firmly. "Recruitment is and always will be the responsibility of departments." The president was uneasy. "Funding originates here," he motioned to the group, "but the faculty hires its own." He pointed to the red book. "I suggest you re-read page eight tonight, Patrick, before you enter your dream world of power politics." He looked down. "And you might try a few pages of the Bible. I can recommend several excellent sections on Christian humility." He looked directly at the dean. "We may be the guardians of the flock, but we are not their masters."

Maxwell broke in. "I don't think we need a Sunday School lecture today, Oscar." He smiled at Patrick. "I did concur with the dean's request for extra funds. Especially for the humanities which need bolstering." He pulled out a yellow sheet. "These ideas for strengthening the literature department are particularly compelling."

"For instance?" asked Oscar. This was the first he had heard of new money for that department. "I don't recall any request from Walter Henry."

Now there's a man who knows something about appearance, thought the president. Good man, Henry. And he throws a damn good cocktail party too.

"Walter and I spoke about his new needs last week," said Patrick. He was conciliatory. As the president did not risk a confrontation with the dean, Patrick was not yet ready to risk one with Oscar. The faculty respected the preacher too much. It would take more time to undermine that man's position, but it would be done. In the meantime, Patrick tried to be sweetness and light even in the face of Oscar's supercilious moralizing.

"The literature department is one of the strongest on the campus. And with the pending promotion of Smith or Mann, it will insure keeping a good young man." Oscar waved pipe smoke away as he spoke. "As a matter of fact, I've urged Walter to promote both of them." He looked at the dean. "And we have the funds already in the budget to handle two promotions in that department." He turned to the president. "I'm deeply distressed with your action, Richard. More than anyone else here, a political scientist understands the need for a clear chain of command." He sipped water. "Very distressed. We can't allow precedents like this." Again he stared at the dean. "End runs may be fine on the football field, but they must not be tolerated here. If we don't have credibility with the faculty, we have nothing."

"Nonsense," interrupted Patrick. "Give them a raise every year and they'll be happy enough. As long as we don't tread on their perks, they don't care what we do." He laughed. "Try to take away their sabbaticals and summer research grants. Then they'll raise a ruckus. Otherwise, they're a bunch of spineless sheep." Patrick spat out those words. He flicked his wrist at Oscar. "Don't give me that crap about credibility. Faculty are among the most selfish beings on the planet." He laughed again. "On any planet."

An awful silence engulfed the room. The president and the other deans silently considered words of conciliation, terms of a truce between two men whose mutual antagonism started the day Dean Patrick Donovan arrived on the campus.

The president spoke. "Enough, gentlemen. I think we understand your respective positions." Maxwell weighed which of the two would be the more dangerous adversary. He looked at the provost. "Oscar, you're absolutely correct about protocol." Patrick frowned. "But there are times when protocol is simply not the most expedient course to follow." The dean nodded. "Patrick's request is one of those times." Donovan smiled. The president tried to sound statesmanlike and solemn. He thought of the reporters waiting in the outer office. "There will be no promotions in the literature department this year. Our resources will be spread over the next three years to recruit in the areas of greatest need over there. And the hiring will be from the outside. One a year for three years." He folded his hands. The provost winced. "That's the way it's going to be." He shook his head sagely. "And my decision should not be interpreted by any one as a negative comment on either Mann or Smith. I've met them both, and I concur that they're young men of great promise. Yes sir, lots of potential there. But they're not going anywhere right now. Not like Wilma Crouse who everybody wants. We'll let them ripen before we promote them." He shrugged. "I don't want any hasty promotions on my watch."

Oscar made some notes in his diary. "I plan to fight this one, Richard. I want you and the deans to know I cannot let this decision go unchallenged." He held up the red book. "It might be wise if we all re-examined

112

chapter nine which makes crystal clear the protocol for bringing a challenge to the university senate. I hope it won't come to that, but if the president doesn't reconsider his decision, I'll be left with no choice." He closed his diary.

"Afraid of losing credibility with the boys and girls of instruction?" Patrick did not smile.

"Yes, Patrick. But I'm even more concerned with losing my own self respect." Oscar thought of an appropriate passage from the good book, but he realized it would be a waste of fine words. "And now, gentlemen, I must attend to the business of the university." He nodded to the group and left the room.

Maxwell shook his head. "God, but it's difficult being a president." *Journal* headlines crossed his mind. "You better come up with an unassailable presentation for the senate, Patrick."

"You don't really think he'll go that route, do you?" Patrick leaned forward. "It was just a power play, pure and simple. The pious owl doesn't want our dirty laundry washed in public." The dean held his hands out. "When the chips are down, he'll do what's best for the university. Believe me, Oscar will think better of going to the senate." He lit his pipe. "Our good provost will sleep on it and see that the president's right. His gamble didn't work. Richard didn't cave. Trust me, this little tempest in a tea pot is over." He smiled. "If Oscar would allow me a metaphor that includes such strong drink."

No one laughed.

Adult Education, who had been at the university longer than anyone else in the room, straightened his tie and cleared his throat. "I hope you're right, Patrick, but Oscar has a history of standing on principle." He hesitated and glanced at Maxwell. "Remember that it was Oscar who toppled the last president."

"Almost single-handedly," said Graduate School who admired the provost. "He was like a pit bull in that case. Just wouldn't let go. And the faculty came to see that he was right. President Wilcox had bent too many rules, and Oscar Lansing finally stuck it to him. Forced the man to resign." He nodded his head vigorously. "We've got to take him seriously." He pointed at Patrick. "And whether we like him or not, he is incorruptible." Graduate School smiled. "God knows I've never been able to warm up to

Oscar, but I wouldn't want to cross swords with him. You know what they say about the meek inheriting the earth."

The president was visibly shaken by these comments. Attire aside, Graduate School was probably right. Old Wilcox had warned Maxwell about the provost who had a terminal case of scrupulosity. Incurable, he had said. And dangerous. "Let me have a draft of your defense by the end of the week, Patrick."

The dean did not fail to notice the pronoun. God damn it, he said to himself. That preacher is not going to hang me out to dry. He jotted a note to meet with Murdoch and Berlin.

Academic confidentiality being what it is, the news of Oscar Lansing's challenge raced through the campus. The scent of blood was in the air and faculty members sniffed with gleeful anticipation. The president of the senate was ecstatic. He looked forward to standing room only when the shit finally hit the fan. It'll be almost as exciting as Vietnam. He prepared for a second moment at center stage.

In the literature department, no one was more pleased about this turn of events than Mary Bullock. She almost forgot her furniture polish in the excitement. That terrible Irishman was on the verge of getting his comeuppance. She hummed *The Sound of Music* as she opened Walter's mail. A vase filled with yellow roses sat on her desk. As expensive as they were at this time of the year, Mary was preparing for the great victory that seemed close at hand. She smiled at every visitor to the chair's office. She even bought a pint of bourbon to sweeten Jack Williams' tea when he next visited with her. Yes, she kept whispering to herself, we'll have a fine search for a real dean soon enough.

A week passed since the cabinet meeting and neither the president nor the dean backed down. True to his word, Oscar Lansing filed a formal grievance with the university senate. The case would be heard seven days following the receipt of the provost's charges. Chapter nine of the red book mandated a waiting time sufficient for the senators to familiarize themselves with the particulars of the challenge. It was also meant to be a cooling-off period during which the adversaries might reconsider their positions. If neither side communicated a change of heart to the senate president, the case would be heard in an open meeting of the senate.

No word having been received, the senate president sent a memo to the university community announcing that the senate would hear Provost Lansing's challenge on February 14. A bearded sociologist, Horatio Ginsberg, the senate's leader, held several meetings with his executive committee, talked with the adversaries, and sent his best suit to the cleaners.

God, this was heady stuff

Not every one in the literature department eagerly anticipated the senate meeting. Wilma Crouse had her own problems. Wherever she was on campus, pickets were not far behind. They awaited the arrival of her Corvette in the parking lot each morning. They followed her to her office, trailed behind her to classrooms, stood sentry in the hall while she lectured to her students, sat in the hall outside her office, stood silently on the sidewalk in front of her duplex. And the cause of this attack on one of the university's brightest lights? Professor Crouse had spoken unequivocally about ebonics. First on the campus radio station, then in a lengthy interview in the campus newspaper, and, finally, in a debate on the subject before a packed auditorium in the student union.

Wilma was befuddled and frightened. What could be less threatening to black activists on a university campus than a sister's critical assessment of a program which would demean black students? Wilma was in the midst of a crash course in racist politics. Reason and good sense were its first casualties.

If the radio discussion and newspaper interview were not evidence enough of her transgressions against her people, the debate became proof positive for her detractors. As Wilma sat on the stage of the auditorium, she tried to look calm. She was surprised at the enormous turnout. Every seat was taken. The stairways and aisles were crowded with an overflow of spectators. They held placards high in the air. Black students, white students, townies, faculty members all stamped their feet and whistled for the show to begin. A high tech lynching, Wilma thought. She smiled to herself for quoting Clarence Thomas. She had sat on this very stage only a few years ago when she introduced Anita Hill. That night she was a hero to many of the same people now crying for her head. Those were probably the same two television cameras directed toward the podium. Now she believed they were aimed straight at her, the target of the proceedings.

The moderator perused his notes. Horatio Ginsberg never dreamed he'd have two crowning moments in a single semester. Wilma glanced at the other participants. A hefty black woman who wore colorful African garb topped by a matching tall hat. Wilma thought it looked like a headpiece for a Halloween party. The chair of black studies sat next to the woman. He, too, wore a costume that made Wilma suddenly feel wrongly dressed. Smoothing the charcoal gray skirt of her smart suit, she was the only black on the stage dressed in western clothes. The fourth panelist was the chair of the linguistics department. A white man, he wore an African shawl around the collar of his well-cut jacket. Wilma realized she would be the lone dissenter, the only panelist who decried the Oakland school board's folly. She had met the two chairs before, but the heavy woman she had known only by reputation, even though she had seen her often enough on campus. Her reputation was major.

Maxine Jefferson was known as the female Al Sharpton. She even sounded like the New York activist. Some claimed she looked like him too. Maxine was a visible and vocal presence at every campus rally that protested some real and many fabricated slights. She had easy access to senior university administrators as she had become the unofficial ombudsman for black students and faculty. A historian by training, she had found her true calling as an evangelical force for black rights and black separatism. That she managed to reconcile these two commitments with little intellectual trouble generated power among her followers, fear within the administration, and scorn from the majority of the white faculty. But except for her devoted legions, the other two constituencies generally remained publicly mute in the face of her outrages. The administration would do virtually anything to avoid conflict. The faculty feared charges of racism more than dereliction of intellectual duty. They grumbled all right, but only in the privacy of department coffee rooms and the safety of dinner parties. But public statements were few. Those who did rise to the challenge were generally left to hang in the wind. Patrick Donovan was not all wrong about the intestinal fortitude of his charges.

Horatio gaveled the debate to order. The large crowd became surprisingly still. They sat on the edges of their seats. The placards and banners were set down. A palpable tension gripped the room, much like what one would imagine at a public hanging in the good old days before democracy and freedom of expression were accepted features of civilized discourse. Horatio Ginsberg introduced the chairman of linguistics who would lay out the parameters of the program that was to be the subject of the evening's discussion.

Arnold Hefferman strode briskly to the podium. A tall man, he towered over the moderator whose hand he gripped firmly as they exchanged places at center stage. Hefferman turned to the audience and raised his right arm in salute. Wilma shivered as his hand balled into a fist. The room resounded with loud applause, cheers, and whistles. Hundreds of feet stomped the floor in a lengthy rhythmic cadence. The building shook. Now, that's one neutral participant, Wilma said to herself. As she listened to his passionate approval of ebonics and the courage of the Oakland school board, Wilma knew she had been sandbagged. "And those who oppose ebonics and criticize Oakland announce themselves to be the enemies of black struggles all over the world." Wilma looked down at her notes, but she was sure Hefferman turned in her direction when he uttered that demagogic charge. "I probably shouldn't say this, but I'm not sure the detractors of ebonics have a legitimate place at an institution of higher learning." The auditorium erupted in applause. Wilma was sure Hefferman looked at her this time. She turned toward the other members of the platform party. They were all applauding. Maxine Jefferson was on her feet, waving to the crowd to increase the noise level. Wilma didn't even like that at a professional football game. Streams of perspiration ran down Maxine's hot cheeks. Jesus, Wilma muttered, she does look like Sharpton. Sam Singleton, the chair of black studies, applauded and laughed. Horatio Ginsberg clapped his hands in rhythm with the stamping feet. Another dispassionate moderator. Wilma felt isolated. She sipped water and prayed her hands would not shake. She thought of those grand offers she had turned down.

"Thus we see the scope of the question our distinguished panel will debate." Hefferman moved to his conclusion. "And even if the matter seems self evident to the best minds of our country, there remain others who doubt the validity of the Oakland approach. And, amazing as it seems to so many of us, they challenge ebonics itself as being in some way," he paused as if looking for the right word, "inferior." He smiled. "As being second-class. As being something," he paused for a longer time, "that should be relegated to the back of the bus." More foot stamping. "But thank the good Lord, we have among us on this great campus a Rosa Parks for our time, a woman who speaks loudly and clearly. And what does she say? She says no. No. No. No. We've spent enough time in the back of the bus. Enough time." Pause. "More than enough time." He slowly walked to Maxine Jefferson and motioned her to stand up. He embraced her. The room erupted once again. There was a three minute standing ovation. Wilma was torn. The three men on the stage stood up and joined the ovation. What should she do? She knew what she wanted to do, but she stood up. She did not applaud.

Horatio stood before the microphone and introduced Professor Wilma Crouse of the literature department for her opening statement. He read from his notes. Her distinguished background and brilliant scholarly accomplishments fell on deaf ears. They seemed to care not at all that she was a black woman who stood at the apex of a white man's field. Ginsberg held his left arm out to welcome Wilma to the podium. A few people applauded. Most of the large crowd remained silent. Having scanned the audience, she noticed only Jack Williams of her departmental colleagues. He gave her a standing ovation as she took her place at the podium. She smiled in his direction.

She had revised and rehearsed her opening remarks over and over the previous night. Should she yield to the time and place and put aside her lifelong commitment to intellectual integrity? That question haunted her even as she drove to campus that evening. Those bastards are going to humiliate me because I dared speak the truth. For all her fame and years at the university, Wilma had no one to talk to, to confide in, to seek advice from. She toyed with the idea of calling Walter Henry. But the chair, for all his cordiality, remained only a colleague. He had been helpful in arranging counter offers, but she knew she deserved them. Walter was only doing his job. She was not only good, but she was the solitary black in the depart- ment. He had to go out of his way to keep her. Perhaps one of the younger people would understand, but she had little to do with them. Yes, she had been invited to many dinner parties and was clearly on cocktail party invi- tation lists all over the faculty community, but Wilma always doubted the integrity of those invitations. Were they because she was a distinguished critic or because she was a woman of color? It never occurred to her that she was invited anywhere because the hosts actually enjoyed her company, really liked her. She had tried calling Oliver, but only reached his answering machine. She was alone.

Not until she reached the microphone did Wilma decide on her opening remarks. She removed a rubber band from several note cards, took a sip of water, and looked out at the audience. Oliver had taught her to fix her eyes on some object at the rear of the room to keep from smiling at some silly remark made by a fellow speaker. This night she stared at the red exit sign over the rear center door to calm her fear. They want a black woman. Well, they're going to get one.

"I want to thank Professor Ginsberg for his generous introduction. And the committee on campus harmony for arranging this evening's discussion of a terribly important issue." She nodded in the direction of the dean of students who chaired the committee. "I come to you tonight as both a literary critic and a black woman." She had succumbed to the moment. Now, could she use her capitulation to her advantage? "I say this because the question of ebonics is as much a political matter as anything else. If a black person can not speak frankly and candidly about the subject, then the very values this university represents are in jeopardy. Indeed, ladies and gentlemen, if any serious student of letters and culture, black or white, man or woman, cannot speak honestly about the subject, we're in terrible trouble." She pointed toward one of the scores of placards. "If any of you believe that slogans, banners, and," she paused, "intimidation can take the place of reasoned, civil discourse, you are mistaken. That's the road to destruction." Wilma's voice strengthened with each word. "Destruction of reason and reasonableness. Destruction of honest debate. And, my brothers and sisters, destruction of our credibility and, finally, of ourselves." She half turned in the direction of the other panelists, especially Maxine Jefferson. "Education is the great leveler. If young blacks across this country are to become viable and productive members of this culture, they must learn to read and write the English language. They must be brought to see the beauty of words, and the power of words. They must become conversant with the literature and ideas of western civilization as well as of other cultures. Let me pose a question to all of those students who have been hounding me for the last nine days. Can you name a single black leader you admire who does not speak and write the English language with eloquence and with power?" Wilma paced the length of the stage, staring out at the crowd of faces as if awaiting a response. "No, I didn't think you could. Just think of the force exerted by the late great Martin Luther King. And, tell me, what was his greatest weapon in his battle against segregation? I'll remind you. It was his magnificent command of language. Coupled with the inescapable logic of his arguments, Doctor King was invincible. Not even an assassin's bullets could defeat the force of his eloquence." Wilma looked directly at Maxine. "King didn't speak ebonics or threaten those who challenged his ideas. No. Oh no. Just like Jesse Jackson and Maya Angelou, Doctor King towered above his detractors precisely because of his incredible ability to articulate his beliefs. His rhetoric was his greatest weapon. Martin Luther King did not slouch around wearing untied Nikes. He didn't wear his cap backwards and think he was cool. He didn't father kids and then take off. He didn't burn down buildings when he believed an injustice had been perpetrated against his people. He didn't cheer rap music that demeans black women and foments violence. He didn't believe that his enemies, or his friends, could be distinguished only by the color of their skin. He didn't believe in self-imposed and self-destructive segregation. And he knew that calling it by any other name, black nationalism or separatism or community, was only a quick fix bastardization of both language and logic. It was segregation and it was evil. As evil as the glorification of ebonics. Black English is simply bad English. Ebonics is simply the latest attempt at black suicide." Wilma wiped perspiration from her brow. Her eyes glistened. "And any one, black or white, male or female, who tells you otherwise is either foolish or malicious. When you hear an apologist for any position which says we blacks are simply incapable of serious intellectual activity, ask yourselves what possible motive could the speaker have? What's the speaker's real agenda? Don't accept second class citizenship in this great country. Don't believe that the best we can do is throw a ball or run a race. For your own sake, and for the sake of our race, rise up and say no to such arguments. We can succeed at anything and at everything."

Wilma's eyes searched the audience. "But we can succeed at nothing if we believe we are inferior. For God's sake, don't buy into those treacherous arguments. Don't rally around ebonics. Rise up against it. If you don't, who will? You're the cream of this generation's crop. You've given yourselves to university training. If you can't see the folly of ebonics, we may truly be lost." Wilma replaced the rubber band around her note cards. "Later, I'm sure, we'll get into it." She smiled sweetly and walked toward her seat.

There was an eerie silence in the crowded room until Jack Williams shouted, "Atta girl, Willie." He stood up and began a rhythmic clapping. He nudged the people on either side of him. They stood and joined him. He didn't care if they were motivated by conviction or his whispered threats. "Get off your ass or I'll beat in your fucking brains." Others stood throughout the auditorium. A minority to be sure, but enough to make an impression. Wilma could at least enjoy the illusion that she was not alone.

Maxine Jefferson shuffled to the podium. She seemed to be slow dancing. She smiled broadly at the audience and held her hands up high as if she had just won a race. At the microphone, she looked to the ceiling and began singing. *We shall overcome* echoed throughout the building as several hundred voices joined Maxine's magnificent alto. At the conclusion, she removed her Halloween hat and gripped both sides of the podium.

"I begin with that great song that became the anthem of Reverend King's crusade. May he rest in the heavenly peace he so richly deserves." She bowed her head as if in prayer. "I mention King only because his name has been taken in vain by the previous speaker." She pointed a finger at Wilma. "Hypocrisy is thy name, Professor Crouse. Neither sister nor truly black, your name is duplicity." Still pointing, Maxine continued. "How dare you come before us this evening, claiming to be a black sister? Your entire existence has been a white life." She turned to the audience. "I didn't say a white lie. I said a white life." Several amens and that's right rose from the crowd. Maxine nodded enthusiastically in the directions of the speakers. She laughed a hoarse, throaty laugh. There's nothing she'd like better than to turn the room into a revival meeting, to turn the crowd into a chanting, foot-stamping congregation. And Maxine knew she could do it. She waved her hands in encouragement. More voices shouted that's right, amen, I hear you, right on sister. "Does she have a right to challenge ebonics?" A chorus of no, no, no. "Wrong, my brothers and sisters. Sure she has a right to her opinion. Even if it's wrong." She laughed again as a chorus of laughter bounced off the walls and ceiling of the auditorium. "She's as wrong as all her white friends, those so-called intellectuals, who don't believe we have a right to a language system that reminds us of our African roots." She turned once again to Wilma who was now furious. "So, don't come parading into this gathering, dressed like some fine white lady on her way to work at a fancy law office in New York City, and try to tell us you're something other than what you really are. Yes, sir," Maxine was almost chanting, "some New York law office cram filled with lawyers bent on denying us our rights." She laughed again after another chorus of amens and that's right. "My mammy gave me special x-ray eyes so I could always see what's what in this world."

Has she no shame, thought Wilma.

"And let me tell you, brothers and sisters, this one, " she shot her thumb over her right shoulder in Wilma's direction, "this one is no sister. Act white. Can't be right." She urged the crowd to join her. "Act white. Can't be right. Act white. Can't be right. Act white. Can't be right."

Maxine quieted her flock and returned the hat to her head. "But we have more important things to talk about tonight than the hypocrisy of Miss I-wish-I-was-white-instead-of- black over there. She's small potatoes compared to the struggle to legitimize black English. That's our goal and that's worth fighting for." She left the podium and walked to the front of the stage. She wanted to get closer to her audience. "It's all right, isn't it," she spoke in a stage whisper, "for the Jews to have their Yiddish. They probably speak it in those law firms I mentioned. And the Hispanics can have their Spanish, the Indians their Native American tongues, the Irish their Gaelic. Germans and French and Russians and everyone else can have their language except the blacks. Do you understand? Do you hear what I'm saying? Everyone but the blacks." She shrugged a great exaggerated theatrical shrug. "So what else is new?" Maxine returned to the microphone. "But we're here to say that will not do. The status quo will not do. What are we going to do? I'll tell you what we're going to do. We're going to make damn sure that black English gets its day. Remember, my brothers and sisters, the word ebonics arises from ebony and phonetics. What could be more legitimate and beautiful than that combination of words? That one," Maxine motioned again toward Wilma, "that so-called scholar, says we should teach our children the beauty and power of words. Well, what could be more beautiful than ebony? What could be more powerful than ebonics?" Maxine dropped her head. She was done with her opening statement. She glanced at Wilma. "See, white lady, no notes." She laughed and walked to her chair, acknowledging the enthusiastic applause. The chanting began again and continued until Maxine sat down. "Act white. Can't be right. Act white. Can't be right."

A single loud boo came from the back of the room. Jack Williams stood with his hands cupped before his lips. "Boo. Boo. Boo. Bullshit," he shouted over and over. Again he nudged and threatened the students on each side, but they ignored him. They had grasped the arms of others and were weaving to the chant of "Act white. Can't be right." Jack left his seat and marched down the center aisle. Still shouting, he mounted the stage. "Fuck you," he shouted at Maxine. "In spades," he spat at her. He bent over a trembling Wilma. "Come on, kiddo, let's get out of here." He gently placed his hand on her arm. "This is no debate, Willie. It's a crucifixion." He urged her to stand.

Wilma smelled the booze on his breath. But she was grateful he was there. She nodded her head slowly as if dimly comprehending Jack's words. She yielded to the pressure of his urging and she stood up.

"Don't let the bastards know you're scared. Don't let them think they got to you. Give them a look that'll freeze them in their seats. And then we walk down that aisle with all the confidence in the world. Can you do that, Willie? You've got to do it or they'll never get off your case."

Wilma stood up and smiled at Jack. "Thanks, my friend." She wanted to kiss him. Together they left the stage and walked out of the auditorium. The chanting and foot stamping continued even after they entered the lobby.

"I've got just the place to unwind." Jack lit a cigarette and coughed. "Got to give up these damn things." He looked the length of his Marlboro, intentionally moving the subject away from the horrors of the evening. He wanted to bring up *Heart of Darkness*, but that could wait. He had been thinking of that Conrad novel all evening. "We can pick up your car later."

It was only a short drive to the King's Arms, Jack's favorite watering hole. Everyone knew him there.

"How's it going, professor," greeted the bar tender. "Nice table by the fire, Jack." He pointed toward the rear wall.

Wilma looked around the place. She had passed it a hundred times and thought it must be seedy. She was surprised. The King's Arms was old and warm. Crowded with late night drinkers, the bar was noisy. It also exuded the comfort of an old English pub. Royal crests covered the red velvet walls. Comfortably upholstered oak chairs surrounded gleaming glass topped wooden tables. The massive fireplace was set in a white brick wall. A friendly fire dropped gold and orange embers on the grate. Wilma was glad to be there, and she was happy the place was crowded.

"So, what's your pleasure, Willie?" asked Jack. When the barmaid arrived, he ordered white wine for her and Jack Daniels on the rocks for himself.

"And what else would it be?" the waitress laughed. Jack slapped her ass when she walked away. "So what do you think of my hideaway?" He lit another Marlboro.

"It's very nice." Willie reached over and touched Jack's arm. 'Thanks for everything."

"Thanks? It was a pleasure." Jack rolled his eyes and chuckled. "Quite a show." He looked into her still moist eyes. "Want to talk about it, kiddo?"

"Not tonight. Can we just sit here for a while without saying anything?"

"It's your call, Willie. Whatever you like."

Wilma sipped her wine and looked around the room. Her gaze paused at the bar. "Who's the guy with Walter?'

Jack glanced over. "His boyfriend," he said matter of factly.

"His what?"

"Dennis Collins. A local kiddie doc."

Wilma shot a disbelieving glance at Jack.

"Our chair's discovered he swings both ways." Jack smiled. "Walter and I go back a long way." He dragged on his cigarette and waved for another drink. "Christ, I knew he was bi years ago. Probably long before he realized it himself"

"Does his wife know?"

"I doubt it. Maggie's too busy with other things. But if she does, she's one terrific actress."

"Isn't he worried?" Her eyes took in the room. "Doesn't he worry about being seen?"

"Not here. I'm the only one who hangs out in this posh place." Jack grinned at the room. "And he knows he can trust old Jack Williams. What the hell. I couldn't care less what makes him happy. He's even introduced me to the doc."

"And what if he sees me here?"

"I'll vouch for you." Jack said this with no irony. He was sure Walter's secret was as safe with Wilma as with himself. "I only worry about some prick like Murdoch finding out. Or that little weasel, Billy Mann. Otherwise, it's just you, me, and Mary."

"His secretary?"

"But of course. My pal Bullock knows everything."

The lights were on in Jack Williams' small house when he pulled into the driveway. He smelled the fresh coffee as soon as he walked in.

"And how long did you spend with your cronies tonight?" asked Mary Bullock. She bustled around the kitchen as if she were expecting a crowd for dinner. "Tomorrow may be one of your non-teaching days, but I have to go to work." Her anger was not genuine. "Well, sit down and get some nourishment. I bet you haven't eaten a thing since lunch." She motioned to a chair at the kitchen table set for one. "And your refrigerator is pathetic as usual. What happened to the shopping list I put in your mailbox?"

Jack did as he was told and began drinking his coffee. "Ah, Mary my darling, what would I do without you?"

"You'd starve. That's what you'd do." She placed a bowl of chili stew on the table. "Dig in, Williams, but don't make a pig of yourself. I made enough so you'll have dinner tomorrow too." She dropped a basket of warm sour dough bread before him as if she were angry. Pouring a cup of coffee, she joined her longtime, dear friend. "Well, do I have to pull teeth? What happened at the debate? Did they lynch her?"

Jack ate and related every event of the evening. "God, this is good, Bullock." Ever since he spent a year as visiting professor at the University of New Mexico, he had developed a taste for spicy food. All he ever had to do was tell Mary about his culinary desires and they would appear on his table. For as long as he could remember, Mary had acted as his confidant and surrogate sister. After each of his two failed marriages, it was Mary who gave him her shoulder and devotion.

"I could have told you that no real discussion could take place with the likes of that Maxine Jefferson on the stage." She sipped her coffee and took one of Jack's cigarettes. Only in his house did she smoke, but not even then with pleasure. "I got her number the first time I laid eyes on her." Mary never inhaled. It was smoking like Clinton, she liked to say. "Another phony if there ever was one."

"Who are you talking about now? Bill Clinton or Maxine?" Jack shook his head. "For someone who's worked in our department for centuries, your pronoun reference still stinks."

"Both of them. They're both politicians." She put out the cigarette. She looked at her watch.

"I gotta go, Williams. You be a good boy and finish your stew. And make sure you spend your day off working on your book."

"The book's going to be published in a couple of months."

"I know that. Begin a new one." Mary put on her coat. "You want those young bucks thinking you're over the hill? And no drinking tomorrow before five o'clock. You hear?" She bent over and kissed him on the cheek.

"Promise, mother." He got up to walk her to the door. "You drive carefully. And don't let them get to you tomorrow. Give 'em hell, Bullock." He patted her arm as she left the house.

Jack carefully spooned the rest of his dinner into the large bowl, covered it as Mary had taught him to do, and placed it in the refrigerator. "It is sort of empty," he admitted. He took a glass and a bottle of Jack Daniels to his den, turned on CNN, and settled in for serious news and drink.

"Start a new book tomorrow. Jesus, Bullock, give me a break." He looked up and saw a weeping Paula Jones on the screen. "Give it to him, lady. Fucking bubba." Jack lit a cigarette. He blew smoke in the air and thought of Wilma Crouse.

Wallace Lounge was abuzz on Monday morning. Even faculty who showed up at the shop only on Tuesdays and Thursdays were there. Eager to discuss the ebonics debate which made the front page of Sunday's paper, they had an added attraction this day. The department had monopolized yesterday's paper. Beneath the large photo of Professor Crouse standing before scores of placards was one of Mitchell Murdoch. "Local Critic Wins

Prestigious MacArthur Genius Grant." The academics' plate was full. As they drank coffee and gesticulated dramatically, their sharpened swords were being readied for the kill.

Exaggerated righteous anger at Maxine Jefferson, fulsome mock concern for Willie, deep bitter envy of Mitchell permeated the discussions. There was too much at stake to keep the professors from pouring into the lounge.

"That woman should be fired. Who the hell does she think she is?"

"Did you read what she said about Wilma?"

"Uppity black bitch!"

"What the hell was Jack Williams doing at that thing, anyway?"

"Do you think we should march on the black studies department?"

"Do you suggest we wear white sheets?"

"And Willie's our most distinguished colleague."

"Not if you read about Murdoch."

"Those MacArthur people must be crazy."

"You can't even understand the crapola he writes."

"You actually try to read his stuff?"

"The man is an absolute enemy of literature."

"He must have screwed every woman on the committee."

"Next they'll give an award to Maxine Jefferson."

"Why not? How much worse can this frigging profession get?"

"Christ, we're all diminished by such an award going to Murdoch."

"How much money does he get?"

"I think a million bucks."

"A million?"

"Good. Maybe he'll take his snake oil show to some other campus."

"Let him take the video queen with him."

"He doesn't give a damn about Beverly."

"That's for sure. He just needs another vote." "What a price to pay. Imagine hanging out with that lightweight."

"Tell it to Maxwell."

"That man creams in his pants every time he reads about those frauds in the *Times*."

"So, smart ass, when's the last time you were mentioned in any paper?"

"That's not the point, pal."

"I smell sour grapes all over this room."

"Fuck you."

"No, fuck you."

"Oh, fuck both of you," said Jack Williams, putting himself between the two men. "Neither one of you could land a punch anyway." He had a hand on each man's chest. "Probably pull every muscle in your body if you tried." Jack moved to the center of the room. "Calm down, all of you," he shouted. "Don't let the outside world know what a bunch of spoiled brats we really are."

"But Jack," Billy Mann whined, "you know what a charlatan Murdoch is."

"Of course he is." Jack looked with distaste at Billy. "So what else is new? What do you think, Billy boy? You think Mitchell Murdoch's the first jerk to be honored?" He laughed. "I'd be a rich son of a bitch if I had a fin for every schmuck who had some academic medal of honor wrapped around his neck." For a moment, Jack looked menacing. "Now, behave yourselves, for Christ's sake." He went to the coffee pot. "As bad as this junk is, it's better than what I make at home." The remark helped ease the tension in the room. He unpacked a large brown bag he had brought into the room. Four dozen assorted donuts. "I figured you folks would burn up a lot a calories this morning."

Abraham moved closer to Jack. "But it's a good question someone asked. What did prompt you to go the debate?"

"And why not?" Jack was unexpectedly coy. "One of our most esteemed colleagues was on the panel." He bit into a lemon filled donut. A quick sugar fix brought him back to his old self "And anyone not completely brain dead knew she was headed for trouble. All you had to do was look at the list of participants." Jack bent over the Dunkin' Donut box. "You think this one's got raspberry filling?" He bit in and smiled. "Right again." He looked squarely at Abraham. "Besides, I like Willie."

There was something in Jack's manner that surprised Abraham. Not known for reading people very well, as Eleanor kept reminding him whenever he became too enthusiastic about people too soon, he thought he detected more than mere collegial interest in Jack's words. Well, that's something I'll have to try out on Eleanor tonight.

"And what do you make of that, buddy boy?" whispered Billy who had sidled up to the donuts. "Me thinks the old guy's got the hots for dark meat." He pulled Abraham aside. "A pal of mine said he saw the two of them hoisting a few at the King's Arms after the debacle." Billy offered a wink that sent a chill through Abraham. Billy continued. "And Jack's not the only lush on campus, you know. One of my neighbors, a sot from the budget office, heads over there after he and his shrewish wife finish screaming at each other. Full of apologies that loser is when he sees you the next morning. Hope we didn't disturb your evening, he says without ever looking you in the eye. Disturb your evening? No, not at all if you're stone deaf. God knows what it does to his kids. Whenever I hear them go at it, I'm glad we don't have any. Not that we ever keep the neighborhood up. Sally and I have perfected the ice cold silence method." He smirked. "But, of course, you and your little lady never squabble. Isn't that right, Abe?" He pulled Abraham into a quieter corner. "It was that lush who told me about Jack going to the Camptown races." Billy looked around furtively. "And he saw someone else at the joint that night." He lowered his voice almost to a whisper. "Our chairman, that great defender of morality, was at the King's Arms. Can you imagine elegantly clad Walter Henry at a dump like that?"

"So?"

"What do you mean, so? Don't you want to know who he was with?"

"Not really." Thoughts of Walter drinking with some young chippie briefly illuminated Abraham's imagination. "Why should I care who Walter had a drink with?" He didn't like to hear malicious gossip about people he liked.

"Oh, shit, don't be such a sanctimonious square. You threw yourself into all kinds of scurrilous stories at the Russian Cafe. Your gossip level is pretty selective, pal. Anyway, Walter was there with a man."

"What are you driving at, Billy?"

"And not some academic sharing Walter's time after some dreary university meeting." Billy's mouth nearly touched Abraham's ear. "No sir. Dear old Walter was at the bar with a local pediatrician. And my neighbor said they sat very, very close to each other." Billy smirked again as he moved away. "Now, what do you think of them apples?"

"I'm not surprised at all. I guess Walter was having a drink with his new neighbor. As a matter of fact, we met Dennis and his wife last week at the Henrys." Abraham enjoyed his new-found upper hand. "They just moved here from Winchester and their new house is just a block from Walter's." Abraham was pleased at seeing the surprise on Billy's face. Obviously the Manns were not on the Henrys' guest list. It was clear that all this was news to Billy. "Besides," Abraham decided to turn the blade, "Dennis specializes in adolescents. Both the Henry boys and my kids are new patients of his." Abraham wanted to sound superior. "And he's a very good doctor." He moved closer to Billy and grasped his wrist. "So, buddy boy, I don't think you should be so quick to sully reputations."

Billy was chastened. He colored slightly which infuriated him. "Big deal," he tried to recover gossip's high ground, "you don't find it odd that they sneak away to some bar on the other side of town? Neighbors or not, doctor or not, why didn't they have a drink at home?" Billy was pleased with his counter attack. "So, buddy boy, what do you say to that?"

"Let's skip it." Abraham turned to the crowded room.

"Okay, okay, but don't forget our crusade." Billy tried to sound relaxed. "We still have operation Murdoch and Berlin to work on."

"Aren't you afraid people will talk if they see us huddling together?" Abraham turned away abruptly and joined the applause for Willie whom Jack had to drag from her office. She entered the room on Jack's arm.

"Think they're rehearsing for the wedding?" Abraham heard Billy say. "Maybe Walter and his new neighbor can be the bridesmaids." Abraham's neck turned hot.

Willie was suddenly a star in the midst of colleagues she rarely saw in a room she rarely entered. She much preferred the coffee maker in her office. She was mobbed by suddenly solicitous people who only last week ignored her completely. Wilma was not a favorite, even though every one in the lounge used her name when trying to impress professors from other universities. "And, of course, Wilma Crouse is also in our department. Yes, yes, every one tries to raid her, but she prefers the stimulation of our place."

Now she was the one everyone wanted to corner. "An attack on you is an attack on all of us," intoned old Calvin. "We can't stand by and allow this outrage to go unanswered." He recalled Walter's support during the awful harassment ordeal. "No, we must carry the fight to the highest reaches of the administration." His wife's admonitions notwithstanding, the old bibliographer touched Wilma's arm as gently as he could. "I'd be happy to speak with the provost. Oscar and I belong to the same astronomy club."

"Sure," laughed Billy, "maybe he'll ask the little green men to abduct Maxine?" He took his turn before Willie. "Forget taking the case to the owl. The thing you want is revenge. Remember the old adage," his voice rose in order to gain a larger audience, "don't get mad, get even." He preened as if he were the author of that cliched maxim.

"And what do you suggest?" asked Ben Rosenthal.

"Well, Ben, my dear friend," Billy put his arm around the older man's shoulder. "I think we ought to lynch the cunt." His lips were as close to Ben's ear as they had been to Abraham's just minutes before. "That's what I'd do. But I doubt you civil liberties types would care for that idea. Probably counter by singing your beloved Billie Holiday song. You know, Ben old bean, strange fruit and all that shit." Billy was on dangerous ground even if he was right in his assessment that old Rosenthal would sooner vote for Hitler than for him. But he was careful to say all this in hushed tones. After all, the object of his phony solicitude was of the singer's persuasion. "So, Willie," he resumed his loud performance, 'just give the word and we'll teach Al Sharpton's sister a thing or two."

Wilma tried to ignore the young man. She paid exaggerated attention to the box of donuts Jack presented for her perusal.

"Try the yellow one," Jack said. "It's the right color for the nonsense that twerp's been suggesting." He glowered at Billy.

Fearing Jack's tongue and still hoping the lush's good sense would surface at tenure time, Billy retreated to another group. He had no intention of being skewered in front of so large a gathering. Most of them were dumb turds, but they had votes to cast. He wanted to discuss strategy with Abraham, but he was dismayed to see him in warm conversation with Walter who had just entered the room with Mitchell Murdoch. A new star had risen on the conversational horizon.

The chair asked for quiet. It was time to deliver the congratulations of the department to the winner of the genius award.

Overly loud applause greeted Walter's short speech. The crowd pressed around Mitchell, leaving Wilma and Jack alone in front of the coffee table.

"Thank God, Doctor Gobbledegook saved me from more of our colleagues' commiseration." Wilma tried to sound light hearted.

"Come on now, you've been in this racket long enough to know these birds. They seem worse than they are. Some of them are actually pretty decent." Wilma raised an eyebrow. Jack laughed. "Okay, so one or two of them. You should have heard their heartfelt clucking after each of my divorces." He scanned the Dunkin' Donut box, but thought better of trying a third. Perhaps he worried about Mary Bullock's interrogation later that afternoon. "And what was your terrible diet today?" she asked whenever he sat down in her office and lit a cigarette. They never could get down to the serious business of trading stories until Bullock castigated him for his unwholesome eating habits. "Maybe their zeal to lambaste or their crocodile comforting tears stem from deep-seated anxieties about their own inadequacies. God knows, they're riddled with them."

Wilma was surprised to hear Jack launch a serious monologue, especially in a corner of the Wallace Lounge which was brimming with the objects of his analysis. "Am I witnessing the kinder, gentler side of terrible Professor Williams?" She held up her coffee cup in a toast.

"You saw that side the other night," he said sweetly. "But I accept your toast anyway." They touched cups. "May this be the first of many toasts. And may they be with something more appetizing than Wallace Lounge coffee." Jack looked deeply into Wilma's eyes. She met his gaze. "Maybe we should go out on a real date." Jack blushed. "What do you say? A real date. Not the King's Arms after a stunningly serious academic seminar." He placed his hand on her shoulder. "Really. I'll even put on a suit and tie." He nodded. "And we'll have dinner at the Ambassador. Best dining room for miles. Just name the night, Wilma, and we'll do the town." Jack spoke rapidly. He felt like a schoolboy.

"Do they serve us Aunt Tomasinas?" Wilma tried to ease Jack's endearing discomfort. She wondered when he had last asked a woman for a date. "I'd be happy to have dinner with you, sir."

Jack breathed a deep sigh of relief. He felt perspiration on the back of his shirt. "Friday night?"

Wilma nodded. She was delighted. Haven't felt this good since I've been in this town. "And I'll dress to the nines. We'll be the handsomest couple in the place." She heard an insistent pulse in her right temple as she half worried about, half anticipated the journey she was beginning. Jumping light years ahead, she thought of introducing Jack to her parents. He and her father were about the same age. What would they say about their baby girl dating an old, twice divorced white man? And a heavy drinker no less. Her father always had a drink when he came home from the hospital and he had wine with dinner, but she had never seen him tipsy. And smoking. Both parents had given up cigarettes years ago. She recalled their seeming tolerance of Uncle Ted's cigars whenever he visited and their grumbling when they emptied ashtrays and deodorized the polluted air. The pulse became louder. She wondered if Jack could see the throbbing. She placed her hand over her temple in an attempt to conceal it.

Mitchell Murdoch was not one to humbly accept congratulations. Used to the glow of center stage, he pranced from group to group to enjoy the fruits of his fame. Of course he knew that beneath the congratulations seethed envy and hatred. But he was interested now only in the delicious fluff that adorned the surface of things. He himself had always found it difficult to swallow his envy whenever he was forced to react to another's good fortune. Oh yes, he had pumped the hand and slapped the back of the smiling victor. And he, too, had thought what a fortunate fool the celebrated colleague was. And he, too, had offered his nasty comments only minutes later to like-minded audiences. But today was his day. Who else among them had won a MacArthur? No one, that's who.

"Yes, the president's already called," he said to Peter Chase. "As a matter of fact, Richard's asked me over for a drink this afternoon." He smiled almost benignly at the younger man. Both knew they shared the same woman, but Mitchell was impressed by Peter's demeanor. You have to hand it to the kid. He asks me about the president's response to the grant while his mind must be filled with images of me fucking his wife. Mitchell didn't know if he admired or scorned the sort of relationship the Chases had. He knew Alice didn't try to conceal their relationship from Peter. The word bothered him. He didn't correct Alice when she invoked that term, but whatever he and Alice had, it was not a relationship. That was something he had with his wife. Alice was merely a diversion. One of several diversions that kept him happy. He looked into Peter's smiling, open, handsome face. He shook his hand and moved to another adoring group. He looked back at the cuckold who seemed totally unperturbed by their meeting. He wondered. Was the man that good an actor? Alice told him she never discussed their meetings with Peter. Was that true? Did she never deliver a pornographic narrative over a drink or in bed? He worried only that Peter might be a better lover than he. Sometimes he tried to imagine the young couple having sex after one of Alice's recitations. Strange world, he thought as his hand was grasped and his back slapped by more disappointed colleagues.

"Oh, I don't know what I'll do with all that money. After all, the magnitude of the whole thing is still sinking in." In fact, he had thought only of the award since the telephone call last Friday.

The first things he did after telling Isobel was to call the local newspaper to set up an interview ("and make sure there's a photographer") and to inform the president. Then he thought of the money. As exciting as that was, it was a distant second to the impending spotlight which would follow him wherever he went for the foreseeable future. He couldn't wait for the children to get home from school. Several faculty kids were their classmates. How delicious it will be for the Murdoch offspring too. They can't learn early enough how to co-mingle abject humbleness and overweening pride. He expected great things from them, too. "Yes," he said in his best Uriah Heep fashion, "it is a great honor." The genius was the soul of Umbleness.

"Hey, look out the window," shouted Billy Mann. "The bastards are marching on our building." The crowd surged to the windows.

There on the mall were scores of placard bearing students led by Maxine Jefferson. She wore the same Halloween hat and carried a bull horn. "Act white. Can't be right" echoed through the morning light. Windows opened all over the building. Students and faculty poked their heads out. A few shouted epithets at the marchers; some applauded.

Walter rushed to his office to call the campus police.

Billy took off his jacket and carefully draped it over a chair. "If it's a fight they're looking for, let's go." He rolled up the sleeves of his Banana Republic olive green shirt.

"Hold on, Billy," said Abraham as he ran to the door as if to block his colleagues from engaging the enemies below. "That's the last thing we want now." But, as he recounted later, his theatrics were unnecessary. The literature department was not about to challenge Maxine's hordes in combat.

If Wilma weren't still in the lounge, Abraham told Eleanor, I dread to think of the insults my esteemed colleagues would have dropped on the protesters. Instead, they cackled and wrung their hands. The closest to downright racism was old Calvin. He pissed and moaned about the evils of affirmative action. "It's not like the old days," he lamented, "when young men and women came here for an education." Billy was in his element. "Now they're here to study Terrorism 101." He loves confrontations, especially when he's in the safety of a spectator's seat. "Their term project is to burn their own communities." You should have seen him racing from group to group, trying to egg them on. I think only Jack Williams had a head on his shoulders this morning. "Let's go out and talk to the pricks," he suggested. "Inelegantly put, but correct," said Ben. "And what language do you suggest our delegation speak?" asked Calvin dourly. "Perhaps their beloved ebonics?" I never knew just how conservative he is. I thought the only thing that interested him was his damn footnotes. Ben thought I should join him and Jack. "But not Wilma." he said, moving to her side. "She's been through enough with those hoodlums." Jack threw him a grateful look. And do I have things to tell you about those two.

Against the bellicose bellows of Billy Mann who had carefully placed his tie over his jacket, the room endorsed the idea of a delegation.

Walter returned to tell his charges that the campus police were on their way. Ben rushed his delegation out in order to beat the cops to Maxine's army.

The three professors faced a heated Maxine who continued to scream her mantra. She paused only when they were within inches of her. "And where's the white flag?" she taunted to the cheers of those students closest to her. "You are surrendering to the truth, aren't you?" She waved her troops to louder applause.

Ben seemed nervous. He tried to smile. Maxine, too, was a member of the local ACLU chapter. "Not surrender, Maxine. We're here to talk over our differences."

Jack interrupted. "And we better talk fast before the cops get here." It was the wrong thing to say.

"Did you hear the professor?" Maxine shouted. "They've called the police." She put the bull horn to her lips. "When white men can't stand the truth, they call out the troops." She pointed her finger at Ben. "Another fake civil libertarian. All for equal rights as long as they're whites' equal rights." She put down the horn. "We've seen liberals like you all our lives. You're the type that wanted order restored in L.A. after your kind caused the troubles. And after your white jury found Rodney King's attackers innocent. And you whined about racism after that courageous jury acquitted O.J. before a white jury lynched him. And now you call the cops when you can't intellectually counter something. Sure, you're all for the poor darkies helping themselves as long as it fits the liberal white man's agenda. But God forbid that us poor black folk try to better ourselves on our own terms." She turned to the crowd and shouted. "Act white. Can't be right." Maxine conducted them as if she were a cheer leader at a football rally. The chant got louder and louder. She laughed in Ben's face. "Go back to your text books, Professor Rosenthal, and leave the real world to us. We understand it better than you ever will."

"But Maxine," Ben raised his voice in order to be heard, "if we don't talk, we're all doomed."

"A lot of good talking with the Nazis did for your people, Rosenthal. And now you act like the Nazis with my people. Haven't you learned anything from your books?" She turned away. Ben's shoulders sagged. He looked even older than his sixty-six years.

Jack tried to turn Maxine around. He placed his hands on her shoulders. "We've got to talk before the police arrive," he implored. Jack was as angry at her unwillingness to talk as he was furious at her invocation of the holocaust. To equate this squabble over bad English with that terrible, dark period in history was an affront to his sensibilities.

"Take your hands off me," Maxine screamed as she shook herself away. "I'm no slave you can manhandle. And you're sure as hell not my master." She turned to her charges again. "Did you see how that white man laid his hands on me? Do you see how little things have changed in this country?"

"Then go find a better one, you fat black bitch," someone shouted from a window of the humanities building. Abraham shuddered when he saw Maxine turn slowly and coldly scan the crowd of faces that filled the window frames. Deliberately, she raised her arm, almost majestically Abraham thought, and offered the black power salute in the direction of the anonymous voice.

Raised fists flew into the air throughout the mall like a flock of black birds suddenly ascending. As if prepared for the salute, several white pro-testors wore black gloves. "Power to the people" ricocheted off the building's facade. Jack smiled ruefully when his eyes made contact with the glowing coals on Horatio Ginsberg's red, steaming face. "So much for an impartial moderator," he shouted at the president of the senate.

Ginsberg lunged at Jack, his fists flailing long before he reached his target. Abraham and Ben rushed to block the furious attacker. They grabbed Ginsberg and wrestled him to the ground. Ben was panting loudly as he held the mad man down with one hand while the other groped for his glasses which had fallen from his head. A tall black man methodically ground them into the frozen grass. "Now try to read your Talmud, Rabbi," he sneered. Abraham recognized him as a student in his class. In the midst of his fear and concern for Ben, he said half aloud, "And I gave him the benefit of the doubt on his last paper."

Turmoil all around him, Abraham visualized the cover sheet of the essay. "Images of Peace and Solitude in the Poetry of Robert Frost." So much for the liberating arts. At the time he had wondered what term paper mill the student had used. But racial sensitivities had prevented him from looking too carefully at a paper he surely would have chal-lenged if turned in by a white student. Never again, he muttered, but he knew he would do the same thing the very next time it happened. We've all been frozen by the fear of being labeled racist. He shivered. Fear and loathing of the situation collided with his own cowardice. But he would never agree with Calvin regardless of his own culpability in lowering standards. Eleanor had called him wrong-headedly paternalistic when-ever he agonized over papers like the one turned in by Maxine's storm trooper.

Two squads of campus police officers arrived before more damage could be done. At the sight of the cops, an avalanche of rubbish rained down on the protesters and the police. Students were throwing shredded paper, used styrofoam cups, chalk board erasers, rolled balls of textbook pages, bits of uneaten lunches, anything that was not valuable to them. Cheers, applause, and catcalls erupted form the windows.

Billy Mann came running into the crowd, shouting obscenities, and challenging Maxine. Walter Henry hurried to the police captain.

"What do you suggest, Professor Henry? Do you want to file charges?"

"No, no. no. Just clear them out of here and let us get back to our business without any more interruptions."

"Are you crazy?" Billy screamed. "Are you going to let them get away with this?" He refolded a shirt sleeve which had fallen down in his rush to do battle. "You can't do this, Walter." He looked around, beseeching his colleagues who had now joined the police. "They'll just do it again. We can't let them get away with it."

The chair ignored a now crazed Billy Mann. "No charges, Captain. I'll take the matter up with the dean." Before he turned to go back into the building, he shook hands with the officer. "My thanks to you and your men for preventing the situation from becoming even uglier." He left an exasperated Billy still trying to cajole his colleagues into some sort of counter-attack.

Meanwhile, Abraham and Jack were calming a panting Ben. They worried about the strain on his heart. "Are you sure you're all right?" asked Jack, remembering the man's by-pass surgery the year before. "Should we take you to the emergency room?"

"Fine, fine. I'm really okay. Just a little winded." He grasped Jack's hand in appreciation for his concern. Ben smiled. "A little excitement is good for the system." He took hold of Abraham's arm. "This surely beats thirty minutes on the treadmill." He sat down on a bench. "Give me a couple of minutes and I'll be just fine."

The other two members of the failed delegation flanked him on the bench and watched the crowd disperse. About a dozen officers slowly moved the protesters away from the building. The chanting was now intermittent. Only a couple of fists remained raised. A few half-hearted shouts of "pigs" punctuated the forced retreat.

Maxine walked toward the delegation. Her face showed no signs of earlier anger. She joined them on the bench. "Quite a show, wouldn't you say?" she said in an almost amiable tone. "And I am sorry about your glasses, Ben." She touched the top of his hand. "Really." Removing her hat, she ran her hands through her thick black hair. "I must look a mess." She laughed. "But show biz is show biz."

"Are you saying this was all a play, a performance?" asked Abraham.

"Well, it's a performance all right. But not a play. After all, a play's only a representation of reality. What happened here today," she waved her right hand at the littered mall, "that was reality. Believe me, young man, that was real." She leaned forward to see all three of the men. "Now we can talk."

Ben shivered as the late morning sun moved behind a dark cloud. "It's too chilly out here. And the performance, as you call it, has tuckered me out."

"Let's find a more suitable time," said Jack, "and an agenda." He lit a cigarette and stared at Maxine over the fresh white smoke swirling between them. "What the hell was all this about anyway?" He drew deeply. "Surely not about ebonics. Or about Wilma Crouse. Christ, Maxine, you know what a load of horse shit bad black English is." He continued to look directly at her.

"Just listen to yourself when you're not cheerleading. Ebonics? Not on your life. You sound like me, not some burlesque Rastus." He awaited a response, but Maxine just smiled.

"Can I bum a cigarette?" she asked. "Gave up smoking years ago, but I still love bumming one every so often."

"So what's the agenda?" Jack asked again while he held his lighter to Maxine's cigarette.

"Equality. Freedom. Respect. Affirmative Action. That's all." Maxine obviously enjoyed the smoke. She examined the bright red end of the cigarette as if she expected to discover something. "It is a pleasant thing, this smoking." Her face was relaxed, almost friendly. "I want you guys in the literature department to support us. You know I never see more than one or two of you at our rallies. And I know you've got the biggest department in the college." She ground out the cigarette. "For starters, that's all I want. Support. And I don't really care what motivates that support. Just as long as it's public and on the record. You support us and I'll call off the dogs from Wilma." She looked hard at the three men. "And I won't go public with all kinds of goodies I have about some of your classically educated preachers of the great western moral tradition." She gave them an exaggerated wink. "I've got spies in lots of places." Maxine lifted her large frame from the bench. "It is getting chilly." She put on her Halloween hat. "No need to get up, gentlemen. And no need for a meeting about my agenda. You've heard it."

"And what exactly do you expect us to do?" asked a now calm Ben.

"Have the literature department march to your next demonstration?" Jack looked at Maxine as if her request was loony. "You know the odds on that one. You've got to be reasonable."

Maxine adjusted her hat. "No, not the whole department." She pointed to them. "Just you three and that loud mouth who wanted to beat me up. Oh yes, that one's got to march with us. And, of course, Professor Crouse." She was quite serious. "One more thing. The next time we have to demonstrate for our rights, I want a letter from Walter to the campus paper. I want the chair of the literature department to throw the weight of your pale white western tradition behind the just demands of people of color."

"Well, I don't know if. . . "

Maxine interrupted Ben. "And if he needs persuasion, tell him my kids and his go to the same pediatrician." Once more, she gave them the same theatrical wink. "Enough said, men. You have a nice day, now. You hear." She walked briskly along the path away from the humanities building.

"What's that business about a pediatrician supposed to mean?" Ben asked.

"Some other time," Jack said quietly. "Some other time."

"My children see Dennis Collins, too" said Abraham, "and I don't get it either."

"Let's get inside where it's warmer," said Jack. "We can talk later. We've got a lot to discuss." As the three men walked slowly to the building, Ben suggested they have a drink at his house that afternoon. "While things are still fresh in our minds, let's talk over a drink in front of a roaring fire."

They agreed. Ben's place at five.

By the time Abraham arrived home at three, Eleanor had heard about the ruckus. Joyce Rosenthal had called. "She said she's been cooking up a storm and invited us both to stay for dinner." She kissed Ab on the cheek. "That is, after you three heroes compare battle notes over your cigars in the drawing room." She saluted. "Don't forget your pith helmet, general. Now, tell me what happened."

Abraham recounted the morning's events. "And I have a few other things to tell you, too."

"Gossip?"

"The juiciest. First, though, I've got to tell you again how much I hate that creep, Billy Mann."

"So why do you keep meeting with him? He's a worm."

Abraham frowned. "Only because we have common enemies. And, I hope, a united front against them."

"All right. I won't mention it again, but politics does make strange bed fellows."

"I have no intention of crawling into bed with him. Don't worry. Strange bedfellows, though, are what I want to tell you about."

"So who's sleeping around now?"

"How about Walter and Jack?"

"No."

"Yes. I think Jack's got a thing for Willie Crouse."

"Jack and Wilma? You're kidding."

"Wait. You ain't heard nothing yet." Abraham looked around. "The kids are still out?"

"Oh, this is going to be rich. Triple x-rated?"

"Exactly. Walter Henry has a boyfriend."

"Walter?" Eleanor laughed. "Don't be absurd, Ab. Maggie would cut it off. Besides, who told you that tall tale?"

"It's true, believe me." Abraham looked around again to make sure he couldn't be overheard. "Jack Williams had to confide in me and Ben. Not only is Walter ac-dc, but Maxine Jefferson is threatening to blow the whistle on him." He leaned forward. "And guess who the lucky fellow is?"

"Not in a million years. Even if I believed Jack's story, I'd never be able to come up with a name. It's too crazy." Eleanor saw that her husband was serious. "Okay, okay, so who is his alleged boyfriend?"

"Want to try twenty questions?"

"No, I don't. Just tell me."

"None other than our kids' doctor and Walter's new neighbor."

"Dennis Collins?"

"Exactly."

"Now I know the story's loony. Dennis Collins is certainly not gay."

"How about bi?"

"Come on, Ab. We spent an evening with them. There wasn't a thing about that guy that wasn't one hundred per cent masculine."

"Well, he doesn't have to wear a tutu, you know." Abraham fixed himself a drink.

"Be careful with that stuff," Eleanor warned. "We're expected at the Rosenthals soon."

"If things go as badly as they might, this may be my last refuge. You want one?" Abraham now spoke at a normal conversational level. "Trouble's a brewing at the shop, my dear. Between my plotting with Billy Shithead and Maxine's blackmailing the department, this should be an interesting semester."

Billy was furious when he arrived home. One look at him told Sally it had not been a good day. Still in rolled-up shirt sleeves on such a chilly day, Billy dropped into his over-stuffed chair. "Would you make me a martini, please."

Sally went to the bar, still having said nothing. She knew Billy was in one of his moods. He'd tell her everything in his own sweet time.

"Thanks, honey," Billy said. He took a long swig from a drink he normally sipped and savored. "What a fucking day this has been. Would you believe I actually looked forward to going to my afternoon class. I was grateful to face those dimwits and try to tell them something about po-etry." He held out his empty glass. "I talked about poetry. That's all. Po-etry. No departmental politics. Not a word about affirmative action and the half-assed demands of a bunch of hooligans. No Mitchell Murdoch and his genius award. No mealy mouthed chairman kissing the ass of big mama Maxine Sharpton. No do-gooding pap from ACLU Rosenthal. And no apple polishing by Honest Abe Smith." He drank from his replenished martini. "What a day." He looked directly at Sally for the first time. "Not a single thing went right until I entered my classroom."

He got up and walked into the dining room. His mother's posses-sions had a way of settling him down. He opened the top drawer of the oversized ornate buffet and removed a blue cloth from its plastic bag. He polished the already gleaming table top. Replacing the cloth in its drawer, Billy gazed at the dinnerware and goblets neatly arranged behind the glass doors of the hutch. He counted the plates silently. "There are very few certainties in this world," he whispered to the empty room. But at least, he said to himself, there are always twelve plates and twelve wine glasses. And twelve of everything else. He dismissed the thought of polishing the silver.

Still quiet, Sally watched Billy's ritual. Better than prozac. She was sure that if the count ever went against his expectations, Billy would need professional therapy. The only good thing about all that ugly stuff was that it actually reduced his stress. Long ago she had come to a deeper understanding of Silas Marner. She poured a glass of merlot and waited for Billy's recitation.

He returned to the neutral ground of the living room. "But for the moment at least I need Honest Abe. Only for the moment." The thought of pancreatic cancer resurfaced. "Only for the moment." He smiled weakly at Sally. "And our chairman is a fucking fruitcake, too."

This last caught Sally off-guard as it had Eleanor. She looked at Billy. "Come again?"

"You heard me right. Walter Henry wears his pants backwards for a baby doctor." That information joined pancreatic cancer in Billy's plot-ridden consciousness. "I wouldn't be surprised at all," he said, suddenly cheering up, "if I were the one to get tenure this year." He walked to Sally's chair, bent over, and kissed the top of her head. "I wouldn't be surprised at all." He went through the dining room without giving a second look to any of the treasures inherited from his mother. He entered the stark whiteness of the contemporary kitchen without complaining about motel modern. Looking into the crowded refrigerator, he called, "What's for dinner? I'm famished."

Word of Helen Abrams' rape hadn't yet reached the Rosenthal house. The three men, their conference done, joined Eleanor and Joyce in the comfortable living room. The two women were drinking tea.

"Solved all the problems of the world?" asked Joyce. She motioned the men to the bar. "Everything you need is waiting." Her eyes followed Ben with concern. "How's the gladiator doing?" She looked at Eleanor. "He's too old for battling on the mall." Her voice dropped. "He had trouble taking a deep breath when he got home."

"Your old man's just fine," said Jack. He slapped Ben on the back. "He could have gone fifteen rounds this morning." He filled a water glass with Jack Daniels. "And with that opposition, he would've scored a knock-out in one."

"Do you agree?" Joyce looked at Abraham.

"Oh, sure. Ben was a giant. And he looked particularly fetching in his boxing shorts." Eleanor thought both men were being too obvious. She could tell from the sound of the hushed voices that emanated from Ben's study that they were far less pleased with the results of that morning's fray than they let on. She wanted to say something about protecting the little ladies from the stresses of their men's world, but she bit her tongue. Instead, she batted her eyes and sounded like Dumb Dora. "Will the department be all right, Daddy?"

Abraham colored. He hoped she wouldn't continue the routine.

"Don't you worry your pretty little head about it, mam," said Jack, slipping easily into Eleanor's pattern. "The Duke will take care of everything." He tipped the brim of his imagined cowboy hat and did a passable John Wayne walk to the couch.

"Seriously," asked Joyce, "how bad are things? When Ben clams up, I know there's real trouble brewing." She decided to move from tea to wine and went to the bar. "The last time I saw him so upset by things at the university was when Oscar had it out with the last president." She looked at the Smiths. "The provost put his job on the line. And we like Oscar." She laughed. "Of course he's a little touched, but he's as honest as they come."

Jack was relieved that the conversation had moved away from the day's events. In fact, the delegation had resolved very little. They agreed Walter must be protected, but they couldn't decide on the means. They also gave Abraham the assignment of convincing Billy to support Maxine's next demonstration. Neither decision gave the men much to be hopeful about. "He's touched all right. Personally, I think the guy lives only part-time on this planet. But, you're right, he is honest." He took a long gulp of bourbon. "Or at least as honest as an ET can be."

Joyce called them into the dining room. "It's only a little more than pot luck since I spent the morning preparing some of Ben's favorite dishes. I was going to freeze some of this, but I'd much rather share it with friends." She nodded to the serving plates and bowls on the table. "Help yourselves to the food of my husband's insulated childhood."

Ben smiled at Joyce. "For a shiksa, she sets a mean Jewish table." He passed a bottle of red wine to Abraham. "And she knows more about my religion than I ever did."

144

"The fruits of conversion," said Joyce. "If you need any help identifying the food, just ask. You know," she continued, "Ben is one of the most sophisticated men I've ever met. I sometimes believe he lives more in his beloved eighteenth century than in the twentieth. And I know he feels more at home in England than anywhere else. You should see him help out the Brits when it comes to their own history. And food and wine. He's got a palette that's as fine as his esthetic sense. Yet," she waved her arms at the array of food on the table, "he's never been able to wean himself from this stuff"

"It looks wonderful," said Eleanor.

"Appearance and reality, my dear," said Joyce. "Would you believe I actually took a class to learn how to overcook meat?"

"Come now, Joyce," Ben said good naturedly, "you even like some of it." He looked around the table. "Try her matzoh ball soup, and tell me if it's not ambrosia."

A bowl of soup had been set at each place. A gigantic fluffy, yellowish ball sat in the center of the bowl of chicken soup, bits of carrot and celery floating around it

"God, this is good," said Jack. "Even better than the Carnegie Deli." He raised his fingers to his lips and saluted the cook.

Abraham imagined Jack and Wilma at the Carnegie. Chitlins and gefillte fish perhaps. He winced at his own thoughts which he believed were more suitable to Billy Mann. Eleanor smiled across the table at him. Perhaps she's thinking the same thing, he thought and returned the smile. Ben passed a platter of pot roast surrounded by potatoes, carrots, and prunes.

"What's this called?" asked Eleanor.

"Flanken," said Ben. "Try it, you'll like it."

"One of the few recipes I was able to coax out of his mother," said Joyce. "She thought I was a moron in the kitchen."

'That's right," Ben added as he carefully arranged a piece of meat, a potato, and a prune on his fork. "She couldn't believe anyone needed a recipe to cook." He pointed his fork at Joyce. "Remember the stuffed cabbage?"

"How could I ever forget?" She turned her attention to her guests. "You'll never believe the scene. There I was, pen in hand, sitting across the kitchen table from his mother while she tried to tell me about that delectable dish."

"You start with a head of cabbage."

"How large a head?"

"What do you mean, how large? A nice head. Not too large and not too small."

"You can guess how successful that meeting of the chefs was. Seasoning? A little of this; a little more of that. I swear the woman never read a recipe in her life."

"But Joyce finally mastered stuffed cabbage. And more." Ben looked endearingly at his wife. "She indulges me."

"I've actually come to like some of these dishes."

"Maybe we'll have a latke party next December," said Ben. "The last one we went to was at the Berlins."

"Can that one cook?" asked Jack.

"Of course not." Ben growled. "She wouldn't take time away from all those television sets in that sweatshop of hers. Anyway, Martin does most of the cooking in their house. He's probably the only person in her employ who isn't robotized before a screen." He stabbed a carrot. "Scholarship she dares call it."

"That's enough, Ben," said Joyce. "It was a very nice Chanukah party. And Marty made delicious latkes."

"With apple sauce," Ben said and shook his head.

"He prefers sour cream, but they try to eat healthy, as Martin says."

"Healthy?" Ben guffawed. 'Trust me, folks. If Beverly thinks you're important enough to invite you to dinner, stop at McDonalds on the way over if she tells you she's doing the cooking."

"Come on Ben, you know she rarely enters the kitchen of that beautiful house." Joyce waved her husband's comment aside. "And she's very proud of Marty's cooking."

"Important enough?" asked Abraham.

"Sure. You don't think Beverly invites people over for good fellowship and conversation, do you? She doesn't send her Martin into the kitchen for such obviously human purposes, for pleasant dinners with friends. Oh no. That one doesn't do anything for nothing." He ignored Joyce's protestations. "That's one calculating girl."

"We're invited for Sunday brunch," Eleanor volunteered.

"Be prepared. Remember, forewarned is forearmed. Get a Breakfast

Mac on the way over." He laughed. "But Joyce is surely right. Of course Martin will be doing the cooking. And he is very good in the kitchen."

"Please, Ben, let's drop the subject." She shrugged in the direction of the Smiths. "I don't think Eleanor and Abraham want to hear about your dealings with Beverly Berlin. Enough to say that Martin is one terrific cook."

The fact was the Smiths did want to hear, but neither urged Ben to continue.

"And I'm sure," Joyce continued, "neither Beverly nor Martin came up during your skull session in the study."

"For sure," said Jack. "Bad enough I have to see that broad dancing through the halls every time I'm on campus. She really thinks she's hot stuff." He looked at Abraham. "Ever notice how she carries herself? Like she's sucking on a lemon, having to be among us intellectual midgets." Jack jutted his jaw and threw his head back. "I bet she practices walking with a stack of books on her head."

"I dare say that's the only use she puts books to," said Ben.

"You know Murdoch's pushing for her promotion this year," said Jack, moving his empty plate aside and leaning toward his host.

"Another man of letters." Ben growled. "And he gets a genius award. Did you read his last book? Only a monomaniacal swindler would have the gall to call it *Beyond the Mystery of Hermaneutical Theory: A Personal Speculation in Three Parts.* Can you imagine such nonsense?"

"Did you read it?" asked Abraham.

"Read it?" Ben smiled. "You don't read such a book. It's not readable. Rather, you open to any page and laugh or cry. It's garbage dressed up to look like some dense eighteenth-century German philosopher. And I'll tell you something else," Ben nodded vigorously, "when you can actually decipher that crap, you discover that what the genius is saying is simple-minded and mundane. That's what it is. Commonplace analysis produced by a commonplace intelligence." Ben was flushed.

"But will you vote for the video queen?" Joyce asked, trying to move her husband from the subject of Mitchell Murdoch.

"Vote for a woman who spends her time looking at soap operas and talk shows? For a fraud who calls that scholarship? Never. I can name a dozen good critics who do popular culture. But believe me, whatever the likes of Mitchell Murdoch may claim, dear Beverly's not one of them."

"You want to bet she gets her promotion?" Jack took out his wallet. "Five bucks she's promoted."

"Put your money away, Jack." Ben touched his arm. "Of course she'll be promoted. We're surrounded by colleagues who claim that which they can't decipher is brilliant." He sipped his wine. "They're like children. Ready to put the blame of incomprehension on themselves."

"They're so damned scared of not being thought au courant, they're ready to give standing ovations to singers who can't carry a tune." Jack walked to the bar for a refill.

"But only if some celebrated charlatans have dubbed the singers brilliant." Ben turned to Abraham. "Didn't you run into that in graduate school?"

Abraham nodded.

"Christ, I read your dissertation before we hired you," said Jack who stood by the bar. "Damned good stuff." He downed his bourbon. "Did you ever read Murdoch on some of the same Robert Frost poems you deal with?"

Ben laughed. "Wade through his chapter on reactionary American poetry and you'll retch. According to the genius, Frost was a religious fanatic. I heard he tells undergraduates that the sister in 'Out Out' is a nun and the guy in 'Death of the Hired Hand' is Jesus Christ. He even makes a case for Jack Kennedy being a closet fundamentalist for having invited Frost to read at his inauguration."

Joyce laughed. "He once told me the leftists had a mole in the Kennedy camp who arranged for Frost to read with the setting sun blinding the page before him. Mitchell was very proud of that literary espionage. Honest, that was his term for it."

"Some Marxist, that one. He'll probably buy a second Jaguar with his award money." Ben looked at Joyce. "Do we have an appropriate dessert to top off this enchanting discussion of our esteemed colleagues?"

"And what would you suggest?"

"That would make a good party game," said Eleanor, trying to enter a conversation of department elders. She was unsure of the roles she and her untenured husband were expected to play. That Ben and Jack seemed not at all reluctant to lacerate Beverly and Mitchell brought the Smiths into their camp. Or, at least, that was what she assumed. "We can invent desserts that suit different members of the department." She glanced at Abraham. Was she overreaching? And what game might they be playing at Sunday brunch? Would the present company be the objects of attack? God, I wish Ab was already tenured.

"No games," said Jack. "I need an early bedtime tonight. And you too, Ben. Walter's scheduled an eight o'clock meeting of the personnel bunch."

"At least he's promised coffee and sweet rolls," said Joyce. "But I agree with Jack. Dessert tonight is pretty simple fare. Nothing as interesting as Eleanor's suggestion, but I hope you'll enjoy it." She stood up. "Coffee for everyone?"

Abraham spoke quickly. "Maybe some other time for Eleanor's game?" he asked. He wanted to be part of Ben and Jack's wing of the department. And he knew neither one of them cared for Billy Mann. Abraham counted votes too.

Joan Eastland's message was brief. Her voice on the answering machine told Eleanor and Abraham there was trouble. "Please call me as soon as you get home. It's important. Don't worry about how late it might be."

By the time they reached the hospital, the police had completed their interview with Helen. Joan stood in the corridor outside a triage examination room. Her face was ashen. She offered a weak smile to Eleanor as she hugged her. "Thank God you're here."

"How's Helen?"

"Terrible. She was nearly hysterical when I got here." Joan hugged Abraham. "And the police didn't help much, even though the woman cop was wonderful. Helen couldn't stop crying. The doctor just now gave her a shot. He says she should sleep for a while, but someone better be here when she wakes up." Joan began to cry. "Her face is black and blue. The bastard beat her up."

"Do they know who he is?" asked Abraham.

Joan nodded. "Her neighbor. The man in the next apartment."

"Her neighbor?"

"Can you imagine that? The same guy who helped her paint the apartment. The same man she invited to dinner so many times, went to the movies with. Helen even cooked half the dishes for his Christmas party."

Joan sat down on a white bench. "She thought the son of a bitch was a friend."

"How did it happen?"

"I think Helen said he did it in her own apartment. Maybe not. She wasn't making much sense. Just held onto my hand and sobbed." Joan wiped her eyes. "The police kept asking her where it happened. And one smug cop insisted on asking about their relationship. That is, until the woman officer hustled him out of the room. Each time he asked that hideous question, poor Helen's eyes widened and she sobbed even harder."

"You know what he was suggesting?" said Eleanor.

"Of course. He was trying to fix the blame on her."

"Did she invite him into her apartment?" Abraham was immediately sorry he had asked that question.

"Oh, Ab. They're neighbors. They've been in each others' places many times."

"Sure," said Joan, "Helen invited him to rape her." She put her hand on Abraham's arm. "I'm sorry. I didn't mean that."

"You know how they're going to make it look?"

"Except for the bruising," said Eleanor. "Consensual sex doesn't include getting beaten up." A nurse came out of Helen's room. "She wants to see you," she said to Joan. "The shot's calmed her down even if it didn't knock her out."

They all entered the room.

Helen was deathly pale, lying in bed, dressed in a green and white hospital gown. Her face bore one large purplish splotch and a few smaller ones. The bruising was less severe than either Eleanor or Abraham expected.

'Hi, kid,' Joan said softly. She bent over her friend and kissed her forehead. "How's it going?"

Helen's eyes filled. She reached out for Eleanor's hand. "Thanks for coming." She tried to smile at Abraham. "Both of you." She propped up her pillows and raised her head. "At least it's a Friday. I'll have a couple of days to recuperate before I have to explain all this," she touched her face, "to my students. Maybe I can blame it all on Patrick Donovan. I'll tell them the dean beat the shit out of me when I asked him for a raise."

They all laughed more heartily than they should have.

"Some great line, huh? I bet there's not a single student in my classes who even knows who Donovan is." Clearly, Helen would rather talk about anything but the rape.

"Don't worry about your classes," said Abraham. "Between Joan and me, they'll be covered for as long as you need." He hesitated. "Do you have a lawyer?"

"A lawyer?" She offered a hoarse laugh. "Why should I need a lawyer? He's the one who's going to need a lawyer. I've got the d.a. and the cops on my side."

"Of course," said Eleanor, angry at her husband's question. "Have the police arrested him?"

"They were on their way to the apartment after they finished with me."

"Is he the one we had dinner with at your place?" Abraham asked. "The computer engineer?"

Helen trembled.

Joan answered. "Yes. Larry. The guy we all thought was a sweetheart."

"Some sweetheart," said Helen. "I'll never understand."

"Not tonight," interrupted Joan. "Not tonight, sweetie. There'll be plenty of time for analysis later on. Now, just rest."

"Do you want us to call your folks?" asked Abraham.

"Please, God, no." Helen was again on the verge of tears. "They're the last people I want to know about this." She wiped her eyes. "The last thing they have to hear is that their little girl was attacked in her own apartment. Their little girl nestled in the secure surroundings of this Christmas card of a college town in the safe midwest. And by a friend, no less. They actually met Larry the last time they visited. He even helped my father unload the car. They brought me my winter clothes last November." Her eyes overflowed. "We all had dinner that night. My mother thought he was such a nice young man. I'm sure she thought I had a thing for him. No, please, don't call them."

"I don't think that's a story she should tell the police," said Abraham as he and Eleanor drove home.

Eleanor nodded in the dark car. "Some people will make mung out of poor Helen. They're the cretins who always assume it's the woman's fault."

"And in her own apartment." Abraham turned into their driveway. "Strange, isn't it. Joan's the one who always wears those short leather skirts and Helen looks like a corporate lawyer."

Eleanor winced. "Even the so-called emancipated among us aren't immune from that kind of thinking," she said tartly.

"I didn't mean. . ."

"I certainly hope you didn't. But imagine what some of the great unwashed, to use one of your friend, Billy's, terms, might say."

Chastened, Abraham didn't reply.

As they entered the house, Eleanor asked if they should call Walter.

"I guess we should. But tomorrow morning. God, this has been a long day." Abraham took off his tie and jacket. "I'll check on the kids while you put on a pot of coffee."

Eleanor took a pack of cigarettes from their hiding place behind the nicorettes in the buffet. She set the coffee maker going, sat down at the kitchen table, and struck a match. The first long drag relaxed her tight throat. It has been a lousy night. She held the cigarette before her and watched the smoke curl from its tip. I wish these things were good for me. She took a second long drag. People who never smoked don't have a clue. Two streams of smoke cascaded from her nostrils. She leaned back and closed her eyes. Poor Helen.

"Both kids are sleeping like babies," said Abraham. He dropped into his customary place at the table, the only chair with arms. "Christ, Ellie, you promised to give those things up."

"So I promised. So, punish me. But, please, not tonight." She looked at the cigarette again. "Now, just let me enjoy my crime. It's the first pleasant moment I've had all night."

"Didn't you have a good time at the Rosenthals?"

"Only for a while. Then I felt like a child at a grown-ups' party. I ended up sounding like a waif who wanted to be allowed into the rich folks' ball." She shook her head. "I felt like a damn dunce with that stupid party game suggestion."

"Then why did you do it?"

"Because I know how important it is to you to be one of them."

"But I always thought you liked Joyce."

"I do, but we're never going to be best buddies. For heaven's sake, she's old enough to be my mother. God, all three of them are old enough to be our parents."

"I do want to be on their side." Abraham placed his hand over Eleanor's. "And I want them to be on my side when the vote comes."

"But, Ab, didn't you feel like an outsider when Ben and Jack were talking about Beverly's promotion?"

"We should be pleased that they were willing to talk about her and Mitchell in front of us."

"Yeah, like plantation owners talking in front of a couple of slaves."

"Come on, you're exaggerating. I think their talk suggested I'd soon be a fully franchised member of the department."

"Jesus, you sound like Walter Henry in one of his clumsily formal moments." She lit another cigarette. "It's me, Ab. Remember me? Ellie, the devoted faculty wife and helpmate. You don't have to use that lofty style. Fully franchised member. Bull shit." She stubbed out a half smoked cigarette. "And don't worry. I won't smoke in front of the kids." She refilled their coffee cups. "But enough about your move up the corporate ladder. Let's get back to Helen. At the moment she's more important than the contest between you and Billy. Or whatever plot you two are hatching." She looked directly at Ab. "Who's the object of your plot, anyway?"

"I thought you wanted to talk about Helen."

"I know you don't want to divulge the nature of your machinations, but you can at least tell me who's the focus of your scheming. I still can't figure out what could have brought you and Billy together."

"Murdoch and Berlin."

"And we're going to the Murdochs for brunch this Sunday?"

"I thought we were going to the Berlins. You said. . . ."

"I just wanted to fit into the conversation. No, it's the Murdochs. So what do you and Billy plan to do? Plant bombs in Mitchell's and Beverly's houses?" Eleanor laughed. "You know what I think about academics being able to work in the real world. Christ, you two would probably blow yourselves up in no time."

"We better talk about Helen."

"There you go again. Changing the subject whenever you're challenged. Did I hurt your feelings? It's true, you know. Most of you people are inept. Totally incapacitated for surviving in the nine-to-five, workaday world. All I can say is that your plot better involve only words. That's the only universe you guys are comfortable in."

Abraham stood up. "I've heard that tired song too many times. Isn't it time for you to record a new one?"

"Oh, come on, honey. Indulge me my views of your profession. You know I exempt you from my charges."

"One would never guess that." Abraham was angry. "Be honest."

"So, exempt from most of the charges." She stood up and hugged him. "How's that? Honest enough?" She kissed him.

"Which charges remain?"

She touched his fly. "I'd rather focus on the exemptions. You must be one of the few professors who can still get it up. And certainly one of the very few who know what to do with it."

Abraham was mollified. Intimations of sex always brought him out of snits caused by Eleanor's attacks on his profession. He was critically astute enough to recognize Eleanor's repertoire, but he could only succumb to complimentary words about his manliness. "Are you trying to seduce me?" He kept her hand over his hardness.

"Not tonight, Ab." She removed her hand and kissed his cheek. "But it's nice to see that willie is alive and well." She returned to her place at the table. "Frankly, with what's happened to Helen, I couldn't get in the mood." She lit a cigarette.

"That's the third one since we got home." Abraham was disappointed. He adjusted his pants and sat down. "So what can we do for her?"

"For starters, no talk about the contrast between her clothing tastes and Joan's."

"That was a dumb thing to say. I'm sorry."

"Good, because those hyenas at your joint will have a field day come Monday."

Abraham nodded. "It'll be the dessert after this morning's entrees of Wilma's debate and Mitchell's MacArthur."

"You got it right. Today's warm-up will have them raring to go at Helen. But perhaps you and Walter can deflect them."

"And Jack Williams. You should have seen how he protected Wilma today."

"And Ben?"

"I'll call them all tomorrow.

"Thank God Helen's not standing for tenure this year. Billy would do a terrible number on her. Can you ask him to ease up? It's a perfect vehicle for his sophomoric chatter."

Abraham frowned. He rubbed his forehead as if he had a headache. "I almost forgot I've been delegated to get Billy to march in Maxine's next protest."

"Billy Mann marching with blacks in support of affirmative action?" Eleanor shook her head. "Lots of luck. I don't know how you can manage that one. Is there a bribe rich enough to get him onto that kind of picket line?"

"There may be. I haven't yet agreed to his plot."

"Which is?"

"I still don't know. Honest, I don't."

Self-aggrandizing talk at brunch was almost overshadowed by the news of the rape. Almost. There were too many heavy hitters present to be thrown off their game by the change of pace which had come so unexpectedly. The suffering of a young woman was finally no match for academic puffery.

Abraham and Eleanor were a trifle uneasy about visiting the Murdochs so soon after witnessing, mute though they were, Ben's hostility toward Mitchell. But even the seemingly most moral among us must swallow scruples when tenure is still in doubt. Neither Abraham nor Eleanor was about to abandon the field to Billy Mann.

"A lot of cars," said Abraham as they looked for a parking space. "This is no intimate brunch they're throwing."

"I'm sure the guest list swelled since he got the MacArthur." Eleanor pointed out the caterer's truck in the driveway as they walked up the front stairs. "You don't hire that four-star outfit to feed a few friends on a Sunday afternoon." Eleanor looked down at her jeans and sneakers. "Isobel told me to dress casually. Just having a couple of good people over to share a bagel and let our hair down. Those are her exact words." She hesitated on the porch of the big, old house. "Should we go home and change?"

"We're here. Let's just go in. We won't be the only ones not wearing top hats and tails."

"And if we are?"

"Then we'll add a touch of class to the joint." Abraham examined his wife. "I think you look terrific. If half of those dames had your body, they'd be wearing jeans too."

The house was crowded with colleagues, administrators, and a smattering of important locals. White vested waiters moved through the rooms with platters of finger foods. A bar was set up in the foyer.

"A casual brunch for a few folks?" Abraham said.

"Well, old buddy, when you win your MacArthur, will you do anything less grand?" Billy had been standing behind Eleanor. "He may not write a lovely English prose, but he sure knows how to throw a party. You've got to try the rumaki. Delicious. And the shrimp toast is out of this world." He put his fingers to his lips. "I'd love to eat like this every Sunday."

Sally Mann joined them. She was a knockout in a black silk jump suit. Eleanor hated her on the spot. "Is my Billy still raving about the canapes? He's planted himself at the front door like an official greeter." She kissed him on the cheek. "Isn't he too much?" She smiled a bit too warmly at the Smiths.

"Yes, Sally, he is too much." Eleanor words were icicles. "Is he handing out campaign buttons as well as gastronomical advice?"

Sally's eyes narrowed for a split second. "Oh, Eleanor, you're just too funny." She turned away and joined the small crowd around Richard Maxwell.

"I didn't know presidents voted in tenure cases," Eleanor said aloud. She felt naked in her sweater, sneakers, and jeans.

"Aren't we making a fashion statement?" It was Beverly Berlin who was wearing a sweater and slacks. "Either we didn't know Mitchell and Isobel were running a formal ball or we're deep into casual chic." Beverly hugged Eleanor in greeting. "Which story do we want?" She nodded in the direction of President Maxwell. "You see what good company we're in." Barbara Maxwell, rich as Croesus, stood talking to the mayor. She also wore a sweater and jeans. Eleanor's spirits rose. "I think that's the way their set dresses on Sunday afternoons in the Hamptons," Beverly continued, still holding Eleanor's hand. "If a stranger looked at Billy and Sally scoring points with the first family, I bet he'd pick the Manns in their fancy duds as the president and first lady."

Still surprised by Beverly's warm greeting, Eleanor had to agree with her sartorial assessment. Sally, in her shiny black, and Billy in a gorgeous pale blue flannel jacket over a deep blue shirt and floral ascot surely looked more impressive than the Maxwells. Not having joined his wife in jeans, the president was wearing a boldly patterned sport jacket and chinos. Eleanor was glad to see he wore sneakers. Had she fully understood Maxwell's scholarly interest in attire, she would not have been surprised at the care he had taken in selecting an outfit he thought critically appropriate for brunch with a genius award winner. He would surely explicate his clothing choices before brunch concluded.

A photographer wandered the house, snapping pictures of the notables assembled to congratulate Professor Murdoch. A *Journal* reporter trailed her colleague, noting the names of those photographed, and asking questions. The article and pictures would be the lead in tomorrow's section two.

Abraham joined Eleanor and Beverly. "Billy's right. The food is delicious." He pointed toward the dining room. "They've even set up an omelet station and carvery in there." He was impressed.

"All it takes is money," said Beverly, surprisingly snippy in the home of her greatest booster. "I'll tell you, though, Marty could do it all at half the price."

Eleanor wanted to ask if she rented him out, but thought better of it. If she read Beverly's tone right, the video queen was not enamored of Billy. And who knows, maybe the outside search will come up dry and she'll have to vote for Ab or Billy. As angry as she was at Beverly for her desire to bypass both of them for an outside appointment, there was still a lot of time for the search to go bad. You can never be sure of the house before it actually votes, she said often enough to Ab, and never count anyone out too soon. So Eleanor smiled warmly at Beverly. "Yes, I've heard your husband is a great cook."

"One of the best," said Walter Henry as he joined the women and kissed them both. "Some party, isn't it? And I'm famished." He patted his stomach. "Ran three miles with the boys this morning."

For a second, Abraham wondered who exactly the boys were. He looked away from Billy's smirk and raised eyebrow.

"Looks like they didn't forget anyone," said Walter as he returned smiles and waves. "That's the chairman of the board of trustees standing next to Mitchell."

But Eleanor had already noted that several people had been forgotten. Her examination of the house failed to find the Rosenthals or Jack Williams, but she saw Wilma just entering the foyer. Mitchell and the chairman of the board, arm in arm, moved toward Wilma. "I want you to meet one of the real stars of our department, Professor Wilma Crouse." Mitchell was expansive in his greeting. "Wilma, meet Jason Whitaker." He left the two in pointless conversation and moved away to continue working the room.

"I've heard a great deal about you, Doctor Crouse," said Whitaker, an elderly, tall, handsome man. "I know I speak for the entire board when I tell you how honored we were when you turned down those most attractive offers." Accustomed to flattering audiences, he smiled benignly at the black woman. He dropped his voice as if he were about to divulge a confidence. "Let me tell you that our deliberations in your case were among the briefest on record."

Knowing that Whitaker was a prominent lawyer and former U.S. Senator, Wilma realized how insincere his words were. Her smile matched his in practiced mendacity. She was no newcomer to cocktail party effusiveness. "Why, thank you so very much for those kind words. You'll never know how much they mean to me." Wilma smiled as she thought what Jack's comments might sound like in a similar situation. But she knew he'd be proud of her performance.

"I was distressed, however," said the chairman, sipping white wine and trying not to be overheard, "by that article in the *Journal*. Terrible stuff, this ebonics business." He nodded his head vigorously. He placed his left hand on her arm. "And a terrible way to treat a distinguished scholar. Terrible."

Wilma nodded her thanks. She wondered, however, what the old pol's lamentation might have sounded like had he been addressing his cronies. Better not wonder too deeply about that, she said to herself, and Wilma extricated herself from Whitaker's concern. She made her excuses and headed for the bar.

Billy Mann intercepted her. "Let me get you a drink, Willie," he said as if they were old friends. Few colleagues called her Willie. "What'll it be?"

"Thanks just the same, but I'd like to see what the bartender's got in stock." She gave Billy a version of the smile she had bestowed on the chairman of the board. "What are you drinking?"

Billy was upset by her rebuff. He was also irritated by the fact that she did not call him by name. I should have asked her if she wanted the same as at the King's Arms. Should've asked her if she got laid that night. "Oh, I'm having my usual." He tried to sound debonair.

"And what might that be?" Something sweet to coat that bile of yours, she thought. You officious little twit. Why don't you roll up the sleeves of that expensive shirt and pick a fight with a cripple.

"I always have Pym's Cup at Sunday brunches." Billy desperately wanted her to ask him what that drink was.

"Really? My father loves Pym's Cup." Wilma smiled mischievously, having correctly read Billy's thoughts. "When I was a small child, I loved the sound of that name."

"Wilma, my dear, how good to see you at a social event." Beverly Berlin fluttered in between her and Billy. Stung by the fact that Mitchell had introduced her to Whitaker in a most perfunctory manner, but desperately wanting Wilma's vote in her coming bid for a full professorship, Beverly was sweetness and light. She had decided before leaving home that morning that the buffet was to be her garden to cultivate. She told Martin, who was unloading the dishwasher, that she planned to sow seeds all over the place. Some fast growing plants and some slow. Wilma fell in the former category; Eleanor in the latter. Marty had wished her a green thumb, which he thought a wonderfully inventive turn of speech, and asked what she'd like for dinner. "I'm in the mood to cook up a storm tonight." Beverly told him the choice was his, but he should make enough for tomorrow's lunch for her assistants. "Remember, Monday's our planning session time. And they adore your culinary magic." She blew him a kiss and left for the garden.

Billy stared at Beverly's back. How dare she interrupt like that? Who does she think she is? He moved to her side so that he could see both women, and both women could not help seeing him. "I was just telling Wilma about my favorite Sunday brunch drink."

"Really, how interesting a subject that must be." Beverly smiled at Wilma.

Clearly hearing the dismissive tone, Billy decided not to be deterred. If Beverly were a lost cause, Wilma surely was not. Could she ever forget his defense of her when those thugs attacked their building? He thought not. It was worth more than a tenure vote, he had told Sally.

"And what might that drink be? Pablum on the rocks?" Beverly smiled at Wilma again.

"Now that's funny," said Billy, swallowing his anger. "I'm sure you're referring to the enormous difference in our ages," he counter thrusted. He, too, smiled at Wilma as though she were the judge at this duel. "I guess from your vantage point, I must seem a mere baby feeding on pablum." He drank from his glass. "And what's the favorite brunch drink with the geriatric set?" Billy was now on the offensive. "Shall I ask the bartender to fix you a prune juice cocktail?"

"Prune juice? They're serving prune juice?" Old Calvin looked at his plate of cheese omelet, roast beef, potatoes au gratin, shrimp, Greek salad, and sour dough bread. "I think I'm going to need a prune juice cocktail after all this." He blushed at his insensitive remark before the women. "Well, you get what I mean."

Billy's eyes lit up. He thought he had the perfect plan if only the venue were right. He raced off to share this serendipitous moment with his partner in conspiracy.

Billy broke into Abraham's conversation with Walter. "I've got to show you something outside." He grabbed Abraham's sleeve and pulled him away. "Believe me, it's important."

Eleanor noticed them talking on the back patio, Billy gesturing wildly, Ab smiling enthusiastically. She shook her head in agreement with Beverly's obvious surprise at seeing those two apparently enjoying each other's company. "I can't figure it out either," Eleanor said. Beverly's ears would be burning if the old wives' tale were true. But before their conversation could continue, Richard Maxwell was asking for the floor. He was flanked by Mitchell and Chairman Whitaker. The Murdoch children were banging forks against glasses, doing their bit to insure the proper deferential stillness for the words of praise for their father. Mitchell tousled the hair of his son and beamed at his guests.

The president launched into a hymn to his MacArthur fellow. His words were directed as much to the local audience as to the board of trustees.

They would have to be impressed by the genius grant. Indeed, it was Maxwell himself who had invited Whitaker to the brunch after he learned there was to be a large gathering. "It isn't many universities who have the honor," the president concluded, "to rub shoulders with a bona fide genius. We all think we're geniuses, of course," he laughed, "after all, that comes with the territory in academe. But few of us ever receive the certificate of authenticity the MacArthur people have conferred on Mitchell." He turned to the ecstatic genius and urged him to acknowledge the applause of the crowd.

Mitchell feigned embarrassment. He did everything except say "aw, shucks." But the president prevailed. "How can I refuse such a heartfelt request," he began. "And from the great president of this great institution." He shook Maxwell's hand. Beverly thought he was about to plant a kiss on the president. He said all the expected things in a half humble, half arrogant manner. "Carefully rehearsed," Beverly whispered to Eleanor. At the conclusion of his remarks, after saying he couldn't have been so successful without the aid of Isobel and his beloved children, "and all those women he fucks," whispered Beverly, he asked for a moment of silent prayer for Helen. Beverly said she was going to puke. "One of our brightest young colleagues is at this moment experiencing great personal anguish which must taint our pleasure on this day. I know you all join me in sending Helen Abrams our deepest heartfelt wishes." He dropped his head as if to pray. "Helen is one of my most cherished colleagues." Eleanor told Beverly she was about to join her at the vomitorium.

Maxwell spoke once again. "That was lovely, Mitchell. We all share those feelings." He placed his arm on Mitchell's shoulder. "Think about it, my friends, at so singular a celebratory moment, our host had the sensitivity and grace to remind us of one less fortunate. Very impressive." He squeezed Murdoch's shoulder. "Very impressive indeed." The president turned to Whitaker for a few words.

"I just want to say how proud the board of trustees is of Professor Murdoch. President Maxwell and the board will be hosting a banquet in Mitchell's honor next month. Black tie and all. We plan to do it up right. And if we're lucky, the governor and first lady will grace the occasion. It's not every day that we can rub shoulders with a genius." Whitaker beamed as *The Journal* photographer snapped away.

Having heard the conclusion of the ceremony, Billy said, "That's it.

That'll be our venue." He laughed as he pumped Abraham's hand. "What a show it'll be." Both men laughed like kids.

After brunch, the Smiths drove to Joan's house. Helen was going to spend a few days there, rather than return to the scene of the rape.

Eleanor carried a box of food Isobel had prepared when she learned Helen was being discharged from the hospital that morning. "Do you think she remembers what Helen looks like?" Eleanor asked Abraham.

"Does Maxwell even know who she is, the object of his great solicitude?"

"You mean Mitchell's dear young friend?" Eleanor sneered. "At least Isobel put together a neat care package. There's enough here for them to survive a blizzard."

They found Helen lying on a couch in Joan's small living room. She looked much better than on the previous night.

Joan brought in coffee and opened the Murdoch's box.

"So how's the genius doing today?" asked Helen.

"The question is how are you doing today?" asked Abraham. "We can talk about him later."

"Much better. Really. I'm surprised at how much stronger I am. Even called my folks as soon as Joan got me here."

"And?" asked Eleanor.

"They were terrific." Helen smiled for the first time. "Mom actually cried. Wanted to take the next plane out. Even Dad said he'd come." Helen made an exaggerated tremble. "But I convinced them there was nothing they could do. I promised to phone them every day until it was all over."

"Better a telephone relationship," said Joan. "I keep my folks at bay by making the obligatory weekly call. It's a lot easier to be family when you know they won't be here after you hang up."

"They may think the same thing," said Abraham, momentarily brooding over the thought of his two children one day talking like that.

"Oh, I'm sure," said Helen. "The last time they came out here, my dad kept looking at his watch as if he had a train to catch. They were staying four days and he kept looking at his watch."

After a long pause, Eleanor asked, "So, do you want to talk about it?"

Helen nodded.

"It's good to try to exorcise the monster," said Abraham. "Maybe closer to my religious training than yours, but it is a good idea. Shrinks do the same thing." He smiled at Helen. "Confrontation can be healthy."

"I still can't believe it happened," Helen began. "Rape is something that happens to other women. And I liked Larry." She bit into now cold shrimp toast.

"That's the first thing she's eaten today," said Joan.

"Larry's always been so kind and helpful. And he's such a nebbish. A nice nebbish." Her eyes filled. "But he was crazy the other night."

"Was he drunk or high, do you think?" asked Eleanor.

"I think so. His eyes were wild when he came into my apartment. He told me he loved me. And when I said something inane like we're just friends, he punched me. Just like that. No warning. He just hauled off and punched me in the stomach. And when I doubled over, he began hitting me in the face. All you elitist broads are the same, he kept shouting. Fucking intellectuals think you're so good. Well, he shouted, I'll give you something that none of your fucking professors can give you. I was terrified. I screamed. He said he'd kill me if I didn't shut up. He ripped off my blouse and stuffed it in my mouth."

Helen threw up her hands. "Crazy as it sounds, all I could think of was those rape-defense classes I attended. Don't struggle. Don't resist. Your best chance of survival. But theory goes out the window when you're in the midst of the real thing. Even with the blouse in my mouth, I still tried to scream. I fought the son of a bitch with strength I never knew I had. But it was useless. Larry's stronger than he looks. He dragged me into the bedroom. He threw me onto the bed. And he kept threatening to kill me."

"You don't have to go on," said Joan quietly.

"No, no, I want to." Helen sipped her coffee. "Then he did the strangest thing. He said he wouldn't hit me anymore if I promised not to cry out. I nodded, hoping I could at least buy time. I really believed my life was hanging by the thread of his insanity. Larry got off the bed and took off his shirt. I was horrified. There in the center of his hairless chest he had printed my name. In the middle of a heart." She almost smiled. "An awful purple color. He flexed his muscles as though he thought he could impress me. He even told me he'd been working out for months just for this moment."

Helen looked as if she were going to be sick. "Like a schoolboy with a summer crush, he was planning for this moment. He asked me what I thought of his physique. I was beside myself. I knew he was crazy. Terrific, isn't it? he kept asking. I nodded, terrified that any negative comment or movement might kill me. Well, you ain't seen nothing yet, bitch. He stood over me and removed his pants and briefs. How's that compare with those pansies at the university? Wouldn't they kill for a prick like this? Them with their intellectual little dicks." Helen sobbed. "He came all over my face. It was horrible. He laughed. When he was done, he rubbed it all over my cheeks."

"Then he began to slap my face. Harder and harder. Then he stopped and sat on the edge of the bed. His voice was almost gentle. He stroked my hair. Now, wasn't that a beautiful massage. He caressed my cheeks. They'll be so smooth now. Suddenly, he commanded that I strip. It's time for the real thing, he snarled. I pleaded that he use a condom. He snapped at me. What, and be like one of those pussy professors. He strutted around the room, almost chanting as he rubbed himself. Real men don't use rubbers. Real men don't use rubbers. Real men don't use rubbers." Abraham thought of Maxine Jefferson's mantra. He imagined Maxine and the rapist leading a march on the humanities building.

"Then he raped me. It hurt like hell, but, thank God, it was mercifully brief"

"Did he leave then?" asked Eleanor.

"He dressed very methodically, almost calmly. I thought the drugs or whatever were wearing off. When he was done, he walked to the door. He turned to me and smiled. Almost the nice friendly smile I had come to expect from him. I hope I didn't ruin your blouse, he said. I couldn't believe it. You don't have to get up, he said as if we were an old couple. I can let myself out. I lay there until I heard the front door open and close. I rushed into the living room to make sure he was gone and then I locked the door and called the police and Joan. Suddenly, I was terrified again, thinking Larry had hid in the kitchen. But he was gone. It wasn't until I got to the hospital that I broke down."

The Pines Hotel glistened in the bright morning sun. Hints of spring were in the air as Jack and Wilma sat at breakfast in the rustic dining room. They held hands across the table.

"Penny for your thoughts," said Wilma. She caressed Jack's hand. "It wasn't that bad, was it?"

"Bad? It was wonderful." Jack brought his napkin to his face. "I haven't blushed since grade school." He was relieved when the waiter brought their food. "I'm hungry enough to eat a horse." He colored again at the awful cliché. "*The New York Review* says I write like an angel and you've reduced me to kid-simp prose." He lit a cigarette.

"Your eggs will get cold." Wilma was delighted with Jack's embarrassment. She motioned the waiter for more coffee. "Doesn't this look good?" She took a mouthful of Belgian waffle.

"And thank you for changing the subject, dear lady." He stubbed out the cigarette and began eating eagerly. "God, I love breakfast. My favorite meal." He combined ham and eggs on his fork and groaned happily as he chewed. "Did I ever tell you Bullock makes a great western omelet."

"She makes you breakfast?" Wilma's sudden possessiveness surprised her. How can she be jealous of an old spinster? But the chair's secretary was no older than her lover. "Bullock cooks for you in the morning?"

It was Jack's turn to be delighted. "Of course she does." His eyes twinkled. "Especially after nights of passionate sex." He laughed. "Can you imagine Mary in bed with anyone?" He reached for Wilma's hand again. "She and I have a very special relationship. But, honest, no sex." He turned serious. "I think it's fair to say that Bullock and I love each other. The kind of love those assholes would never understand." He continued to eat. "Those maggots who gather every morning in the lounge to feast off the remains of one of their beloved chums. They'd make something soiled and unclean about us." He lit another cigarette which made Wilma think once again of her parents and Uncle Ted's cigars. "Fact is we go back a long way. Even me, one of the old farts of the department, I found her here when I hit the campus, a green kid with stars in his eyes about a career in lit-ra-ture." He looked out the picture window at the pond, surrounded by tall pine trees. "Oh, yea, I was going to live the life of Mister Chips." He returned his gaze to Wilma. "Rich, isn't it. This broken down old man sharing a meal with the most wonderful woman in the world believed he was on his way to a lovely life of literary studies." Jack paused, hoping Wilma would contradict him, but she sat silent, waiting for him to continue.

"Anyway, there she was when I walked into the literature department for the first time." He sipped his coffee. "Not in that green tiled crapper we call home, but in an old red brick building left over from the early days of the university. A wonderful building." He stared at the pond again. "It had character. Oiled wooden floors. Dark paneled walls in the offices. All different sizes and shapes. Not the identical cubby holes we have now. And the classrooms gave you a sense that you were at a university rather than some assembly plant that turns out kids who all look alike and think alike. And, believe me, our product, that's what we produce these days, you know, products, were different." He held up his hand to silence the expected interruption. "Sure I'm romanticizing the good old days. And sure, I pissed and groaned then, too."

"How could it be otherwise?" Wilma smiled. "Big bad Jack Williams not finding something to carp about?"

"What I wouldn't give for that building and those times again," he said, almost wistfully. "It was a hoot, Willie. And best of all, I thought it all mattered. I was the young professor of a thousand dreams. You should have seen me then." He lit a cigarette as the waiter filled their coffee cups. "I actually wore tweed jackets. With leather arm patches no less. I smoked a pipe. I carried my papers in a green book bag slung over my shoulder. I was Joe College. And I was good." He blew a perfect smoke ring. "They loved me. My students thought I was hot stuff and one day they could be too. The ticket was to love books and learning as much as Prof Williams did. Honest to Christ, Willie, it didn't matter what I talked about. They listened like they were pilgrims at Mecca. It's almost frightening when I think about it. They were mine. And I loved it. When I read a poem in class and we discussed it, my God, it did matter. To me and to them too. We all believed our lives could be better, that we'd be better people, you hear, fucking better people, if we attuned ourselves to the great writers. And in those days before the barbarians took over the academy, there was agreement about which writers and which works we should talk about. Not just here. Hell, this was a frigging cow college when I hit town. Everywhere. There were great and important books educated people simply had to know."

"The writers you and I still write about," Wilma said. "You'd love Oliver. I don't know if I would have ever made it without him."

"Or you'd be team teaching that miserable ebonics with Maxine Jefferson."

"Or watching television with Beverly."

They both laughed.

"Or sharing a MacArthur with that charlatan who wouldn't recognize a lovely sentence if it embraced him. You should try reading the genius' last book."

"I did." Wilma stuck her finger into her mouth.

"Jesus, Willie, things have changed. I can't wait to retire and get out of this racket." He was sorry he mentioned retirement. The last thing Jack wanted this morning was to appear as old as he was. "Of course," he said sheepishly, "there's still a way to go before I hang up my typewriter." He looked for a response.

"I surely hope so. We need you to stick around." She had almost said we younguns. "And wait until they read your new book. It's truly wondrous."

"Read it? Those new types don't read real books. Their lips get tired just from glancing through reviews. That's what they'll look at before they offer their hollow congratulations when Walter throws one of his official cocktail parties for a new book. And the slimiest cocksuckers will actually throw a line at me from a distinguished reviewer. Even if they hate my old-fashioned stuff, they want to be part of that day's cognoscenti. What a business."

"Some of them will actually read the book. I was surprised when I talked about my last book at a faculty seminar. Some of the questions made it clear they had read it. Read it with care. I was impressed."

"I bet you could tell the bull-shitters from the real thing."

"Of course. Those are the ones who want to impress the students in the audience."

"Or one-up the expert."

"Them too." Wilma stared at the opposite corner of the dining room.

"Are you all right? You look like you've seen a ghost." Jack grimaced. Another cliché.

"No ghost. Only Walter Henry. In jeans and sneakers yet."

"Walter's here?"

"At a table over there." Wilma nodded her head in the chair's direction.

"Is he alone?" Jack knew the answer to his question. He and Wilma weren't the only lovers on a mid-week tryst at the Pines.

"No. He's with a man. Do you think?" Wilma thought of the rumors Jack had mentioned.

"Of course. We're too far from the campus for them to be part of some university conference. And even mid-week, this place is too pricey for academic gatherings. Has he seen us?"

"I think so. He's glanced over a couple of times." The dining room was not crowded on this off-season Wednesday morning. Wilma and Jack had made a few adjustments in their teaching schedules to capture these couple of days. Had Walter done the same?

"I guess we can't make believe we don't see him." Jack sighed, and suddenly chuckled. "He may be as surprised at seeing us." He turned around in his chair and waved in Walter's direction. The chair returned the greeting.

"Should we stop at his table?" Wilma smiled. "I'm not up on the protocol of these situations."

"And I'm an expert?" He took Wilma's hand. "Why not. Let's just behave like characters in a Noel Coward play."

"In collaboration with Oscar Wilde maybe?"

They walked toward Walter's table. As they got closer, they could see the chair was uneasy.

"Small world, Walter," said Jack as they stood before the two men. Several raunchy greetings had passed through his mind, but he settled for something neutral.

Walter raised himself half out of his chair. He motioned for them to sit down. "Why don't you join us. By all means, join us."

Jack and Wilma sat down.

"Only for a moment or two," said Wilma. "We've got to stretch our legs after all that food."

"And I've got to hit the men's room. Coffee does that to me in the morning." Jack wanted to sound casual. As if this happens everyday, he thought. The chairman shacking up with his baby doctor and me with the black beauty of lit crit. He smiled at Walter's companion. "Jack Williams," he said, "I think we met before." He extended his hand. "And this is Wilma Crouse."

"Forgive me," said Walter, regaining some sense of composure. After all, he had said to himself, it could be much worse. When he first saw his colleagues, he had thought with horror of some others enjoying the morning. Jack Williams, he knew, was safe. He could be counted on to keep a secret. "Forgive me. Let me introduce Dennis Collins." He left it at that. No groping for an explanation or, worse, a lame lie. They certainly could guess.

"Good to see you both." Dennis spoke easily. Not a hint of embarrassment. Jack liked that. The doctor's reaction was no different from what it would have been if they had been introduced at a backyard barbecue at the Henrys. Even Walter didn't appear shocked to see Jack and Wilma at breakfast. You don't have to be a MacArthur genius to know they had spent the night. Who would drive sixty miles for breakfast?

A waiter asked if the new arrivals at the table wanted coffee. At the same instant Wilma and Walter said yes, Jack said no. "Of course you'll stay for at least a cup," Walter said and nodded to the waiter. He had decided to speak frankly to Jack and Wilma. Even though it wasn't exactly a comparable situation, after all neither of them was married, Walter wanted to tell someone. He and Dennis had occasionally talked about the freedom they might experience if a few discreet friends knew about them. Why not this morning? Why not.

The waiter brought two fresh cups and a carafe of coffee. The silence was oppressive as each seemed to wait for someone else to speak. Jack stared into his coffee as he stirred it deliberately. Wilma silently willed him to stop stirring and say something.

"It's a beautiful place, isn't it?" Dennis finally spoke. "Have you been here before?" Innocuous enough, thought Jack. Sure, I come here every week with a different chippie. How about you? Is Walter this week's prize? Christ, what a subject. But he responded. "Beautiful." It was that. He didn't add that he had spent his second honeymoon at the Pines. Bitch, he said to himself. That marriage had lasted only two years. Frigging alimony number two and I had a wonderful time here. And where'd you take your little lady after you promised to love and obey? He was immediately sorry for his churlish thoughts.

"We're here for a couple of days of R and R," said Walter.

Is that what it's called these days? Poor fucking Walter. R and R. Oh

God, my dear chair, fess up, for Christ's sake.

"We're here together," said Dennis. He blushed. "As if you couldn't guess."

Walter was scarlet. It wasn't going to be as easy as he had hoped. "Dennis and I met a couple of months ago. In Winchester when I was having lunch before a trip to the used book shop."

Please, don't give us your history, thought Jack. Next he'll tell us what they do in bed. Please God, spare us the details.

"I know that book store," said Wilma. "Great collection of nineteenth-century first editions."

"You go there often?" Walter asked as if the two of them were exchanging professional tid bits over coffee in Wallace Lounge.

Jack became increasingly uneasy. Either we get to the nitty gritty or we should clear out, he wanted to say to Wilma. In the best of times, he hated meaningless chatter. He had enough. "So how long have you two been an item?"

The suddenness of the question surprised Walter. Wilma was embarrassed.

"Just a couple of months." Dennis answered in an even, friendly voice. "It's become a friendship we both needed." He smiled at Walter who was twisting a napkin in his moist hands. "It's difficult," Dennis continued, "even in our so-called emancipated age. You know, it's tough to be bi-sexual in a world that doesn't really understand."

"Or doesn't want to understand," said Wilma.

Dennis shot her a grateful glance. "Yes. There's so much to lose. People just don't understand." He looked at Wilma. "Or don't want to understand. Profession, family. There's so much at stake. And only because our genetic makeup is a little different from what they believe is normal."

Walter wanted to interrupt. He hated the words. Gay, bisexual, different. He wanted to say he was as normal as anyone else. He was as straight as the next guy. Just needed male companionship. He loved Maggie and his sons. He was a good husband and father. He wasn't queer. But he said nothing.

"Walter and I see each other as much as we can," Dennis went on.

"But never at the expense of our families," Walter added quickly.

"There's nothing in our friendship," he could not bring himself to the word, relationship, "that really interferes with our devotion and responsibilities to our wives and children." He sounded as if he were reading from a prepared statement.

"Do they know?" asked Wilma.

"My wife's known for a long time that I'm as attracted to men as to women." Dennis spoke matter of factly. "The kids, though, are too young. Maybe when they get older."

"Maggie would die if she knew," Walter said morosely. "The boys would never get over it." He voice was a quiet whine.

"She doesn't suspect?" Wilma continued her interrogation.

"No, nothing."

"We're even neighbors now," said Dennis. "And Maggie and Norma have become fast friends. Norma's my wife. I've got the best of both worlds." He was embarrassed by these words of his good fortune when he looked at the anguish his lover was suffering. "I hope Walter will feel as lucky some day." He tried to ease the other's distress.

"We don't do some of those awful kinky things you read about in gay novels." Walter's eyes pleaded with his colleagues to think well of him.

Shit, he is going to tell us what they do in bed. Jack pushed his coffee cup toward the center of the table. He wanted to shake Walter by his shoulders. Who the hell cares what you and Dennis do. I don't care if you fuck pigs. Just don't tell me about it. For all his colorful language and reputation, Jack had a strong Puritan streak. He despised pornography and hated hearing stories about friends' sexual peccadilloes. Do it, but for Christ's sake, don't talk about it. He even cringed in the presence of medical discussions of both male and female problems. He was glad he and his two wives had never had children. He could never have been the patient parent explaining the facts of life to hormonally active, pimply faced teenagers.

Dennis was also not happy with Walter's remark. He tried to laugh it off. "I don't think Jack and Wilma are much interested in that. Hell, who knows what they call kinky."

Jack was suddenly afraid Walter was going to inquire about their bedroom preferences. He thought of the straightforward sex he and Willie had. Nothing awful about their missionary position. But, he felt himself get warm, it was wonderful, even if Willie questioned his desire to always do it in the dark. The way it should be, he said. Daylight destroys the mystery. He thought of the bitch who always insisted on seeing everything. Intellectual prudery she said for the two years they tormented each other.

"You will keep this quiet," Walter asked. "You can't imagine the fear I have of everyone knowing.

"I'll only tell John." Jack laughed. "Your father-in-law will be delighted. He probably thinks you're queer anyway."

Walter looked away.

"Oh, for Christ's sake, don't worry, boss. We're not going to tell anyone. Especially if you give us big raises next year." He held up his hand. "Just kidding, Walter. Just kidding."

"And I won't tell anyone about you two."

Jack and Wilma looked at each other. Would they care if anyone knew? "Nice of you, Walter, but what's to keep secret? The worst that can happen is Maxine Jefferson'll have another reason to go after Willie." He took her hand. "She's the best thing to happen to me in a very long time." He spoke so sincerely Willie's eyes filled with tears.

"But you know the way people talk," Walter continued. "Look at the way they gossip about Mitchell. And he's a MacArthur fellow."

Wilma laughed until she realized the chair was serious.

"The schmuck really believes Murdoch is a genius," Jack said as he and Wilma left the dining room.

Walter eyes followed them out of the room before they filled with tears. His finger tips touched Dennis' hand. "I'm so scared." He was suddenly sobbing.

Dennis rushed to his side and put his hands on Walter's shoulders. A waiter ran to the table. "Is he all right?"

"He'll be fine, thanks," said Dennis. "Just the flu."

The president was in a jovial mood as he hosted the small gathering. Richard Maxwell loved planning celebratory occasions almost as much as the events themselves. He sipped his sherry and smiled at his guests. It was the end of the day when the president enjoyed opening the black lacquered oriental cabinet and offering drinks all around. He was careful to schedule only appropriate visitors to his inner sanctum after five o'clock.

He savored a baronial elegance in such intimate cocktail hours in his office. The knowledge that invitations to these intimate meetings were treasured by his faculty made Maxwell's noblesse oblige expansive. He touched arms, nodded appreciatively at effusive thank yous, laughed generously at lame witticisms, spoke words of praise softly into ears eager for such acknowledgment from on high. Whenever possible, that is, whenever his secretary had presented him with advance notes, he used nick names and inquired about wives and husbands by name. His terrible memory was rarely perceived by guests. The president's secretary was very good.

"So, Mitch, are you over the first flush of celebrity?"

No one ever called Murdoch Mitch, but the MacArthur genius beamed. Son of a bitch, he thought. What does he mean, first flush of celebrity? Does he even read the books and offprints I send him. Autographed no less to our distinguished president. Distinguished my ass. What has he ever written other than a stupid book on presidential diseases. First flush of celebrity my ass. "Still basking in it, Richard." He had called Maxwell by his first name since they met. It pleased Mitchell that the president looked irritated on that fall day when he first visited the literature department. Everyone else kowtowing to Doctor Maxwell or Mister President. But not me. Nice to meet you, Richard. Welcome to the campus, Richard. Swell article you wrote on the political symbolism of clothes, Richard. Hope to see a lot of you, Richard. Murdoch's eyes narrowed. Fuck you, Richard. "As a matter of fact, *The New York Times* cultural affairs editor is flying out next week to interview me."

"Part of the article they're doing on this year's MacArthur winners, I believe," said Oscar Lansing. "Bernstein called me about it." The provost smiled benignly at Murdoch. "Too bad you have to share space with all those others." He turned to chat with Beverly Berlin and Patrick Donovan.

"And how are your television sets operating?" He held up his club soda to the dean. "Good afternoon, Patrick. Any end runs today?" The owl was surprisingly loose. He had just come from a meeting with Horatio Ginsberg who had unsuccessfully urged him to drop his charges. As soon as Lansing heard the president and the dean wanted an out-of-senate compromise, he knew he had them by the proverbial short hairs. A thrill of recollection of his battle with the former president rushed through his body. The astrological charts had been correct. Not a confrontational man,

Oscar had to admit to himself that the adulation of his colleagues had been exciting. He believed he was on the verge of another moment in the spotlight. No president to bring down this time, but his distaste for charlatanism in any guise had forced his extreme measures. The added bonus this time was his profound dislike of Patrick Donovan. He knew he could always handle Maxwell who did not want to be bothered with the daily operations of the university's academic life. Occasionally stroking his ego was a small enough price to pay to keep him from meddling. Donovan was a horse of another color. His ambition was limitless. Oscar knew he coveted the provostship as the necessary step to the presidency. He knew also that the dean was totally unscrupulous. He had to be stopped. And it had fallen to Oscar W. Lansing to derail Donovan's ruthless plans.

The dean smiled at Beverly. "Our illustrious provost obviously refers to the on-going search for a suitable candidate to join you and Mitchell in invigorating the moribund department he's so fond of." Patrick touched Beverly's shoulder as if to confide in her alone, but he did not lower his voice. "Old men have old ideas." He raised his glass of Irish whiskey to Oscar. "I toast your devotion to lost causes with this marvelous nectar Richard stocks for my late afternoon pleasure." He winked at Beverly. "Beats whatever extra-terrestrial fluid you're imbibing, Oscar. Which abductor laid in a stock of that stuff for you?" His snicker was malicious. "Of course no offense meant. But most of us have enough on our plates simply dealing with this wonderfully complex world God has given us. Little green men in silver space ships are luxuries we can't indulge." His eyes twinkled. "Perhaps we can save the literature department by transporting their old men to another planet. I think I'll have to talk to Walter about that. I'm sure you can suggest an appropriate galaxy, Oscar, can't you? Western literature in translation might be a popular subject for those dear creatures of yours, don't you think?" Patrick had rarely been so frontal in an attack on Oscar himself.

But the provost was not to be bested by such transparent mischief. "Oh, I'm confident the good Lord created the entire cosmos, not just our little corner. Why don't you visit my Sunday school class some time, Patrick. You're so fond of invoking God, my students would surely enjoy a lecture from you. It's not everyday that I could actually introduce the anti-Christ to them." The twinkle in Oscar's eyes more than matched Patrick's. Neither man erased the smile from his face.

"How good to see you two getting on so well," said Maxwell as he joined the trio. He nudged Beverly. "Those two have great trouble getting along, you know. But these little gatherings," he waved his hand at the small group, "have a wonderfully salutary effect on frayed nerves." He clapped his hands. "Why don't you all fill up and take seats around the table. I'd like to get on with plans for the banquet." He took Beverly's arm. "I've asked you to join us today not only because of your scholarly sympatico for Mitch's work. I think it'd be great for the board of trustees to tour your operation while they're here for Mitch's celebration. You can put on a good show for them, can't you, Bev?"

She was flattered. "Sure. They'll finally have an opportunity to see what their generosity has produced."

"Good. Let's pencil in late morning on that day. Make sure you see my assistant about putting out a good spread for them. Maybe a buffet lunch at your place, then cocktails at my home before the banquet. I certainly hope you and . . . " he glanced at a card he carried, "and Marty will join me and Barbara for cocktails." He touched Beverly's arm again. "No black tie in the afternoon. Tell Marty he can save his monkey suit for the evening's festivities." Richard cast an appraising eye at Beverly's pants suit. "Of course, some of you women, I'm sure, will really put on the dog for drinks at the president's house as well as for the banquet later on."

"We'd love to come."

"Easy for the men, isn't it? They can wear the same tux for every affair, while you fair ladies have to rush home to change for the banquet."

Beverly realized she'd have to buy another evening dress. Her black one can't serve her all day. If the president didn't bother to read their publications, he could be counted on to note his charges' apparel.

Richard took his seat at the head of the table. "Now let's get down to making sure that the celebration of Mitch's MacArthur will be as special as the award itself. The entire board will be here for the great event. And," the president lowered his voice, "there's a good chance the governor will attend." He nodded as if to underscore the importance of a possible visit from the state's most significant political figure. "And we know how important to us all a good impression can be." He nodded again before asking for suggestions for the gala week-end. Only Patrick Donovan had a prepared list of recommendations.

As the meeting droned on, the guest of honor kept looking at his watch. He had a dinner date with Alice Chase. They were going to toast his award with an evening at an out-of-the-way inn three towns away. Mitchell had been toasted by several women at that place. This was the first time Alice would be so honored. Murdoch smiled. Isobel had taken the children for an overnight in the city. Good old Peter would probably spend the night laboring over his book. That's life, he thought. He removed his watch and placed it on the table. He did want to arrive at the inn before Alice.

Peter Chase decided not to have dinner alone. He finished grading a few student papers, poured a glass of wine, and sat in the empty living room. Where to dine was on his mind. He hated eating alone in a restaurant. He felt guilty of some nameless sin whenever he said "only one" to a maitre'd. He invariably felt like a fool for including that gratuitously foolish only. He used to take a book when he ate alone, but he felt eyes on him as he sat reading in a crowded restaurant. He had taken to going to carry-outs, but there was something seedy about eating alone at home out of cardboard containers with a white plastic fork. More recently he visited pubs on Alice's nights out. They were not as brightly lit as most restaurants and single men were not uncommon patrons. There was even a hint of camaraderie. The less pretentious, the more comfortable he found them. His mind was made up. He put his glass down, went to the bathroom, took two aspirins, checked his wallet, punched in numbers on the security system key pad, and left the house.

It was a short drive to Tony and Theresa's. Peter had found this working class bar to his liking. No puffery, no academic oneupsmanship, no malicious gossip. Just honest guys trying to forget their troubles as they drank beer and talked about sports, cars, and sexual fantasies. There was a juke box in the corner, but Peter had never heard it playing. It simply sat there like an alien presence, encased in its multi-colored neon frame. He felt it glowering at its unbeatable competition. Three television screens faced the patrons. Each showed the sports channel. If the country went to war, they'd probably not hear about it until they left the easy comfort of Tony and Theresa's. Peter was not yet a regular, but the bartender nodded with a hint of familiarity. "How're you doing, professor." Peter had made the mistake of answering honestly when Tony had asked him what he did for a living. Apparently he had a good memory. Not many university types frequented the place.

Peter carried a draft beer to a small table against the wall and read the menu neatly printed on a green chalkboard. Tonight he did not want to eat and run. He wanted to savor the pleasure of this male watering hole. He glanced around the room. Theresa was the only woman there. He was surprised by how many customers there were at what was in most homes the dinner hour. *I wonder how many other wives are getting fucked by a genius.* But Peter was not terribly jealous.

At first, he was angry about the open marriage he and Alice had decided to try. With the passage of time, they had fallen into an accommodation they could both live with. He used to envy the traditional marriages his friends had. He would bristle with a mixture of anger and jealousy when he saw happily married couples on television commercials. Worse, when he watched love scenes. He yearned to trade places with those actors, but he had made his bed. Peter smiled as he thought of the phrase his mother was so fond of invoking whenever she talked about people who had made bad choices. Yes, he had made his bed.

Tony intruded on his musings. "Another beer, professor?" The heavy man stood before the table. He had a good face. Peter enjoyed watching Tony. He laughed easily, made small talk sound friendly, patted Theresa's ass when she walked by him. *They love each other,* Peter decided. *A nice life. Work like bastards, but together.* He looked at Tony's large hands holding an order book and a menu in front of his long white apron. *He'd beat the shit out of anyone who screwed around with his wife.*

"Sure, another Bud, please, Tony." Peter smiled at the man. A genuinely warm smile. How different from the face he had to put on every time he entered the humanities building or the fraudulent smiles and feigned interest in Wallace Lounge. He felt good here. "And I'll try the shepherd's pie." He looked up at Tony. "It's good tonight?"

"Good every night." He motioned to Theresa behind the bar. "She makes it herself. So, how could it be anything but terrific. Had some myself this afternoon." He kissed two fingers. "Terrific. You'll love it, professor. The wife out with the girls tonight?"

Peter's face darkened. "Yea, out with the girls."

"You just relax and enjoy." Tony looked at the garish Miller's High Life clock. "Good game starts soon. Bulls and Pistons. I'll have that beer to you in a jiffy."

Peter saw Tony talking to Theresa as he drew the Bud. Peter was sure the old pro had diagnosed the situation and was confiding in her. Literary critics weren't the only ones who could read a context. Out with the girls. Bull shit. That was probably an in-house metaphor. He went to the cigarette machine and pulled the Marlboro button. On his first visit he had looked for something mild, but there was no such thing. Real men don't smoke low tar he figured. Peter hated cigarettes. He threw the nearly full pack into the rubbish as soon as he left the pub. But he wanted to fit into the ambiance of the place. And puffing even inexpertly on these coffin nails gave him something to do as he drank his beer. Imagine if I brought a book into this place. He smiled. Maybe Murdoch's personal essays. Maybe he should leave it in the men's room. What would all these guys make of that piece of shit.

Tony returned with the shepherd's pie. "Theresa didn't grow up in England for nothing," he said. "Mangia."

What an odd combination of menu items, Peter thought as he looked once more at the chalkboard. But even that amalgam of cultures was attractive here. Fish and chips, bangers and mash, pizza, strombolis, burgers, and Tony's special fries. Behind the bar were draped three flags. The stars and stripes was flanked by the union jack and the red, white, and green vertical bands of Italy. Tony was right. The shepherd's pie was delicious. Peter was relaxed and enjoying himself. He held up his empty glass. Why not? He felt like getting a buzz tonight. Almost like being an undergraduate fraternity man again. He remembered those beer drinking bouts when the only object was to get blind drunk. He didn't plan to go that far, but the beer did taste good. And the place was perfect. He slipped off his jacket. Yes, he'd stay a while.

"Peter?" The voice came from the front door.

Peter looked up from his food. He was surprised to see Billy Mann.

"What a surprise to see another effete intellectual in Tony's. Let me place my order and I'll keep you company for a few minutes." Billy walked confidently to the bar and spoke to Theresa. Peter heard her say, "about ten minutes." Billy sat down at Peter's table. "So, when did you discover this place?"

Peter put his napkin to his lips and laid his fork on his plate.

"No, no, don't stop. I know that dish is too good. Don't let it get cold." Billy looked around. "Is Alice here?"

"I guess I'm baching it tonight. She's out with the girls." Please don't let him ask me which girls. "I like this place a lot."

"Oh, it's great. But Sally won't step foot in it. She makes me come down for take-out. Tonight it's fish and chips. Have you ever tasted his fries? Great. Really great."

"Want a beer?" Peter asked.

Billy shook his head. "No, I've got to get home as soon as the food's ready. We're trying to make an early movie. The new Woody Allen flick."

Peter looked closely at Billy. He was hoping for any hint that he night have been wrong in his initial assessment that Billy was totally straight.

But Billy's return gaze was simply open and friendly. He had liked Peter from the start. He was, in fact, the only new faculty member to receive a dinner invitation from the Manns.

Peter decided to test the waters. "If you go out alone often, give me a ring. I'd love to hoist a few with you."

Billy's suspicions about Alice suddenly surfaced. "Does Alice give you that much slack? Sally likes to keep me on a short leash."

"We both have our little secrets." Peter tried his most intimate smile. He gripped Billy's arm tightly for a brief moment. "'We all need breathing room, you understand." He looked away coyly. "You know, men and women sometimes have different needs." Peter feared he was entering dangerous ground. He liked Billy, but he had been around long enough to know Billy had a loose, malicious tongue.

"Sure. I sometimes go out with my neighbor for a drink. Especially after my better half throws a snit." He winked across the table. "Retreat is the better part of valor." Billy raised his hand as he heard his name called. He stood up.

Neither Peter's smile nor broad suggestions seemed to have any effect on Billy. Hopelessly straight. Too bad. Peter thought Billy would have been a grand prize. "Well, enjoy the movie." Again he tried to sound light-hearted. "By the way, is there any late news about Helen?"

Billy sat down. "Terrible, isn't it. I'd have thought it would be Joan who would attract some crazy, not Helen."

Peter raised an eyebrow.

"Christ, it's Joan who wears those short, tight leather skirts. Whenever I see those two walking together, I get half a hard-on watching Joan. Then the thought of dowdy Helen brings it right down." He stood up once again. "Can you imagine any guy actually wanting to screw her? That's why it was such a surprise to hear she got raped. Frankly, I was more interested in learning something about him." Billy realized he was sounding crass. "But to answer your question, no, I haven't heard anything new. Sally's going to visit her tomorrow so I'll get the latest scoop." He shook Peter's hand. "Enjoy what's left of your dinner." As he walked away, he turned. "Let's all of us have dinner again soon."

Peter was even more depressed than when he first arrived. Billy was a lost cause. No more fantasies to build on there. There's always Walter, he thought. But he's homely, and he's no kid. He motioned for another beer. Given my batting average, I may be completely wrong about him too. I should have asked Billy. If there's a red letter on anybody's chest, he'd know about it.

He wondered if Alice and Mitchell had finished their dinner. Strange feelings gripped him. Fright and anger. He was afraid he might blow this job if he weren't more careful than he had been with Billy. I'm surprised he was so obtuse. At the same time he was angry at the thought of his wife and Murdoch together. Perhaps it was Billy's rushing home to have a quick meal with Sally and then go to a movie. Or maybe he'd just had enough. His eyes smarted as he thought of a traditional marriage. Of course I'm romanticizing it, but I think I want to try it. Hell, doesn't mean I have to be celibate. It's different with men. Getting my rocks off with some stranger is something I can handle. Women invest too much emotion in that shit. They talk about love and relationships. We see it for what it is. He looked for the right word. Right, a release. That's all it is. A release when the tensions become insistent. No love. No relationship. You zip up your fly and go home. Period. End of tension. Relaxed, you go about your business. It's not even being unfaithful. Can't be called adultery if you spend a couple of minutes with another guy. What Peter decided he wanted was a wife like Sally. No more show and tell. No more wondering about every moan and groan. No more of that shit. That's what he was going to tell Alice tomorrow morning. Don't tell me about your night at the Inn with the genius. And don't ever do it again with him or any other stud. From now on we're going to try a new thing. We're going to be a regular young married couple enjoying only each other and supporting each other. Except, when those tensions creep up on me. And then it'll be my business only. Alice will never know about those times. Peter felt good. He was excited about the new life ahead of him. The only problem now was how best to present his case. He hoped Alice wouldn't be a hard sell.

Billy was not on his way home, nor were he and Sally going to the new Woody Allen film. Instead, Billy headed for the humanities building where he and Abraham were to have their third top secret meeting. It was Billy's turn to supply the food.

Wanting complete privacy, Billy had decided that they meet in their offices on week-end nights when there would be little chance of being overheard. Not even their wives were to know of their plans. "The last thing we want is to make them accomplices before the fact," Billy kept insisting. "We've got to give them deniability." Even though Ab thought his accomplice was being overly dramatic, he went along with Billy's veil of CIA secrecy. When he jokingly said they should wear long trench coats, Billy was not amused. "Jesus Christ, Abraham, don't you understand the stakes were playing for here? It's a fucking criminal offense we're planning."

"Two, as a matter fact," Ab added.

"Right. Two criminal offenses. We could end up in jail. Never mind being booted out of the university."

Ab thought Billy enjoyed looking around furtively and covering his mouth when he whispered. He was as eager as a kid playing counterspy. Excitement and fear exhilarated him.

Abraham was torn between pushing ahead and bailing out. He did not have Billy's adolescent enthusiasm for the great capers. But his anger, too, had escalated since he heard of Murdoch's and Berlin's machinations. He wanted to punish them. When Billy came to him with his plans, Ab was more than ready to agree. His second thoughts were bred of fear, not lack of desire. Billy's plots were delicious. Ab also knew this alliance with Billy would bind them together in a frightening way. Successful or not, they would be forced to depend on each other for a very long time. Even their wives, never meant to be friends, were curiously linked now in their mutual curiosity. Eleanor and Sally knew only that their husbands were meeting secretly to discuss projects they were not allowed to inquire about. The two women now talked on the phone about these strange actions. In a turn of events none would have ever predicted, each of the four was involved in the fates of the others.

At home, Abraham was tight-lipped about the entire matter. All he said was that Eleanor must not worry. "There's nothing going on that I won't tell you about when it's all over."

"God, but I hate that enigmatic Yankee stiff upper lip. I'm your wife, for Christ's sake." She poured herself a stiff scotch. "What's so special about this big secret, anyway? And since when do we keep secrets from each other?" She paced the living room. "I went through hell with two miserable long labors to produce our beautiful kids. And you were there with me every lousy hour, holding my hand, urging me to breathe, telling me to push. We were a team. Just like that crummy job I took to help put food on the table while you took forever to finish the dissertation. But we were a team. And who held your hand through all those depressions? In graduate school, and now with this tenure hearing hanging over your head. Christ, who gives you blow jobs when you're really down in the dumps. Me, that's who." She took a long drink. "Do you really think I enjoy having a dick in my mouth? Well, think again. But I know how much you like it and how it relaxes you. So, I do it. Gagging and all, I do it. Why? Because we're a team." She kissed him on the top of his head. "And damn it, Ab, because I love you. But now I'm not allowed to know what you and that creep are doing at those crazy hours in an empty office building." Eleanor sat down opposite Abraham. "Of all the people in the world to confide in, I never thought it would be Billy Mann. What the hell are you doing with that guy?"

"I thought you liked blowing me."

"I don't believe it." Eleanor took a package of cigarettes from the drawer of an end table. She slowly removed one and lit it. "Every time I think you're different, really different, from all those brutish men out there, you come up with a line like that. Honest, Ab, I can't believe it. Here I am asking about something important, and what do you fixate on? A passing remark. A parenthetical remark that has nothing to do with what we're talking about." She took a deep drag. "Sometimes I think I've got three children."

Abraham feared making any comment about her smoking.

"Okay, okay, let's clear up that subject so that we can return to you and Billy. I'm sorry I said anything about the other thing. For the record, let me say, your honor, that there are few pleasures in the world more satisfying to me than sucking your magnificently beautiful pecker. I was guilty of perjury a moment ago. Forgive me. And, your honor, there are few taste treats that can surpass your delicious cream as it spurts from that manly appendage of yours that is surely the envy of the western world. If only Michelangelo were alive, you'd be his model. Not David with that little thing. No sir. He'd sculpt Abraham Smith." She ground out her cigarette. "He'd want to run away with his model, he would." Eleanor stood up. Hands on hips, she looked imposing. "Now, dear sir, does that clear the air? Can we now return to whatever it is that you and Billy Shit are up to?" She laughed. "If for no other reason, I've got to know so that I can terminate those terrible telephone conversations with Miss Perfect. Come on, Ab, what's going on?"

As tempted as he was to confide in Eleanor, Abraham knew Billy was right. Deniability was essential. If things went very wrong, Eleanor must be ignorant of the entire thing. "Honey, trust me. I've promised. I'll tell you everything when it's all over. Now, please, let's talk about something else."

"Like what? Your cock?"

Ab laughed. He tried to sound light-hearted. "Well there are worse subjects. Just ask Michelangelo."

Abraham was thrilled to hear the front door open and the voices of his children. He loved them even more at that moment.

Eleanor went to greet them. "It's only a reprieve, stud. Only a reprieve." She whispered, "Truth seekers, indeed."

Even though Billy told Sally nothing about the plots, he enjoyed circling the subject at every opportunity.

"You can't imagine how rich it all is." He rubbed his hands together as if he were out in the cold. "Rich. That's what it is." He put his arms around his wife's waist and held her at a distance. "I can't wait to tell you what I've dreamed up."

"At whose expense this time," asked Sally. There was no scolding in her question. Sally enjoyed Billy's skewering of enemies. She had always been amused by his pranks in graduate school. A valley girl by breeding and inclination, Sally's great strength was not intellect. She still laughed whenever they recounted the crazy glue in office locks on commencement day. Tears streamed down her cheeks. "Their caps and gowns were in there, behind doors they couldn't open." Or she would hold her sides in painful laughter when they recalled the whoopee cushion Billy had placed on the guest of honor's chair at the dedication of the Creativity Center. "Remember the look on the president's face when he sat down?" Laughter. "Or the giggles that every one was trying to hold in?" More laughter. "And when he sat down again after that awful speech of his?" They hugged. "When no one could hold it in any longer."

"Oh, no, I can't tell you that." Billy chuckled. "If I told you who my targets are, you'd be half way to being an accomplice before the fact." He winked at Sally. "When the cops and the FBI interrogate you and that cold bitch, Eleanor, I don't want you to have to lie. If you don't actually know what Honest Abe and I are up to, you've got deniabiity."

"I still can't imagine what you and Abraham Smith can have in common."

"Not much," Billy replied and he thought of pancreatic cancer. "But on this one occasion, we do have a common purpose." He chuckled again. "It's almost time. I've got to stop at Tony and Theresa's for tonight's chow." Billy headed for the front door. "Enjoy the Woody Allen flick."

As usual, Billy arrived at the office first. Wearing sneakers, he walked the corridor silently, ears cocked to hear the slightest sound. He smiled and nodded his head at the quiet office wing. He was satisfied that only a few graduate students in their wing shared the building with him. He knew there was no reason for any of them to leave their ghetto, especially since a few of them actually lived illegally in their offices. They'd be sure to keep out of sight if they knew a couple of professors were in the building. At their first meeting, Wilma Crouse surprised them when she came out of her office. Her curious look had not bothered Billy. "She's got enough worries of her own and no one to gossip with anyway." On the night of their second meeting, they discovered a custodian mopping the floor. "You guys working late, too," he had said. No curiosity at all.

There must be a correlation, Billy thought, between intellectual pretension and perverse assumptions.

Billy opened his brief case and removed a small tape recorder. He tested it to make sure the batteries were good, slipped it into an empty cigarette package, and then into the breast pocket of his blue denim shirt. He patted the recorder. Always one to plan carefully, Billy wanted a tape of every conversation with Abraham. Should the need arise, careful editing could suggest Honest Abe had been the fomenter of the outrages. He laughed. Stupid schmuck. Now ready for the meeting, Billy arranged the fish and chips. He took two still cold beers from the briefcase and placed one before each white bag of food. One more dip into the briefcase produced a small bottle of vinegar. Finally, Billy placed the manila folder before him. It bore only the letter R on its tab. R for revenge. Perfect.

Ab arrived right on time. They were about to enter the final stretch of their planning. Of course they knew their plots smacked of sophomoric pranks, but even Abraham was coming to enjoy the anticipation. Billy loved every minute of it. At night in bed, he often imagined the results of their labors. He reveled in them.

"Have you lined up the tapes?" asked Abraham.

"Check," said CIA Billy.

"And the drug? Are you sure it'll do the trick?"

"Check again."

"Where do we get it?"

"Not to worry. Sally's brother's a pharmacist. He's sending me enough to do the entire campus."

"And careful directions?"

"Check. The best. It's as harmless as Ex Lax."

"But it'll do the job?"

"In spades. And very quickly."

"No after effects?"

Billy shook his head. "Don't worry so much, Abe. We're not going to kill anybody." He giggled. "They might even feel a lot better the next day." Billy sprinkled vinegar on his food. "Don't you wish we could be flies on the wall that night?"

"I just want things to go smoothly." Abraham was getting nervous again.

"They'll go smoothly as long as we follow our plans." Abraham nodded his head.

"As long as we do everything by the numbers and remember our assignments, it'll be a piece of cake," Billy tried to reassure him. "Now eat those great fries before they get too soggy." He reached over and patted Abraham's hand. "For Christ's sake, don't worry so much. The worst that can happen is nothing will work." He giggled again. "But the best is they'll never forget that Saturday."

Abraham ate his food. As much as he hated to admit it, Billy did have a way of calming him down. And the fish and chips were delicious. As he ate, the sounds of a string quartet floated down the center hall from the graduate student ghetto.

"You know some of them live in this building." Billy grimaced. "One Saturday when I stopped by to pick up my mail, the fucking place smelled like a cheap Indian restaurant." He looked at the door. "Is that Mozart?"

"No. Beethoven." Abraham thought of Eleanor's whispered words and his dream of the concert at the chapel. "Having borne witness, you will go forward to carry to the multitudes, each in your own way, the promise of my words." What the Christ am I doing here? Why am I planning these pranks with a snake like Billy Mann? He stared into the hall as if expecting the glorious sounds to materialize.

"Now what's bugging you?" Billy asked impatiently. "You better shape up or we'll never get this show on the road." He slammed the office door shut, half to waken his colleague and half to let the squatters know they weren't the only ones in the building. "Give those bastards an inch, and they'll take over the whole frigging university." He returned to his place behind the desk. "Can you believe Sally wanted to invite them over for a Sunday meal? She's too good, that's what she is. But naive. Shit, is she naive. You wouldn't believe the airhead goody-goody she can sometimes be." Realizing that the tape was running, he quickly added, "but always for good causes. Always wants to help people out. And I'll tell you, Abe, I love her for it." He smiled at his recovery. Those last words should make Sally happy when and if he ever plays the recording for her. Lots of good reasons for that never to happen, he thought, as his attention returned to his wavering cohort. "All right, let's set an agenda for our next meeting."

"Why do we need an agenda?"

"You are hopeless sometimes, do you know that? We need an agenda so that nothing goes wrong. Understand? Plans go awry because some dope didn't plan every step of the caper." He reached across the desk and grabbed Abraham's arm. "Are you with me, Abe? Do you follow? You understand why we need a plan? You finally get the picture?" He opened the manila folder on his desk. "I've worked out some points we mustn't overlook." He handed the paper to Abraham. "I call it an agenda. Get it? Our code for a plan. You never know who might be listening." He winked. "Now, let me hear you read the agenda. Out loud. Loud and clear. That way the words will make a stronger impression than if you read them silently to yourself."

Abraham took the sheet of single spaced items. "I can read it to myself."

"Sure you can," Billy replied, having known in advance that Abraham would balk at reading out loud. "But indulge an author who loves to hear his own words." He winked again. "So indulge me."

Abraham decided it was easier to read than protest any longer.

Billy patted the recorder and smiled. He had become a minor expert at editing tapes.

THREE

Richard Maxwell could not have asked for a better day. Giddy as a child, he laughed out loud while he sat at his breakfast table.

Except for the soft steps of the maid, the house was quiet. It was early even for the president who jogged every morning while his faculty still slept. If not the sleep of the righteous, he thought as he ran the tree lined streets of the wealthy neighborhood, then at least the fitful sleep of his obedient faculty.

Maxwell enjoyed jogging at dawn for reasons that transcended the esthetic pleasure he experienced when he rounded Mansion Ridge and saw the sun's first pale red haze rising above the town nestled in the valley below him. He always stopped at that point. Two miles into his run, he sat on a stone bench under a spreading horse chestnut tree. Sometimes his examination of the town and his campus to the north was interrupted by other early morning joggers. He knew them all by name, of course. Because this neighborhood was patrolled by a private security force, outsiders did not take their constitutionals in Mansion Ridge Estates. Maxwell always sucked in his gut and waved return greetings to the prosperous runners. He enjoyed their "Good morning, Doctor Maxwell" or "Mister President." Those were appellations to be savored. The few who called him Richard were almost all exalted humans of accomplishments nearly equal to his own. A few bankers, an investment broker, a couple of physicians. And that awful dentist who recently moved up in the world. The nerve of him to wave his stubby fingered hand and offer a panting "How's it going, Dick." A high pitched voice yet. There was nothing attractive about the dentist. Even his sweat stained bargain basement warm-up suit was tacky. Surely, none of the Maxwell family would ever allow that little fat man's hands to enter their mouths.

The return run was lovely. The damp grass which bordered the path now glistened as it picked up the sun's first rays. Lawn sprinklers oscillated gently on expansive green front yards. Then the turn into the president's house. Surely the most handsome home in the area, it had been built long before the developers offered grand sums to the university for the acres that originally formed an estate worthy of a titled baron. Maxwell always stopped to admire the large Georgian house. No sign, thank heaven. Those who didn't know it was the president's home obviously had no reason to know. If his sprinklers were on, Richard admired the sun's play on the swaying watering pattern.

Juanita asked if he wanted eggs.

Richard nodded. "Scrambled with bacon this morning, por favor." Thank God she's not black. What would Maxine Jefferson and her gang of racist cutthroats say about a black maid at the president's house? He shuddered. Or the hostile journalists who watched his every move? No one seems to mind Juanita. Even Maxine partook of the canapés the Hispanic woman served at the last presidential reception for the black students honor society. So much for affirmative action for everyone. Sanctimonious hypocrites.

"The governor will be here today?" Juanita asked as she scrambled eggs.

"Oh yes, and the entire board of trustees." Richard beamed as he held out his cup for more coffee. "It'll be the greatest constellation of political power ever assembled on this campus at one time." He looked at the plate of eggs and bacon. Maxwell took an English muffin from a multicolored straw basket. "Delicious as usual, Juanita." While he ate, Richard scanned the day's schedule which lay next to the morning paper.

"You want I should lay out your clothes, Richard?"

The use of his first name by a domestic servant who never completed grade school was his grand gesture toward an egalitarian household.

He loved explaining his democratic sensibility whenever a guest raised an eyebrow upon hearing Juanita address him as Richard. At first, he had asked to be called Ricardo. Upon reflection, however, he decided that was a bit too ethnic. Yes, Richard was quite as far as he wanted to go.

"Remember, Juanita, there'll be three changes today, but you'll have to lay out just two. One for the luncheon at Professor Berlin's television extravaganza and, of course, a tuxedo for tonight's banquet."

"You'll wear the same things for the cocktail party this afternoon?"

Richard had given a good deal of thought to that question. If he changed from the casual elegance of the Berlin affair for cocktails with the governor and trustees, would he be the only man to do so? He decided no one would really have time to change clothes for drinks with the Max-wells. There'll be plenty of time after cocktails for them all to shower and dress for the banquet. "Yes, I'll wear the same until the banquet." He had bought a new Harris tweed sport jacket which he'd wear over gray flannel trousers. Country squire British, he thought. The tattersall shirt and wool tie will add the final smart touch. Right out of *Town and Country*, he thought. Expecting the pols and trustees to be garbed in dark blue busi-ness suits for the afternoon, he anticipated the grand contrasting state-ment his attire would make. After all, they might be movers and shakers in the worlds of commerce and politics, but, damn it, he was the president. They might have written fat checks, but he had written a book.

"I wonder if the governor will arrive in a limousine?" Richard ad-dressed the question to his wife who had just entered. "Wouldn't the neigh-bors love that?"

Barbara Maxwell poured a cup of coffee and joined Richard at the table. "Did you enjoy your run?"

"It was perfect. That is, until that grubby dentist broke the spell."

"Did he call you Dick again?" Barbara laughed. "Don't let that little man bother you so much. After all, he does own a house here. It's not as though he's an interloper."

"I know that, Barbara. But a dentist in a cheap sweat suit?"

You don't have to marry the man, Richard."

"Marry the man! I'd prefer never to set eyes on him again. Damn tooth mechanic with a white jacket. That's all he is."

"I don't think it's the end of the neighborhood." Barbara lowered her voice and catered to her husband's sensibilities. "At least he's white." She patted Richard's hand. "And his wife seems very nice."

"Where'd you meet her?"

"At the farmer's market last week. We had a lovely little talk over some beautiful home grown tomatoes. I almost invited her and her husband for drinks."

"You didn't." Richard offered a mock gasp. "What could we talk about? Overbites and fillings? Really, Barbara, do you think they've ever read a book?" He chuckled. "Probably spend their time watching sit-coms on a forty-five inch television set. I bet it's even in their living room." Richard shuddered. "No taste at all." His speculation about the TV had quickly become a fact. "Oh yes, I'm sure that ostentatious set is the focal point of the living room. And their designer? Sears, do you think? Or Montgomery Ward perhaps?"

"Oh, I'm sure she reads real books. As a matter of fact, she's enrolled in one of your adult education courses. Something about philosophy and literature."

As always, Richard ignored a remark that exploded his perception of a situation. "Time for a shower. Have to get the show on the road soon." He patted the top of Barbara's head as he passed by. "Don't forget to check with the caterers about the cocktail party. And a final call about tonight's arrangements wouldn't hurt."

Richard went up to shower and dress for the morning's activities. Outfit number two.

Billy had made several trips to nearby towns to buy the video tapes. He paid cash for each one. Seven tapes for Beverly's seven viewing stations.

"You should see them, Abe." Billy's eyes shone as he extolled the pornographic virtues of his purchases. "I was scared to death about being seen at any of those video stores. But I was lucky. I guess the local boys and girls patronize their neighborhood porno parlors." He touched the backpack lying innocently on his desk. "What a selection of salacious smut."

"Did you watch any of them?" Abraham asked.

"Any of them? I watched all of them." He shook his right wrist. "And are they ever terrific. I'll tell you, I had a hard-on for a week after those seven movies. I bought tapes for every taste." Billy laughed like a titillated school boy. "Most of them are he-she fucking, but I also got one she-she and one he-he. Those are actually the categories they advertise. There's even one called *Hand Jobs Around the World*. Nothing but shots of different cities and close-ups of guys beating their meat." He made a masturbatory gesture. "I'd love to see Richard Maxwell's face when a big prick fills the screen and comes right at the camera."

"You know this is all sophomoric," Abraham chided. "But she deserves it." Abraham smiled broadly. "Don't you wonder how dear old Beverly will explain it all to the luminaries gathered to witness the research they've so generously funded?" Abraham, too, was excited by the prospect of replacing the tapes Beverly Berlin had so carefully selected to show off her scholarly enterprise.

"Remember, timing is everything. We'll have a good hour before the arrival of the caterers. Should be plenty of time to make the exchanges. But just in case, I bought two white jump suits for us to wear. You know, in case the florists or other hired help arrive early."

"You want us to synchronize our watches?" Abraham asked, returning to the secret agent mode Billy enjoyed. "And make sure we have cyanide capsules in case we're caught?"

"We're not going to get caught. Nine sharp we show up and we're out of there by ten."

"Then?"

"You've forgotten the plan already? Then we lay low until we hit the banquet hall. I've already seen the menu. They'll be preparing enormous vats of fruit salad for the appetizer. It couldn't be more perfect. Maxwell's wife asked for raspberry liqueur as one of the ingredients. They'll never taste our stuff."

"And the rest rooms?"

"I've killed that plan. Too risky to put crazy glue in all those stall doors. Besides, there aren't enough bathrooms to accommodate the crowd that'll be celebrating the genius' award. The only fly in the ointment is that we won't be able to see any of our handiwork at either place."

"We'll hear about both, believe me. I wouldn't miss the Wallace Lounge on Monday morning for anything. Then we can tell our wives?"

"A ticklish problem, Abe. Maybe we should wait until the smoke clears. A couple of weeks sounds about right. Just in case the investigation takes in the whole faculty. And there will be an investigation. With the shit-eating governor as one of the victims, the frigging state police might get involved. I think we should wait before we tell our better halves about the capers."

Abraham nodded his agreement. "I still don't know how Eleanor will take it."

"My Sally will be tickled. She's always enjoys my pranks. But she has very loose lips."

"You better impress upon her the seriousness of this one." Abraham could imagine Sally gossiping with all those women she's been cultivating since she hit campus. Little Miss Perfect could blow the whole thing. He was worried.

"I'll take care of Sally. She'll be careful or I'll threaten to cut her off." Billy offered one of his smarmier smiles. "No reason why you should know this, but she loves our bedroom activities."

Abraham was grateful Billy dropped the subject at that point. The last thing he wanted to hear about was Sally Mann's sexual exploits. He was surprised, however, to learn she had an erotic side. He had imagined the Manns' bedroom activities were limited to modeling their expensive wardrobes. Sally often said there was a fine art to dressing appropriately for every occasion. Abraham believed the Manns shared genes with their distinguished president.

Beverly Berlin was a wreck at dinner the night before her big day.

"Imagine the audience I'm going to have tomorrow. Marty, do you know how important their visit will be to my position at the university."

"And to the full professorship."

"After tomorrow, the promotion's in the bag. I've arranged a show that'll knock their eyes out. Just let the food be as good as my presentation and there'll be nothing for any of those philistines to complain about."

"And speaking of food, what do you think of this feast?" Marty had prepared some of his wife's favorite dishes. "Sort of a pre-celebratory dinner." He was proud of the meal Beverly seemed not to have noticed.

"Yes, it's fine, Marty. Very good."

"Just fine. Just very good?"

"Excellent. How's that? Truly excellent."

Marty smiled. "In a way, we're celebrating more than your big day."

"Namely?"

"I sold the Hammond estate this morning." He looked for Beverly's congratulations. "Do you know what the commission is on a property like that? Why don't you try six percent of two million dollars. How's that grab you, professor? Your Richard Maxwell doesn't make much more than that in a year. Six percent of two million. A pretty decent day's work, wouldn't you say?"

Beverly was always embarrassed by Marty's recitation of his real estate transactions. It was bad enough when they were alone, but she could never discourage him from talking real estate prices and commissions with her university colleagues. She nodded her head approvingly and tried to change the subject. "This Beef Wellington is maybe the best you've ever made. Even better than the salmon en croute you served at the dinner party last week."

"Why do you always change the subject whenever I talk about my work? You think there's something dirty about the six figure income I bring home every year? Something degrading about Berlin Realty being the classiest in town? Even when we began listing properties for Sotheby's you weren't impressed. So I'm not a professor. So I read the stock reports instead of PMLA. That makes me a lesser person?"

Beverly was about to interrupt, but Marty held up his hand. "You know, Bev, it's not as if you came from some fancy aristocratic family." He held up his hand again. "No, let me finish. Your father was a crummy insurance agent who never brought home in a year what I sometimes earn in a week. So he went into hock to put you through a fancy college. That was nice of him. Really nice. But he was no Rockefeller. And neither are you." He pointed his finger at Beverly. "You didn't mind my bankrolling your television project before you started to get all those grants. You never said a word about my buying that house you use for Professor Berlin's research empire, or all those television sets and VCRs. Never mind the furniture and even a guest suite for visiting scholars. And did I want to do all those things? Of course I did. And why? Because I love my wife. Is that a crime, too?"

"Oh, Marty, you're over-reacting."

"No, Bev, I am not over-reacting. Do you think I'm blind? Do you think I don't see your face when I spend a minute or two talking real estate with your intellectual friends? And I'll tell you something. They enjoy discussing real estate. They want to know what properties sell for and how many square feet so-and-so's house is. And I'll tell you something else. They salivate over those big expensive houses I sell. They may pooh-pooh my crass business world, but they'd love to be able to afford those houses. You professors have very expensive tastes, you know, and very low salaries. But every one of you would love to be rich. Oh yes, rich on your terms, of course, so you could still look down your noses at all us work-a-day slobs who toil in the commercial world. Or, I guess, your kind would refer to it as the commercial milieu. Did I pronounce it right or did I embarrass you again?" Marty's face was crimson. Sweat rolled down his puffy cheeks. His eyes were full. "So I'm not handsome and elegant like Mitchell Murdoch. I see how you fawn all over that guy. But I'm not some poor schlep because I don't have a Ph.D." He rose from the table and went into the kitchen. Marty didn't want his wife to see his tears.

"Come back to the table," Beverly called. She tried to sound warm and comforting. "Your beautiful dinner will get cold." She grimaced when she heard him blow his nose. For Christ's sake, you'll ruin my big day, she thought. "Come on, Marty. Don't be a big baby." Her voice took on a scolding edge. "Of course I appreciate everything you've done for me." She feared he was on the verge of bringing up the matter of children again. Whenever he got into one of his feel-sorry-for-Marty moods, the sad song about their childless state was never far from his lips.

"Kids would have made all the difference in the world." Beverly mouthed the words as Marty lamented from his hide-out by the kitchen sink. She nodded her head to the familiar rhythms of his old melody. "If we only had a family." Beverly returned to her meal which was truly excellent. She wasn't very hungry, but she ate. Better not give him more to complain about. And he better snap out of it by tomorrow. She smiled ruefully as she cut her meat and envied the dinner conversation she imagined at colleagues' homes. Enlivened intellectual talk about books and ideas. She shuddered at Marty's talk of the Hammond estate. God, but he's bourgeois.

Marty came back in. As always, he was sorry for having upset his wife. He stood behind Beverly's chair and put his arms around her shoulders. "Please forgive me," he whispered as he kissed the top of her head.

"I've been a pain in the ass again, I know. But every so often I just feel lousy."

Every so often? Beverly thought. She smiled. Every damn day would be more like it.

Marty read the smile as incorrectly as he misinterpreted so many of her comments and gestures. "I'm glad you're not too angry, Bev." He sat down and began to eat the meal he had worked on all afternoon. "It is a good Wellington, isn't it?" He looked for even the slightest hint of agreement which would signal the end to their squabble.

Please don't let this lead to how happy you would have been to cook for a large family. Please don't. This is not the night for me to have to comfort you. Why can't you understand this is the night before the day I wow the world. Can't you be considerate for once in your life? "Yes, Marty dear, it is one of your best." The words were the right ones even if the voice was icy.

Marty was mollified. Tonal qualities meant nothing to him at that moment. Only the words mattered. And Beverly's words were the right ones. Once again, she had pressed the right buttons. The skirmish was over. Marty's eyes were dry. The subject could now return to Professor Beverly Berlin.

The great day arrived. Richard Maxwell might start his morning with the familiar jog through the streets lined with great maples and houses Marty Berlin sold, but nothing so normal was on the schedule for the other principal players.

Mitchell Murdoch sat in his study rehearsing that evening's speech. Not too complicated or erudite. Just down home folksy humility and gratitude. Something the governor and Maxwell could appreciate. There would be time later for him to come out with both critical guns blazing when he actually accepted the MacArthur. For that audience Mitchell planned to be scintillatingly brilliant.

Across town, Billy and Abraham, clad in white coveralls, were already into phase one of their project.

Beverly Berlin had thrown up twice before seven o'clock. She had slept fitfully and was in no mood for Marty's eggs benedict. She worried every detail, not the least of which was her face. How to look fetching after such a bad night's sleep was the first item on her agenda. She ignored Marty's call to breakfast.

At the Berlin video project, seven research assistants prepared for the grand show. They worked around the caterers already setting up for lunch. Poor graduate students, Beverly's assistants ingratiated themselves with the caterer's young helpers and sampled shrimp, lobster salad, asparagus wrapped steak, and melon and prosciutto.

At the faculty club, only a couple of hourly helpers had arrived early. Two were busily preparing a variety of fruits for that evening's starter. A third inspected small cut glass bowls as he removed them from cardboard boxes. No one paid any attention to the two men in white who moved among the minimum wage caterer's helpers. Billy and Abraham were careful not to speak. Billy's orders had been explicit. Voices can be clues too. Silence was their credo as they looked into the large pots of fruit, nodded their approval, and secreted vials of colorless liquid into the fruit medley. They were finished in minutes. Their work completed, the two men walked calmly to the men's room, removed their costumes, shook hands, and separately left the building.

"The eggs are getting cold, Bev. Shake a leg or they'll be ruined."

Staring at her tired face in the mirror, Beverly grimaced in the direction of Marty's call. "In a minute," she yelled. She could hear him making intentionally loud pots-and-pans noises in the kitchen. "I'll be down in a minute." She didn't try to conceal her irritation. There are more important things this damn morning than your cooking. She smiled at the mirror and was horrified at the strained unhappy semblance of a friendly face that looked back at her. An undertaker could do better. And probably has something healthier looking to work with. She glanced at her watch which sat on the dressing table surrounded by the jars and creams Beverly hoped could transform her into the vision she had of her best moments. At least I've got time. She threw on a robe and swept out of the bedroom.

Fresh flowers from his greenhouse adorned the breakfast table. A handmade greeting card sat propped up by the coffee cup at Beverly's place. To match the flowers, Marty had used blue and yellow crayons to inscribe his wishes for the day. Beverly pushed the card aside in order to drink her coffee. "Maybe this will give me the jolt I need to get going." She did not comment on the flowers. "What's this?" she asked as she picked up the card.

Marty placed two plates of eggs benedict on the table. He rushed to the oven for a skillet of his famous hash browns. "It's probably overkill, I know, honey, but you do love these." He artfully arranged potatoes around Beverly's eggs. "There you go." Beverly silently mouthed the next words. "You know what they say about breakfast being the most important meal." She grimaced. "Mangia," her proud husband said to the accompaniment of Beverly's quiet rehearsal of the word. She nodded her head more in acceptance than appreciation. "Read the card," Marty said. "Read the card."

"I thought you wanted me to eat. Weren't you afraid the food would get cold?" Beverly shook her head. "Why don't you make up your mind?" The tone was not pleasant.

The smile no longer on his face, Marty sighed. "Do what you want, Beverly." He ate quickly, another irritant to his wife. "Eat. Read. Don't eat. Don't read. Do what you want." He finished the last of his meal and stood up. He looked at the clock. "I've got to run anyway." He took a last sip of coffee. "Showing a couple of houses this morning." He patted Beverly's shoulder. "Sure you don't want me to come to your joint later?" She didn't answer. "Okay, okay, I'll be home in plenty of time to dress for the president's cocktail party. Don't worry, I'll look great. And I won't forget to pick up the tux at the cleaners." He talked as if there had been a dialogue. "And, Beverly. . . "

She looked up.

"Break a leg, kid." Marty smiled as broadly as he had learned to do in the face of indifference for many years. He had become adept at faces for all occasions.

Beverly picked at her food. She heard the garage door open, the car door slam, the engine start, the car leave the garage, the door slowly close. But she was paralyzed by her own concerns. She wanted to rush to the garage. She wanted to thank Marty. But she remained seated. Beverly's eyes suddenly filled with tears. She put her head in her hands and sobbed. Why in God's name am I such a bitch?

The shaken professor went to the counter and poured another cup of coffee. She looked out the window. The lawn Marty cared for so diligently looked perfect. The envy of the neighborhood, he said every time he finished cutting the grass. But isn't that precisely the problem? The man is so predictable. I know every comment in his paltry repertoire. There's never a surprise. Never any mystery. Never a witty turn of phrase. Marty just wasn't clever. Beverly sat down at the table. Every time I do an inventory of that man, the list is the same. Every time I measure my life against those of my colleagues, mine sounds good. But they don't know the boredom of sharing a life with such a tedious man. She smiled ruefully. I know most of them probably envy me. The house, the money, the doting husband. They can't possibly know of my routinized existence. He always says the same things, does the same things. Christ, he even cooks the same dishes because he thinks they're my favorites. My favorites. Tears flowed again. Even sex has been boring for years. And for the same reason. He thinks I like it the way it's always been. Was it good for you, Bev? Did you enjoy it, Bev? One day I'm sure he'll ask if the earth moved for me too.

She hadn't enjoyed sex for as long as she could remember. She hadn't really enjoyed an evening alone with Marty for God knows how long. She doesn't even listen to most of the things he has to say. She nods and thinks of more interesting or important matters.

You better watch it, Miss Smarty Pants, mama used to say. You better watch it or you'll find yourself out in the cold. All alone you'll find yourself with your books and papers to keep you warm. She'd shake her finger at her daughter. He may not be Clark Gable, but Marty's a good man. You take care, do you hear, or you'll chase him away with all your fancy ideas.

But Mama, Beverly spoke to the empty chair opposite, the chair her mother used to occupy every morning of her infrequent visits. Mama, you don't understand how different my life is from yours and dad's. It's a different world. And Marty would be happier in yours than mine. He'd be more comfortable sitting at your table with you and dad, with Uncle Izzy and Aunt Bella, with your friends in the apartment house. He'd rather spend a week with all those cronies of yours at the beach than with my colleagues at the university. He just doesn't fit in here.

So he's not a professor. Big deal. But those teachers you love so much don't buy houses from him? They don't ask him for advice about real estate, about investments? Your father always said Marty had a good head for business. And this place? She'd wave her arms as if to embrace the large house. Those teachers can afford a palace like this? I bet your dressing room is bigger than their living rooms. You think this is something to sneeze at, to look down on, to be ashamed of? She'd shake her finger again. I'm telling you, Beverly, you better watch it or you'll end up sorry. You think your friends have better lives? You really know what goes on inside their little houses? Inside their bedrooms? Inside their minds? You should think again. You could do a lot worse than being Mrs. Marty Berlin.

It was different with you and dad. You had the same interests. Your friends had the same interests. When you all sat on the piazza and talked on those wonderful summer nights I used to love, everyone participated because everyone was involved. Everyone had the same interests. Everyone understood the rules of the game. But the world I live in is different, Mama. Marty's the odd man out when we sit around with my friends. Oh, sure, he talks. But it's always about real estate or his golf game or gardening or his cooking. It's never about what the rest of us want to discuss.

And what may that be?

Ideas, Mama. Ideas. He's just not interested in the intellectual world.

You mean watching all those television screens every day is the world of ideas? That's intellectual? She'd shake her head. If that's the wonderful world of ideas Marty doesn't want to talk about, I think he's a lot smarter than you think. If someone stole my TV I don't think I'd miss it. Except for the news, I hardly watch it anyway. And if it's so important to you that Marty Berlin should be as smart as you and your friends, why don't you teach him? You're a teacher, aren't you? Give him lessons. Tell him what books to read so he'll be an intellectual too.

Oh, I've recommended books to him, Mama. I've given him things to read. He just doesn't enjoy them. I've even left books written by people whose houses we were going to visit. Read them, I'd tell him. I'd say, you'll understand the conversation better if you get a head start by reading this book or that article. She'd shake her head just as her mother had. But he never read them. Didn't even try to read them. He'd thank me and smile. I'll just wait until they talk about something I'm interested in, he'd say and pat the back of my head. Believe me, Bev, if nothing else, they'll eventually get around to real estate. You'll see, everybody loves to talk about houses.

So, is he right or wrong?

That's not the question, Mama. Of course people want to talk about real estate and money. But they also want to talk about important things. And that's when Marty just sits there like a lump or says something he thinks is cute. I see the smirks on people's faces. I cringe at the patronizing comments they make.

And do you defend him?

Of course not.

And you're not ashamed of yourself for not saying anything when they make fun of your husband?

I am, Mama. But I'm even more ashamed when I realize that if it were someone else, I'd smirk too. I'd make the same sort of smart-ass comments and look around the room to enjoy the selfish, easy pleasure of my compatriots. It's terrible, Mama, but it's true.

Beverly sighed. I'll make it up to him later. Always sorry immediately after she hurt Marty, she always remembered he was an easy mark. By evening, he will have dressed his wounds and regained the adoration of his princess. He'll accompany her to the Maxwells for cocktails and the banquet for Murdoch and act as if the breakfast quarrel had never occurred. Beverly could count on that. And it was that certainty which allowed anger at herself and pity for Marty to dissipate so quickly. She returned to her dressing room to repair the damage of a poor night's sleep and prepare for the video show. After all, there were more important things on the agenda than Marty's tantrum. She hummed an old Judy Garland song as she worked on her face. And when will I reach the other end of that damned rainbow? she asked aloud. Yes, I know, Mama. You think I'm already there. But let me tell you something. I've got a long way to go. A long way.

The president, now wearing his country squire tweed jacket and tattersall shirt, walked from his car to Beverly's studio. Noting several cars already parked in the drive, Maxwell was pleased. He never enjoyed being the first arrival. He never relished small talk with small groups whose eyes kept scanning the front door for glimpses of new arrivals. Better other eyes should look over conversation partners' shoulders to see him, the president of the university, make his entrance. Richard enjoyed entering a crowded room. He liked working his way around a crowd, smiling here, waving there, touching a shoulder, grasping an outstretched hand, all the while knowing he was bestowing privileged status to those so acknowledged. Body language often told him someone wanted a few moments of his time. This, too, the quietly spoken confidence in the corner of a room, titillated him. He knew others were watching and he was invariably pleased to be the focus of their attention regardless of what else they were doing or with whom they appeared to be in conversation.

He liked the garden Beverly had planted in front of the long ranch house that was home to her well-funded research projects. Although not the best residential part of town, the street was pleasant. Its great attraction was its proximity to the campus. Several larger homes had been converted to rooming houses for students. Some specialty shops, a Barnes and Noble bookstore, a few small restaurants, the best coffee house in town, and a newly opened foreign film cinema were scattered throughout the neighborhood. Richard always enjoyed wandering here. He often walked from the administration building to lunch at one the area's ethnic places. Dining at a restaurant filled with university people gave him the same high he got from entering a crowded room. He always took a corner table that allowed him a good vantage point from which to see the whole dining room. And from which he could be seen by the whole room.

Beverly greeted the president effusively. She had been keeping her eye on the front door since guests began arriving some thirty minutes earlier. Even though one of her assistants was stationed behind a small table in the foyer, checking the guest list and dispensing lapel name tags, Beverly wanted Richard there to do the introductions. That is, she wanted him personally to introduce her to the notables who milled around the house, drinking coffee and enjoying delicious pastries from the Russian Coffee House. She breathed a great sigh of relief when he finally entered.

Beverly was proud of her factory. Marty had given her carte blanche when he bought the house. He had hired the best architect in town to carry out her wishes. The results were impressive.

Having gutted the interior of the house, the architect created a large open workplace for Beverly's staff. Seven white formica desks and chairs sat in a semi-circle on pale gray carpeting. Low white dividers stood between work stations, each of which housed a twenty-five inch television monitor, a VCR, and a computer. Research assistants sat poised at every desk. Each had heeded their professor's orders and dressed up for the great event. No jeans and sweatshirts today.

Beverly's office now stood in what was once the bedroom wing. Worthy of the director of a major foundation, it was the envy of all who saw it. Expensively but tastefully furnished, the office boasted a small collection of fine contemporary art on the walls and in two glass cases. Behind her massive desk, also white with gray accessories, the wall was almost completely covered with framed copies of the many grants and critical reviews the video project had received.

The kitchen served the staff and guests, the dining room was now a conference room, the garage had been converted into a private suite for visiting scholars. This latter was coveted by every one of the graduate students. A sitting room with fireplace, a bedroom, a full bathroom with skylight and Jacuzzi tub was more than any of them could hope for on their small stipends.

"Have all the members of the board arrived yet, Beverly?" Maxwell asked as he grasped her hand particularly warmly. He knew that added touch would be appreciated.

"They're all here, Richard." Beverly was almost demure. "And, of course, just everyone has been awaiting your arrival." She glanced at her workstations. "Would you mind terribly if I introduced you to each of my research assistants?" Beverly actually batted her eyes. God, I'm shameless today, she thought.

The chairman of the board embraced Richard. "Couldn't have asked for a prettier day." He smiled broadly at Beverly. "And is this the little lady who runs this show?"

Beverly was only slightly chagrined at not being remembered from the Murdoch brunch. But he'll remember me after today. She smiled back, but decided not to be as blatantly flirtatious as with the president. After all, the chairman of the board heads home tomorrow; Richard Maxwell stays.

"You remember Jason Whitaker, don't you, Beverly?"

Of course I remember him, you silly schmuck, Beverly wanted to say. The question should be directed at Whitaker. He's on my turf now. "Of course I remember someone so distinguished." Beverly batted her tired eyes again. She extended her hand, half expecting the courtly ex-senator to kiss it. "Beverly Berlin," she said warmly.

"And Professor Berlin, was this splendid place paid for with all those

hefty grants you've received." He looked around. "It surely is most grand."
Whitaker raised an eyebrow and shot a glance at Maxwell. "Most grand
indeed."

The president interrupted quickly, realizing the chairman thought
state funds were expended on the restoration of the house. "Oh, no, Jason.
Not a dime of state or grant money went into this. Not a red cent." He
touched Beverly's shoulder. "Every dime spent on the purchase of this
property and its transformation into a first-rate research facility came from
a private source." He moved his hand to Jason's shoulder. "Beverly's husband footed the entire bill."

"Is that a fact," said the chairman. "What a wonderfully generous
husband you have." He smiled at Beverly. "And what does Mr. Berlin do?
Or is he Doctor Berlin also?"

"No, no," said Maxwell. "Beverly's husband." He looked at her.
"Martin."

"Of course, Martin. How could I have forgotten his name?"

You forgot it because your secretary didn't prepare a cheat sheet for
you. Beverly continued to smile.

Maxwell continued. "Marty," he enjoyed using the nickname, "is
one of our leading realtors. He's probably handled more houses in Mansion Estates than any one else. No, not another Doctor Berlin. That one's
in big business."

"I see," said Whitaker, "so your husband's a member of the merchant class."

There was something in his tone that Beverly had heard since she
was old enough to detect anti-semitism. But this was not the time to challenge anyone. And if the truth were told, Beverly was no Helen Abrams.
She had never confronted anti-semites. She had learned to roll with the
punches. The best revenge, she had convinced herself, was to succeed.
Marty had always disagreed with her tactics. This subject had prompted
the few substantive quarrels in their years together. Beverly even objected
to the several obviously Jewish organizations Marty supported. Give them
your money, she often said, but must you receive their publications? Beverly
did not want such magazines and newsletters delivered by their mailman.
She was embarrassed each time she collected them from her mailbox.

"Maybe I can pick up a few tips from him." Whitaker winked at

Maxwell. "He must know a great deal about the stock market." He and the president laughed.

Beverly was mortified. She changed the subject. "When the program begins, you'll see what the board's generosity has produced." She looked at her watch. "I better make a final check. Don't want anything to go wrong today." She had regained her composure. "Not with so many important people gracing my little shop." She nodded at both men. "I know you'll excuse me now so we can begin on time. Almost eleven already." She walked toward the semi-circle of workstations, the flush leaving her cheeks. She'd show those bastards what a merchant's wife can do.

After a quick check before the bathroom mirror, Beverly went to the center of the room. The assistant at the door rang a small bell. The room quieted, Beverly folded her hands before her and smiled at her guests. She looked casually smart in a blue blazer, white shirt open at the collar, and dark gray slacks. "I'm very happy to welcome you here this morning," she began. She scanned the thirty or so people standing before her. Except for the members of the board of trustees and the governor's assistant, the great man would arrive later, she recognized the others. Members of the university administration and two faculty members. Walter Henry nodded to her. Mitchell Murdoch whispered to the president who obviously enjoyed the clever remark which passed between them. She did not miss Patrick Donovan's having insinuated himself between Oscar Lansing and the chairman of the board. "Before you have an opportunity to see first hand exactly what we do here, I'd like to introduce you to the dedicated graduate students who really make my projects the great success they are." The seven research assistants stepped forward as Beverly read their names and the undergraduate colleges from which they came. "As you can see by the variety of fine institutions they represent, the fame and reputation of my projects are widely appreciated." She offered a sedate bow to the applause begun by Richard Maxwell.

For the next few minutes Beverly explained in very broad and general terms what she and her assistants were looking for as they culled hundreds of television programs from all over the country. "One of my assistants is fluent in Spanish so we can monitor the growing number of Spanish language stations. I'm particularly happy about the cross cultural study that allows." She moved to the semi-circle of desks. She placed her hand on a VCR. "We've selected a cross section of the sorts of programs we monitor and the kind of fascinating findings they lead us to. Each work station has a carefully edited tape that will make clear to you the kind of work we do. The assistant at each desk can answer your questions relative to the materials on his or her screen." She smiled again. "You have to realize that what you'll be seeing are distilled versions of literally thousands of hours of research. This project is a twenty-four hour a day operation. When we're not here in the building, our VCRs are quietly taping programs. Each tape is date and time coded so we can reference particular moments that suit our inquiries. Now, before we start the tapes rolling, let me read the most recent review of our work." She nodded to the chairman of the board. "Work that has been so generously supported by our board of trustees as well as by four different scholarly foundations and six smaller organizations." She put on her rose-colored half glasses and read from a review of her work which appeared in the Video Research Foundation Newsletter. Filled with words like groundbreaking, fresh, exciting, fascinating, the review was everything Beverly could have wanted for the occasion. "Now, ladies and gentlemen, please gather around the desks and our presentation will begin."

Richard Maxwell shouted, "Lights, cameras, action." Everyone laughed and applauded. Beverly nodded to her staff. The large monitors were ready to come alive in brilliant living color.

Small groups of honored guests gathered around the monitors and listened intently as the assistants explained the particular aspect of the current research project which would be presented on their screens. They turned on the VCRs and the room grew quiet.

. Then gasps of horror, nervous laughter, and Beverly Berlin's piercing scream filled the room of astonished viewers. The graduate students stared in disbelief at their screens and then at their mentor. An angry cacophony of shouts, loud talk, questions, recriminations, and even a few wolf whistles broke around Professor Berlin. Her face a deathly white, Beverly held her hands out in despairing confusion. She was about to speak when she fainted into the arms of a flushed chairman of the board of trustees.

"Thank God the governor isn't here to witness this outrage," said the nervous assistant to the state's leader. The slight man fidgeted with his necktie as he rushed from monitor to monitor, from group to group, offering the same prayer that his boss was not present.

Richard Maxwell stood transfixed and mute as he gazed glassy eyed at a handsome young couple copulating before his eyes. He groaned when the man extracted his extraordinarily long penis from the woman and ejaculated all over her stomach. "My God," the president whispered, "I've never seen anything like that in my whole life." He quickly shook himself back to the reality of the terrible situation around him and sought appropriate words.

"Say something, for heaven's sake," said Oscar Lansing. "Pull yourself together, Richard, and say something."

Maxwell moved to the center of the room and cleared his throat, but he seemed unable to frame appropriate remarks. He simply looked from television screen to television screen as if he hoped for salvation on at least one of them. He perspired heavily. He could feel the fine fabric of his tattersall shirt stick to his clammy back.

Patrick Donovan lurched into the power vacuum created by Maxwell's catatonia and Lansing's reluctance to bail out the president. The dean wanted to kill Oscar who seemed to be enjoying the administration's humiliation. Patrick rushed to the president's side. He clapped his hands together to gain the attention of the crowd which appeared unable to free itself from the screens. Even George Watson, the governor's prissy assistant, was stopped dead in his tracks before *Hand Jobs Around The World*. He wiped his brow with his now twisted tie as, slack jawed, he stared at a tall black African who danced and masturbated. When the camera zoomed in on the muscular native's private part at the climactic moment, the assistant seemed ready to join Beverly in a swoon. His knees buckled. "It is true," he said aloud and moved even closer to the monitor. He had recovered only for a moment when the video announced a visit to the land of the rising sun. Three obese sumu wrestlers dropped their diapers and, jumping up and down, rubbed their members in grotesquely unlovely choreography. They grunted in rhythm with the jumps and hand motions. "It's so ugly," the assistant spoke aloud again. "And they're so small." For a quick moment he felt empowered. Wanting to see more, he hardly heard the dean's call to attention.

Walter Henry glanced sideways at a he-he tape while trying to give the impression of being disgusted. Two beautiful young men were fondling each other. Walter thought for an instant of what his life might have been like if he had yielded to his impulses when he was their age. "But it was a different world then," he whispered.

"Yes, it was," said an older member of the board who stood next to him. "All our lives might have been different if we hadn't been so frightened." He spoke those words as if he understood Walter's whispered comment.

Walter turned to the elderly man and nodded his head. Their eyes met in sympathetic understanding. No further words passed between them, but Walter suddenly felt an instant bond of kinship that he would remember for a long time. In a curious way, this crazy moment in Berlin's video factory had been liberating. For only a fleeting moment, but Walter felt good.

The two female members of the board moved from screen to screen. They held each other for support. "This is absolutely fascinating," said the older woman. A grandmother in her late sixties, she had never before seen a pornographic film. "I actually believe I've learned something this morning about a large segment of the population that had been unknown to me." She laughed nervously. "My grandson teases me about my ignorance of popular culture. How can you run a college and be so square about the interests of its students?" She grasped the arm of the younger woman more tightly. "Understand, I think all of this is just terrible. Certainly not my taste," she laughed, "but an awful lot of people like it."

The younger woman, a business executive in her early forties, was appalled by the large mindedness of her companion. "I've never been able to understand you, Thelma. How can you laugh this off," she shuddered and pointed at two women wrapped in each other's arms, "this obscenity?"

"I guess you can chalk it up to wisdom gained with the years."

"I doubt that very much. We've locked horns on too many issues for me to buy that malarkey. Even if you make it sound sympathetic. We're just ideological opposites. The trouble with you, Thelma, is you believe conservatives are just not as worthy human beings as you liberals. And that, dear Thelma, is simply a crock." She squeezed the older woman's arm. "But you know I still like you."

"I do?" Thelma smiled. "Now I guess we ought to listen to the dean try to weasel out of this one." Both women turned to Patrick Donovan who continued to clap his hands.

Having watched the visitors staring at the seven television screens, Patrick had devised a strategy for deflecting their public outrage while understanding their silent fascination. He nodded in the direction of an ashen Beverly Berlin who sat trembling in a chair in the corner of the room. She sobbed audibly when Marty entered the room.

He waved to her and pointed to the door where two tuxedoed waiters carried a case of chilled Dom Perignon and a box of Swedish champagne glasses he had specially ordered. Each bore an inscription to celebrate Beverly's great day. A memento for each guest to carry away, this was Marty's surprise gift for his wife.

Before he could make his way to Beverly's side, Maxwell, his voice a mere whisper, introduced Marty to the chairman of the board. Whitaker put his arm around the merchant's shoulder and forced him into the garden where the caterers were busily readying the tables for lunch. "Only your expert advice about the market can salvage this day for me," Whitaker said hoarsely. His face was flushed.

Marty comprehended none of this, but his business instincts could not let him miss an opportunity to further ingratiate the Berlin clan with so important a person. Marty had actually voted for Whitaker in his last race for the senate.

In the ten minutes they sat together at a table, to the consternation of the caterer whom Whitaker continually waved away, Marty lectured the chairman. Whitaker took a few notes, calmed down, even smiled at this man who obviously knew more than he did about the stock market. Marty motioned a waiter to open a bottle of wine and bring two glasses. He pointed to the inscription. "On the occasion of Professor Beverly Berlin's presentation to the board of trustees."

"My God, Marty, how did you get so many words on such a delicate glass?" Whitaker asked in obvious admiration.

"Well, Jason, as I've been saying for the past few minutes, money is the name of the game. In this case, if you know what you want and you're willing to pay for it, you can have anything done." Marty laughed. "The glass people I worked with are so brilliant, I could have had the Declaration of Independence on each goblet."

"And I bet you could have," said Whitaker. He held his glass up to Marty. "Many thanks for the lesson, professor." They clinked glasses. "And may I call you from time to time?"

"Of course."

Jason Whitaker's hostility to Beverly's presentation had been ameliorated by visions of financial gain.

Still faint from the morning's disaster and seething over Marty's arrival, Beverly would never know how fortuitous her husband's presence had been.

Patrick slowly moved to the center of the milling, loud crowd. He cleared his throat and smiled benignly as though he were about to gently chastise his congregation for misreading that morning's sermon. He spoke softly, calling on every nuance of his beloved brogue. At times like this, Donovan was at his most captivating. That accent could make even mundane commentary sound like mellifluous poetry. "Yes," he began as if he were continuing a conversation with his flock, "yes, Professor Berlin's presentation was a surprise. Perhaps, at first, shocking to some. But I'm sure," he smiled the smile of a con man bringing his marks into his fold, "only at first. Professor Berlin realized that such a knowledgeable audience was quite familiar with the older work she was doing, groundbreaking as it was, by virtue of your study of the full and brilliant documentation you examined prior to your generous funding. She and her team decided to risk involving her guests in a darker, seamier side of American, indeed, international, popular culture. And a gamble it was, but if not at a university research center and before a group as sophisticated as you," he spread his arms to embrace them all, "then where? Pray tell, my good friends, where indeed?" He scanned the room, his eyes making knowing, warm contact with each person now listening intently to his every word. He nodded sympathetically to each face he read as already in his camp. Donovan had warmed to the brilliance of his own extemporizing. He knew he was soaring, as a jazz virtuoso climbing higher and higher into an outrageous, daring riff on a familiar tune.

The dean relished the audacity of his own gamble as he continued to scan his audience. He knew he was making in-roads. Even the governor's assistant, having removed his now mutilated necktie, nodded his head and scribbled notes for the chief.

Donovan placed his hands before him as if in prayer. He swayed slightly, intoxicated by his own performance. He closed his eyes, smiled to himself, and decided to go for broke. "In conclusion, I must underscore the importance of the bold research we were privileged to observe this morning. I can think of no better way to convey this than by invoking others in whose mold we can now place our university's own Professor Berlin."

Beverly brightened as she listened to Patrick's words. Marty pressed his hands into the back of her shoulders to the rich rhythms of the dean's syllables. He beamed with pride. Marty even winked at Jason Whitaker.

"Researchers who were not only ahead of their time," Patrick continued, "but risked public condemnation." He paused and began to recite his luminous list slowly and solemnly. Jonas Salk. Copernicus. Gallileo. The Wright Brothers. Madame Curie. Alfred Kinsey." He knew, of course, there were neither historical nor disciplinary connections or logic to his list, but he continued naming great figures from his audience's collective historical consciousness. "These as well as the scores of artists and writers who broke new ground for the ultimate benefit of us all." Donovan was aware of the nodding heads before him as he tolled the august names. His auditors could not have failed to nod their heads in respect for the roster of great names, if not in comprehension of the dean's logic.

Patrick paused after every invocation and savored each name. He moved toward Beverly Berlin as he spoke. Breaking loose from Marty's proud grip, she stood to meet her savior. Reaching her, he placed an arm around her waist. Beverly was now actually blushing and batting her eyes once more. As Patrick recited the last of the list of her intellectual ancestors, he threw caution to the wind and whispered hoarsely in mock humbleness of that final name. "Jesus Christ himself was willing to risk all for the greatest good of mankind." The dean bowed his head for a moment. He body gave only the slightest hint of a genuflection. He did not have to look at the congregation to see the effect of the invocation of Jesus by a member of his order. He straightened dramatically and looked at the crowd with clear-eyed confidence in his mission. He moved a few steps away from Beverly and extended both arms in her direction. He smiled broadly. "It is with the greatest pleasure and most profound admiration that I once again present to you our own Professor Beverly Berlin." As he passed her to join the applauding crowd,

Patrick kissed Beverly on the cheek and whispered, "you owe me big time, lady."

Maxwell began shouting enthusiastically. "Brava, brava." He had been totally enthralled by his dean's brilliantly conceived and delivered nonsense.

Oscar joined in the applause, but muttered to Walter Henry. "I'm surprised he left out Washington, Lincoln, Martin Luther King, and Frank Sinatra."

All applauded, but most remained skeptical, others confused. Nevertheless, Patrick's words went a long way to salvage the morning. Gone were the images of genitalia, copulation, masturbation, cunnilingus, and fellatio. Gone were the he-she's, she-she's, and he-he's that Billy Mann smuggled into town in his canvas backpack. In their place, because of Donovan's intellectual alchemy, were serious discussions of the value and propriety of Professor Berlin's project. Donovan had moved the discourse to a respectable plane, even if the participants remained convinced that the materials of the study were themselves disgusting. Or, at least, they claimed they were disgusting. That, after all, is the proper public response to pornography among genteel, well-bred men and women. In the privacy of their cells, they often thought the opposite.

"It's just like Robert Mapplethorpe," Maxwell, now recovered from his earlier paralysis, said to Thelma and Jason Whitaker. "He offended much of the public's sensibilities, but ultimately we came to realize he was a wonderful photographer."

"If you like big cocks and butt fucking," Murdoch whispered to Walter.

Walter blushed. Was that comment aimed at the president or himself? He laughed, but wanted to say "never butt fucking!" He thought of his meeting with Jack and Wilma at the hotel when he had wanted to tell them that he and Dennis never engaged in what he considered abhorrent practices. God, he had told Dennis, I don't think we do much more than James and Jeremy do in the privacy of their rooms. He had shuddered at the invocation of his own sons' names in such a context.

"A penny for your thoughts, Walter," said the dean, now working the room still glowing with his rhetoric. Patrick smiled at the literature department chair. Even a penny for that man's thoughts is gross inflation. The dean was adept at carrying on two conversations at social gatherings where he was expected to mingle in behalf of the administration as Maxwell often exhorted his senior administrators to do. His private monologue was fraught with castigations and unflattering evaluations of the people he spoke with so amiably.

Murdoch laughed. "He's still fixated on the videos."

Walter blushed again.

At first, Mitchell was as amused as Oscar about this fascinating and grotesque turn of events. But his glee turned to concern as he was torn between the low comedy of the scene and chagrin about how it might rub off on him. He'd already begun framing an essay on the collision of two cultures from the vantage point of an observer in the center of the clash of sensibilities. There were wonderful titles floating through his fertile mind. He savored the alliterative sound of Pricks and Prigs: A Problematic Passion Play of Prols and Patricians. While he worried other possible titles for a piece he thought perfect for *The Journal of Popular Culture*, the caterer announced that lunch was being served in the garden.

Beverly was now radiant. Fully recovered from her morning's near disaster, she moved confidently and almost seductively among her guests. Walking from table to table, nodding and smiling, exchanging small talk with the most important, she flirted outrageously with Chairman Whitaker and then with the governor's assistant. This was a Beverly Berlin few of her colleagues had ever seen.

Mitchell nudged Marty's arm. "What the hell did you feed her this morning? You must have laced her orange juice with one terrific aphrodisiac. And if you have any left over, ship it to my house." He punched the befuddled realtor in the arm, much as a teen-ager might in honor of his best friend's losing his cherry. "I never thought I'd envy you, Marty my man, but you must have a hell of a good time in that enormous bedroom of yours."

Before an embarrassed Marty could say he was as surprised as Mitchell, the genius pointed at Beverly pawing the governor's assistant. "Well, get a look at her now. I bet that twerp never had a woman in his monkish little life."

Beverly sat next to the nervous young man and appeared to hang on his every word as she held his arm tightly. Even from a distance it was clear that George Watson was embarrassed.

"Oh George," Beverly cooed. "I'm sure the governor will understand completely after your brilliant discussion of the videos." She stroked his arm. "I saw all the notes you took this morning."

Beverly's behavior surprised even herself. Only in her fantasies had she been as coquettish as she now was in actuality. In fact, she not only enjoyed her new role, but she seemed unable to stop. She was propelled by a mad desire to be outrageous. Perhaps it was the video show, but she knew better. Dirty pictures had never interested her. When her college friends gathered around the television set to smoke pot and watch *The Devil and Miss Jones* or *Deep Throat*, she was more repelled than involved. Indeed, one of Marty's most attractive traits, perhaps the only one in addition to his wealth, was his sexual innocence. He had been a virgin when she first met him. Although he did not divulge that fact until long after they were married, she had guessed it after the first week-end they spent together. Clumsy and apologetic, he had groped her inexpertly. He remained a lousy lover, which she let him know in her most vicious moments. That and the small size of his penis were among the most damaging of her attacks. She had laughed out loud when he seriously considered an operation. She recalled how earnest he had been when he showed her an advertisement for penile enlargement. "Gain two inches in length and girth" was the promise of the bold headline. He had crushed the piece of newspaper in his perspiring hand when she laughed. "Do you really think it would make any difference?" she asked. He was demolished. The subject never came up again. But she still sometimes asked if he didn't have Japanese ancestors. Beverly always knew exactly where to plant the stiletto as she always knew Marty would return for new attacks. "I'm some sort of dominatrix," she had once confided to her shrink. "And it's about the only thing in our relationship that turns me on, and even then it's not much of a turn-on." Once she wept. "But when you're married to Marty Berlin, I guess even low heat is something to be grateful for." Marty had never known his wife saw a psychiatrist. That the shrink's advice echoed her mother's did little to comfort Beverly. She did not like sex.

"But the governor isn't like that, Professor Berlin," George Watson quietly protested.

"Call me Beverly, please. We're all members of the same family here at the university." She sipped champagne from the specially inscribed glass.

"Call me Beverly and I'll call you George." She allowed the tips of her fingers to brush his. "Is it a deal, George?"

More embarrassed than ever, Watson looked away. "Yes, Beverly," he mumbled. He pulled his hand back and dropped it to his lap. "I'll try."

"Of course you'll try, George." She smiled intimately. "And I know you'll succeed brilliantly. After all, George, we've all heard of your great success in the state capital." In fact, Beverly had never heard of George Watson before that very day. She blew him a kiss and moved to another table.

"I'd love to know what line she fed that guy," Mitchell said to Marty who sat opposite him at their round table.

He looked up from the plate of grilled shrimp on a bed of salad greens and shook his head. "Don't have the slightest idea. But if it gets her more funding, who cares?"

Beverly took an empty seat at her husband's table. Riding her high, she kissed Marty's cheek. "Hi, honey. Enjoying yourself?" She winked in Murdoch's direction as if they were conspirators. "Your speech ready for tonight's do?" She smiled across the table. Not waiting for a response, her expansive mood returned to Marty. "Those champagne glasses were a master stroke. How did you manage to keep them a secret from me?" She looked at Murdoch again. "He can never keep anything from me." She kissed Marty's cheek once more. Beverly's gaze invited the table's other diners into her conversation. "We share our day's adventures each night while Marty prepares dinner." She nodded to the table. "And I can assure you, this man's one great chef. Isn't that right, Mitchell? I'll tell you all something if you promise not to tell him." She glanced at Marty and laughed almost affectionately. "If there were a MacArthur grant for cooking, this guy would win it walking away."

Marty blushed. He couldn't remember another time when Beverly praised him for anything in front of strangers. And affection in public? Never before. A couple of busses on the cheek in full view of the world was something Marty couldn't fathom. Just because he brought some champagne and glasses? No, he thought, it had to be something else. But once the embarrassment passed, he enjoyed this new experience. He brought Beverly's hand to his lips and gently, gallantly, kissed it. She did not pull away. Marty was delighted. He smiled broadly at his luncheon companions. This was his wife, the star of the morning, who was willing to share her spotlight with him. At that moment, Marty Berlin would have done anything for Beverly.

Beverly led her husband away from the table to a private corner next to the buffet table. "Dear," she cooed, "would you do me a favor on your way home and stop at the drugstore for some magazines?"

Marty nodded. "Sure, Bev, which ones?"

The professor looked around to make sure she couldn't be overheard. "Just *Hustler*, *Playboy*, and *Penthouse*." Her new found confidence still strong, she did not look away from Marty's questioning eyes. "I'll tell you all about it later. I promise. It's the start of a whole new set of projects."

"Okay, if that's what you want, but I'm not going to buy them at our drug store. Everybody knows me there."

Beverly's impatience surfaced. "I don't care where you get them. Just get them." Realizing that eyes might be on them, she smiled and kissed Marty on the cheek. "I'll see you at home soon. And don't forget to pick up your tuxedo at the cleaners." She turned back to the tables which were arranged artfully under a great awning on her lawn. She looked back at Marty for a moment. "And don't forget we go to the Maxwells for drinks at four." Images of the new porno queen of academe cascaded through her mind as she walked toward tables she hadn't yet graced. She returned George Watson's wave. The jerk probably has had a hard-on since I left him. She was delighted by his smile. She blew him a kiss. Get me a big sweet grant from your boss, George, she whispered to him as she passed his table. He looked up at her adoringly. Some conquest, she muttered to herself.

Billy Mann was surprised to see the Henrys at the College Wine Shoppe. What the hell are they doing here on a day crammed with so many events for the two pricks? he thought, as he waved to his chairman. "I thought you'd be resting up for the big banquet," he greeted Walter.

"Plenty of time for that, Billy. Besides I can't miss the old Shoppe's semi-annual sale. He pointed at his shopping cart. "How can you not buy this great merlot for only sixteen bucks? Maggie already had a couple of cases of a very nice shiraz loaded into the car. Twelve dollars a bottle if you get it by the case. Our favorite Aussie wine."

Rich son of a bitch is what Billy wanted to say, but he merely nodded his agreement. The Henrys liked their wine. Billy himself was here to stock up during the week-end sale. Happy at least that he hadn't yet loaded his shopping wagon with the liter and a half inexpensive wines he had circled on the store's advertising flyer, Billy mentioned a very expensive margaux he had adored at the only dinner party he had ever been invited to at Walter's. He smarted at the recollection of Abraham's inclusion at several such dinners. "I think I'd like a case of that," Billy said off handedly.

"I don't believe they carry that label any longer. When we bought it, I was told it was the end of the run. We were lucky to get the last few cases."

Lucky to have married a rich bitch is what you really mean. Billy offered his practiced warm smile. "Well, win a few, lose a few. I guess I'll just have to wait for another dinner party at the Henrys if I want to taste that one."

"Oh, I'm afraid it'll be a long wait," Walter laughed. "We finished that one some time ago." Walter ignored the hint for an invitation.

Billy imagined Walter and his boyfriend, the baby doctor, drinking that delicious rich margaux as they sat by Dennis' pool. He let his imagination play with the scene for a few seconds. Before it became triple X rated, Walter pointed to Maggie and Sally chatting by the shop's food counter.

"We better get over there before the ladies decide to spend the national budget on caviar." Walter turned his wagon toward the delicacy corner. Billy and Sally always enjoyed browsing and trading admiring comments about the delicious looking displays. It was the part of the store they reserved for window shopping only. The prices were as high as the products were beautiful to behold. "Don't worry about Sally. She loves to make her own canapés."

"I guess that's right," said Walter. "Maggie's always telling me what a talented cook your wife is. She runs the gourmet club, doesn't she?"

Billy nodded. "And speaking of food, how was the lunch at Beverly's video factory?" Billy had waited as long as he could. He had wanted to ask Walter about that morning's show from the moment he saw him pushing his wagon of expensive wines. Food, he thought, was an innocent enough prelude to the real question.

Walter's momentary hesitation buoyed up Billy's expectations. "I guess the food was good enough," Walter began. "But the video program was something else."

"How so?" Billy tried to sound as innocent as a new born. As Walter recounted what had happened, Billy's emotions rose to the great high he had anticipated and then were dashed by the unexpected turn of events that seemed to actually save the day for Beverly Berlin. Billy's face was pale as he questioned the chairman. But as disappointed as he was by the news, he managed to control both his tone and his questions. He tried to sound incredulous and scandalized. "Are you telling me Beverly actually showed dirty pictures to those people? Is she crazy? Is that what she does over there?" Billy shook his head. "Were they really pornographic movies?" He thought of the videos he had watched so many times. Be careful, he said to himself. He moved closer to Walter. "What were they like?" He tried to leer. "I haven't seen a dirty movie since I was an undergraduate." That's far enough, he warned himself. Don't say another word.

Walter nodded. "Oh yes, they were as rough as I imagine they can get. I'll tell you, I was glad Maggie wasn't there. She can't even stand dirty jokes."

Billy smiled to himself and bit his tongue. I could tell her a few, he thought. He laughed to himself. Have you heard the one about the Shakespeare scholar and the pediatrician? That's under the he-he heading, Maggie.

The two men were now beside their wives. Billy wanted to arrange a meet with Abraham. He had to tell him about that prick, Donovan. They now would have even greater reason to despise the dean. But, he would comfort Abraham, all is not lost. There's the banquet. And not even Patrick's forked tongue can save the night. Billy smiled as he imagined that night's scene.

Richard Maxwell, clad only in a white towel, stood before the bathroom mirror. The cocktail party over, he was ready for a short rest before dressing for the banquet. He could hear Barbara in her dressing room. "Went wonderfully well, didn't it?" he called to her. "And nobody mentioned the bloody videos." He examined a small pimple under his bottom lip and wondered if he should attempt squeezing it. Which was worse, he debated. A small red mark or the possibility that the little white head would grow larger during the evening. That literature chair would probably convene one of his ridiculous task forces to study the problem. Richard laughed.

What a bunch of cretins. His disdain for his faculty gave him moments of small pleasure. He sighed. It comes with the territory. He wondered if it would be any different at the more prestigious places he planned to head. "I think we had a pretty classy bunch here this afternoon," he called out. "I don't know if I could have kept quiet about the dirty movies if I had been a visitor to Berlin's porno factory." Still no response from the dressing room. "Barbara, are you listening to anything I'm saying?"

The president's wife entered the bathroom. "Of course, I'm listening. Heard every word you said." She patted his flat stomach. "And I agree with everything you said." She scanned the bottles and creams neatly arranged by her sink. "Thank God, no one talked about it. And thank God I wasn't there. It's enough I have to go to all these boring dinners with you."

"But tonight's special."

"I know, I know. A genius award for Mitchell Murdoch." She made a face. "You know I never liked him. And a genius?" She looked at Richard. "Come now, we know better than that. I couldn't even decipher the introduction to that last piece of drivel he gave you." She scoffed. "Genius, my foot."

The president sighed again. "Probably true, Barbara. That's why I protect myself by not reading any of the stuff my faculty send over."

"At least you've got a secretary who culls the reviews for you."

"A heck of a lot easier to read reviews than books."

"You almost sound like your impossible Dean Donovan. He always has a few pithy comments about every new book the faculty publish. I know his secretary feeds them to him."

"Why not? We're far too busy to read their publications. And is Patrick on your hate list too?"

"You know I don't care for him. Much too slimy for my liking. And remember, dear, he's out there gunning for your job."

"Well, of course he is. Isn't that what provosts and deans are all about? Every administrator wants a presidency. Don't forget the route we took to get here." He stared at his pimple. "Patrick's probably smarter than most of them." He tested the pimple. "And he saved our asses this morning. Don't forget that."

"All for the greater glory of Patrick Donovan, my dear. Don't you forget that."

"So what's wrong with helping us and himself at the same time." He fingered the pimple.

"For heavens sake, Richard, either squeeze the damn thing or leave it alone. The world won't come to an end if the president shows up with a blemish on his chin." She chuckled. "Not even your friends at the campus paper could care less about your complexion."

Richard suddenly embraced Barbara. He let the towel drop to the floor.

In a moment they were in bed.

Richard sat up in bed and held a condom before him. "Do you realize what a market there would be for designer condoms?" He unwrapped his common drugstore Trojan. "A fortune. That's what the right entrepreneur could reap." He moved slowly into his wife. "Designer condoms." Every syllable matched a thrust. "A fortune." His speed increased. "Imagine a condom boutique at fashionable Barney's in New York. A discrete, sedate Episcopalian counter at Rogers Peet. A casual corner at Eddie Bauer. A chic, hip display at Ralph Lauren. A popular knock-off line at The Gap." Richard got harder and harder. Barbara moved faster and faster beneath him. She gasped "yes" after each mention of a condom line and a store's name. At the moment of climax, Richard shouted "bejeweled ringed condoms at Tiffany and compan-ee-ee." Barbara screamed "yes, yes, yes."

Hands above his head, the president stretched his long, lean frame. He looked down at his firm body and slapped his flat stomach. His morning runs had paid off. Richard opened the top drawer of his night table and reached for his pack of Carltons. He smoked only after sex, and only low tar cigarettes. A pack lasted a long time. He lit the cigarette, blew two streams of smoke through his nose, and turned to Barbara. "God, I love this yuppie sex."

She placed her head on his stomach. "Designer condoms indeed."

Richard offered a passable imitation of his wife. "Yes, yes, yes," he whispered. He sat up, viewed himself in the mirrored wall of closets, and continued puffing away. "Yes sir," he said to his image, "there are many sides to this president." He stood up and admired himself. "I am one complicated son-of-a-gun." He saluted the mirror. "And tonight, my dear," he turned to Barbara, "we'll be the best looking president and first lady this campus has ever seen. Yes sir." As he retired to the bathroom, he said aloud, "too bad there won't be a search committee there to check us out." He examined his blemish under Barbara's make-up light. "Yes," he said to the pimple which had not grown larger, "tonight's festivities could snag me an Ivy League presidency."

The faculty club looked splendid. It had been transformed from the drab eating establishment for wrinkled professors, frustrated by the realities of their careers. If not quite the glittering grand ballroom of the Waldorf, it was handsome enough to make even the guest of honor smile. "Well, ain't this something?" Mitchell exclaimed to Isobel as the handsome couple entered the club's dining room. He nodded and waved in the direction of the smattering of applause which greeted him. "You'd never believe this is the same room I lunch in when I have to eat on campus."

The usual dining tables and chairs had been removed for the evening. Most of the two hundred guests, drinks in hand, were already milling around. Mitchell knew better than to arrive too early, perhaps the only thing he had learned from Richard Maxwell who had not yet made his entrance. Tuxedoed waiters expertly moved through the room, carrying canapés and trays of champagne glasses. Rosy pink fluorescent lamps had replaced the glaring white lights. A large candelabra adorned each serving table. Candle light flickered on silver trays laden with tastefully arranged delicacies. No university food service had put together this spread, Mitchell thought. The president had been surprisingly generous tonight.

"Remember," Isobel said, "Maxwell's out to impress the out-of-town bigwigs."

"Stop it," Murdoch snapped. "Let me at least think it's because of my grant." He shot an angry look at Isobel. Isobel shrugged. "I think it's time for us to work your room." She smiled at a nearby group of beautifully attired people. "Plenty of time later for petty arguments," she said through her smiling lips as she passed Mitchell. Her smile still painted on her lips, she looked back at the genius. "If you get lucky, champ, you may even screw some important broad in the rest room." She waved a return to a greeting. "Beats renting a little room in some quaint country inn." Isobel waded into the crowded center of the room. Over the years, she had become expert at singing her husband's praises at such gatherings. But even

Isobel felt a special twinge of excitement tonight. The MacArthur was different. And it paid handsomely.

A jazz trio played in a corner of the room. The musicians had been hired and paid for by the genius himself. Intellectuals of the Murdoch type think it's cool to prefer jazz, especially if performed by black musicians, to more traditional classical music. Just as they would rather gyrate alone on dance floors, arms and torsos flailing in clumsy attempts to move to the rhythms of rock music. They know little about such music of course, but they believe it provides a link between them and a hip younger generation they court and pander to. Not that they know anything more about jazz, even though they're fond of words like cool, dig, and groove as they relish talking about Louis, Trane, and Dizzy. If the truth were known, Murdoch and his ilk rarely put jazz or rock CDs into their expensive sound systems, except when colleagues in musical oneupsmanship visit, or as Beverly Berlin prefers, oneupspersonship. But she also insists on herstory for history and refuses to call her doctoral classes seminars, obviously believing the term has something to do with that white viscous fluid men are so fond of spilling. No wonder she's the darling of the womens studies program.

The jazz game reminds old prof watchers of baseball which was once the academic intellectuals' sport of choice. After all, Updike and Cheever and Algren and even Bart Giamatti were fans, weren't they? How they love to use first names, even better, nicknames for people they never met. Yes, John and Bart wrote about baseball. So it was that the Murdochs of academe knew a great deal of diamond lore without actually appreciating or even enjoying the beauties of the game. And so it was that their musical knowledge embraced biographical data, song titles, nicknames of celebrated performers, even discographies, but hardly touched the intricacies of the music itself. They could name ten jazz saxophonists. They couldn't identify a riff by a single one of them. In private, they'd much rather listen to a Strauss waltz or a Sousa march. Thus they postured about jazz in their world where appearance was king. And they unrhymically bounced around the floor in their masturbatory dancing when, in reality, they'd much prefer to hold partners in their arms and slowly sway to the strains of an old standard fox trot in a darkened ballroom, spots of light reflecting from the glitter ball gently turning high above them. Perry Como crooning *When You Were Sweet Sixteen* in such a setting gave romantic promise. But they knew that was square. The solitary arm wagging, jumping around they appeared to favor produced only sweaty clothes and fallen arches. But it was cool. And since their total public persona was predicated upon appearance, reality remained a hidden private pleasure.

Thus Mitchell Murdoch had hired a jazz trio of talented black musicians to provide the background for the cocktail hour which would precede his banquet and, more importantly, his moment in the spotlight. That no one actually paid any attention to the music mattered not at all. Everyone would know it was jazz and they could see the three black musicians. The statement would be made and registered in the collective consciousness of the two hundred guests. Appearance would be served. Murdoch had even toyed with the idea of having the trio play an appropriate tune when he was introduced, but gave it up when he and Isobel could not agree on a song everyone would know. For if the tune were not obvious, the point would be lost. But he and Isobel had a lovely short list. *It Had To Be You, King of the Hill, My One and Only*. None from the classic jazz repertoire, but played by fine black musicians, anything would sound good. Isobel thought *Jealousy* would make a terrific inside joke.

The candle-lit head table was radiant. It was the only table in the faculty club's ballroom so handsomely adorned. Before each place setting a delicate, small silver vase contained two miniature carnations, one blue, the other white to remind the honored guests of the university's colors. Larger bouquets sat as center pieces on the other twenty tables. The head table was flanked by great sprays of the same color combination. Only Isobel's chastening words about Maxwell's motives prevented Murdoch from complimenting the president on the beauty of the room.

Richard leaned across Mitchell in order to speak to the governor. "The flowers all come from our provost's greenhouse. Gorgeous, aren't they?"

In response to the pol's nodded agreement, Richard continued. "Never was much of a scholar, but the man sure has a green thumb." He pointed toward the Lansings who sat one table removed from the head. "Always like to invite old Oscar to big parties at the president's house, you know. He might not be the best conversational partner, but you can count on his bringing some really great flowers."

Mitchell colored slightly as he sat between Maxwell and the governor. Why can't he ever leave well enough alone? Murdoch shook his head and wanted to throttle Maxwell. Isobel's quiet faux coughing fit stopped her husband's head shaking. She shot him a look that quickly replaced his turned down lips with a broad smile. Nodding at the television cameras which were panning the room, she mouthed, "remember, you're on candid camera."

He wanted to whisper his thanks to Isobel, but the maniac who had set out the place cards had separated husbands and wives at this head table. Mitchell couldn't understand why the three central seats were occupied by men whose wives were not at their sides. Still, he was pleased that he sat at the center and on the occasion of his honor, he was flanked by the president of the university and the governor of the state. He really shouldn't complain.

But Oscar Lansing did complain to everyone at his table. "Can you understand why the dean is seated at the head table and the provost is not?" To the baffled silence that greeted his complaint, Oscar explained that he was the provost of the university, a position that outranked a mere dean. "It's certainly not a question of vanity," Oscar continued. "Frankly, I'd much prefer sitting with you fine people than with them," he gestured to the head table. "No, it's a matter of protocol." He shook his head deliberately. "Without protocol, there are no standards. And without standards, the university is rudderless." He surveyed the other nine people at the table. "Surely, you understand my point."

The provost's wife smiled warmly at her husband. Irene Lansing knew exactly what Oscar meant. She touched his arm in agreement. "You see," she said in her gentle, soft southern voice, "my husband is a great believer in doing what's right." She had the table in her quiet grip. "Not what some might consider expedient." She sipped her wine. "No," she continued as if answering a question. "Oscar Lansing will never be a university president." She accented that title in an ambiguously insinuating tone that only a well-bred southern lady could get away with. She put down her glass and leaned toward the others. "You see, Oscar is not only an honorable gentleman of the old school," she laughed lightly, "even if he is a Yankee intellectual, but he also believes in God. Not a very fashionable thing these days, you know." Waiting for a response that didn't materialize, Irene continued. "Yes indeed, Oscar teaches in our church Sunday school." She touched his arm again. "Hasn't missed a class in eight years." She pointed at her wine glass. "Just about the only thing we don't agree on." She held the glass out to her neighbor for more white wine. "And I'll tell you something else that will keep Oscar Lansing from a presidency." She lowered her voice dramatically. Irene knew exactly how to manipulate an audience. "We believe in extra terrestrials." She nodded her head smartly. "Well, now, what do you think of that?" She clinked her glass against her husband's glass of soda water. Irene winked mischievously as her table's conversation picked up.

This was a new audience for the Oscar and Irene show. At least one faculty or administration couple was seated at each table. Ostensibly designed to welcome the university's guests and talk about academic matters, the Lansing table conversation turned to an animated discussion of unidentified flying objects, Roswell, and Oscar's favorite, the relation between intelligent life out there in space and his profound Christian belief in divinity.

Maxwell was surprised, but delighted by the sight of such robust conversation at the provost's table. For a moment he wondered if he had misjudged the man.

"The owl seems to have caught the fancy of his dining companions," Patrick Donovan pointed toward the provost. "Tell me, Richard, which bible lesson is the old bird teaching this evening.?" Patrick laughed. Wanting to pursue a skewering of the enemy, he was interrupted by a waiter who placed fruit cocktail before him. He looked down at the glass bowl of fruit sitting in a larger silver bowl of crushed ice. He shrugged. There'll be plenty of time later to score a few points against such an easy mark. It'll be a long evening. He took a spoonful of the tempting fruit. He turned to the governor's wife. "They must have flown some of this in. I haven't seen such beautiful melon or kiwi even in the best of our local markets."

She nodded. "I could listen to you all night, Dean Donovan. I just love the way you Irish speak." She ate some fruit. "You make everything sound like poetry. When Bill and I were in Dublin last year, I was enchanted with the accents."

Patrick smiled benevolently at Mrs. Richmond. "Mary, if I may. . . "

"Of course dean. . . "

"Patrick, please. Patrick. I was about to say that if this were a more intimate occasion, I'd serenade you with that great George M. Cohan song that bears your name." Patrick smiled at his own excess. But, alas, isn't this what university presidents must do?

"Eponymous." The governor's wife looked into Patrick's twinkling blue eyes. "Isn't that the word you all use in the British isles? Eponymous? I heard that for the first time last year. I do love that word. Eponymous." She touched the dean's arm and smiled broadly.

The woman is a blithering idiot, Patrick said to himself. "Quite right, Mary. Quite right." He returned his attention to his fruit salad. He looked to his left and smiled at Isobel Murdoch who had overheard his *tete a tete* with the governor's wife. He tried to read the thought behind Isobel's return smile.

He knew she was smart. He didn't know what she thought of him. He'd be wary as he felt her out during dinner. A supporting letter from Mitchell Murdoch couldn't hurt when the time came. Who cares if anyone could really comprehend his work. He was a figure of substance. Even the folks on the other side of campus, the hard scientists, knew that Murdoch was a celebrated critic. And those people don't read anything.

When Wilma Crouse entered the ballroom, the first people she noticed were the two camera operators who were recording the event for posterity. Wilma assumed they were the same cameras that captured her infamous debate. Of course she knew exactly why she had been invited to such a glittering event. She was tickled by the visible surprise of some, not only because of her presence, the only black guest, but also because she was escorted by Jack Williams.

"Fuck them all," Jack whispered. He held her arm tightly. "Walk like a queen. Act as if you own the place." He smiled over broadly at a woman whose looks he immediately disliked. "Overdressed rich bitch," he muttered through an exaggerated smile. "I bet she doesn't know the difference between a sonnet and a salami."

Wilma giggled. But she did walk like a queen. She wasn't even embarrassed when Jack bowed regally before the governor. "Wouldn't vote for that guy if he promised me a life long sabbatical."

"With full pay?" Wilma teased.

"Well, that might change the equation." Jack waved to the Henrys.

"But he's still a reactionary bastard."

By the time they found their table, they were the last to be seated. Jack helped Wilma to her chair in another grandstanding display of ostentatious formality. He looked at his dinner companions. "Jack Williams of the literature department," he said, "and this is the jewel in the department's crown, Professor Wilma Crouse." It was always easy for him to move between elegant formality and street corner vulgarity. Wilma found that duality refreshing and often charming. Jack rarely misread his audience. His cussing usually seemed just right. Jack Williams, too, was a consummate performer. Wilma knew he would be on his very best behavior when he met her folks next summer. If she could keep him from the booze at the annual Crouse fourth of July barbecue, she was sure her family would approve of her old white man. Whether they would love him as much as she did only time would tell. But she had told her mother all about Jack. Together, she and her mother were already laying the groundwork for the surprise Willie was going to spring on her extended family gathered to celebrate Independence Day. Her vein pulsated after each call to her mother.

After a round of exchanging names and handshakes, Jack grimaced as he looked down at the fruit cocktail. "I've always hated fruit salad," he said. "Ever since I was a kid, I've hated it." He lit a cigarette. "My mother thought it was a really elegant dish." He blew smoke in the direction of the woman he had hated instantly earlier that evening. She sat opposite him. "You'll never know how awful those dinners were with all my relatives. And on every one of those terrible occasions you can be sure there was this." He pointed at the dish before him. He casually pushed it a few inches away. "Anyone want a second bowl of Mrs. Williams' specialty?" He smiled when the hated woman looked away.

A middle aged man next to Wilma spoke to Jack. "I was in your class a hundred years ago. No reason you should remember me, but I sure do remember you."

The hated woman snorted. "I'm sure you do." She gave her husband a superior look. Jack wanted to punch her.

"Oh yes," the former student continued, "it was a great course." He looked at Elizabeth Crowell, the hated woman, "the twentieth century American novel it was." He extended his hand for the second time to Jack. "Bob Johnson, class of '71. I recall so fondly your lectures on Roth and

Mailer and Malamud What a wonderful crew. And that great building that housed the lit department in those days. My wife, Jane, and I wandered through the new humanities building yesterday." He made a face. "What an awful place to talk about great books."

Jack was pleased. "Yes indeed. A real shit house," he shot a glance at Mrs. Crowell to see if his appellation had its desired effect. He was gratified to see a slight redness overtake her powdered cheeks. "Another monstrosity approved by our distinguished board of trustees." He looked directly at Mrs. Crowell. "Their taste is up their asses." Jack chuckled. You like that one, lady? Up their asses. Stick around and I'll really give you something to cluck about, you sanctimonious cunt. "And I'll tell you something else, Bob, the students were better then, too."

"Oh, I'm not sure that's true," Mrs. Crowell entered the conversation. "My son tells me he has wonderful students."

"Where's that?" asked Jack. "In kindergarten maybe?"

"At Yale," she said haughtily. "I'll have you know my son has an endowed chair at Yale." She shot Jack a smug look. "Only thirty-nine and he has a chair." She looked at Wilma. "I'm sure at least you've heard of him. Anthony Crowell. After all, he is in literature." She pointedly ignored Jack's academic affiliation.

Wilma nodded. "Oh yes, I'm familiar with his work."

Mrs. Crowell nudged her husband's arm. She beamed. "Of course you are."

Jack continued his conversation with his former student. "And what brings you to this fancy dress ball?"

"I'm representing the northeast alumni association. They tried to get as many alumni groups here tonight as they could. We thought it'd be a nice trip back. Jane's an alum too. Never had any of your courses, but she was also a lit major. I went to law school after I graduated. She got her master's and teaches at a local community college just outside of Boston."

"I think it would be great if any of my students ever talked about my courses the way Bob does about yours, Professor Williams." Jane had a nice voice, Jack thought. "But I know they won't. I agree with you about student abilities and interests. They've changed. But the profession has changed too."

"You ought to see how depressed she is when she comes home from a day at the library," Bob picked up his wife's train of thought. "Something's happened since those halcyon days when I studied literature."

Jane nodded. "I don't even understand some of the articles in the journals I now only occasionally read. And half of them aren't even about books. They seem to be exercises in solipsism."

Jack liked this couple.

Jane lowered her voice. "I don't know if I should say this here, but." She looked toward the head table. "I hated his last book." She nodded in the direction of the genius. She colored slightly. "I guess I shouldn't really say that I hated it. Frankly," she leaned toward Jack, "I couldn't understand it."

Jack laughed. "He calls the language he writes English. But we know better, don't we?" He winked at the alums.

"Well, I'm sure my son would have loved to be here," Mrs. Crowell asserted. "He very much admires Professor Murdoch's work."

"You know his work?" Jack whispered to Wilma.

"Oh yes. He's one of Mitchell's fellow travelers."

"Figures."

"And he would have so enjoyed the music. Anthony is devoted to jazz. My son has an extensive collection of recordings. He trades and buys on the internet. I think he knows every recording by heart." She stared at Jack. "A very valuable collection."

"I wonder why that doesn't surprise me," Jack muttered.

"And what is that supposed to mean, professor?" Believing she now held the upper hand, the endowed chair's mother was spoiling for a fight.

Jack put his mouth to Wilma's ear. "Two to one she's also a knee jerk liberal. Probably writes fat checks to all the correct organizations."

Before Mrs. Crowell could comment on the professor's rude whispering, the entree was served. The presentation was handsome. Medallions of roast lamb in a mint sauce. Medium rare with gorgeous pink centers. The plate held Murdoch's favorite sides, which had been suggested by Isobel: snap peas and polenta. All the tables having been served the entree and fine red wine, the room became quiet, the only sounds being occasional soft murmurs of appreciation for the splendid food.

Suddenly, the overbearing Mrs. Crowell farted. A long resonating blast. She was mortified. No one spoke or made eye contact. Jack was ecstatic. He nudged Wilma and smiled broadly. Mrs. Crowell farted again. She quickly pushed her chair from the table and rushed from the room.

At the head table, Maxwell was chatting amiably and he thought winningly with Jason Whitaker when the chairman of the board suddenly turned scarlet and cut a monstrously loud fart. Maxwell tried to ignore it. And while he continued to pursue his train of thought, Whitaker shat in his pants. He stood up, dark stains overspreading his trousers. Not saying a word, he waddled from the room.

Maxwell was appalled. He turned to his wife, only to see her white faced. "Richard, I've soiled my dress. I'm afraid to stand up. But I must." Richard saw the brown spots seeping throughout her backside as she raced out of the dining room. Before he could gather his thoughts, Richard felt a terrible cramp envelop his stomach and he farted even more loudly than the chairman had. He blushed and looked down at his untouched entree. The large room was suddenly filled with farts. Sounding like gunshots, they came from everywhere. Shot blasts. Longer wet drum rolls. The stench was nearly unbearable. Beverly, who a moment earlier had scolded Marty, was now sitting in her own shit. For the second time that day she fainted. From every corner of the dining room, guests were rushing to the rest rooms. But the bathrooms could accommodate only a fraction of the frantic diners. The blasts continued. Uncontrollable shit flowed into the tuxedo pants and evening dresses of the celebrants of Murdoch's genius award.

Mitchell himself sat at the head table with only Patrick Donovan. They both sat in their own excrement. As miserably uncomfortable as he was, the dean managed to speak while holding a handkerchief to his nose. "No use moving, Mitchell," he said in resignation. "There'll be no room in the toilets." He almost smiled. Murdoch nodded his head, a tear rolling down his cheek as he surveyed the stinking shambles before him. He reached into his jacket pocket and touched the pages of the speech he would never deliver. "And even the governor himself was sitting next to me."

That august chief executive had joined the crowd rushing from the room. His fussy assistant, himself in great discomfort, tried to clear a path to a toilet stall for the governor. But no one would yield a place in the disgusting lines. "But, he's the governor," the now hysterical assistant was shouting.

Perhaps trying to make up for that morning's catatonia, Maxwell had placed an urgent call to the athletic director. Buses were on their way to take the guests to the gym whose shower rooms awaited, as was a rag-tag collection of warm-up suits and sports uniforms. Following the call, the president placed Oscar in charge of moving people to the gym. Wearing their long coats, Richard and Barbara left the faculty club and walked quickly to the president's suite in the administration building to shower in private.

Naked in the presidential bathroom, drying each other with thick university towels, Richard whispered, "Condoms at Cartiers." Barbara whispered back, "Yes, Cartiers." And the lights went out in the president's suite.

Driving home, now clean but still clad only in coats, their clothes wrapped in towels and piled in the car's trunk, Richard spoke deliberately. "Whoever is responsible for this will wish he had never been born. I'll hound that bastard until I find him. I'm telling you, Barbara, there won't be a hole deep enough for him to hide in." He lit a cigar Jason Whitaker had given him. "He'll pay for the humiliation he's caused me."

"And the university," added Barbara.

"Of course the university. Do you realize what price we're going to pay for this day of infamy? Dirty pictures would have been bad enough. God damn Berlin and her stupid video project." He bit on the cigar. "At least Patrick bailed us out of the morning fiasco. But tonight. Can you believe what happened tonight."

Barbara nodded. She didn't speak. She wept quietly.

"Tonight was impossible. No one would ever believe it if they read it in a novel."

"It's even on video tape." Barbara sobbed.

"All because of your God damn fruit cocktail," Richard muttered. "Couldn't go with plain old shrimp cocktail, could you?"

She sobbed louder. "Richard, you're not being fair. Someone poisoned the fruit."

"Well, of course, someone did." Richard touched her arm. "I didn't mean to blame you." He bit harder on the cigar. "I'm not myself right now. It's that poisoner I'm going to get." He touched her arm again. "But it wasn't a total disaster, was it?" A hoarse laugh caught in his throat. He leered at Barbara. "It might not have been breakfast at Tiffany's, but it sure was dessert at Cartiers."

FOUR

Monday morning broke cloudy and cool. The promise of rain in the low, dark clouds was a perfect complement to the mood in the president's office. Maxwell's staff, heads down and eyes averted, worked silently. The president himself was closeted in his suite, huddling with representatives from the state and town police and senior officers of campus security. Coffee and donuts had been brought in all morning. Big things were happening in Maxwell's inner sanctum.

Richard's executive assistant did not dare look up from her desk in the tastefully appointed alcove immediately outside the president's office. Even she of such impeccable poise had smiled when her eyes made earlier contact with one of her secretarial staff. There was nervous laughter hovering beneath the surface of Maxwell's outer offices. Everyone had heard of the Saturday disasters.

The mood was very different at the literature department. Boisterous shouts and gales of laughter spilled into the corridor outside the Wallace Lounge. The regulars had gathered to share rumors and trade information. The return of Helen Abrams was overshadowed by the events of the weekend. For this Helen was grateful as she entered the lounge.

Billy Mann rushed to her side as if he were her dearest friend. He hugged her and in a loud voice announced her presence. "Look who's returned to our happy family."

Several of her colleagues applauded; others took slight notice and continued their pleasurable gossip.

Jack Williams took Helen's arm and moved her to a vacant couch. "So, how're you doing, kiddo?"

Helen knew his concern was real. She nodded her head. "Could be better, Jack. But all other things being equal, which they never are, I'm doing fine."

Jack examined her face and looked directly into her eyes. "And what are they doing about the guy who did this to you?"

"It's in the hands of the court now," she shrugged.

"As if any punishment to him can heal you."

Helen was surprised at Jack's understanding of her pain. "And what about you and Willie?" Her inclusion of Willie seemed natural. "From what I hear, you had quite a banquet." Helen smiled weakly. She wasn't yet back to her sparkling good humor. "Joan's report of the week-end did more to lift my spirits than you'll ever know."

"Are you still bunking out at her house?"

Helen nodded.

"I'm fine," Jack said, slapping his stomach. "Never liked fruit salad. But Willie's still feeling lousy." He lit a cigarette and smiled, still trying to read Helen's eyes. "I don't think she'll ever look at fruit again."

"So, who's the culprit?" She and Joan had gone through the department roster over their Sunday morning coffee. They came up with several who would have loved to get Beverly and Mitchell, but they couldn't settle on anyone with the courage to score two hits on a single day. That took planning and nerve, both of which they decided were in short supply among the lit faculty. But if the hero weren't someone from their department, half the fun would be lost.

Jack shook his head. "Don't have a clue. But whoever he is, he's got big balls."

"Or she?" Helen raised an eyebrow. "And who's on your list of suspects?" she asked of Abraham and Billy who took chairs facing the couch.

Billy giggled. "I would have loved to do it." He glanced at Abraham who sat stony faced. "Wouldn't you love to have been a fly on the wall at Beverly's factory?" He giggled again. "Can you imagine their faces when her video machines started up?" He rubbed his hands together. "God, I'd give anything to see a tape of that crowd staring at porno films."

Afraid Billy might go too far, Abraham interrupted his partner's obvious glee. "We may never know who did it," he said glumly. "It seems pretty sophomoric to me, anyway." He tried to look disapprovingly at Billy. "I wouldn't even want to see what happened at Beverly's."

"You wouldn't?" asked Jack. "Christ, we'd make a small fortune if we had a tape of all those tight asses looking at *Deep Throat*."

"That wasn't one of the films," Billy said. He flushed at his blunder. "Or, at least, I heard that none of them were flicks any of us ever heard of." He shot a nervous glance at Abraham who stared into his coffee cup.

"You must have good sources," Jack said. "And what else did you hear?"

"I want to know how you and Wilma are," asked Abraham, clumsily changing the subject. He, too, was flushed. He did not look at Billy.

"What's the matter with you two?" asked Helen. "Do you both have the flu? I can't believe you're embarrassed by dirty pictures."

There was a long silence before Billy spoke. "Well, face it, Helen, there's got to be more than a little embarrassment. After all, we know some of those people." He looked at her almost pleadingly. "You know, Walter in particular. Can you imagine him in such a situation?"

Helen was surprised. Could this be the same Billy Mann who made a career of skewering his colleagues now demonstrating charity to them? She furrowed her brow. Is it possible? Could this be the counter attack Eleanor had hinted at? Was the heavy artillery pornography and poison? Abraham an accomplice in all this? She shook her head. It was just too implausible. Perhaps Billy. But Abraham. Never.

As if reading her thoughts, Billy continued. "I met Walter at the wine store Saturday afternoon and, I'll tell you, he was still reeling." Billy shook his head in an exaggerated show of concern for their chairman. His eyes did not leave Helen's face as he looked for any sign that she found his solicitude convincing. "I'll tell you something else. Whatever differences I've had with him in the past just evaporated when he told me about his discomfort." Billy's fabrication might have continued if Jack didn't interrupt.

"You were concerned about Walter?" Jack laughed. "And what other fairy tales are you going to tell us." He was immediately sorry for his choice of words, especially when he saw Billy's quick facial response. Just a slight twitch of his lips and a sudden alert widening of his eyes told Jack that Billy had caught the reference. *I hope the little prick doesn't think I was taking a cheap shot at Walter. And if I ever did, it surely wouldn't be for Billy Mann's benefit.* "So, you're now sweet William." Jack looked at Abraham and Helen. "And to what can we attribute the great conversion? From scurrilous, malicious gossip to saintly solicitude in a single weekend? Remarkable."

Abraham felt he must bail out his new accomplice. The last thing he wanted was a battle in which Billy might blurt out something incriminating. He touched the older man's arm. "Come on, Jack, relax. Let's leave it alone. I think it's pretty darn swell of Billy to feel that way about Walter."

"Pretty darn swell?" said Helen. A hint of her old self broke through. "What gotten into you? Pretty darn swell? When did you become a flapper? This isn't the twenties, you know, and we're sure as heck not in Jay Gatsby's mansion." She looked at both men facing her. "What's happened to you guys?" Her mind filled with images of Abraham and Billy as the desperadoes who pulled off both capers. *Could it be?*

Walter Henry entered the lounge with two men in dark blue suits. "Can I have your attention, please," he shouted in order to be heard over the rambunctious din. "Let me introduce Captain Gerald Manley of the state police and Lieutenant Gary Bolton of our campus security." He pointed to the two men who nodded smartly at the now quiet room. The campus cop smiled at several of the faculty members he knew. Captain Manley looked severe and, Abraham thought, threatening. "I know most of you have heard by now of Saturday's . . . " Walter looked for a word, ". . . incidents." He smiled weakly. "The governor has placed Captain Manley in charge of the investigation. I know all of you will give him and his colleagues from university security and town police your full cooperation as they try to get to the bottom of those. . . " Walter shrugged, ". . . incidents." He looked at Captain Manley who moved to the center of the room.

"Good morning, ladies and gentlemen," the state policeman began, "I'm terribly sorry to have to be on the campus today, but both Governor Richmond and Doctor Maxwell have ordered a full probe into last Saturday's events. As a matter of fact, I've just come from a long meeting with President Maxwell who has pledged his complete support and assistance to our investigation." Manley peered over his glasses at the assembled faculty. "You understand, of course, that we were extremely fortunate that no one became seriously ill. The foreign substance that was introduced into the fruit salad at the banquet has now been analyzed." He peered at the group again and paused dramatically. "And I can tell you the state toxicologist reports that the substance was strong enough to have caused significant harm to individuals who were allergic to it. We were very lucky that no one seems to have suffered from such allergies. In any event, we aim to get to the bottom of the . . . " he glanced at Walter, ". . . the incidents. I remind you these were serious crimes. Especially the poisoning which the attorney general is calling attempted murder. There could have been fatal results if enough of the foreign substance had been ingested. Fortunately, the perpetrators added it to the fruit salad which contained enough liquid to dilute it sufficiently. But," he peered again, "had they introduced a greater concentration or placed it in a more dense food, the results might have been tragic. Tragic indeed, ladies and gentlemen. The point is that this is a serious matter." The captain smiled briefly. "The other event, that is, the morning incident, is far less serious, but serious nonetheless. There are, after all, in addition to breaking and entering, obscenity laws in this state. And those laws were violated at Professor Berlin's studio." He smiled again. "I should also tell you that at least three of the participants at the video presentation have threatened individual legal actions against those responsible for causing them great emotional trauma."

"Is he kidding?" Billy whispered to Abraham. "Don't let him scare you." Billy snickered loudly enough for the detective to hear.

"Have I said something amusing?" Manley looked at Billy.

"Well, as a matter of fact, captain, I think it's pretty amazing in our time that anyone could claim emotional trauma from watching a couple of porno flicks." Billy looked around the room, smugly proud of his declaration of support for the first amendment. "I mean, censorship is anathema on a university campus." He did not drop his eyes before the penetrating gaze of the detective. Abraham prayed he would shut up, but Billy thought he was on a roll. "I should think," the sarcasm dripped from his words, "that our state police would have something better to do with their time than bust some dirty movies."

Helen did not miss Abraham's blush. She also noticed the slight tremor in his arm.

"And who might you be?" asked Manley.

"Professor Billy Mann," Billy responded truculently. He was now spoiling for a fight.

"And were you present at the video presentation?"

"Oh no. I'm just an assistant professor. My status isn't exalted enough to rate an invitation to such events. But I know what's wrong with bluestockings whose delicate noses can be put out of joint by images on a screen."

The captain jotted Billy's name on his yellow legal pad. "Regardless of the opinion of your resident civil libertarian, we are taking this seriously. And Professor Henry has volunteered his office and secretary for the duration of our investigation." He removed a copy of the department roster from his brief case. "We'll be interviewing every member of the literature department. Ms. Bullock is now working on a schedule of appointments that won't clash with teaching assignments and office hours. You'll find appointment times in your mailboxes. We'd very much appreciate your taking these crimes as seriously as we do. Let me thank you in advance for your cooperation. The interviews will be short. And, I promise, painless." He looked at Billy. "And I can assure you, we won't use rubber hoses or truth serum." He laughed at Billy as derisively as he had been laughed at. The detective returned to the side of the chairman.

"Thank you Captain Manley," said Walter. "I can assure you that every member of this department will cooperate fully." He scowled at Billy. "Even Professor Mann, unexalted though he may be, will, I'm sure, give you his full attention when his turn comes. Isn't that correct, Billy?"

"But of course," Billy said. "I'd never think of doing otherwise." Billy wanted to say something about pigs on campus, but he bit his tongue. Images of his own undergraduate days filled his mind. Heady times when, at the slightest provocation, he'd march to protest police harassment. Why should this pig be any different even if he wore a decently cut business suit instead of a riot helmet. "Pigs are pigs," he whispered to Abraham and Helen.

"Why don't you stow it," Jack said to Billy. "This isn't one of your dumb-assed student rallies. Just do as you're asked and we'll get the damn thing over with." He nodded in the direction of Ben Rosenthal. "And if you need advice from a genuine civil libertarian, check with Ben."

Check with that jerk? Billy wanted to say. Instead, he offered a slight wave in Ben's direction. You old shit. You and Williams can both suck my dick. I'll get tenure without either of you. Billy's count of the promotion task force still gave him a positive vote without either of those dinosaurs. He could smile at them with impunity.

"I think we better talk as soon as possible," Abraham said to Billy after Walter and the cops left the room. He looked haggard. "I'm worried."

Billy grasped Abraham's arm. "Just relax. And for Christ's sake, don't panic. We're home free as long as we don't panic. They can't touch us unless we screw up."

"You two plotting again?" asked Helen. She was now pretty sure they were the university's most wanted.

Would she have something to tell Joan tonight. But she worried about Abraham. He looked so scared. She wanted to put her arms around him and tell him everything would be all right. But that would never do. Not now when all those sharks were circling. She looked at her colleagues now in animated conversation once again. Fortunately, none seemed to notice Abraham's condition. She put her arm in his and walked him to the coffee maker. "Buck up, Abraham, things could be much worse."

He shot her a curious look.

"At least no one kicked off." Helen squeezed his arm. Her concern for Abraham pushed aside her own troubles. "But what made you hook up with that slime-ball?"

Abraham was nearly panicked by Helen's apparent knowledge. He stammered, "How do you know?" He searched the room for sight of Billy. Relieved when he saw him smiling and chatting at the other end of the lounge, Abraham kissed Helen on the cheek. "God, I'm glad to be able to talk to someone other than Billy about this thing." She returned his chaste kiss. "And I'm glad it's someone I can trust. It was a stupid thing to do, but it was a lark. A way to get even with Berlin and Murdoch. I had no idea it could get so bollixed up." He shrugged. "State police, attorney general, law suits. Who knows how it'll end? And I can't tell Eleanor anything."

"Why not?"

"Billy says we can't tell anyone, especially not our wives. He says they've got to have deniability in case things turn sour."

Helen thought for a moment. "For a change, I think he's right. The fewer people who know, the better your chances to beat this rap."

For the first time that day, Abraham smiled. "You sound like some gangster in a bad mystery. Beat the rap, indeed. So, you think I shouldn't tell Eleanor?"

"Not yet. Wait until the investigation comes up dry." Helen nodded. "And, believe me, it'll come to a dead end. Remember, these guys aren't the FBI. They're cow state hicks." She paused. "You guys didn't make any mistakes, did you? Like leaving finger prints?"

"We wore surgical gloves."

"Or a trail they can follow back to whatever junk you got for the fruit salad or the porno videos?"

"We were very careful." Abraham felt some of his burden lift with those words. "Billy planned it all with enormous skill. He was really impressive," Abraham snickered, "even if he overplayed his cloak and dagger bit." The more Abraham thought about Billy's insistence on details, the more optimistic he became.

"It must have been quite a day," said Helen. "After this is all ancient history, I want to hear everything. Everything, you hear? But don't put anything in writing. You'll have to rely on your memory. The first rule has to be nothing in writing. Don't ever let anyone use your own words against you." Helen thrilled at suddenly being a co-conspirator. "Here I am offering advice to Al Capone. Can you beat that?"

Billy sauntered over. "You've got the magic touch, Helen old girl." He pointed at Abraham. "When I left this guy a few minutes ago, I thought he was about to faint. Must have been his guilty conscience about all those high grades he doles out to every victim in his class." Billy winked. "But I won't tell the gumshoes."

Abraham thought better of opening the running debate he had with Billy about minority students and guilt. He did think for a moment, though, of the student who attacked Ben Rosenthal. And of his assignment to get Billy involved in Maxine Jefferson's next march.

"I checked my mail box," said Calvin Willoughby as he poured a cup of coffee. "My appointment is for this afternoon." He looked distressed. "I was sure they'd run their interviews alphabetically. After all, Captain Manley did have the department roster."

"Maybe it's by seniority," Abraham suggested.

"Or scholarly distinction," Billy said with a nasty smile. "Or," he winked again, "perhaps they're interviewing all those with rap sheets first."

The bibliographer looked befuddled.

"Come on, Calvin, you've got a record." Another wink. "You can't have forgotten that hearing before Judge Bull Dyke." Billy was enjoying Calvin's obvious distress.

"Oh, surely the state police wouldn't have any knowledge of that," Calvin said seriously. "Purely a local campus matter, that was."

"Don't be too sure. The feminist militia has a long arm." Another wink. "I wouldn't be surprised if they had a pipeline right to the attorney general."

"He's joking," said Helen, aware of the older man's concern. She frowned at Billy.

Why don't you mind your own fucking business, Billy thought. Here I am having a little fun with this old geezer and you have to butt in. What a bunch of losers in this joint. After I get tenure, they'll have to jump through hoops before I vote for them. But he was chastened, especially as he saw Jack approaching the coffee table.

"So, Professor Loudmouth, are you done playing to the crowd?"

Jack pushed past Billy who stood in front of the coffee maker. When their shoulders touched, Billy thought Jack was looking for a fight. His fists clenched. What I wouldn't give to belt him right in his fucking mouth. He looked at Jack's thick middle. Or one punch to that paunch and the drunk would double up like a pretzel. I've got twenty five, thirty years on that lush. Could take him easy. His fists tightened. One more word, and it'll be curtains for you, Jack Williams. No fucking your black princess tonight after I get through with you.

But Jack simply filled his coffee cup and walked away.

Once again translating fantasy into reality, Billy unclenched his fists and smiled at Helen. "All talk, that guy. No guts when the gauntlet is dropped. I thought I'd have to deck him right here."

This man is crazy, Helen thought. She worried again about Abraham's association with a back-stabber like Billy Mann.

Mary Bullock entered the lounge and posted an interview list on the bulletin board. "Just in case some of you don't check your mailboxes today," she snapped. She had learned years ago that her faculty were forgetful in their self-centeredness. But never on pay day. Then every one of them went to their mailboxes. You can bet on that. Or if they're waiting to hear from journals to which they've sent their articles. Dear Jack had threatened to write a short story about them and their mailboxes. You'd get a glimpse into their paltry minds by having an observant narrator report only on them and their mailboxes. He'd have to be an omniscient narrator, of course, so that his readers might get a look into all those envelopes and notes. It'd be rich, you can bet on that. Mary smiled as she thought of the never written story. Just another one of the many dark plots Jack had tried out on her. If only I had the talent of a Joyce. God knows, the material is all around us. These clowns would make it easy. Every one of them is a Little Chandler. Even those few of us with real talent, he'd laugh, live fantasy lives infinitely richer than the frustrated, mean-spirited little world we actually inhabit. The more Jack drank in Mary's office or at home after one of her bountiful meals, the more morose would his reflections become. And, she reminded herself, this from one of those talented ones. "Any questions about the schedule," she barked, "see me or Walter. He'll be sharing my office for the duration." Much like a queen taking leave of her subjects, she walked from the room without looking to the right or the left.

Upon her departure, there were no nasty remarks from her subjects. If they feared anyone in the department, it was Mary Bullock. A good friend to some, she could make life miserable for those who crossed her. More than once she had intentionally misplaced mail her surly subjects were eagerly anticipating. She was known also to have altered teaching schedules to the great inconvenience of those she chose to punish. Always playing innocent when gingerly reproached for such transgressions, Mary would stare down her questioner. After such confrontations, she'd take out the can of Pledge and vigorously polish her desk. Jack would, of course, hear of each encounter. His admiration for her increased with every such recitation. Give 'em hell, Mary, give em' hell.

There was an immediate crowd in front of the bulletin board.

"She knows I play squash every Tuesday afternoon," wailed Billy. "She even reserved a court for me." He pursed his lips. "Isn't that right, Peter? Christ, we had a game set for tomorrow." He looked around for support. But no one spoke. "Believe me, she knew," Billy pouted. "She knows my Tuesday schedule. Squash and a swim."

"Poor baby," said Jack. "Gonna miss a day at the play-pen? Give me a break. Some lunatic's out there, or in here, for all we know, and this one's crying about a dumb game. The point is, Professor Billy, we have to help catch the bastard." He turned to get a fuller view of his colleagues. "Most of you weren't at the genius' banquet, but, I'll tell you, it was terrible." He pointed a finger at Billy. "A lot of people were very sick that night. Let's not forget that, buddy."

Ruined your night, old man? Pity. But, once again, Billy elected not to challenge Jack. There'll be a time and a place, believe me, to throttle you and your quick mouth. Oh yes, I'll lay you out. But good. Billy shook his head, as if a dim student had just offered another stupid answer. "You ought to try that dumb game, Jack. It'd get you in shape." He patted his flat stomach.

Jack rubbed his slight paunch. "In shape for what?" He tapped his head. "It's what's up here that counts. And here." He pointed to his heart. "One without the other doesn't cut the mustard. And this," he patted his stomach again, "this, my little squash boy, is a very distant third."

Ben Rosenthal, recognizing a tone he feared in Jack's voice, moved between the two. "Enough," he said, looking at Jack and ignoring Billy. "The last thing we need right now is a brawl. I think we've had quite enough bad news around here. A fist-fight in the literature department would be just perfect after Beverly's porno show and Murdoch's poisoned dinner." Ben's little smile made clear he had trouble taking the week-end's incidents very seriously. "I don't mean to make light of all this, but," he smiled more broadly, "with apologies to you Jack and the others who suffered at the banquet, but it does read like a bad burlesque." His laughter escaped his attempt to stifle it. "Especially since no one was seriously ill, it is the stuff of comedy." His eyes now crinkling, he looked at Jack. "You do see that, don't you?" He laughed again. "Old codgers like me, all dressed up and acting like serious patrons of culture, staring at dirty movies. It's rich is what it is. And then the banquet. I almost think we should give the engineers of such exquisitely deserved pain medals instead of the jail time Maxwell is screaming about." Jack remained impassive. "Come on, Jack, can you think of more deserving targets than those two? I heard our dear video queen fainted a couple of times. Wonderful. And the genius with a shit stained speech is perfect. Probably the most accurate criticism his prose has ever received. I'd gladly suffer a few stomach cramps to have seen the show."

Billy was elated by Ben's words. A medal would now play prominently in his fantasy recreation. But he had to maintain his pose. "Those sentiments from the ACLU? Shocking."

"I think they were terrific," said Helen. She blew a kiss at Ben. "Three cheers for the sanest comments I've heard today."

"Watch it, kiddo," Jack finally spoke. "The untenured among us life-long appointees should be more careful. Some of these good folks," he made a wry face at the room, "love to play all sides. Believe me, Beverly and the genius will hear everything said in this room before the day is over." He patted Ben's arm. "It's okay for him to say whatever he wants. He can't be touched. Besides, they know he can't stand either of them. But some of these weasels who want to score points will be on the phone as soon as they get back to their cubby holes." He was serious as he nodded his head in agreement with his own words. "Take care, kiddo." He looked at Billy. "That one was born teflon coated." He waved away Billy's attempt to interrupt. "Sonny, you get away with murder. Only God knows how or why, but so far, you've lived a charmed life around here." Jack shook Ben's hand. "You're probably right, but I'm still too close to it." He walked toward the door. "I'm going to see how Willie's doing."

As soon as Jack left the room, Billy mimicked, "see how Willie's doing." He scanned the room. "What do you think of that couple?" He moved his right forefinger in and out of his cupped left hand. "Now, that's what I call multi-culturalism," he smirked. Disappointed that no one picked up on his obscene gesture, Billy pushed the issue. "You all think it's just fine and dandy that a broken-down, white drunk is making it with the darling of the black academic establishment?" Still no responses. Billy whistled *The Camptown Races* as he shuffled out of the room. "Well, Andy," he said, "I guess we be in safe territory." He stopped at he door and turned to his colleagues. "Yes, Amos, we sure be safe here." He slammed the door behind him.

"That young man is headed for one big fall," said Ben to Helen and Abraham. "And I want to be there when it happens."

Abraham nodded his head, torn between loathing of Billy's behavior and fear of the future he and his partner faced.

"He's a loose canon," Helen whispered. "You better watch your back at all times, Ab. I wouldn't trust him if my life depended on it." She blushed. "And yours, my friend, may well depend on keeping Billy Mann in check." She looked at her watch. "I don't envy you, but if there's anything I can do, just give a holler. Now I've got to face my first class since you know what. I know everyone of them knows what happened." The momentary return to her old form evaporated. Her face darkened. "I don't look forward to it."

Abraham put his arm around Helen's waist. His own problems put aside for the moment, he walked her into the corridor. "It'll be fine. Don't worry. They're a lot more sensitive than that gang in the lounge." He strolled with her to her office. "You want company in class today?"

Helen shook her head. "It'd be even worse if they thought I needed a bodyguard. But thanks, anyway."

Abraham walked very slowly to his office. The last thing he wanted to talk about this day was the poetry of Robert Frost. Billy's door was closed. Probably licking his wounds and staring into his mirror. And to top off a perfect few days, I've got to convince him to march in Maxine's next rally. Abraham's head was throbbing. He wanted to go home and stretch out on the living room couch. He imagined the quiet house and the cooling effect of Eleanor's furnishings. But there were students to teach and office hours to keep. Worse, he had interviews scheduled with three of the Murdoch brigade. God, he moaned, what indignities will they subject poor Frost to this morning? Abraham entered his office, closed the door, and dropped his body into the desk chair. He reached for the aspirin bottle and shut his eyes. He could see no light at the end of the tunnel. Abraham shook his head. I can't even see the tunnel.

Walter Henry opened the bottle of tranquilizers as he sat at his desk. How can I write such a letter? he kept asking himself. He swallowed a valium, turned his chair to the window, and imagined Maxine Jefferson marching across the mall, emboldened by the support of the chair of the literature department.

The conversation with Jack and Ben had been terrible. Walter had felt the strength drain from his body when his two old friends told him of Maxine's threats. No judgmental hand wringing or words of disappointment at Walter's involvement with Dennis. Just measured, gentle analysis of the present predicament. And what choice did he really have? There were no options. He had to write the letter and trust a person he had no reason to trust. For God's sake, he had said, that woman's history is fraught with duplicity. She's double-crossed everyone who's ever dealt with her. How do I know she won't do the same to me after I write the letter?

But Jack and Ben convinced Walter. He had no choice, just as he had no guarantee Maxine would keep her word. Ben was more confident than Jack about Maxine's promise. "I think she'll do as she says. You remember, Jack, how matter of fact she was about her actions. She knows exactly the role she plays around here. Even her language is part of the performance. When she's not on stage, Maxine is someone you can deal with." Ben nodded his head. "At our ACLU meetings, she's a different person. There, she's the well-spoken, serious historian, not a rabble-rousing harridan. Yes, I think we can trust her. Besides, she has absolutely nothing to gain by outing Walter." Ben did not lower his voice or blush when he said this last. He had stared directly into Walter's eyes. At that moment, Walter knew he could trust Ben with his life. He was grateful to have these good men on his side.

"And there's the matter of Billy Mann," Ben said quietly. He looked down at his folded hands and pondered that problem.

"Billy Mann?" Walter asked.

"Yes," said Jack, "he's another piece in Maxine Jefferson's package." He looked at Ben to continue.

"She insists Mann must march in her next rally." Ben looked out the picture window and thought of better days.

"Billy Mann marching alongside Maxine?" Walter's voice rose. "Have you forgotten his little act when she marched on our building? He'll never do it." A new round of terror shook Walter's body. "Have you broached it to him?"

"We're leaving that to Abraham," said Ben.

"You mean, young Smith knows too?"

"Yes," said Jack, "but don't worry, Walter, he's all right. He's a good kid."

"But he's vulnerable." Walter trembled again.

"We're all vulnerable," Ben mused, still observing the campus scene below him.

"You know what I mean," Walter snapped. "He's at the mercy of too many of them. Abraham's hoping for tenure this year." Walter put his head in his hands. "I'm sorry, Ben. This hasn't been easy." He looked up at Jack. "What if Maggie and the boys find out?"

Jack walked to the window, his back to Walter. "Maybe it's time to tell them." His back stiffened as he awaited Walter's response. Silence. "Maybe it's time for you and Collins to come clean with your families." He was glad his back was to the room. No one could see his unease at his choice of words.

Ben's gaze went from the window to Walter. "Jack may be right. Speaking to Maggie may be the most liberating thing you can do."

"And it removes the possibility of her hearing about it from someone else." Jack sat down. "Wouldn't it be better to clear the air yourself than to have some malicious prick whisper in Maggie's ear?" He lit a cigarette. What he really wanted was a drink. "Of course it won't be easy, especially with your sons, but Ben's right. You'll be free."

Walter was pale. He smiled tightly. "So I tell my students with such smug confidence. The truth shall set you free." Tears filled his eyes. "Just words. Beautiful words." He stroked Shakespeare's bust. "But just words." Walter looked at Jack. "How can I tell them I love them, but I also love another man? Do you think Maggie will pat my head and tell me everything's fine. That we'll just continue our lives as if nothing's changed? And the boys? What'll happen to the boys when they learn their dad's a fairy? A fag. A homo. A queer." He spat out each word as he would a curse. Tears rolled down Walter's cheeks. He cried quietly but uncontrollably.

Jack wished he were anywhere else as his chair suddenly became unbearably uncomfortable. He glanced at Ben. The older man rolled his chair next to Walter's, leaned forward, and hugged him. Both men stood up, continuing to embrace. Ben patted Walter's back as one might a crying infant's. "It'll be okay. It'll be okay," he crooned as he kept rubbing Walter's back. "This, too, will pass, old friend. This, too, will pass."

Jack's eyes suddenly filled with tears. He thought this was one of the most beautiful things he had ever seen. He stubbed out his cigarette and joined the other two men. Together the three hugged and rocked to the soothing cadence of Ben's words. The intercom clicked on and Bullock's voice announced the arrival of Captain Manley. Jack leaned toward the speaker without removing his arms from the other two men. "Not now, Mary. Not now."

Bullock heard the desperate plea in Jack's voice. She dispatched the state police officer and wondered what was going on in Walter's office. She reached for her Pledge.

Sitting at his desk, the president finished reading Captain's Manley's report. He sighed as he closed the blue binder. He stared at the state police logo embossed on the cover. "Morons," he spoke aloud to the empty office. "All of them. Morons. I told them to call in the FBI. What do these hicks know about investigations?" He brought his fist down on the folder. "Damn traffic cops. That's what they are." He pressed the intercom. "You can send them in now." Richard stood up and walked to his spot. His back to the wall of kudos, he straightened his tie and painted a weak smile on his face.

The president's secretary announced Dean Donovan and Professors Murdoch and Berlin. Maxwell greeted the trio with forced affability. He was in no mood to listen to petty academic squabbles while perpetrators were still on the prowl.

"So, Richard, what have the gumshoes come up with?" Always shrewd, Patrick knew which button to push. Let him get it off his chest before they get to the subject that brought them all together on this crystalline morning. Beverly had wanted to say something about the beautiful weather and how glorious the campus looked, normally a perfect line to please Richard who spent an inordinate amount of his executive time on landscaping. The appearance of the university was as important to him as its academic mission. The president was fond of showing off the grounds to visitors, especially to prospective benefactors. Nobody's going to donate a plug nickel to a run-down, depressing campus. He worried the appearance of the university as he did his own apparel. First impressions, he would lecture his senior administrators, are lasting. Don't ever forget that. There's little you can do to overcome a negative first impression.

Richard generally pursed his lips after dispensing that piece of wisdom as he disapprovingly surveyed the attire of his subordinates. He had often thought of giving them Christmas subscriptions to *Gentlemen's Quarterly* instead of the usual bottle of expensive booze. That he did not grew out of his unhappy belief that they were sartorially a pretty hopeless bunch.

"You wouldn't believe the incompetence of Manley's minions," he smiled at the alliterative power of his prose. "Those traffic cops couldn't find the proverbial needle in the haystack."

"I don't think most of us could," Mitchell said dryly. He was rarely impressed by Richard's metaphorical prowess.

The president looked at him curiously, not sure about the professor's comment. Why the hell can't they ever say in plain English what they mean? Intellectual snobs, all of them. Gobbledygook's what it is. Thank God I don't have to read their whining memos. Richard's crackerjack secretary was adept at summarizing. At least she speaks English. "You know what I mean, Mitch."

Murdoch winced. My name is Mitchell, for Christ's sake. Mitchell. Is that too hard for you to manage? Two syllables shouldn't tax even your minuscule brain. But he said nothing.

"They've come up dry," the president continued. "Can you believe that? More than two weeks on the case. And with an army of investigators. State police, town police, campus police. An army of investigators and they don't have a clue." He pounded the folder again. "Nothing. Nada. Zip." He glowered at the folder. "Not a clue." He continued to look down at the impressive logo of the state police.

No one spoke until Patrick broke the silence. "Well, Richard, one can never tell when the clue will turn up that will break the case." His measured cadence was meant to comfort his superior. In reality, he no longer cared about the investigation. Once he had made it home that Saturday night, showered, and poured a large Irish whisky, he enjoyed replaying the evening. His fine moment, after all, had already passed. It was he who had stepped in to salvage the grotesque morning when Maxwell was overcome by paralysis. The banquet fiasco was no blot on his resume.

Murdoch was the chief victim. And Patrick had little affection for him. That Richard suffered a second humiliation in less than twelve hours, and before everyone who mattered in Patrick's quest for the presidency, could only further the inevitability of that longed for goal. As he sat, dressed in a handsome silk dressing robe, whisky in hand, the dean realized it had not been so bad a day. "Yes, Richard," the brogue more pronounced and slower with each syllable, "you can never tell when the police will get lucky." Patrick looked up from his folded hands. "And you've certainly done everything one could ask from a chief executive."

Richard nodded. "That's true, isn't it." He offered a half smile to his dean. "But do all of them out there," he pointed to the window, "realize how diligent I've been?"

"Of course they do." Patrick spoke even more deliberately. He felt like a Sunday school teacher trying to convince his charges that God loved them. He thought of Oscar Lansing teaching his little people about the Lord and the Martians. Patrick chuckled to himself. Richard would probably be enchanted by the owl's speculations about extra terrestrials and divinity. The sooner he leaves the presidency, the sooner will this become a great university. Billy Mann was not the only campus citizen with a finely tuned fantasy life.

Patrick's words had a salutary effect. Richard covered the police report with a pile of travel folders. "Barbara and I have got to get out of here for a few days," he said as he pointed to a glossy photograph of a palm-lined beach. "I think Acapulco would be nice," he mused. Images of designer condoms struggled with the memo he had received from the trio awaiting his attention. "All right," he sighed, "let's get to the latest squabble among the guardians of humane learning." The president glanced once more at the waves breaking on the white beach before he opened a green file containing numerous letters about the literature department's recruitment. He looked half imploringly, half belligerently at Patrick. "I still don't know why a university president has to be bothered with such matters." Maxwell stood up and went to the window. He kept his back to his visitors. "The last time I looked at Oscar's little book of regulations, or whatever that thing's called, I read that the matter you're all hot about falls within the purview of the provost." Alliteration again. He turned away from the window. "Why did you insist that we meet without Lansing here?" He pointed a finger at Patrick. "Of all people, you should know better than that." He wagged the finger at the other two. "You should know better, too. Oscar's a stickler for protocol. He'll fry your asses if he thought you were plotting another end run." Richard looked at his watch. "You've got exactly ten minutes to make your pitch before the provost arrives." He held up his hand to silence Patrick. "Ten minutes and no more. I'm not going to get involved in some stupid battle over protocol." Richard sat down at his desk. He took his wrist watch off and placed it before him.

"Nine minutes."

"This is outrageous," said Patrick. "You led us to believe that we would meet without Oscar."

"And so we are," Richard replied sweetly. "Eight minutes. I suggest you get going." He enjoyed Patrick's rare display of discomfort. You think I don't know what you really want? Squirm, you little bastard. When the chips are down, dear dean, I'm still the head honcho around here. He glowered at Patrick. And head honcho I will remain until I decide to leave for greener pastures. Not, my dear dean, because some mackerel snapper decides for me. He tapped his watch. "The second hand is sweeping, folks."

Beverly spoke. She had never seen Patrick so furious. Veins pulsated on his forehead. She was afraid of what anger might prompt him to say that would upset their plans. "Richard, I assume you've read the latest proposal from Mitchell and me." She awaited the president's response.

Maxwell nodded. He held up their letter. A summary of its points was clipped to the first page.

"The situation hasn't changed since we last met about the future of literary studies on this campus."

Oh yes it has, thought Richard. We're now a center for research into culture and pornography. He wanted to laugh.

"Beverly is quite right," Mitchell spoke. "If we leave literary studies to old-fashioned scholars, there'll be no future. Just more of the same tired stuff." He gave Maxwell one of his most ingratiating looks. "And I know you don't want to be the custodian of outmoded methodologies. Certainly not someone like yourself who wrote such a groundbreaking book. You in particular understand how important it is to encourage new approaches and to bring in fresh young minds." Murdoch disappointed even himself. How could he serve up such silly stuff? "You surely recall the unflattering comments the tired, entrenched establishment offered about your book." He smiled knowingly. "But time and keener minds proved you correct." Yes, indeed, Mitchell thought, they proved you were an idiot. "You see, Richard, your personal vantage point is exactly the reason we know you'll understand what we're talking about."

Richard's amusement at the dean's continuing unhappiness was no match for base flattery. His defenses crumbled. The president pondered his finely manicured nails while he examined his options. He thought of the dentist's fat fingers. No genius could ever praise that man's work. So what if Murdoch's words were as fraudulent as his scholarship. They were now on the record. Nixon's mistake was that his recordings were found out. Not so with this president. Not even his secretary knew of the existence of the superb recording system he had installed in the handsome desk. Some New York whiz-kid had set it up when the Maxwells bought the desk on their last Manhattan shopping spree before moving west. What was that line about having your name in print even if it's misspelled? Richard nodded at Mitchell and snapped on his intercom. "Have the provost wait when he arrives." And for the benefit of his visitors, "Offer him carrot juice or whatever those bible thumpers drink." He smiled broadly as he placed his watch back on his wrist. "Now, what were you saying, Patrick?"

The dean cleared his throat to insure a mellifluous register. Regaining his fawning mode, he winked at Mitchell. "We must follow the lead of Mitchell and Beverly in this matter." He smiled benevolently at the president. "There must be a number of stellar appointments from the outside if the literature department is to be saved." He raised his hands as if to deliver a benediction. "And there can never be a distinguished university without a distinguished literature department."

"And what makes a distinguished department?" asked Richard, knowing what the answer would be.

"One that the profession as a whole admires," said Mitchell.

"I thought Walter Henry's group was admired," the president responded, playing devil's advocate. "At least that's what Patrick's annual reports always claim."

"That's true enough," said the dean. "But times change and Walter's department has not been willing to acknowledge those changes. Henry himself is surrounded by a cadre of old men. And while most of them had respectable reputations once upon a time, they've now been passed by."

Not wanting to be left out of the action, Beverly interrupted. "Even a younger so-called star like Wilma Crouse mines very old territory." Beverly batted her eyes.

"But everyone wants her," Richard said. "Look at those rich offers we've had to match." He wished he could return to his vacation brochures.

"She does have other things going for her." Mitchell's voice was insinuating and arrogant. "You understand that, of course." He was patently condescending to the president.

Of course I understand that, you self-congratulatory bastard. "I might suggest, as a layman to be sure," Richard spoke sweetly, "that one of her greatest attributes is her wonderful prose style." He walked to a book shelf and removed Wilma's book on Dickens. "I really enjoyed this one." It was one of the few faculty books Richard had actually read. He did not say it was required reading in Barbara's monthly book group, or that his wife led the discussion of Wilma's study at a meeting which took place at the Maxwell house. Richard thought it would be marvelous public relations for him to be present and join in the discussion. His reading had not been motivated solely by intellectual curiosity. But it was true that he enjoyed Wilma's discussion of one of the few nineteenth-century novelists he knew something about. He liked motion pictures made from classic texts.

Of course you'd like her work, thought Murdoch. Simple minded judgments about a writer and his age. She should have been a historian. Or even a sociologist. But a critic? Never. He often held Crouse's work up to his doctoral students as examples of the wrong-headedness of a profession gone soft, and of the excesses of affirmative action. "No, Richard, I was not referring to her style which, by the way, I would call flat and unimaginative." The arrogance was apparent again. "I was referring, of course, to her race. We already have well-known women in our midst," he nodded in Beverly's direction, "but a black female humanist is still a rarity." He waved his hand in a dismissive gesture. "They usually go into something like political science or sociology, you know."

"And the assistant professors your plan would punish?" asked Richard. His question exasperated Murdoch. Since the president had already approved the announcements of vacancies which would be prominently displayed in several leading publications, and which had so inflamed Oscar, Mitchell wanted this puerile game to end.

"They're not going anywhere." Mitchell glanced at his watch. "They'll still be here whatever we do. And to answer your question, both Mann and Smith are chips off the old geezers' block. Young men with old ideas."

"But good enough to lend balance to the people we hope to bring in," added Beverly. "And they'll certainly be promoted one day. We surely aren't punishing Billy or Abraham. Far from it. In the long run, their careers will profit from association with the quicker, more contemporary minds of new colleagues."

Murdoch smiled. Beverly was in good form today.

The intercom crackled on Richard's desk. "Doctor Lansing has been waiting for fifteen minutes. He has another meeting in a half hour."

Richard shrugged at his visitors. "Please ask the provost to join us."

Oscar was surprised to see the other three already engaged with Maxwell. It was plain to him that the meeting had begun without him.

The president waved him to his customary chair to his right. As always, Richard noticed Oscar's impeccable attire. "New suit?" he asked.

Lansing nodded without a smile. "Yes, as a matter of fact."

"Got a big date tonight?" asked Patrick. He winked at the president.

"I'm having dinner with the president of the alumni association."

Maxwell's eyes narrowed. "What's the occasion?" He wondered what mischief his second-in-command was plotting now. Ever since he had yielded rather than risk a defeat at a senate inquiry, he noticed the provost's manner was more confident. Even Patrick had agreed that it would be prudent to avoid a senate skirmish over protocol. Especially since they had already won the battle. A bit of groveling and a few mea culpas at a private meeting with the owl were preferable to a full-scale hearing. Only the president of the senate wanted to press on, but Horatio Ginsberg's freshly cleaned suit would have to await another great moment.

Lansing's smile chilled the president. "No occasion. Just an opportunity to clear up some misunderstandings," he looked at Beverly. "Misunderstandings about what we do at this university." He opened his brief case. "Now about the literature department."

But before the discussion could return to the business of the day, Mitchell stood up and rushed to the window. "What in Christ's name are they marching about today?"

The others joined the genius. There before them was a large group of protesters moving across the beautifully manicured mall toward the administration building. Richard's first fear was that they would ruin the grass.

"Maxine Jefferson again," growled Patrick. He looked to Richard. "What's her grievance today?"

Maxwell spread his hands. "I haven't any idea." He asked his secretary to send in his administrative assistant. "Roger's not in the office right now. He got a call and raced out. I'll send him in as soon as he gets back."

"I think it must be the student union business," said Oscar.

"Oh God," Maxwell groaned, "I've forgotten all about that damn thing." He put his hands to his head. "How can I be bothered with that in the midst of everything else?" He shook his head. "I've got a bellyful of tension with the rape, the dirty movies, the mad poisoner. Now this." He sat at his desk. Acapulco looked more attractive than ever. "I sent that Jefferson woman a reasonable counter offer. Even Ben Rosenthal and the ACLU endorsed it." He returned to the window. "So now she's got them protesting. Not even a reply to my offer. Another march on my building." He snapped on the intercom. "Get campus security over here now."

Beverly and Mitchell looked to Oscar for clarification. "Maxine Jefferson demands a black student union building. Richard countered with a promise of a minority student union building." Oscar shook his head. "Even the university lawyers advised against it. They're sure a union for minority students wouldn't stand a court challenge. And, believe me, there'll be a challenge."

"My counter offer was a decent one. It would satisfy all minorities without giving special treatment to any one of them." He pointed at the advancing crowd. "But do you think that would satisfy her? There's your answer. She thinks she can get whatever she demands. Can get? Should get is more like it. Well, lady, not this time." Richard bellowed at his secretary. "Where the hell are the police?"

"Probably chasing down the monsters who ruined their day," said

Oscar, nodding at Beverly and Mitchell. A slight smile played on the provost's face. The corners of his eyes crinkled.

"You think it's humorous, do you?" asked Patrick. Never missing an opportunity to challenge the owl, the dean was about to continue his scolding when Mitchell interrupted him.

"Am I crazy or is that Jack Williams marching next to Maxine? I don't believe it."

"And there's Ben arm in arm with Abraham Smith. What are they doing there?" Beverly was genuinely horrified. "And Wilma Crouse."

"Humiliated at their debate, and now she marches with them?"

"Hold on," said Beverly. "Will you look at who's running across the mall to join the march."

"Is that Billy Mann?" asked Patrick.

"It is," said Mitchell. "I'd have bet my house against that guy ever joining forces with Maxine. Not too long ago he wanted to kill her. Now he marches with her. I don't get it."

"And your department wants to promote those two?" Richard was furious. "Well, this takes care of them all right." He pointed a finger at Oscar. "I don't want to hear another word from you about Patrick's recruitment plan. Those two traitors will just have to cool their heels for a good long time." He was livid. "I only wish I could get their tenured buddies." Oscar thought better than challenging the president at this moment of his irrationality. He ignored the dean's smug look in his direction. Oscar knew there'd be a proper time and place to deal with this entire matter. He did not take the president's charge seriously, nor was he afraid to take on the dean. But he, too, was curious about a literature department delegation marching with Maxine Jefferson.

"It's about time," said Maxwell, as a horde of campus police formed a line in front of the administration building. He moved closer to the window, folded his arms across his chest, and smiled broadly. He hoped the protesters could see him. He wanted them to know he could not be intimidated. Richard waved the others from the window. He wanted to be seen alone, facing the mob, in case there was a photographer below.

The president's administrative assistant entered the office. "You've got to see this," he said, out of breath, holding up the next day's edition of the campus paper. He thrust it at the president. "Look at the front page." Richard's jaw tightened as he read. "What the hell's going on here?" He threw the paper on the desk for the others to see. A bold black border highlighted Walter Henry's open letter to the university community. "Have they all gone crazy in that department?"

"I don't believe it," said Beverly. "It must be a gag."

"Walter writing such a thing?" asked an astonished Mitchell. "It doesn't make any sense." He laughed nervously. "They're all committing suicide."

The dean rubbed his chin. "This is no mere coincidence," he mused. "At least five of them marching and now this odd letter from Walter." He looked at his audience. "Why are they doing this? That's a mystery every bit as interesting as your pornography and poison." The dean was at a loss as he tried to find an easy explanation. "But we will get to the bottom of this puzzle also," he said.

Beverly was chilled by Patrick's ominous tone. She feared for the future of her department. And, more immediately, for her promotion. She looked for comfort from Mitchell, but found none. He was as befuddled as everyone else in the room.

The president began to wave to the crowd now stopped before the police line. He continued to smile. "Make sure you stay away from the window," he said through his smile. "I want those bastards to think I'm all alone here in my office and not the least bit frightened of them." He thought of the board's rejection of his request for bullet-proof glass. Richard made a mental note to ask again. He snapped on the intercom. "Get Roger out there to take pictures. And tell him to be sure to get those literature people. I want a photographic record of all of them." He slid open a large window in order to better hear the crowd's chants.

"Yo, yo, yo, Maxwell's gotta go. Yo, yo, yo, Maxwell's gotta go." It was Maxine's voice booming through her bull horn that led the chanting. "Yo, yo, yo, Maxwell's gotta go. Yo, yo, yo, Maxwell's gotta go." She waved her left arm and urged her followers on. Protesters raised their placards in rhythm to the words. Richard's smile tightened as he read the banners. Richard Maxwell is a Dick. Screw Maxwell. Richard the Faint Hearted.

"That one must be a history major," Mitchell laughed.

The president shot a dirty look at the genius. "I don't think this is the time for jokes," he snapped. "Don't you realize the mischief those thugs can cause."

"And the job they can do to the grass," Oscar said wryly.

"Do you see your professors' lips moving? They're yelling right along with Jefferson." Richard shook his finger at Patrick. "You better get to the bottom of this. I want a report on my desk tomorrow morning. What kind of a game are those whackos playing?" The president stared at the dean. "You better find out what's going on in your little domain."

Out on the mall, the representatives of humane letters were far less comfortable than they appeared to be from the president's suite.

Jack Williams moved next to Wilma. "Can you believe what we're doing to protect Walter?" He returned Maxine's insistent look in his direction. "Okay, okay, don't get your water hot." He raised his voice and joined the cadence. "Yo, yo, yo" he shouted, "Maxwell's gotta go. Fucking Jesse Jackson's turned protests into rhymed nonsense."

"But you sound like you're into it." Wilma nudged Jack. "It's like being at a football game." She joined him. "Yo, yo, yo, Maxwell's gotta go. All I need now is a pom pom."

None of the literature department members was willing to carry a placard. "That's where we draw the line," Ben had said to Maxine. "Our agreement was only to march." She had nodded her assent. In fact, she was delighted they were there as she was satisfied with Walter's letter which she had read before its delivery to the paper. It was Maxine who had placed the professors in the first row of march. She, too, had a photographer in tow.

Billy Mann pushed his way to the front of the marchers and now stood next to Abraham.

"I was afraid you'd backed out," said Abraham. He nodded to Maxine. "Yo, yo, yo, Maxwell's gotta go," he shouted. "What the hell, Billy. We've got nothing to lose anyway." Abraham was sure their days were numbered at the university. Each time the telephone rang, his heart skipped a beat. He was sure it was only a matter of time before the state police would come for him. Eleanor had been frantic about Abraham's erratic behavior before he violated the agreement with Billy and told her everything.

"You did what?" It was after breakfast and Eleanor and Abraham were alone in the house. The children had left for school and Abraham had no classes until that afternoon. "You and Billy Mann were responsible for all that?" Eleanor turned white. "What in God's name were you thinking? Were you crazy?" It was not the way Abraham had hoped the conversation would begin.

The sun reflected off Billy's gold earring. "Might as well dress for the occasion" he had told Sally as he modeled his outfit before leaving the house. She hugged him. Billy had also broken his silence. Sally knew everything and thought Billy's caper was his best yet. "You'll never be caught." She gave him a long, deep kiss. "You're just too clever for them." For Sally, the events of the now infamous Saturday were just further evidence of Billy's genius. She had hungered for every detail. When Billy told her of the tape recordings and his plans for them, Sally was beside herself with joy. "God, it gets me hot." She rubbed against him. They ended up in bed. Giggling and fucking away the afternoon, she thought it a grand time. He feared it might be their last intimacy until he was allowed a conjugal visit.

"Finally got that earring?" Abraham said. "Either you're now sure of your masculinity or you just don't give a damn." Believing he was doomed, Abraham felt liberated. "Why not? We've nothing to lose."

Billy shot him a glance. "You told Eleanor?"

"Yes. Seemed pointless not to now. And you?"

Billy nodded. "Sally knows everything."

"How'd she take it?"

"She thought it was sexy stuff. We hopped into the sack." He shrugged. "The confession was a frigging aphrodisiac. And Eleanor?"

"She thinks we're crazy."

"And that's it? Not even a hand job?" Billy laughed.

Instead of the anger Abraham usually felt at Billy's dirty comments, he joined his partner's laughter. "No, not even a smile."

"What the hell are you two laughing about?" asked Jack. "President Goofy is watching us," he pointed to the third floor window, "and his factotum is snapping away." He looked in the direction of the short, fat man with a camera. "I'd like to shove that thing up his ass."

"Except he'd probably like it," said Billy.

"At least you'll take a great photo," said Jack. He shook his head as he examined Billy's get-up. "What rodeo are you entering?"

Billy extended his arms and did a full circle. "Pretty snazzy, don't you think?" He was a vision in denim. Except for the lizard boots and earring, he did appear dressed for a rodeo. Jeans, denim shirt and jacket, even a blue and white denim bandanna around his neck. A black cowboy hat completed the outfit.

"I think he looks wonderful," said Wilma. She touched the earring. "I wish I had one just like it."

"Ask your boyfriend. Maybe he'll get you a pair." His sense of finality allowed him that comment, but neither Jack nor Wilma seemed to mind. Billy smiled at Maxwell's assistant who was at that moment aiming his camera in his direction. He waved his hat and struck a pose. "Come out from behind those cops and I'll really give you something to take a picture of." He thrust his pelvis at Roger.

Ben was appalled at his younger colleagues' levity. "Come on, men. At least act as if you're serious. The last thing we need is for Maxine to add new conditions to this awful arrangement."

"Like what?" Billy snapped. "Having our great chairman and his pediatrician do a little sixty nine in front of Maxwell's office?"

Ben was unhappy to learn that Billy was aware of Walter's problem. He shook his head at Jack. "Now this whole distasteful exercise may be for nothing." He grabbed Billy's arm and pulled him aside. They stood at the periphery of he line of march. "That's enough of that. Do you understand? The only reason we're doing this is to protect Walter and we're not going to have him outed by a self-serving little bastard like you shooting off his mouth." Ben was trembling with anger. "One word from you and I'll make sure your career is over. And I mean in the entire profession, not just here. Have I made myself clear? Not a word."

Billy smiled sweetly at Ben and snarled. "Fuck you, Rosenthal. I'll say what I want whenever I want." He was jaw to jaw with the older man. "And while we're at the warning stage, let me warn you." He poked Ben's chest with each word. "If I go down, your beloved Walter Henry goes down with me." He snickered. "Not on me. With me. You get that, Mister ACLU? I don't give a fiddler's fuck about what you think of me. But you better make sure you vote right at tenure time or I'll blow the loudest whistle you ever heard. It'll be Walter Henry who'll find it hard to get another job, not me."

Ben pushed Billy's hand away. "You are a hateful viper." He wiped his forehead. "But even the devil must be dealt with."

"You're sweating, old man." Billy's smile did not leave his face. "I guess we'd call this a Mexican stand-off, wouldn't we? You vote for me and I keep my lips buttoned about the fag." He extended his hand for the handshake that would seal the bargain.

Ben pushed Billy's hand aside.

"Watch out for that bad heart of yours, old man." Billy put out his hand once again. "Either you shake or I'll make a fucking bee-line to Maxwell's office right now." He whispered nastily, "you see, Rosenthal, I have absolutely nothing to lose. And, I promise you, I can blow that whistle without feeling one pang of guilt about what happens to good old Walter."

"I'm sure that's true," said Ben, who was now struggling to breathe deeply. The color had left his face moments before. He reluctantly shook Billy's hand.

"That's more like it," Billy said. He put his arm on Ben's shoulder. "Now, don't go into cardiac arrest. I want you to take good care of yourself." The two men looked like old friends, shaking hands and talking in low tones. "At least until the tenure meeting is over. After that, you can drop dead for all I care." Billy felt his earring and adjusted his cowboy hat. "Now I have a march to continue." He took Ben's arm. "Shall we dance?" He offered an exaggerated, grotesque wink. "I think this has been a fruitful conversation, don't you, Ben?" He blew a kiss and rejoined Abraham in the front line of the protest. And I've got a sweet surprise for you, too, if you dare cross me, you faint-hearted goody-goody.

"What was that all about?" asked Abraham.

"Nothing at all, Abe. Nothing at all. Ben and I were just getting to know each other a little better. That's all. Now let's march. Yo, yo, yo, Maxwell's gotta go." Billy unfurled a yellow cloth and wrapped it around his waist. On it was neatly printed in large blue block letters, "Protest." A smaller word, "under," appeared above the larger. He waved to the president's assistant. "Use your zoom lens, Roger. Get me and my sash." There was no thrusting of the pelvis this time.

Jack pointed to Billy. "See how the son-of-a-bitch is trying to cover all his bases. You see that, Ben."

"You don't know how successful that man's been today." Ben now breathed more easily. "Billy's the devil, Jack, and I just made a bargain with him."

Jack thought Ben was about to drop. He grabbed his arm.

"I'm all right. Don't worry, I'm not going to keel over. It's my soul that just got more tarnished."

Jack looked quizzically at Ben. He waited for him to continue.

"This isn't the time or place to discuss it, but you should know I just agreed to vote for Mann's promotion." Before Jack could respond, Ben moved ahead of him. "Yo, yo, yo, Billy's got to go," he chanted softly. His eyes misted. "Yo, yo, yo, Rosenthal's gotta go."

The marchers now stood face to face with a row of campus police. Hands on hips, Maxine stared at the president three floors above. She brought the bull horn to her lips. "We demand a meeting, Mister President. A public meeting." She pointed at three reporters. "A public meeting with the press present."

The crowd cheered. The police locked arms. The president continued to smile down from his office.

"Well, say something," he whispered. "Say something, Oscar, Patrick. What do you think I pay you for?" He turned away from the window. "It's time for you to earn your keep. What do you think I should do?" He sat down at the desk. "Why won't they just leave me alone?" He looked at the white capped waves.

"I suggest you meet with them," said Oscar. "You don't have the luxury of options." He sipped ginger ale. "Admittedly, she should have responded to your offer of a multi-minority student union in the same professional manner as your reply to her request. But the fact is she did not. She's put you in the position now of either meeting with her or giving the appearance, wrong as we know it is, that you're retreating from some imaginary agreement." He went to the window. "And we know Jefferson is adept at using crowds and the media to serve her agenda. Yes, Richard, I'm sure you must meet with them. But let's arrange the meeting on our terms, not hers."

Privately, Patrick agreed with the provost's remarks, but, politically, he was unable to publicly say so. There must always be clearly articulated differences between him and his chief adversary for the president's ear, and, perhaps, for the presidency itself. Patrick could not take at face value the provost's oft stated position that he had no desire to be a campus president. Had he known how true was Oscar's statement, the dean's rhetorical stances might have been less pronounced. But Patrick believed no one.

"Once again, I must disagree with the provost," he said. "To meet with a mob of rabble-rousers, especially at the point of a gun, or at least at the point of a bull-horn," he smiled to himself, "is to begin negotiations from a position of weakness." He looked directly at Maxwell. "And a president should never appear weak. Strength is all those people understand." The dean took his place now at the window. "Look at them. A disgrace to the university." He moved to Maxwell's side. "A disgrace to higher learning, to rational discourse, to the rule of law." The dean was warming to his rhetoric. Oscar rolled his eyes and sat down.

Patrick walked to the center of the room. How far dare he go? "Those hooligans down there can't even read the president's message about a minority union. They're not students. They're simply attending the university because of this country's wrong-headed, insane, and I must say it, suicidal chase after equality." He leaned toward Richard. "But there isn't any such thing as intellectual equality. Never has been. It's a bootless chase to begin with." The dean clasped his hands and closed his eyes.

The worshipful pose, groaned Oscar to himself. The president was transfixed as usual whenever his dean's words began to soar.

"How can that disgrace to our profession dare suggest, no, demand, anything from us? Nonsense. We must meet her illiterate horde's pathetic display of strength with our legally granted powers. A firm, unequivocal display of strength far greater than theirs." Patrick had been mercifully brief. "No, Richard, send down the word that a meeting at this time is out of the question. Further, that if they do not disperse immediately, you will have them arrested and suspended from this university." He nodded smartly at Oscar. "I am sure the powers of the president that I am suggesting are clearly enumerated in your precious little book of regulations. Are they not?"

Oscar stood up. "They are. But, Richard, they are to be invoked by you only in extraordinary circumstances." He returned the dean's smart look. "These are not such circumstances."

The president swiveled his chair to the window. He placed both hands to his forehead as if in deep thought. He weighed Oscar's rejoinder to Patrick. Only the chanting from below broke the silence of the room. Beverly and Mitchell sat quietly watching the power struggle play out before them. She feared the president would take Patrick's advice. He smiled inwardly at the paltry stakes involved. But he thought it a grand political opportunity if Richard did indeed arrest Ben, Jack, and Wilma. Even, hopefully, Walter too. Mitchell did not return Beverly's worried look.

Maxwell stood up and went to his office door. "Please get the director of public safety on the phone." He put his hand on the provost's shoulder. "I appreciate your concern, Oscar, but I do think these are extraordinary circumstances." He returned to the window. "They will be ordered to disperse immediately or they'll be arrested. Patrick is right. This is no time for weakness. They must be taught a lesson now, or their civil disobedience will escalate. Then this great university will be turned into a battle field." He slammed his fist onto the state police logo. "I will never allow that to happen."

Richard was sure his action would make the national press and only enhance his attractiveness to search committees elsewhere. In these days everyone is looking for a strong leader who's willing to preserve a safe academic environment. Well, Richard Maxwell is willing to stand tall. He began framing a ringing statement that would kick off tomorrow's press conference. The only question now was what to wear. His appearance on television and in the press must convey strength of purpose and informal elegance. An appearance any presidential search committee would admire.

Patrick was delighted that he had bested the provost once again, but he feared the repercussions if protesters, especially, professors, were arrested. He hoped for a personal win-win situation. They must all disperse.

The literature professors now stood arm in arm with Maxine in the front line. They could feel the breath of the officers facing them. Billy taunted a young cop. "Be a hero, man. Go ahead, man. Use your night stick. Get your picture on the eleven o'clock news. But make sure you club one of them. Hitting a white guy won't make it." He laughed derisively at the nervous young officer. "Slug a darkie and you've got it made." Billy moved as close as possible to the pale, grim-faced younger man. He spoiled for a confrontation. His eyes danced. Come on, prick, hit me, they urged. Raise your club and I'll have your badge.

"Knock it off," said Abraham, pulling Billy back. "Leave him alone. For God's sake, he's not much older than your students." Billy's look of hatred startled Abraham. He put his hands on Abraham's chest and pushed him away. "Mind your own fucking business." He glowered. "Don't ever touch me again. Don't you dare put your hands on me again."

The director of public safety arrived on the scene. A tall man, the director now stood between his officers and the protesters. He raised his arms, trying to quiet the crowd. "Now hear this. All of you. Hear this. You must disperse immediately. If you do not disperse, you will be arrested. President Maxwell has ordered that you disperse immediately." He stared at Maxine's legions.

"He's serious," said Billy as he removed his sash. "I'm getting the hell out of here." His manner now conciliatory, he urged Abraham to join him. "Let's go, Abe. The last thing we need is jail." He nodded knowingly. "With all my planning, something might have gone wrong. Who knows what we might have touched without our gloves on. And as of now, they don't have our prints on file." He looked at his hands. "Let's hit the road now." He nudged Abraham's arm. "Now," he said between clenched lips.

Abraham was once again nervous. Billy might be right, but what about the agreement with Maxine?

As if reading his thoughts, Billy scolded, "Fuck Walter. We've got to think about our own skins." He pushed Abraham away from the other marchers. "Do you think he'd risk his future for us? Sure he would. In a pig's eye, he'd go out on a limb for a couple of untenured assistant professors." Billy was pleased by Abraham's willingness to be led away from the crowd. The two men quickly left the field of battle.

"Look at them run." Richard Maxwell was exultant. "And if they try it again, we'll throw them back again." Tomorrow's headlines looked better by the minute as the president watched the crowd disperse before the advancing security officers. Not even Maxine Jefferson's raised fist in his direction lessened Richard's delight. "Run, baby, run," he shouted at the now closed window.

Patrick was as happy as the president, but he kept his pleasure under tight control. The win-win situation was now his to savor. But later with Irish whisky and soft music. Much better that way. Now was the time for a few magnanimous words for Oscar, and, of course, effusive congratulations for the president. Patrick whispered the former before loudly complimenting Maxwell for his heroic stand.

Beverly watched from the window as her colleagues walked away together.

"Did you notice the two assistant professors leave as soon as the warning was issued?" asked Mitchell. "Nothing to worry about there. Those two will take whatever we dish out." He rubbed his hands together. "My dear, I do believe we're home free." Mitchell looked at his watch. "Got to run now." He shook hands all around and rushed from the room.

"I wonder which tart is to service our genius today." Patrick smiled and shook his head. "It's really too bad he can't lead a moral life." He looked to Beverly for confirmation of his judgment, but she remained impassive. "And I do believe Isobel is a lovely woman."

Beverly was not only surprised that Patrick knew about Mitchell's philandering, but that he was capable of such talk. As did so many others, she believed the dean was asexual and hardly interested in anything as coarse as Mitchell's love life. But here he was offering comments worthy of a precocious schoolboy with raging hormones. That he even noticed Isobel interested Beverly. Another item to tuck away for possible future speculation. Could Patrick Donovan have an erotic side? She had recently screened *Priest* for her assistants. The subject of film depictions of the clergy and sex interested her as another project to exploit. She had read an article about it in one of the magazines Marty had bought for her. She recalled the accompanying photos of naked men wearing only clerical collars and cavorting before an ornate altar. God, research is wonderful, she had said half seriously as she turned the glossy pages. Not even Marty's comment that the priests were circumcised disturbed her research. Although she did think that might produce an interesting footnote. She jotted a few words next to a picture of a Cardinal with a hard-on.

Peter Chase was stretched out on the couch, trying to read the inelegant prose of his doctoral students. "He's cloned an army of them. Why did I ever assign that charlatan's book to the seminar?" he shouted to Alice who worked in the kitchen. "This one tries to write just like him." He threw the typed pages onto the coffee table. Peter yawned and put his hands behind his head. Life had been much better since Alice agreed to their becoming a typical suburban couple. No more overnights without Peter. Their open marriage was to be replaced by the conventional relationship they used to rail against. Well, almost, said Peter to himself. He now frequented a gym he had recently discovered when he and Alice were shopping at the mall. A respectable health club, he had no need to keep it secret from his wife. In fact, he often asked her to come along and join the women's aerobic classes. Even if Alice, who disliked exercise, decided to accompany him, there would be nothing to hide. The men's showers, whirlpool, sauna, and lockers were separated from the women's by a large co-ed swimming pool. Peter sometimes wished the pool were for men only. Hell, you can't have everything. He could still show off his great body and stroke when he did laps. And the brief racing suit he wore surely added a touch of mystery for those who might be interested in meeting him in the men's quarters. True to his word to himself when he opted for a traditional marriage, Peter's encounters at the gym were infrequent and discreet. Since he had convinced himself that adultery must involve another woman, he could also convince himself that he remained faithful to Alice. He did not break the rules of their newly formed monogamous union.

When the telephone rang, Peter was not surprised to hear Alice refer to the caller by name. "No, Mitchell. No, not tonight. Please believe me. I was serious when I told you it was over." Alice carried the cordless phone into the living room and sat next to Peter. She smiled. "I know, Mitchell. I really do want to remain friends." She shook her head. "No, not even one for old time's sake." She laughed. "I'm glad you can laugh too." She put down the phone. "I think he's finally got it." Alice leaned over and kissed Peter's head. "Dinner in about ten minutes," she said as she got up.

Peter was delighted by Alice's new-found openness. Formerly, he could only guess that Mitchell was on the line. Either Alice would be cryptic or whisper into the telephone. Sexual secrets had now vanished. At least those that had to do with adultery as defined by Professor Chase.

The family meeting at the Henry house had been carefully planned by Walter. Even Howard had agreed to fly out for the event. His long telephone conversations with his professorial brother-in-law convinced him that the poor guy would need every bit of support he could muster. "Why not mom and dad too," he had joked. Not even the obvious jest kept Walter from trembling. "That's all I need," he tried to sound light hearted. The image of John Taft sitting in on the family conference was terrifying. There he'd sit in his favorite chair by the fireplace, glass of booze in his hand, spitting out obscene comments about queers and fags. I knew it all along, he'd smirk. Walter could see his sympathetic glances at Maggie and the boys. He might even suggest the boys come to live with their grandparents. They might not write books about Shakespeare, but at least they were straight. And good Christians. Walter was sure his in-laws were in the fold of some self-righteous televangelist who spoke of the good Lord's message while he screwed young girls in motel rooms. The thought of John's presence was too grisly to contemplate.

Dinner on the day of Howard's arrival was the first scene in Walter's passion play. He picked at his food and fidgeted with his napkin as he thought of the words he and Dennis had scripted for the after dinner confessional. Walter seemed the only one at the table who did not eat with relish. Not even Howard appeared the slightest bit apprehensive. After the boys helped Maggie clear the table, Howard winked at Walter. "Don't worry, buddy, everything's under control." He smiled warmly. "Just wait and see." Walter gazed blankly at his brother-in-law. What could be under control? He was about to fracture his family and Howard smiled. Perhaps everyone was mad.

Howard shut the dining room lights and carried in a cake decorated with burning candles. He placed it in front of Walter who looked around with the confusion bred of a time warp. This was not his birthday.

"Read the cake," urged Howard. "Just read the cake before you tell us it's not your birthday."

Walter tried to focus on the blue and yellow cursive script that flowed over the white frosting. His heart beat wildly as the words finally made their way into his consciousness. Could this actually be happening to him? He felt the intense flush of his cheeks. His eyes filled with hot tears.

At their uncle's prompting, Jeremy and James raised their wine glasses. Howard smiled broadly at the scene he had orchestrated.

Walter could not believe he was not living a deliriously wonderful dream. He made no attempt to wipe away the tears. A sappy smile broke across his homely face. He looked at everyone with love and thanks. He feared he might faint.

"Well, read it," Howard urged again. "It took me a hell of a long time to come up with those few simple words." He clinked his fork against his wine glass. "And I'm dying to taste that beautiful cake. Come on, Walter, read it. You can't cut it before you read it out loud."

Walter's eyes now focused on the inscription and he cleared his throat. He didn't know what control he'd have over his voice. He blew his nose. "All right," he said hoarsely. "I wouldn't want Uncle Howard to starve for the want of a slice of cake." For the first time since the lights went out, Walter smiled. Even he knew his joke was lame, but it did break his silence. It also convinced him that his voice was operational. Walter removed his reading glasses from their case in his breast pocket. He could see the inscribed words well enough without them, but the slight delay gave him another moment to control his emotions. The half glasses now in place, he read aloud. "We love you dad, and we know you love us. What could be better than that?" Once more, Walter's eyes filled with tears. "You mean I don't have to deliver the speech I agonized over?" Walter now lowered his eyes. "But how did you know?"

"Dennis, Norma, and I had some pretty intense conference calls with your family," said Howard. He motioned to Maggie and the twins.

"Norma?"

"Yes, Norma," said Maggie, her hand now resting next to Walter's. "She's known for a long time." Maggie forced herself to smile for the boys' sake. "You'll never know how many talks she and I have had over late afternoon tea. I think she had a great deal to do with all this." She pointed to the cake. "Now, why don't you cut that thing and make my brother happy." She handed Walter a cake knife. "Jeremy, I think you can call them in now."

Walter was astonished to see his son lead Dennis and Norma into the dining room. "They've been waiting in the kitchen ever since Uncle Howard brought in the cake."

Howard pulled up two additional chairs.

Walter's cheeks flushed again. He glanced at Dennis and Norma and then looked away. He was speechless.

"I think Maggie's advice is excellent," said Norma. "Why don't you just cut the cake, Walter."

How can they all be so understanding? Walter kept thinking as he slowly placed cake on dessert plates. How can they take this so calmly? And the boys. What's actually going through their minds? Dare I ask?

As if reading his mind, Howard prompted Jeremy and James. "I think your dad would like to hear from you two." He urged them on with an upward shake of his right hand.

The boys had rehearsed the words Howard had scripted with them, but they were both nervous now that the moment had arrived. For the past few days they had talked about nothing else but the news of their father's situation. After Howard's carefully worded explanation to them, they had retired to their rooms in a state of embarrassment and shock. Their father? Their dad and Doctor Collins? The same doctor who examined them. "He touched my balls when he asked me to cough." What were they to say to dad? And to their friends? Was this all to be a family secret or was dad really going to come out?

"Are gay fathers interested in their own kids?"

"Don't be stupid."

"What do you think he and Dennis do?"

"Probably nothing more than we've done to each other."

They giggled nervously. "But we were just experimenting. Everyone does that. Besides, we were much younger."

"You mean much younger when we started playing with each other."

"Don't make a big deal out of it."

"But Dad's an old man."

"Do you think he does it with other men besides Dennis?"

"What about Mom? Do they still do it?"

"She says he loves her."

Long silences separated their comments.

"What about Uncle Howard? Has Dad made it with him too?"

Nervous laughter.

"Can you imagine what Grandpa will say."

More laughter.

Now they blushed as they raised their wine glasses and began their words to Walter.

"Dad," James began, "we want you to know that we love you very much."

"And," Jeremy continued, "Uncle Howard told us some men can love women and men."

"And still be great dads. . ."

"And husbands. . ."

"We learned all about it in sex education last year. . ." James lied.

"And we've read a lot of books. . ." Jeremy also lied.

James blushed. "You see, Dad, all your harping on us about reading paid off."

Howard raised his glass. "Here's to education." He drained his wine. "I wish my father read as much as you guys." He filled his glass. "I think you two are great sons." He looked adoringly at the boys. "Do you realize what a good world this would be if we could bottle this stuff?" He wiped a tear from his eye. "I don't know when I've been so proud of my nephews."

Maggie kissed each boy's head before she moved to the sideboard. "More coffee, anyone?"

Walter went to Maggie's side and put his arms around her. He held her very tightly even though she did not reciprocate. "I'll never be able to tell you how much I love you," he whispered. "And how grateful I am to you." He raised his glass to the table. "Thanks to you all for making this night so memorable. I want you to know I dreaded this meal." He dropped into his chair. "And it turned out to be so wonderful." He smiled at Dennis. "You said I had a great family. You were right." Turning to his sons, "I want you to know how much I love you and your mother." He colored. "And I want you to know I'm not a dirty old man." He held up his hand as Maggie tried to interrupt him. "No, they should know I don't go prowling at night, dressed in an old trench coat and slouched hat. They have nothing to worry about. They're not going to read about their old man in the police report." His voice lowered. "You see, boys, I have a very special relationship with Doctor Collins." He looked across the table. "And only with Dennis."

"I think your father wants you to understand," said Dennis, "that his feelings for me and," he looked into Walter's eyes, "mine for him don't lessen our love and devotion to our families. Not to our wives. Not to our children."

"But not everyone can understand that," Howard said. "Some people will say very terrible things. And you have to prepare yourselves for that. You're both old enough to realize that. Even if your dad doesn't run an ad in the local paper about all of this, some unpleasant people will learn about it." His voice trembled slightly. "Perhaps even some of your own schoolmates will talk." He poured more wine. "It's not going to easy to ignore them. But, believe me, it's best to ignore them." His eyes remained fixed on the boys. "I know better than most. You've known for some time, I'm sure, that I'm gay." Walter's heart sank at the first mention of that word.

"I know you've heard my own father say awful things about me. Christ, he says them when I'm in the room. I can only imagine what he says when I'm not present." He sipped his wine. "My point is that if one's father can be guilty of inflicting such hurt, you can imagine what strangers might say. Ignore them, boys. Just be strong in your knowledge that your parents love you." He touched Maggie's hand. "And they love each other."

Maggie looked away. Her face was ashen.

Walter knew that several real issues had been skirted by everyone, but he remained grateful for the evening. There'll be time for the rest. He still dreaded the private conversation he knew must take place with his sons. He worried about his ability to soothe their concerns and, even more troubling, answer their questions. Only God knows what they've been talking about. And Maggie. Could it ever be the same between them? Could she really understand he loved her as much as he ever did? He hadn't dare touch her in bed since the news broke. Nor had she turned to him in the dark with hands or words. Walter suddenly left the table. In the bathroom he washed his face with cold water and wept. His entire body shook. What had he done? His desire for a man's body, for dear Dennis, had turned his world upside down. Now sitting on the toilet bowl cover, he put his head into his hands. He was too lightheaded to stand up. He flushed the toilet in the hope that the sound would carry into the dining room. He reached over and ran the water tap at full force. He must return to the fold. And he must look good. Walter shook his head and wept again.

At first, Jack and Wilma wanted a quiet wedding in the judge's chamber. Quick, easy, private. But the more they talked about it, the more they thought a public ceremony was necessary.

"I don't want those bastards to think we slinked away and got hitched." Jack and Wilma were sitting at his breakfast table. "The last thing I want is for them to think we're ashamed of anything." He lit a cigarette and sipped coffee. "God, Willie, I'm so proud you agreed to be my wife. I want the world to know I love you." He reached for her hand.

"And I do love you with every fiber of my decrepit body." He laughed. "I'll never forget the look on your father's face when we came down to breakfast that first morning."

"The matching bathrobes weren't as great an idea as when we bought them. He didn't know what to say. The poor dear was tongue-tied. If mom hadn't complimented the robes, I think he'd still be looking for something to say. And what do you think of those beautiful robes, she prompted him. You remember how he nodded his head in agreement and returned to his French toast. It must have taken him three or four bites before he looked up and smiled. Willie's mom's French toast is terrific. The best you'll ever taste. Only then did he get up and kiss me and urge us both to dig in."

"But I'll give him credit. Once he got over the shock, his performance was first-rate. As it was at the dinner party they threw for us." Jack shook his head. "And he was right about your mother's French toast. Best I ever had."

"You were pretty good yourself. Surrounded by so many of my relatives, you put on a show that wowed them. By the end of that night, they all loved you." She blew a kiss. "Almost as much as I do."

"Yea, I was pretty good, wasn't I?" Jack nodded his head in agreement with his own statement. I really liked most of them." He looked intently at Wilma. "Do we have to invite all of them to the wedding?"

"You mean do we have to invite Aunt Helen?"

"She did hate me from that first meeting at the front door, didn't she? You're old enough to be my boyfriend. What a greeting. And when she stared at me and asked me to open my mouth. Like a frigging dentist. Well, at least your teeth look good. What kind of endorsement is that? But you're pretty thin in the hair department. Then she clucked a few times, shook her head, and asked your father for a stiff drink. Oh yes, Helen is a real pistol."

"But she doesn't like anybody."

"I gathered that pretty quickly. She ordered that poor husband of hers as if he were some sad sack in her platoon. Horace, get me another drink. Horace, save some white meat for me. Horace, bring me a clean plate. I'm surprised she didn't ask him to examine my teeth."

"We still have to invite her. But she won't travel all the way out here to see her favorite niece marry a honky. You probably won't believe it, but

Helen was on her best behavior that night. She's as rabid a racist as Maxine Jefferson. Someday, if you're a good little white boy, she'll show you her college scrap book."

"She went to college?"

"Are you kidding? Helen's down-home mammy routine's just one of her weapons in her war against whitey. She was a magna history major at Smith. I think Northampton breathed a sigh of relief when she left town. If there was a protest, there was Aunt Helen. The scrap book is full of her exploits. Pictures, newspaper articles, even two police reports of her arrests. She's proudest of them."

Jack was incredulous. "And Horace? What was he, a Nobel laureate in physics?"

"Far from it. Uncle Horace never finished high school. But he was an organizer for the Southern Christian Leadership. That's how they met. Helen went to Georgia to work for voter registration and the rest is history. Love at first sight, she says." Wilma smiled. "Tough to believe it when you look at them now, isn't it? So what do you think, professor? Will we be like them after forty years?"

"Forty years? Sure. Forty years from now, you'll be collecting my TIAA pension and living it up with all those young graduate students." He dragged on his cigarette. "Let's get back to the invitation list before I get too jealous of them. Those earnest young men with firm, fresh peckers. Too bad they don't know what to do with them."

"Don't you wish," Wilma laughed. "Okay, the guest list. I don't know how we got so far from a quiet ceremony in Judge Winston's study."

"I still don't want to invite the whole department. Maybe we can run a cocktail party for them a week or so after the wedding."

"So whose feelings are we going to hurt?" Wilma filled her coffee cup. "I know the rejects will be absolutely crushed." She rolled her eyes. "And think of the gifts we'd be missing if we don't invite everybody."

"I want to keep it manageable. Maybe fifty at tops. The Rosenthals have already offered their house."

"Joyce's gardens are beautiful. What a grand setting it'll be. She wants to rent the tent and tables. Says that'll be their wedding gift to us. Isn't that sweet?"

"Good people, Joyce and Ben. How big's the tent?"

"As big as we need. She won't rent one until she knows how many guests they'll be." Wilma doodled on the list.

"At least Aunt Helen can't complain about the festivities taking place at an ACLU house."

"She's not nuts about Jews either."

"Remind her that Joyce was born a true believer. Only Ben's a genuine Christ killer." Jack put his hands together in prayer. "Please let there be no race riots at our wedding."

"What about Dennis Collins? Do we have to invite him and his wife?"

"She hates gays too?"

Wilma nodded.

"Let's just have the show at the local Bethel church and get it over with. Maybe we can convince Farrakhan to officiate."

Wlima shook her head again.

"He's on her shit list too?"

"Aunt Helen can't stand him." She smiled. "But Jesse Jackson would be just right."

"I'll see what I can do. A marriage in rhymed couplets would be another first for this town."

Jack and Wilma's nuptials were the talk of the department from the moment the announcement was made. Even after the wedding, the subject titillated the literature faculty. Conversation in Wallace Lounge vacillated from obscene speculations when Jack was absent to proper polite congratulations when he was in residence. As usual, Billy Mann was the most indefatigably outrageous commentator. His repertoire ran the gamut from racism to smut. From bad imitations of Amos and Andy to speculations about white men's penis size and disappointed black women, he was the star of the minstrel show. He loved every minute it. Not even Ben chastised his bad taste. Rather, the senior scholar left the lounge abruptly whenever Billy went into a routine.

"Oh Lordy, I've offended the saintly sensibilities of our resident civil libertarian once again." He rolled his eyes. "Massa just don't like us white boys making fun of his darkies." Billy pulled out a red bandanna from his jacket pocket and arranged it expertly on his head. He had rehearsed the

Aunt Jemima routine at home to the fevered delight of Sally. "Shucks, you white folks just ain't got no rhythm." He pranced about the lounge, stopping before embarrassed colleagues and striking coquettish poses. "It's not just hot cakes I makes, you knows." He stroked the cheeks of old scholars and squeezed the thighs of others.

Peter Chase spread his legs as Billy approached him. "It's right here waiting for you, mammy." Peter ran his hands up his legs and grabbed himself. "This white boy's ready and waiting." Smiling lasciviously, he slowly rubbed his crotch. If you only knew how serious I was, I wonder what you'd do, he thought as he became excited.

"Why, Peter Chase," Billy sang as he pranced around the young man's chair. "I declare. I never knew you blond types hankered for black pussy. I thinks we needs to make some beautiful little ones together." He laughed and thrust his pelvis back and forth. Billy acknowledged scattered laughter with bows in every direction.

Removing his head dress, he dropped into a chair and continued to laugh. "You see how sanitized our humor has become because of Rosenthal's sanctimonious sermonizing." Billy turned serious. "Political correctness will destroy us all." He looked around the room, pleased that he still held center stage. "There's no way we can talk about American culture in his terms. I mean, we all teach that great books course. Take *Huck Finn*, for instance. Ben would probably want us to refer to African-American Jim for Christ's sake. I'll tell you, gentlemen, we're in danger of losing our intellectual balls."

"You're right, you know," said Peter, not yet willing to risk standing up. "And it's a lot closer to my field than yours." Although he had reservations about Billy's view and certainly about his racism, Peter wanted to announce his public agreement. He smiled to himself. Hope does spring eternal, he thought. He returned Billy's nod.

"Perhaps true," said Calvin Willoughby, pipe in hand. "But you do push things too far." He blew a puff of aromatic smoke into the air. "That mammy stuff you just did, for example." The old bibliographer bit on his pipe stem. "You must admit, Mann, it was pretty gross business." Calvin looked around, hoping for support. He thought his criticism was fair and measured. But no one endorsed even so mild a rebuke. Calvin colored. "Well, I was just saying. . . ."

"You were just saying you don't want to see or hear what you your-self think every day." Billy pointed a finger at Willoughby. "We've all heard you grumble about affirmative action. Christ almighty, how many times have you lamented the loss of the good old days at the university." He pointed again. "We know what you were really saying."

"And what might that be?" asked Jack Williams who had entered the room shortly after Billy's show.

Billy paled only slightly when he looked at Jack, but his voice re-mained controlled. "Calvin's complaint is every rational academic's com-plaint. Standards have gone south as we try to make the university an arm of the social welfare state. Come on, Jack, you've been here almost as long as Willoughby. Face it. The student body's just not the same as it used to be." Billy stood up and began pacing just as he did in the class room. "We admit too many unqualified kids. And why? I'll tell you why." He moved closer to Jack. "Because we've been corrupted by the preposterous claim that in some magical way the university can make this a better and fairer country by spoon feeding the untalented and unqualified while at the same time boring the shit out of the truly talented kids." He spread his arms. "And does anyone benefit from this misguided and," he dropped his voice to a dramatic whisper, "tragic idea?" He looked around the room, neither expecting nor wanting a response to his rhetorical question. "No one, that's who. Qui bono should become the new slogan for higher education in our country."

He now stood directly in front of Jack. "And let me tell you this, Jack. I don't believe there's a single person in this room who doesn't want a better and fairer society. Calvin there's a Republican, I'm a Democrat, only God knows what kooky party Ben sends his checks to, but all of us want a better and fairer America. The sixty-four thousand dollar question, how-ever, is how do we reach that better place. I made as much fun of Reagan as anyone, but I'll tell you, Jack, I, too, would love to see the good old U.S.A. become that shining city on the hill." Billy sat down. "But it sure isn't going to happen by flushing standards down the toilet."

"You surprise me, Billy," said Jack, not retreating an inch from their face-to-face position. He dragged deeply on his cigarette. Two streams of white smoke flowed out of his nostrils and surrounded Billy's flushed face. Billy didn't flinch. He would surrender no advantage. "I never knew you were so concerned with standards." Jack leaned forward, now almost touching Billy's face. "Standards of any kind." His smile made his disdain clear.

It had been an awful day for Abraham. The seminar turned into another match between the blessed angels of critical good sense and Murdoch's dark minions. Once again, Abraham was forced to play the referee rather than the purveyor of sweetness and light. How he hated the sneering tensions of his seminar. And how much his role contrasted with his now barely breathing ideal of the literature professor. Not even his brief visit to Wallace Lounge before heading home eased his acidic stomach. He found the room empty. The late afternoon sun filtered through the faux Tiffany windows. Normally, the undulating orange shadows, the fine old oriental rugs, the comfortable oversized chairs, the dark beamed ceilings comforted him. Wallace Lounge had become the last remnant of the idealized professorial life he prized. A tattered remnant to be sure, but it still had the power to create a rounded softness that momentarily shielded him from the angular harshness beyond the door. The harshness that circumscribed his troubled life.

The coffee was still drinkable at a few minutes before five. Mary must have made a fresh pot for the late afternoon instructors. Happily, she disliked Sanka as much as he did. Abraham sat in his favorite chair and shut his eyes. He tried the deep breathing exercises Billy had taught him during their meetings in the empty building. Relax, he said to himself, relax. He opened his eyes to gaze once more on the artifacts of the life he thought he was entering when he left graduate school. He imagined a Mozart divertimento playing softly on the stereo, civilized tweedy colleagues quietly discussing serious issues of pedagogy, good will and love of literature palpably permeating the lounge. Aromatic pipe smoke mingled with the aroma of good coffee. The provost's silver service glistened. Students were nowhere to be seen in Abraham's hallowed place. Thoughts of obscene videos and poisoned banquet guests were out of the question in such a setting. Tenure, rape, Mitchell Murdoch, Beverly Berlin, a tortured chairman, Maxine Jefferson, Billy Mann. All were gone. None was possible in this lovely, hazy dreamworld of university life.

Abraham stretched his long frame and yawned. He rubbed his temples. But that's not the way it is, he said aloud. The lump in his throat threatened to strangle him when he swallowed the last of the coffee. Thank God there's no one else in the lounge. Abraham was in no mood to make small talk. The seminar had been only the start of his terrible day. There had been too many confidences shared with him. Ben's recounting Billy's minstrel show and the older man's pained confession that he had been bludgeoned into supporting a man he loathed. Jack's fear that he had backed away from a confrontation he had wished for since he first met Billy and smelled sulfur. Billy's supremely confident gloating over having annihilated all adversaries. And if these weren't enough after three trying hours in the seminar, there was Joan, his last visitor of the day. One look at her face told Abraham the news was not good.

She had shut the door and dropped into a chair by his desk. Joan's eyes were weary, her face drawn. "Helen's in bad shape," she said quietly and began to weep. She took a tissue and a pack of cigarettes from her purse. "It's got me back to these damn things." She tried unsuccessfully for a breezy tone. Lighting a long filtered cigarette, she inhaled deeply.

Abraham said nothing about his aversion to smoking in his office. He placed a plastic cup before her. "What's happened now?"

"She found this in her mailbox." Joan handed him a sheet of ruled notebook paper.

As he read, Abraham absent mindedly tore the tabs off the left side of the paper where it had been ripped from a spiral binder. He shook his head in disgust. "It's a prank. Awful and insensitive, but only some stupid sophomore's idea of a rich joke." Abraham folded and refolded the sheet neatly, carefully and deliberately pressing the edges of the paper. "She must have expected something like this, didn't she? She must have known it couldn't be kept a secret forever." Abraham wanted to go home.

"Sure she knew. But she knew it only intellectually. When it actually happened, rational expectations went by the board." Joan lit a second cigarette. "It's easy for us to see that damn mash note for what it is." She drew deeply. "But not for her. It's too recent. Too fresh in her memory." Joan stood up and paced the room. "Imagine some little son of a bitch writing something like that? And to be so graphic about fucking his professor. With that obscene cartoon, too."

"Tell her to forget it," said Abraham, becoming more anxious to escape. Where would he begin a rehearsal of this day to Eleanor?

"Of course I told her that. But she's not even sure it was a student who sent her the damn thing."

"Not a student?" Abraham began packing his bag.

"She's been going through the department roster, trying to come up with someone who might have done it." Joan sat down again. "Ab, what can we do to help her." She placed her hand over his. "I mean it, Ab. Helen's in deep trouble. I persuaded her to move back in with me, but I just don't know how to get her out of her depression. And she's got to testify again next week. I just don't know how she's going to get through it. She's now talking about a leave of absence. Or even resigning. She doesn't know how she can face a class again. Says she's afraid to make eye contact with any male in her classes."

Abraham pulled the cord of his green bag and stood up. "I really have to get home." He put his hand on Joan's shoulder. "Let me talk to Eleanor. She'll call you tonight." He held the office door open for Joan. "We'll be in touch." He knew he sounded like an uninterested stranger, but he was desperate to escape this last encounter of the day. Yet he almost laughed as he thought of Zero Mostel's line in *The Producers*. How do they find me? He walked Joan to the stairs before he sought a moment's solace in Wallace Lounge.

Until he turned onto his street, the ride home had been the best part of the day. His favorite FM radio station flooded the car with a Beethoven quartet. So preoccupied with his immediate problems, he failed at first to realize it was the same music that had filled the chapel of his disquieting dream. When he finally recognized the music, it was too late to dwell on the terrible fate of the truth teller touched by his lord.

His heart sank when he saw a state police car in his driveway. His first thought was to keep driving. But escape to where? They'll find me wherever I go. He felt cold sweat overspread the small of his back. Abraham shook with fear. It's over, he said to himself. Resigned to disgrace and years in prison, he pulled in next to the blue and yellow police car.

Eleanor and a detective sat in the living room, drinking tea and apparently enjoying a pleasant conversation.

Abraham turned from the sight of his wife, suddenly transformed into Mata Hari, and stared at his harried face in the hall mirror. God, I even look guilty. He wet the palms of his hands and tried to smooth his hair. Might as well look as good as I can for the ride to prison. He smiled weakly. He cleared his throat. He entered the living room to face the music.

"I told you he'd be home about this time," Eleanor said brightly to the detective. "Honey, this is Bob Everett. He's from the state police." There was nothing in her voice to suggest worry or fear. Eleanor stood up to kiss her husband's cheek. "It's all pro forma," she whispered. "Don't worry. He's really very nice."

"Happy to meet you, Professor Smith." The detective stood and extended his hand. "I'm sorry to bother you at home, but we've got to interview every member of your department by the weekend." He opened his notebook. "And you had a busy schedule today." He glanced at a page headed Abraham Smith. "There was no way I could catch you at the university." He smiled. "And today was R, S, and T day for me."

Eleanor handed Ab a martini and waved him to her side on the couch. "Mister Everett already turned one down. On duty, you know." She laughed softly, thinking of how many times she'd read that line in mystery novels.

Abraham drank half the martini in a single swallow and looked at the detective. "So what can I do for you?" Why didn't Billy mention a visit from the cops? If they're up to S, he'd already had his interrogation. Son of a bitch. Abraham smiled at Everett and lifted his glass. "Sure you wouldn't like to join me?" He was suddenly surprisingly relaxed.

"Just a few questions about the events of that Saturday everyone's talking about." He looked at his notebook again. "Any ideas about who might be responsible for all that stuff?"

Abraham shook his head. "Not a clue." He now casually sipped his martini. "And you? Do you have a suspect?"

It was the detective's turn to smile. "Oh, we have a few notions." He made a short notation in his book. " But we're still a long way from an arrest." He stood up. "But we do think there was more than one person involved. We're pretty sure of that."

Abraham's heart skipped a beat. Did he dare inquire. "Why do you say that?"

"Oh, only because you used the singular. You asked if we had a suspect." The detective smiled again. "As a matter of fact, the caterers recall a couple of men wandering around when they were preparing for the banquet. They don't remember the faces yet, but we're working with them." He took his coat from the back of a chair. "They'll remember." He shook Eleanor's hand. "They always do, you know. Thanks very much for the tea, Mrs. Smith." He nodded to Abraham.

"That's it?" asked Ab. "That's the whole interview?"

"For now," Everett replied. Abraham was sure the detective's tone was ominous. "At this point I've just got to report to my boss that everyone was asked that same question."

Abraham couldn't resist. "May I ask what you wrote in the notebook?"

"Just my reactions."

"Reactions to a single question?"

"Oh, yes. You can learn a lot from a person's manner."

"And mine?"

Eleanor was obviously uncomfortable with Abraham's pursuit of the detective. Why can't he leave things alone? "Really, Ab, Mister Everett's got to go."

"Yours?" Everett laughed. "Everything I expected."

"Expected?"

"Sure. You professors all have been relaxed. If I had to guess, I'd say none of you was broken up. Some of you guys seem to have actually enjoyed it all."

As soon as the detective's car backed out of the driveway Eleanor turned on Abraham. "How could you have been so stupid?" She poured herself a martini. "I mean really stupid. Everything was going along beautifully until you had to open your big mouth." She put her glass down and began pacing the room. "Of all the dumb things to do. Can you please tell me why you persisted in asking those questions? Did you really want to make him suspicious? The man just finished saying how relaxed you professors were when you began your stupid questions." Eleanor stopped in front of Abraham. "I just don't understand how you could have done it. Only God knows what he'll write in his book after that display." She lit a cigarette. "Do you think any of the others asked him such questions? Do you think your darling Billy Mann said anything to make him suspicious?" She dropped herself into a chair. "Well, I can assure you he certainly did not. You can bet your ass he was as cool as a cucumber. Billy wouldn't ask him what he was writing. And he surely didn't ask what kind of impression he made. Honestly Ab, I just can't understand what you were trying to do. I just can't understand."

Abraham felt sick to his stomach. He was sure he was about to throw up. "You just don't understand the day I had." He put his head in his hands. "And then to see that police car at my house. It was just too much."

"So you decided to blow the whole thing, did you?" Eleanor lit another cigarette. "Poor Ab had a bad day." She blew smoke through her nostrils. "Big deal. A lousy seminar makes you take leave of your senses. Grow up, for Christ's sake. Don't you realize the stakes you're playing for? Let's face it, it was you and that creep who caused all this trouble in the first place." She furiously stubbed out the half-smoked cigarette "Now, my man, it's time to act like a grownup. Not like some kid who's been caught with his fingers in the cookie jar. Honestly, Ab, you've got to get a grip on yourself or you'll end up in prison." She stared at her husband. "And what's going to happen to the kids and me when they haul you away for those sophomoric pranks? Have you thought about that? Have you?"

"It wasn't just the seminar," Abraham said softly.

"So what else? Was your tuna sandwich too soggy? Was the conversation in that loony lounge of yours too unintellectual? Did it fall short of your cockamamie dream-world idea of what professors should talk about? Did some undergraduate interloper dare enter that holy inner sanctum? Did you run out of red ink while you were writing your voluminous comments on an innocent freshman's paper? The comments they never read anyway. Was your office too warm or too cold? Tell me. Tell me what could be more important right now than the investigation?"

"You just don't understand." Ab looked longingly in the direction of his study.

"Oh no, buddy, you're not going to escape."

"And you don't have to make fun of me ." He waved away the almost dissipated curling blue smoke. "And I wish you wouldn't smoke so much."

"Fuck you, Ab. This is not the time for feeling sorry for yourself." Even though she didn't want one, Eleanor lit another cigarette. "And these," she aimed the Salem in his direction, "are not at issue right now. You always try to deflect conversation when you feel trapped." She took a long drag. "Do you do that in class too?"

"There you go again with another personal attack." Abraham stood up and walked to the bar.

"Sure, get looped. That's also a terrific way to escape." Eleanor put her arms around him. "I guess I was a little rough on you. I'm sorry. But you must admit you're not the easiest nut to crack when you're in one of your states." She kissed his cheek. "So let's start again." She returned to her chair. "Tell me what happened at the lit factory today."

Abraham was relieved by Eleanor's apology. He had wondered which of them would yield first. In fact, he knew Eleanor would eventually make the peace. She always did. "It wasn't just the seminar." His voice was stronger. He was gaining control of his emotions. This would not be the day of his nervous breakdown. His eyes were dry. The nausea had passed. He calmly told Eleanor about Billy's minstrel show. About Ben and Jack. About Billy's visit to his office. Finally, about Joan and Helen. He omitted his curt treatment of Joan. Eleanor had more than enough arrows in her quiver.

It was Helen's despair that captured Eleanor's immediate attention. "We better get over there right after dinner. We've got to help her."

"You go. I'm in no condition to help anyone tonight." He feared Joan had already reported his behavior to Helen. Abraham felt another tremor of nausea. He was filled with shame. This dispenser of truth had remained silent during Billy's obscene routine in the lounge. He had not said a word in defense of either Ben or Jack when they most needed support in the face of Billy's belligerence. He didn't even offer a quiet word when old Calvin silently beseeched the room for support. And, worst of all, he had virtually dismissed Joan. He was happy that Eleanor had retired to the kitchen to prepare dinner. The children would be home soon and they'd be famished. I do care about Helen, he said to himself. She's always been there for me and now she must think I don't give a damn. "But, Helen," he said aloud, "you can't know the mess I'm in."

The front door opened. "We're home," his kids shouted. He heard their backpacks hit the hall floor. Abraham tried to put on a happy face. It was time to act interested in their recitations of their day in school. Once again, he looked longingly at his study door.

Walter shuffled around the kitchen like an old man. He felt awful. All night he had tossed and turned, unable to sleep. There was no way for him to get comfortable in the king-size bed, now intolerably and insistently empty without Maggie's regular, comforting breathing.

She had left to visit her parents the morning after the coming-out dinner. Alternately envious of and furious at Norma, she was unable to accept her husband's needs with the seeming equanimity of the other woman. Maggie wanted to be as modern as Norma, but she found herself weeping, sometimes uncontrollably, when she was alone in the house. This woman who prided herself for her legendary ability to plan for every eventuality was left rudderless by this turn of events. She who carried a folding umbrella on the most beautiful summer days had found herself completely unprepared for Walter's admission. She had been left defenseless. How could Norma live so comfortably for all those years knowing about Dennis? Why wasn't she furious? How could she have children after she found out? The thought of even being touched by Walter was repugnant. She froze when he turned to her in bed and tried to kiss her. His lips were now tainted. His entire body disgusted her. Could she ever get over this? She could think only of Walter and Dennis doing things previously reserved for her and her husband. She trembled whenever she thought of them together. And she thought of them constantly. She had to get away. Howard's invitation to fly back to New York with him was all wrong. His world was the last thing she needed at this time. But her father's chronic hip problem and his recent surgery gave her a perfect excuse to visit her girlhood home. What could be less suspicious than a visit to help in his rehab? And it would give her necessary time and distance. Walter didn't object. Her parting words to him at the airport resonated in his mind this morning. "This will give you a perfect opportunity to talk with the boys. You be sure to do that, Walter."

Two frying pans were heating on the range. Bacon and eggs, muffins and jelly, hot coffee. He was preparing a hearty breakfast for the three men. Now if he could bring together all the conversational scraps and gambits he had spent the sleepless night rehearsing, perhaps things wouldn't be as awkward as he feared.

He looked toward the second floor when he heard the shower water shut off. They'd be down in a moment. With their mother gone, he wondered if they feared the encounter as much as he. What did they talk about in the quiet of their bedroom? How ashamed are they of me? How much do they hate me?

Walter's eyes misted again when Jeremy and James entered the room. He didn't fail to notice that they made sure to come down together. Hair still damp, they were beautiful. He wanted nothing more than to put his arms around them. Like those great days at the beach when the three of them would pose for Maggie's camera. Those innocent days that could never be recaptured, he thought, as he waved a spatula in greeting. "I hope you guys are as hungry as I am." He tried to sound cheerful. Everything would be fine if he could only control his voice. And those damn tears. He mustn't cry this morning. They think I'm half a woman anyway. He was suddenly ashamed of the blue and green striped apron he was wearing. Maggie's apron. Why hadn't he put on the one he wore for backyard barbecues. The masculine dark gray apron the boys had given him with a picture of some dumb chef holding a tray of hot dogs. Walter rubbed his hands dry on the brightly striped apron and was about to apologize. No, no, that'd be a terrific way to start the morning. Carry on as if nothing were wrong. Christ, I've worn this thing a hundred times. "How do bacon and eggs sound?"

"Great," said Jeremy. His hollow, forced enthusiasm seemed to echo throughout the room. He had never been as proficient a dissembler as his brother. Walter thought James would make a great lawyer. Jeremy, the more serious of the two, a fine scholar in his father's mold. Perhaps not exactly in his father's mold, Walter hoped.

"When's Mom coming back?" Jeremy asked.

"She just left, for God's sake," James chided. He shot a warning glance at his brother. It was clear to Walter that he wasn't the only one who had a script this morning. "I'm really in the mood for bacon and eggs." The lawyer-to-be brought the subject back to breakfast.

The three men sat at the table, quietly eating. Appetites were not hearty this morning. Jeremy kept looking at his watch.

"There's no school today," Walter said "No rush to finish." He poured more coffee. "Would you like me to put on some more bacon?"

Neither boy looked up.

"How about another muffin?"

"That's all right, Dad. We're in good shape." James nodded his head curtly at Jeremy, his eyes urging him to join the meager conversation.

"Sure, we're in terrific shape," Jeremy said without raising his head. His voice was flat.

Walter crossed his knife and fork on his plate and looked across the table at his sons. "I think we should talk." His voice trembled only slightly. "With your mother gone, it's a fine opportunity for us to have some man-to-man talk." Both boys remained silent. "Don't you think?" Walter was becoming nervous again. "I mean, we haven't really had much of a chance to talk about the dinner and all that."

"It's all right, Dad," said James. "We don't have to talk about," he looked away, "all that."

The translation was clear to Walter. They didn't want to discuss their father's treachery. "No, James, we do have to talk." Walter's throat was dry. "I know there's got to be some distance between your words at dinner, words I truly did appreciate, and what you guys really feel about everything that's happened around here." He drank from his water glass. "I mean, no one would have expected you to be completely honest the other night. Not with Uncle Howard and the Collinses at the table." He sipped again. "But now we're alone and I really want to hear what you've got to say." He stared out the window, thinking how much he hated that word, really, and how often he already used it this morning. "What you've got to say about me."

The boys were clearly uncomfortable. Not that they were surprised by their father's wish for a conversation. They had expected it. They talked of little else before they finally fell asleep last night. Walter was not the only one Maggie had instructed. But now, face to face with their father, their rehearsed lines seemed vapid. The fact of the matter was that they were not happy. They were ashamed of themselves, but even more ashamed of their father. And what if their friends were to find out?

In the darkness of their room, Jeremy and James had whispered their secret feelings to each other. Sharing their fears and anger seemed easier in the dark.

"You remember the jokes about Ronnie after we decided he was gay?"

"And we joined in with the guys without thinking anything like that could ever happen in our house."

"The only thing we ever worried about was anyone finding out about Uncle Howard."

"But he's so straight looking that no one who didn't already know would ever guess." Jeremy stared into the dark. "Does Dad look gay? Do you think any of the guys wonder about him?"

"Don't be stupid," James scolded. "Did we have a clue? Did you ever imagine he went down on someone's dick?"

Jeremy's giggle was choked by sudden sobs. He turned his head into the pillow to muffle the sound.

"It's going to be all right." James tried to comfort his brother, but he didn't move from his bed. He was now nervous about putting his arms around Jeremy.

After sixteen years of brotherly closeness and love, they both feared overt signs of affection. Boyhood hugs of joy after a touchdown catch, backyard wrestling, roughhousing in the waves at the beach, holding each other as they practiced the latest dance steps in hopes of impressing the beauties at a school dance. All were now suspicious memories. For the past few days, the boys turned their naked bodies from each other after showering. Their morning erections, always a subject for their teen-agers' robust humor, were now hidden or ignored. Neither Jeremy nor James had talked about these changes.

James felt guilty as Jeremy's sobs continued. His face flushed with shame as he repeated his words. "It's all right, Jeremy, it's going to be all right." Although they were twins, James knew he was the leader. He had always been the stronger, the more daring of the two. Now he wanted to go to his brother's bed and hold him in his arms. His heart broke as he heard Jeremy crying in the dark. But he held back. Christ, we're not kids anymore, he tried to convince himself. We'll be in college in a couple of years. Christ, we're men. He stifled an unbidden groan when he tasted his own tears at the corners of his mouth.

"Jimmy? Jimmy," Jeremy said through his sobs, "what are we going to do? I'm so fucking unhappy. Jimmy, I feel like a kid again, like when I got lost at the beach. And you found me. Do you remember you found me?"

"And I told you everything would be okay, didn't I? And everything turned out fine, didn't it?" James turned on his side to face Jeremy's bed. "And Dad took us to the amusement park that night to celebrate your return. Do you remember, Jeremy?" James made out his brother's form sitting up in his bed. He moved to the far side of his own bed to make room for Jeremy.

The boys hugged. Jeremy's body still heaved with each sob. James kissed the other's cheek and stroked his back. "It's going to be all right. It's going to be all right." He kept repeating this mantra as he rubbed Jeremy's back.

"I love you, Jimmy," Jeremy whispered. The sobs subsided and the young man soon slept.

"I love you, too," said the leader. "I'll take care of you, Jeremy."

The brothers slept until dawn. James awoke to his arm having fallen asleep. His brother's head seemed not to have moved all night. "Jeremy, wake up," he whispered. "We've got to talk about breakfast. Wake up."

Jeremy stretched. He opened his sleepy eyes, blinking them into a recognition of where he was. "If I don't pee, I'm going to burst." He avoided talking about the reason he awoke in his brother's bed. He slipped out of bed and stretched luxuriantly.

"Now, that's a piece of wood if I ever saw one." James laughed at Jeremy's erection. He, too, wanted to avoid last night's events. But both boys knew the awkwardness which had enveloped them had been broken.

"Wouldn't you love to have one that good." Jeremy slapped James on the rump and retired to the bathroom.

Walter poured more coffee. "So, I'm listening." He was more calm than he had expected. After all, *I don't have to admit anything they don't already know.* "Can you understand that my love for your mother and you doesn't change because…" He paused, unsure of the words to follow. *Because I'm gay? Because I have sex with your pediatrician? Because you now have to wonder every time I hug you? Because your father's a creep, a pervert?* "Because of my," he looked away, "bisexuality?" The word almost choked him. But he had said it. Finally, he had been able to use the word in front of his sons. Walter looked directly at the embarrassed boys. "It's not contagious," he laughed, his throat once more dry. "Or genetic, you know. You guys don't have to worry." He was sorry as soon as he uttered those words. Not too smart, Walter. The last thing you want to do is underscore the magnitude of the sin they think you've committed. The treachery.

Walter wasn't surprised that it was James who spoke first. "We know you still love us, Dad."

The *still* was a dagger that pained Walter.

"But why did you have to do it?" James was pale, but he looked directly at his father.

Jeremy glanced quickly at his brother. He was nervous about James' forthrightness, but glad the question they talked about was finally out in the open.

James continued. "We do talk about it, you know, Dad. But we don't understand. We know all about Uncle Howard, but he's always been different. At least that's what Grandpa says."

"And he doesn't have a family," Jeremy finally spoke. "We don't want grandpa making fun of you the way he always does about Uncle Howard." The tremble in his voice was apparent. James feared his brother was on the verge of sobbing again. "Can I ask you a question, Dad?"

"Anything, son."

Jeremy looked down again. "Is Doctor Collins the. . . ." He lowered his voice. "Is he the first one?" He looked at James. "Or have there been lots?"

Walter had not expected that question. His mental crib sheet didn't contain a carefully rehearsed response. "No, Jeremy, there haven't been lots of others. Just Dennis. Just Doctor Collins. But would it really matter if there had been others? I don't expect you guys to understand it all, but some men have needs that require more than women." He didn't want to sound like some pompous, dim-witted sociologist. "That's just the way it is with me. I love your mother. I don't want to live with anyone but your mother." He wanted to be as delicate and antiseptic as he could. "But every so often, I want to be with a man. It's something I've felt for a long time, but I've never done anything about it until I met Dennis and realized he felt the same way, that he had the same needs" Walter sipped coffee to ease the dryness that had returned. "You have to understand that we're not lesser husbands or fathers because of it. I want you to believe that, boys. I'd never talk to you this way if I didn't think you were old enough to understand." He looked directly at them. "You can't understand it all, I know. But I do want you to understand. I want you to know I'm not some dirty old man. I'm not one of those guys you read about or tell jokes about. But I'm sure your friends won't understand. They're just too far removed from our situation." He dared bring them into the fold with the plural pronoun. If only he could convince them that they must share whatever it is their father had brought into their lives. His burden was now theirs also.

The boys nodded their heads, but there was so much more they wanted to ask.

"Does everyone at the university know?" asked James. Unspoken was his fear that others, his friends, would soon know. He toyed with his fork. "Can we keep it a secret?"

Once more, Jeremy silently admired his brother's boldness.

"Only a few people in the department know about it." He reached across the table and touched James' hand. "And they're discreet. You don't have to worry about your dad and Doctor Collins hitting the front page." Walter was at first angry at James' question. But he understood the young man's fears of public disclosure, of being tainted with his father's affliction. For God's sake, he's really only a kid.

"You mean we don't have anything to worry about?" asked Jeremy.

"What he means, Dad," James interrupted, "is that it's tough enough for us to understand and we're involved, but if it got out of our family." He looked imploringly at his father.

Walter could only think of the families he knew when he was their age. Families that tried to hide the mentally ill relative. Even the cancer patient, for heaven's sake, was kept a secret. As if the family would be tainted if others knew. Then it was the alcoholic who was kept secret. Now it's the homosexual. He understood his sons' fears. He hoped only that they wouldn't feel the same shame when they got older.

He thought of Maggie now at her parents' home. God, I hope she can understand. Several times since her departure, he had asked himself how he might respond if she told him she was involved with another woman. How, indeed, would he respond? He realized he didn't know what his response might be. What would Maggie's feelings be now when her father took off on Howard? And Walter knew he would. John couldn't resist venting his frustrations and anger over his son's way of life. The terms were always derisive and vulgar. The more afternoon drinks, the more offensive the comments. Now Maggie would have to defend not only her brother, but, secretly, her husband too. Walter closed his eyes for a moment as he thought of his father-in-law's response if he were to find out.

Neither boy left the table during their father's brief reverie. Always ready to bolt from the kitchen after quickly finishing their breakfast, today they were reluctant to leave. They thought of questions they had talked about in the dark, but they seemed incapable of framing them in language that wouldn't sound insulting or even dirty. Jeremy hoped James would find the right words. There was so much the boys wanted to know. There were so many fears gnawing at them.

Walter opened his eyes and smiled at his sons. "I was just thinking of the job your grandfather would do on me. He's never really liked me, you know. Wanted your mother to marry a CEO of a Fortune five hundred corporation. Yes, old grandfather John had one hell of a time getting used to a literature professor." Walter realized he had never before spoken this way to his sons about their extended family. He hadn't ever actually referred to Howard as gay. He laughed. "Your grandfather's a piece or work. I'll tell you something," he leaned forward, "after you guys were born, that old bastard's only comment to me was, 'didn't know you had it in you, professor.' Kindest thing he's ever said to me." Walter continued smiling in the face of what he realized many might now call John Taft's acuity, if not prescience. "But there's no reason to worry about your grandfather's finding out." Walter returned to the strategy of easing the boys' worries. "Nor for that matter, of anyone else finding out." There was no need to add to their suffering by telling them about Maxine Jefferson and the price she exacted for her silence. At the moment, she remained the only threat on the horizon. Or, at least, the only threat Walter was aware of. "So what else do you guys want to know?"

Jeremy wanted to know exactly what his father and Doctor Collins did, how often they saw each other, where they met, how much Norma Collins knew, whether his little kids understood anything. But he dared raise none of these questions. Nor did James venture into the areas he and his brother hypothesized about in their dark room.

"Maybe we've had enough for a first conversation," Walter said, standing up from the table. "I think we cleared away a bit of the fog, don't you think?" He began moving dishes and silverware to the kitchen counter. "No, no, you guys don't have to help." He waved James away from the sink. "Your dad's got everything under control. Mom would be proud of me."

"Can we talk again?" asked Jeremy.

Walter put his arm around Jeremy's shoulder. "We can always talk, son. You know that."

"I mean about all this. You know, about us."

Walter was immediately moved by Jeremy's use of the plural. He was sure the word embraced the three of them, when only a day before it meant only the two brothers. He wanted to hug the boy, but he did not. He had felt Jeremy's muscles tense when he put his arm around him an instant before. It'll take time, but they'll be fine. He was proud of them. Walter waved the boys out of the kitchen. "Hit the road, guys. There must be a million things you'd rather do on a Saturday morning than schmooze with your old man." He admired their straight backs as they walked out of the room. No slouching like when they had entered. Yes, he thought, they'll be fine. Walter looked forward to cleaning the kitchen. He was clear-eyed with no tears in the offing. He wanted to call Maggie. No, she'll probably think I'm putting on the best face after a disastrous talk with the boys. Better I tell her about it when she calls. He wished it were afternoon when Dennis would be free of patients. Maybe Ben or Jack. His spirits were so high, he wanted to share the elation with someone. He thought of going to his office in hopes of bumping into one of his confidants.

Walter wandered the empty house. He looked at the papers on his desk, but they held no claim on his nervous energy. He returned to the kitchen. Clean as he had made it, he reached for a yellow sponge and wiped the counters again. He looked out the window and thought of working the soil of his rose garden, or fiddling with Maggie's herbs. God, he whispered, I don't know what to do with myself. Perhaps Howard. He poured the last of the coffee and settled into an easy chair in the living room. As he dialed Howard's number, he heard the sound of a neighbor's power saw. He could imagine the aroma of cut wood. Walter breathed deeply. Maybe things will be good, he said aloud. Maybe. But then he thought of his empty bed upstairs and his mood changed. He set the receiver back in its cradle. What a fool I am. One conversation with the boys a better life doesn't make.

Suddenly chilled, he rubbed his hands together. Better read Maggie's note again. She had left explicit instructions about dinners as well as a list of approved restaurants should he decide to take her sons out. Maggie was an expert on which restaurants served food safe for her boys' stomachs. No matter how often Walter had laughed at her obsessive concerns, no matter how often he had reminded her that she couldn't monitor every morsel that James and Jeremy ingested, Maggie remained adamant. She had deluded herself into believing her sons avoided the greasy fast food places their friends frequented. As with her haughty rejection to the architect of Walters's suggestion that the boy's suite have a private entrance, Maggie placed James and Jeremy in a fantasy world of her creation. In most matters, Walter yielded. How could one hope to convince a woman who urged her family to carry an umbrella on the sunniest of summer days? Walter realized that he, too, was a character in Maggie's idealized family world. Just as she read conspiracies against her husband in the most innocuous criticism of his chairmanship, so she had created him as a model husband and father. Walter shook his head sadly. Maggie, dear Maggie. Even without Dennis, I could never have lived up to the character you created. Oh, Maggie, please don't tell your folks about our problems. About my problems. And please, Maggie, come home soon. He gently refolded her apron. He brought it to his lips. I do love you, Maggie. You do know that, don't you. He hung the apron on its hook in the pantry. He caressed the blue and green striped cloth. Is this the closest I'll get to you?

Oscar Lansing sat in a lounge chair on his red brick patio, reading a memorandum from the long range planning director. He frowned as he closed the maroon folder and mouthed the title of the work. The Role of the University in the Twenty-First Century. Oscar gazed at the garden he had cultivated for so many years. Circular rows of plants to guarantee color throughout the season. From the sky, he liked to think his handiwork resembled a miniature crop circle. I wonder if anyone up there has tried to read meaning into it? The role of the university in the twenty-first century? He smiled. If my calculations are right, there won't be any university then. There'll be nothing at all or we'll be drones of some very un-friendly invaders. Oscar once believed the aliens would look kindly on the inhabitants of such a meager planet. But more recently he had come to doubt that optimistic possibility. The more he read the accounts of abductees, the more fearful he had become of the aliens' plans for man-kind. And why not? We don't deserve any better. A bunch of ungrateful, selfish, destructive people. Egomaniacs all of them. And that moron's writ-ing about the next century when he should be preparing for …. For what? Oscar looked to the sky. What indeed? Only Jesus can save us from the calamity that everyday seems more and more inevitable. Please, Jesus, he whispered.

The previous Sunday, the provost had addressed his adult church class on that very subject. Actually, he enjoyed the youngsters much more. Kids who came to his weekly session with so few preconceptions, with so little hostility, with so few frustrations. They loved the bible stories. They listened intently to Doctor Lansing's quiet voice as he offered interpreta-tions that incorporated his devotion to Christian teachings and his belief in extra-terrestrials. Always careful to blend the two subjects in a reveren-tial way so as not to frighten the children, Oscar was beguiling. They adored hearing of cute little ET cavorting in the Judean hills with baby Jesus.

The adults were different. Mostly in their forties and fifties, the ma-jority female, they joined Oscar every Sunday at four in the vestry. At first, he wondered what most of them were doing there. A social event for lonely people? A gaggle of Miss Brills? A place to escape while their husbands watched Sunday afternoon games? A flock of football widows? Whatever the reasons, the group had stayed together for three years with only a few drop-outs. And every year, several more joined with them so that their number now reached over thirty. Oscar had started with the Pentateuch and was working his way steadily toward Revelation. At his current rate of speed, he figured he'd beat the arrival of the new century by a good year at least. Regardless of what might happen, his little flock would be ready.

Mavis Healy was always the first to arrive. Laden with cookies or cake, she started the coffee going and laid out cups and napkins. Mavis had been the first member of Oscar's Sunday afternoon family and re-mained his most devoted pupil. Smelling the brewing coffee as he entered the room, Oscar knew Mavis was on duty. And after three years of asking her to call him by his Christian name, he knew she would greet him as she had on that first Sunday. "Oh, Doctor Lansing," she said, her voice heaving as though she were out of breath, "how nice to see you again."

Oscar thought Mavis had stepped out of a play about a fading southern aristocratic family. A large woman, she carried her bountiful figure with a dignity that elicited deference from everyone who met her. Even the white lace hanky tucked into her right sleeve fit the image of a gracious woman who had seen better days. She managed the collation each week as if she were expecting a gathering of distinguished gentlemen at her father's white columned, green grassed estate. Whether the soft southern accent was genuine or manufactured, no one knew. For as outgoing and hospitable as Mavis was on Sunday afternoons in the church vestry, there was little of her past or, for that matter, her present life that she willingly divulged.

Oscar was not surprised to see Mavis carefully arranging the white plastic forks and spoons on the immaculate green table cloth she carried in her large bag each week. "A wonderful German chocolate cake this week, Doctor Lansing. It was a favorite, you may remember, two months ago." Oscar had learned not to ask who had baked the cake. It was always Mavis Healy. He remembered how offended she had been when he once suggested that other members of the group might like to contribute refreshments. After more than a year, he had prevailed upon her to allow others to occasionally bring Sunday afternoon sweets. "But, mind you, Doctor Lansing, I shall remain in charge of arrangements." She blushed deeply, apparently aware of her forward manner. "That is, I hope you will allow me the pleasure of continuing to arrange the collation." As always, a band of perspiration outlined her gray hair line where it met her pale forehead. The handkerchief, surely perfumed with a delicate magnolia aroma, dabbed at the droplets.

After greeting their brothers and sisters, pouring cups of coffee, readying notebooks and reading glasses, the rest of the class took their chairs arranged in a semi-circle around the provost.

Only here and at home did Lansing feel free to talk about the imminent arrival of the others. There was no Patrick Donovan to hurl snide, arrogant missiles in his directions. No curled lip references to the owl. No rolled-eyed, indulgent glances around the conference table. Here he was surrounded by Christian believers of the apocalypse as imagined by Oscar Lansing. It had taken time, of course, but he had brought them around. Not even the minister objected too strenuously to the strange blend of doctrines Oscar preached. After all, he had argued to the elders, the provost's theories were inevitably in the service of God. One always had to be willing to bring traditional religious teachings into the contemporary world. Even if the minister never preached Oscar's views, he did nothing to discourage them as long as they remained in the church vestry, and only at four o'clock on Sunday afternoons. And because no parent had objected, Oscar's Sunday school stories continued as harmless diversions the innocent children so obviously enjoyed. And they were certainly preferable, as the minister often reminded the elders, to the films on birthing the Unitarian kids watched in their Sunday school classes. At least Oscar's stories were about God.

"I should like to begin today's lesson with a personal anecdote," Oscar began. "I have been engaged in a long standing conflict, perhaps debate is a more Christian term, with another senior administrator at the university." Oscar smiled beneficently. "While I am sure he is the anti-Christ, albeit a seemingly benign man, a Catholic no less," Oscar returned the smiles of his flock and warmed to his subject, "a Jesuit if you please," a murmur of disapproval pleased the speaker, "it is his insistence that there is no possibility of extra-terrestrial life that most rankles me." Oscar nodded his head vigorously. "He is incapable of imagining the possibility of God's dominion encompassing a realm greater than our small planet. However, it is another difficulty I have with this man that I wish to mention as a way of entering today's text." Oscar paused. What he really wanted to do was lacerate the dean before such a receptive audience. With a nod of regret, he thought better of it. "This man of limited vision is convinced that I want to be the next president of the university. Mind you, I've said repeatedly in and out of his presence that I have no such desire. But as he cannot accept our beliefs, he cannot accept my statement for what it says. Deviousness clouds his ability to believe an honest man's honest words. Indeed, my friends, he is so symptomatic of the ills that plague our planet that I worry profoundly about the meeting that will take place between us and alien visitors. Why should they treat us kindly when we seem incapable of treating each other kindly? A good question, is it not? It is the text

I wish to explore this afternoon. Put in other terms, how do we appear to those others whose perceptions and intelligence so far outstrip our own? What can they make of a religious scholar, a priest, whose soul is so be-clouded that he must distrust the simple declarative truth delivered by a humble Christian? So twisted have we become in our overweening sense of self that we cannot view reality as it is. Thus that anti-Christ is emblematic of our dilemma."

Mavis, sitting at the edge of her chair, leaned forward in anticipation of Oscar's next words. Or, thought the provost, was she ready to say that a fresh pot of coffee was now ready.

Jack and Wilma, back from a three day honeymoon in New York, awaited the arrival of their first guests as man and wife. Helen and Joan were coming for brunch.

"Have we forgotten anything?" Wilma asked as she surveyed the table. An heirloom from her grandmother's simple apartment, the table looked good in Jack's dining room. After weeks of his urging her to consider a new house, one free of memories of two earlier wives, Jack had agreed to their starting married life in his house. His only condition was that Wilma oversee the redecorating. "From top to bottom, kiddo, I want our home to reflect you." Wilma was delighted. Happy to leave her cramped duplex, she looked forward to putting her stamp on the house. Painters and wall paperers were to begin work that week. "And after all my stuff's unpacked, we can go furniture shopping." Jack offered a good-natured, mock grimace. "There goes my TIAA annuity." But he was happy. He had told Ben that Wilma's obvious joy was a tonic for his aching bones.

"Why worry? How much do we need on the table for a simple brunch?" He kissed the back of her head. "You could have called Isobel Murdoch, you know, and got the name of her caterer. Remember that brunch I wasn't invited to? The one everybody talked about for weeks." Jack flapped his arms and danced around the table. "Prima donnas." He poured a cup of coffee and stared at Wilma. "God, you're beautiful. I wish you people could blush more obviously. I'd love to see the effects of my worshipful praise."

"Ah, but the mystery of darkness is far more enticing. This way you can imagine the effect you desire." She kissed his cheek. "You professors are good at fantasizing." Wilma intoned a deep southern accent. "And it's a lot better than being shut out by some pale faced honky bitch."

"Touche, Miss Mammy. Let me imagine then."

"You know," Wilma turned serious, "I think this is Helen's first social engagement since the rape."

"Social engagement? Pretty grand for ham and eggs."

"Eggs Benedict if you please. And it's Canadian bacon, not ham."

"Pretty uppity for someone of your persuasion."

"How's that again, Massa Billy Mann?"

Jack laughed. Both of them had heard of Billy's minstrel show. "He'll get his too, believe me. Once I finish working on Ben, I'll make sure we get Billy Mann's ass."

"But Ben promised."

"To hell with that promise. It was extracted under extreme duress. Never stand up in court. Not even in Ben's super moral supreme court. I'll convince him, don't you worry. Little Billy's going to be in for one big surprise."

The door bell interrupted Jack just as he was warming to the subject of Billy's downfall.

"They're here, honey. Please, no talk of this. Let's focus on making it a fun afternoon for Helen."

Helen and Joan came bearing gifts. "For the happy couple," said the guests as all four hugged and kissed.

"You two look great," said Helen. She dropped into an easy chair. "So, which one of the love birds is going to give me a glass of wine? Or is the department's old crone, Bullock, going to show up in a fancy maid's get-up?" Helen's eyes sparkled as of old. She winked at Joan.

"You look like the cat that swallowed that poor little canary." Jack opened the chardonnay. "Okay, ladies, what's the big secret? It's written all over your faces."

"Are we that obvious?" asked Joan. She held up her glass. "It's the famous good news, bad news gambit." She nudged Helen. "You go first."

"Just as we rehearsed it, right?" Helen's cheeks colored slightly. "Not sure whether my news is the good or the bad, but here goes." She sipped her wine. "I propose a toast to me."

"So, what's the occasion? Did they execute the bastard?" Wilma touched Helen's shoulder affectionately.

"From your lips to God's ear. No, his trial's been postponed again. My news is about me."

"For heaven's sake," said Joan. She rolled her eyes in mock exasperation. "Just get to the point." She flung her arms. "She can never say anything without a preamble. If you don't tell them, I will."

"Be my guest," said Helen.

"All right, I will." Joan and Helen clinked their glasses. "Professor Abrams has resigned." She held up her hand to silence any comments. "But she already has a new job. Even if it's in New York City. I mean, how could anyone leave this bucolic wonderland for the big apple? Gotta be crazy to go back to all those theatres and great restaurants."

"And parents. Don't forget them." Helen laughed. "I'll be trading this beautiful respectable distance for the same area code. Only a short subway ride will separate me from the old homestead. Ugh. But the enticements of the city and a new campus make it all worthwhile." Helen's smile faded. "I just couldn't hack it here after the rape. I mean, every class was torture. The kids looked at me as if I were a wounded bird. Not even my standard jokes got any response. And you'll never know how many double entendres can crop up in fifty minutes. It seemed as if everything I said had a gruesome double meaning." She shrugged and held out her glass for a refill. "Every class was a nightmare."

"She got on the phone with her old dissertation director and would you believe it, in a week he lined up a job."

"Pure shit luck," Helen added. "Some poor guy at City dropped dead. Right in his classroom, he croaked. So, good old Oliver got me in as a replacement. I start in two weeks to finish the semester. And they gave me another year besides. You know, to give me a good look before they ship me off to Podunk U. But, hey, it's no different from my position here. The worst that can happen is I'll be on the job market next year. Or, if I'm lucky, they'll give me a three year appointment. I could end up getting tenure there at about the same time as Walter's personnel task force would be considering me here." She drank more wine. "And back in New York I sure as heck won't be an exotic."

"Even if your folks have you addressing campaign envelopes and putting up posters." Joan leaned over Helen's chair and hugged her dear friend. "Isn't this great news?" she asked Wilma and Jack. "Except for my losing my only real compatriot, I think Helen's got a win-win deal. And I'm going to have a place to crash every time I need a New York fix. And believe me, I'll be there even when there's no MLA slave market to attract me." She held up her glass again. "Here's to visiting New York without the company of thousands of professors in black shoes and white socks. What a kick that'll be." Joan's happiness for Helen was conjoined with her own sadness at losing her friend, but she tried not to show the latter.

Wilma kissed Helen's cheek. "That's great news. Congratulations."

"Yes, great news, kiddo," echoed Jack. "Does Walter know yet?"

"Oh sure," said Helen. "He was terrific about it when I gave him my letter of resignation. And he was genuinely pleased when I told him about the job. He gave me a hug and said he wished he could go with me."

"I bet he'd love that," said Joan. "From what I've been hearing, our dear old chair would rather be anywhere but here right now." She raised her eyebrow in Jack's direction. "You going to tell us all about it?"

Jack ignored the question. "Well, kids, have we just heard the good news or the bad news?"

"You ain't heard nothing yet," said Helen. "We've saved the juiciest for last. Even if it is the bad news."

"Save it for table talk. Food's ready," said Wilma.

"It can wait," said Helen. "I'm starving."

Sun filtered in through the skylight over the dining room table as the four friends took their seats. "Looks wonderful," said Joan. "And I love the red roses." She winked at Helen. "I told you old Jack Williams was a closet romantic."

"Romantic? You bet," said Wilma as she stood up and pushed the power button on the stereo. The voices of Peter, Paul, and Mary filled the room. Jack blushed when he heard the strains of *We Shall Overcome.*" Wilma smiled. "He's got a bunch of records from the sixties tucked in behind all his operas and jazz."

They ate in silence for a few minutes and listened to the music. Memories of earlier days filled their minds. Wilma was nearly moved to tears for a lost national innocence.

"Eat up, kids," said Jack, his voice thick. "Those days are over. Long gone. We won the battle and lost the war." He smiled ruefully. "But they were great days, weren't they?"

"We were just kids then," said Helen. "But you were right there, Jack. Right in the middle of the anti-war movement." She stared at nothing for a moment. "It must have been wonderful."

"The ham and eggs sure are delicious," Jack laughed softly, trying to get Wilma's goat and change the subject at the same time. He pushed his chair back, poured more coffee, and lit a cigarette. The three women waited for his response. "Can't win today, can I?" He surveyed the table. "Well, yes, they were the worst of times and the best of times." He smiled. "You know that most of our colleagues would add a literary footnote at this point for the benefit of the great unwashed. But they were wonderful days. We actually ended the war and brought down a president. My students believed they could do anything. Christ, they thought they could change the world. And change it for the better. Believe me, they were beautiful kids. Bright and committed. What a time to be on a university campus. Not like today. What do they believe in now?" He ground out his cigarette angrily. "That's quite a question, isn't it? What do they believe in? What do their professors really believe in? What does our crummy culture tell them they should believe in?"

"I didn't expect an old LP would turn our brunch into a post mortem on the sixties or an analysis of contemporary culture." Wilma's eyes moved from Jack to Helen. Please bring the subject back to her, they implored.

"And you kiddo," Jack said, "soon you'll be in the big city. Won't take long for you to forget all us hicks." He raised his coffee cup. "And may the good gods smile on you all the rest of your days." He blew her a kiss.

Helen was touched more deeply than she had expected by the warmth in Jack's voice. "I'll never forget you, Professor Williams." She paused to throttle the catch in her throat. "I always knew that even in the worst of days, you'd be there. Among all the dead white men roaming the corridors of our beloved shit house, you were always the live one. And whenever I got too big for my britches, I knew you'd bring me down and set me straight with one of your verbal zingers." For a moment, Helen wasn't sure she wanted to leave.

"Thems kind words, kiddo." Jack was taken back to those earlier years by Helen's gratitude. Years when serious kids offered clumsy thanks to their Professor Williams. Years when he truly believed he had a vocation, a calling, rather than a job on an assembly line, turning out little clones of Bill Clinton and Mitchell Murdoch. He tipped an imaginary fedora in Helen's direction. "My father thanks you. My mother thanks you. And I thank you." He stared into Helen's eyes. "I thank you from the bottom of my heart."

At that instant, Helen knew she was listening to the real Jack Williams.

"And having borrowed those words from the great George M. Cohan, I will now offer my rendition of *Yankee Doodle Dandy*." He stood up and moved to the middle of the room. "If you bear with me, I'll also give you my rendition of Jimmy Cagney's stiff legged dancing." He began singing the Cohan song as he danced around the table. The three women joined in the song as a badly winded host completed his performance. Falling into his chair, Jack, breathing heavily, raised his hands to the blue beyond the skylight. "God almighty, those days sure are gone." He lit a cigarette and coughed. "I could have done a few more choruses in the good old days." He took a deep breath as if to prove that he could. "But this old body has been around the track too many times." He pointed to the cigarette. "And I've smoked too many of these coffin nails. But what the hell, it's not been a bad race. And now in my declining years," he reached for Wilma's hand, "I've finally come face to face with an angel." This time he blew a kiss at the sky beyond the skylight. "Thanks, old pal."

Wilma smiled. "Oh sure, Jack, a real angel."

"What declining years?" Joan asked brightly. "Let me second Helen's words. You, my friend, are younger than all those young old men we know and love so well. You're a kid, for God's sake."

Before he became maudlin, and he knew he was only seconds away, Jack forced a loud laugh. "Enough of this requiem for a heavyweight baloney. Now it's time for that juicy news you two kids promised us." He clapped his hands together. "And now, ladies and gents," he blew an imaginary trumpet, "the young-uns have the floor. What say you, Mrs. Williams, shall we give our undivided, rapt attention to our guests?"

Wilma tapped a drum roll with her spoon to accompany Jack's trumpet.

"Well," said Helen, nodding to her musical introduction, "we know who poisoned the fruit cocktail."

"And arranged the triple x-rated movie extravaganza," said Joan. "And won't you be surprised when we tell you."

"If we do tell them," Helen laughed.

'You must," said Wilma.

"Shall we?" asked Helen, batting her eyes in a fair imitation of Beverly Berlin. "Shall we, darling?"

"Oh yes, Professor Berlin, let's tell them even if they're not members of our veddy veddy elite band of literary theorists."

Striking a conspiratorial pose, Helen leaned forward. "Would you believe the villains are that little squirt, Billy Mann, and, hold on to your hats my fine friends, the boy scout of boy scouts, true blue Abraham Smith." She leaned back and folded her arms over her chest. "So, what do you think of them there apples?"

Jack and Wilma exchanged knowing glances.

"Just as we thought." Wilma smiled.

Jack whistled. "We guessed, but we hoped we were wrong."

"At least half wrong," added Wilma. "It would have been too delicious if Billy were the only one."

"And if they hung him by his balls." Jack lit another cigarette. "But Abraham. Why the hell did he team up with Billy Mann?"

"Who else knows?" Wilma asked, trying to stifle the laughter in her throat. She liked Abraham well enough, but the entire episode still was hilarious to her. Even her brief discomfort was worth the enjoyment she had received from watching the creaky wheels of justice trying to turn. And the travail of the principal players was joyous to behold. What trio more deserved such rich humiliation? Wilma couldn't muster a moment's sympathy for either Mitchell or Beverly. Two egomaniacs whose vanity deserved all that crap. And the president? Oh, Maxwell deserves much worse, she'd tell Jack. Her best sympathetic intentions were no match for the hilarity of it all. She laughed. "Really, it's all too funny. I never thought either of them could tie their own shoe laces. Sure, like all the rest of us, they talk a great game. But to actually pull off such stunts? If I were wearing a hat, I'd tip it to them. The keystone cops as successful terrorists. Who'd have thunk it?"

"But they're in for big trouble," said Helen, also trying to overcome the laugher she felt rising. "They're criminals." Her face turned scarlet as the laughter exploded. "I know it's terrible, but, God knows, it is funny."

Joan tried to scold both women. "What about Eleanor and the children? Haven't you thought of what's going to happen to them if Ab's caught?" Her stern look was suddenly overtaken by the others' laughter. Against her best intentions, Joan joined them.

Jack stared at the three women. Tears rolled down their cheeks as they now all shook with laughter. "Hey, ladies, time out." He held up his hands. "This is really serious." He frowned. "We've got to protect Abraham. Even if it means we have to protect that cocksucker too." The others paid him scant attention. Jack put two fingers in his mouth and whistled loudly. "For Christ's sake, come back to reality. Do you think Maxwell's going to send the state troopers packing before they arrest those two jerks? Do you really think Murdoch and Berlin will let this thing drop?" But before Jack could continue, he, too, broke into laughter. "Jesus, we're awful," he tried to continue his scolding of the three women. It was a losing attempt. He rocked in his chair and continued to laugh. He blew his nose and grabbed his chest to keep his ribs from their increasing pain. "Ladies, this is not funny."

All four laughed even harder.

Early Monday morning Billy Mann sat in the provost's sun-drenched waiting room. He smiled at the receptionist each time she glanced over at him. A friendly, warm ingratiating smile that he had rehearsed so often. Like a professional athlete who made even difficult plays look easy, Billy practiced the moves of his public demeanor. He could call them up whenever he wished. He thought of a shortstop's easy glide to his left to start a game ending double play. He, too, was that good. And Billy did enjoy social games.

"Beautiful day," he murmured almost seductively to the young woman behind the white desk. At first glance, he knew she was shy and inexperienced. "Been working here long?"

She smiled at him and nodded. "Six months," she said.

Billy did not fail to notice the slight reddening of her cheeks as she turned back to her computer keyboard. I could get her into the sack by noon if I wanted to, he thought as he checked the knot of his gray silk tie. He had spent time that morning making sure his sincere appearance would be perfect. This would be even better than visiting a dying Abraham Smith at University Hospital. And this is the real thing, he thought. If he could only finish his damn book with the same ease, he'd in be in like Flynn. Wonder where that idiom came from. Oh yes, a completed manuscript accepted by a prestigious university press would be the icing on the cake.

Billy smiled once more at the young woman. Wonder what she'd be like in bed. The thought of deflowering a virgin was another of his fantasies. Not even his wife had been virginal when he first took her to bed. The times, he thought. Everyone fucked like bunnies then. Christ, on weekends, the fraternity house was one big brothel. His eyes undressed the receptionist. Oh yes, she'd be willing. All he had to do was check the reservation list on the inside of his suite's door. Two bedrooms, a bathroom, and four guys. The calendar had been blocked out in hour long grids. "What's your name, anyway?" he asked.

Her blush was redder this time. "I'm Patricia, Professor Mann." Had she looked up, she would have seen the professor lightly run his hand down his zipper, stopping teasingly over his cock. God, he loved games. He imagined putting his name in one of the hour blocks on the grid, perhaps even adding Patricia after Billy. He'd show her what fucking was all about. She'd love it.

At that moment, the provost entered the room. He nodded at Billy on his way to the young receptionist's desk. "Good morning, Pat," he said as he looked at his appointment list which she handed to him. "Be sure to put the president through when he calls." Oscar nodded to Billy again. "Be with you in a few minutes, Mann. Sorry about running late even this early in the day." He disappeared into his office.

Fuck you, owl. I had a nine-thirty appointment, you stupid son of a bitch. Billy frowned at the young woman he had ravished only moments before. If I were one of your tenured stars, I wouldn't be sitting here cooling my heels while you screw around in your office. He removed a cigarette and tapped it against its package. Even though it had a filter tip, Billy thought tapping had an elegant look. Bogart or, better, James Mason or

Orson Welles about to interrogate a Nazi or proposition a gorgeous married woman. Oh yes, it was all in the manner. Appearance was the ticket. He lit the cigarette. So there's no ash tray in the room. Big deal. She can get me one. He waved the cigarette in Patricia's direction. "Ash tray," he said. No smile this time. She had already served her purpose. His manner need be insinuating no longer. He could pass her on campus without even a smile. Christ, she wasn't that good in bed anyway. Who cares if she wants more. He laughed out loud. Let someone else screw her next time. Lots of fresh pussy where that one came from.

"Oh, Professor Mann, the provost doesn't allow smoking in the office."

Allow? Who the hell does he think he is. I bet Beverly cunt Berlin can have a cigarette here. And that dickhead, Maxwell, can light up one of his expensive cigars anywhere he wants. Probably a substitute for his puny prick anyway. Billy glowered at Patricia, now looking nervously at the provost's closed door and the cigarette smoke curling its way toward it. "Just get me one of those styrofoam cups with some water in it." He held up the long ash at the tip of his cigarette. "Either that or I'll just flick it on his cheap carpet." He leered at the poor girl. "Your choice, sweetheart." You'll sure as shit never get into my fraternity house again.

Oscar's door opened and the provost stood there sniffing. He stared at Billy's cigarette as if it were a poisonous viper ready to strike. Oscar waved the smoke away. He sighed. "I never thought we'd need a no smoking sign these days." He crinkled his nose and sighed again. "Why don't you put that thing out and come in." Might as well get this over with. Lansing had not looked forward to a meeting with young Mann

Ought to fix him up with my mother-in-law, Billy snickered to himself. That'd be quite a pair. What I wouldn't give to see those two creeps get it on. Unruffled, Billy dropped the cigarette into the white cup and placed it on Patricia's desk. He nodded at her, hoping that the curtness of the nod made clear their relative positions in the world according to Billy Mann.

Now seated before Oscar's desk, Billy lounged in the black leather easy chair as if he were watching Sunday football in his own living room. He waited for the provost to speak.

"So, Professor Mann, what can I do for you?"

Billy's anger rose again. He had heard that little twerp call Abraham by his first name on more than one occasion. You'll get yours too, yes you will. As much as he disliked the dean, he knew that once he had tenure, he'd support Patrick Donovan in his quest for the presidency. Put your money on the winning horse and you can't lose.

"I'm not happy being here," Billy began, trying to sound somber. He tried a boyish grin, but it had no effect on Lansing. "It's about that awful Saturday." Billy was disappointed by the provost's lack of immediate interest. He had expected an instant show of great curiosity. Instead, Oscar seemed to be perusing his day's schedule while Billy's play-acting went virtually unnoticed.

"And what about that awful Saturday, as you refer to it?" Lansing did not look up. "And why come to me if you have information about it?" He pushed aside his day's agenda and stared directly at his visitor. "As you know, there is an ongoing police investigation of the matter." He stood up and moved toward the door. "I am the provost of this university, its chief academic officer. I am not the police, Professor Mann."

That damn Professor Mann again. He wants me out of here. All right, you fucking owl, let's play it your way. Throwing away his prepared script, Billy went directly to the conclusion he had so carefully planned to lead to, insinuating and hesitating on the way. "I know who's responsible for those events. I know who the guilty person is." Billy now was standing face to face with the provost who had his hand on the door knob.

"Why, then, if I may ask, Professor Mann, do you not take that information to the police?" The provost's distaste for the confidence and for Billy Mann was evident in his tone. "Why do you bring such information to me?"

For a moment Billy was confused. This was not the response he had expected. Expected? Indeed, the response he was sure his news would elicit. Can Lansing be as uninterested as he appeared? Or can he, too, be a superb actor? "Don't you want to know who did those terrible things? Don't you care that it was a member of your faculty?" Billy was now in control again. He sat down once more, his back now to the provost who still stood at the door. Billy fell into a tone of deep respect for the university and their profession. "I wanted your advice, sir, on how to proceed." The sir almost stuck in his throat, but he knew it was perfect for the moment. "I thought,"

Billy stammered in a boyishly innocent way, "we'd want to protect the university." He turned his head sideways. His profile, he knew, was good. "That's why I came to you, sir, rather than the police." He tried to force a blush. "And Abraham is a friend of mine, a dear and close friend."

"Abraham Smith?" the provost inquired softly. He moved back to his desk. "Are you telling me that Smith is responsible for those videos at Professor Berlin's?"

Billy nodded and looked pained. "And the poisoning at the dinner." He dropped his eyes. "Awful, but true, sir." Billy's voice cracked.

The provost was silent for several moments. Not even the intercom seemed to break his concentration. "President Maxwell on line two." Lansing slowly picked up his phone. "Tell him I'll get back to him in a little while." He toyed with a small space ship on his desk. Billy noticed the cross painted on its side. "A gift from my children's study class," Oscar said absently. "And how do you know all this, Professor Mann?"

"Ab told me. More than once before that Saturday, he told me what he was planning." Billy wrung his hands. "At first I thought he was just kidding." Billy looked directly into the older man's eyes. "But when I realized he was serious, I tried to talk him out of it. On more than one occasion, sir, I pleaded with him not to do it."

"And evidence?" Oscar asked. "Do you have evidence of any of this? Otherwise, it's one man's word against another's." Lansing returned Billy's gaze. "And since you're both standing for tenure, one might, uncharitably to be sure, think the worst of your charges." Once again the provost's tone angered Billy.

"Oh, I have evidence."

"And what might that be?"

"Tape recordings," Billy almost smiled.

"You taped conversations with your friend?" Oscar raised his eyebrows. His distaste was now a palpable thing. "What in heaven's name prompted you make such recordings?"

"Protection, sir, protection. I had to defend myself against charges Abraham might level against me." He wrung his hands again. "He was irrational. I was afraid he might go after me, too." Billy tried to stammer. "I'm telling you, sir, he was irrational."

"I just can't imagine Smith irrational." Oscar tried to read Billy Mann. *Whether he's telling the truth or not, this is Uriah Heep sitting before me.*

"What do you suggest we do?" asked Billy. He dropped his voice to a whisper. "Now you see why I couldn't go to the police. How could I turn him in? He's my friend." Billy stood up and put his hand on the provost's shoulder. He squeezed gently. "And we have to consider poor Eleanor and those beautiful young children." Billy thought better of squeezing the provost's shoulder a second time. He retreated to his black leather chair. "What shall we do, sir?" The laughter in his gut was in marked contrast to the plaintive, soulful sound of his words. He cradled his chin in the tips of his extended fingers. *I hope the fucker notices my posture of prayer. Christ, I'd pray to his little green people if they'd guarantee success with this caper.*

Events of the last few days had prompted Billy's decisive action. He was now sure Ab was close to confessing everything. A full frontal assault on Abraham Smith was required. *I always knew he was a wimp. The best defense, after all, is an offense.* The triteness of that thought almost caused Billy to blush.

Oscar Lansing snapped out of his silent contemplation. "Let me consider this, Mann. But I must ask you to keep this conversation confidential. The fewer people who know right now, the better." He stood up. "I'll get back to you very soon. You can count on that." He led Billy to the door.

Not even a fucking handshake. Not even a thank you. Billy pursed his lips and said nothing. He left the office.

"See you later, sweetheart," he said as he passed Patricia's desk. For an instant, he thought of a quick blow job, but there were now a couple of others waiting for the provost's ear. He adjusted his tie, smiled at the room, and left the administration building.

Oscar Lansing made two telephone calls. He wanted a meeting as soon as possible with Ben Rosenthal and Jack Williams. He shook his head. "What a miserable snake he is." He closed his eyes and imagined hostile extra-terrestrials swooping down on the campus and abducting Donovan and Mann. What a delightful thought. Might as well toss in Murdoch and Berlin too. Make a clean sweep of that department. He thoughts went back to the halcyon days of his university administration.

Literature professors who actually spoke English and enjoyed literature. Colleagues who saw teaching as a noble calling. He put his hands to his temples. Where has it all gone? he asked softly. It seems only yesterday that this was a hallowed place. Before the barbarians entered the sanctuary. We never thought it could happen. Now they've donned the high priests' robes. Once beautiful robes now rent and soiled by those grubby beings bent only on preferment and self adulation. Oscar knew he was romanticizing a past that never really matched his imaginings. But those were better days, he said out loud. He looked through a window at the bright sky. Is it any wonder they think so poorly of us. Oh Lord, why are you waiting so long? He touched the small space ship. The children. A slight smile broke the rigidity of his face. If only we can nurture the children. If only we can keep them from the grasp of the barbarians. He thought of Blake's little lambs and visions of an earlier sacred time suffused him. God, it seemed so good then. Oscar depressed the call key of his intercom. "All right, Patricia, get the president on the phone." Another barbarian, thought the provost. The analysis of political attire indeed. He almost chuckled. Lord, but we've become an asylum.

Abraham sat before the television set, but his mind was far from the Sunday morning talking heads pontificating about the state of American politics. Eleanor sat next to him on the couch. The remains of their breakfast were on the snack tables before them.

"Ab, you haven't touched your bagel. And it's one of those everything bagels you love."

"Can't get a good bagel in this town anyway," said Abraham. His voice was expressionless.

"True enough, but these are from the batch Helen's folks sent her. They're the real thing." She moved his plate closer to him. "Try them, you'll like them."

Ab did as he was told and took a bite.

"Since when do you eat a plain bagel? Put some cream cheese on it. And don't forget the lox. And the tomatoes and onions." She nudged him. "What would Helen say about the way goyim have to be taught to eat. You remember the day you asked for jam when we had breakfast at her apartment? The lecture she gave you. You could get killed at the Carnegie Deli if you asked for jelly for your bagel. Like putting mayonnaise on a hot pastrami sandwich."

Once again, Ab did as he was told. He covered the cream cheese with a layer of lox and gently added onion and tomato. Then he left the bagel on his plate, untouched and uneaten. Ab sighed and continued to look at the TV screen without really seeing or hearing Sam, Cokie, and George pepper a senator with questions about the latest crisis in the Middle East.

"Okay, Abraham, let's have it. What's eating you today?"

"Nothing. Nothing at all. Just engrossed by the program."

"You couldn't even tell me what they're talking about. Lying has never been your strongest talent." She touched his arm. "I have learned a few things about you, you know."

Abraham did not answer.

"I bet you didn't hear a word I said." Eleanor was getting angry. "Well, if you don't want that bagel, I'm not going to let it go to waste." She moved the food from his plate to hers. Exasperated, she turned her attention to the television set.

"I think I'm going to cop a plea."

"Oh, Christ, now he sounds like some hood on Hill Street Blues." She shook her head and took a cigarette from the pack she no longer hid. "First he's morose and silent," she blew smoke in his direction, "and now he's Al Capone. Cop a plea yet. Give me a break, Ab. You're going to do no such thing." Eleanor laughed angrily. A short dismissive laugh. "You'll confess over my dead body. And whatever gave you that stupid idea anyway?" She tried unsuccessfully to blow a smoke ring. "Cop a plea," she repeated derisively. "You know, I love you dearly, but, Jesus, you can be an awful dope."

"They're going to find out sooner or later anyway," Abraham said, "and a confession might get me a better deal."

"Sure. You'll avoid the chair."

"I'm serous." He looked at Eleanor. "I've given this a lot of thought. Believe me I have." He turned to her. "I haven't been able to think of anything else lately. You know I can't sleep. My teaching's gone to hell. I don't eat much." He blushed. "And you've surely noticed our sex life hasn't been something to write home about."

"Right, Ab, I always write mom every time we screw. Your scintillating use of the English language has sure as hell suffered. Since when have you become the cliché expert?" She laughed. "Remember that story about the cliché expert testifying? You'll be something else when you cop your plea. And will good old honest Abe take the fall for that toad too? Why not? Might as well go all the way. Why not confess to that murder last week in Centerville too. And don't forget all those thefts from the school lunch program. Might as well show the cops our garage full of that macaroni and cheese you took out of the mouths of all those babes."

"Don't make fun of me." Abraham's trembling voice rose. "I'm tired of your criticizing me. Always poking fun at what I say." He almost shouted. "Can't you realize how serious I am?" He took back the half of his bagel that Eleanor had not eaten. He turned it over on his plate and ground in the lox, cream cheese, onion, and tomato. He sat back and folded his arms.

"Now there's a mature gesture," Eleanor snorted. "You going to empty your cup of coffee on the white rug next? Or stand up and stamp your feet? And what comes next? A rap across my face? Jesus Christ, Ab, I do take you seriously. But that doesn't mean I have to agree with every lame brained idea you come up with. Or applaud dumb-assed clichés as if they were literary gems." She lit another cigarette. "And don't you dare say a word about my smoking." Eleanor inhaled deeply. "Gotta have a few pleasures while you're doing time in the big house." That derisive laugh again. "I hope at least the con who claims you for his wife is cute."

Abraham bolted from the table and rushed to his study. He slammed the door behind him and dropped into his desk chair. He stared at the pile of papers he had promised to return to his graduate students the next day. Couldn't even read them in an afternoon. Probably never have to grade them anyway. Maybe they'll let me work in the prison library. Son of a bitch Billy will probably end up the warden and I'll spend my time in solitary. But maybe he's right after all. Maybe we are smarter than the cops. But they still hang around, asking questions of everyone. And Maxwell isn't going to give up. Abraham thought of the peculiar look the president gave him when they passed each other on campus the other day. Don't worry, Billy said. We are more clever than they are. Just stay cool and we'll be home free. Stay calm and soon we can go back to our battle for tenure. This'll all be ancient history. Bastard. I don't know how he stays so calm. Still smiling. Still dropping one liners about the old timers. Still more concerned about his attire than our troubles. God, let him be right. Let us go back to things as they were. The good old days. The contest for tenure, Walter's problems, the arrogant clones of Mitchell Murdoch who drove him mad, Jack and Wilma, the Maxine Jeffersons of the campus, Helen's rape. All these worked their way through his mind. The good old days. He smiled. What I wouldn't give to have them back on my worry list instead of this. He thought of the ugly seminar room he reluctantly entered each week. Now he longed for it. He looked at the papers again. Maybe I shouldn't cop a plea. Even he laughed at the words. Maybe I should call Billy right now. He did think I had gone over the edge when I told him I was considering turning myself in. No, a telephone call wouldn't convince him. Better I see him tomorrow. Face to face will be better. I can convince him I'm not going to do anything rash. Plenty of time. Tomorrow. Abraham felt relieved. He stood up and stretched.

He walked up behind Eleanor who was doing the breakfast dishes. Abraham put his arms around her waist. "You're right again, honey. I'm not going to turn myself in."

Eleanor turned around and put her wet hands on Ab's cheeks. "Thank God you've regained your senses." She kissed him. "Welcome back to the world of sanity." Eleanor rested her head on his shoulder. "We'll beat this rap together."

The three men looked like conspirators as they sat staring at the small black tape player on the provost's desk. The hollow, sometimes muffled voice was unmistakably that of Abraham Smith.

Jack Williams finally spoke. "You'd think the prick would have had state of the art equipment." He stood up and walked to the window. "What in God's name has happened to this place?" He looked out at the campus. "It looks the same, but it sure as hell isn't. Appearance and reality again." He lit a cigarette, ignoring the new no smoking sign on the wall. "So what do we do now?" The question was directed at Ben Rosenthal who sat, shaking his head in disgust.

"Terrible. This is terrible," said Ben. "I still can't believe young Smith did those things. Simply terrible."

"But this is evidence," said Oscar, pointing to the tape player. "We have to forget for the moment the gross violation of Smith's confidence. The fact is that Mann has produced this tape. And it is Smith planning the entire thing. The video tapes, the poison, the whole thing. And we do hear Mann trying to talk him out of it. And the other tape is even more incriminating. The one after the events. Smith's almost gloating about what he did on that one. And once again it's Mann who tries to convince him to turn himself in, to throw himself on Maxwell's mercy." The provost leaned back and looked at the two other men. "Well, gentlemen, what do you suggest? You know I haven't told anyone else about these tapes yet. But I can't keep them secret much longer."

"Yes, Oscar," said Ben, "we appreciate your calling us first."

"We go back a long way," Lansing said quietly. "A long way back when the university was a more pleasant place."

"You can say that again," said Jack. "I hate to say this, but I think we have to turn the tapes over to the president. Put the thing in his hands."

"But not without first speaking with Abraham," said Ben. "Call it due process, collegial responsibility, friendship. Call it whatever you want. We owe him at least that courtesy."

"What's the point?" asked Oscar. "The evidence is here."

"We must give him a chance to respond to this before we hang him."

"And bringing the tapes to Maxwell will be the first step toward a lynching," Jack muttered. "I don't know what the hell he thought he'd gain by humiliating Berlin and Murdoch."

"And hurting a lot of innocent people in the process," the provost reminded. "These are serious offenses."

"I know, I know," said Ben, throwing his arms in the air. "But all the same, I sometimes think it was a grand scheme."

"Ben, you can't be serious." The provost was surprised.

"I am serious." He smiled at his old friend. "Can you think of two people who deserve it more than those two quacks? Throw in our beloved president and it's a trio that couldn't be matched anywhere for pomposity and plain old stupidity. Three prima donnas who got their comeuppance in spades." The civil libertarian laughed until his face was red and damp. "Wonderful. That's what it was. Wonderful." He nodded to Lansing. "Of course it's terrible too. Of course it can't go unpunished. But in secret delicious moments, I think we ought to give Smith a commendation."

"Only the good lord knows what Maxwell will do to him," said Oscar.

"We must urge him to keep the entire matter within the university. I don't want him to turn the thing over to the police and the courts."

"But remember, Ben, the governor and his assistant were also involved." Oscar was uncomfortable playing the inquisitor's role. "I'm only trying to indicate the breadth of the anger out there."

"The governor." Ben started laughing again. "Another sterling individual who deserved to mess his pants." He wiped his eyes with a handkerchief. "I'm sorry, but it was an event I would have given anything to have attended."

"So why didn't you?"

"Oscar, you can't ask that seriously. I should go to a dinner honoring the greatest of the fakers among us? I should raise a glass to toast Murdoch? Only if his glass was laced with a heavy dose of hemlock would I have toasted that man." Ben's eyes now sparkled. "Not even Beverly's as bad as he is." He started laughing again. "But I would have loved to have been at her video show too. To have seen Maxwell paralyzed by all those animated genitalia would have been well worth any price of admission. Even if I had to bear Donovan's hymn to cultural expression."

"Ben, don't you realize how serious this whole thing is?" the provost asked.

"Forgive me, Oscar." He looked at Williams. 'Forgive me, Jack. I know a young man's future is at stake here, but he is responsible for one of the greatest events of modern academic life. After all, how often in one's life does metaphor become reality? Merde. All has become merde. Remember old Dickens. Merdle is the name of the age. He could have been talking about the world of humanistic study in our time. And to have all those charlatans who spout all that crap actually covered in their own merde. Don't you see how fitting it all is? God almighty, Smith became the performance artist for our time on that Saturday. He deserves the Pulitzer at least. Surely not the condemnation that awaits him." Ben waved down the provost. "Of course I know how serious this is. Of course I do. But for a moment, at least, indulge an old warrior's fancies."

Jack nodded his head. "But the facts remain." He gestured toward the tape player. "The little bastard's dropped a bombshell into our laps and we can't ignore it."

"All right," said Oscar. "I'll hold onto this for another day. That'll give you time to meet with Smith and report back to me." The provost rubbed his forehead. "I did tell Mann I'd get back to him. Who knows how many copies of these tapes he has or when he'll decide to bring them directly to the president or the police. I'll call him this afternoon and tell him I'll take the evidence to Maxwell on Thursday." He glanced at his watch. "You've got better than a day. Use the time wisely, Ben." He nodded at Jack. "Look after our comedic genius here."

Billy's squash game had never been better. He chased Peter all over court and beat him soundly. The two men, panting and perspiring, towels draped around their necks, left the court.

Sitting on a wooden bench in the men's locker room, they pulled off their sneakers and socks. "You beat the hell out of me today," said Peter. "You must have had a great week-end."

"Actually it was a great Monday that got me all revved up." Billy laughed. "You'll never know what a great day yesterday was." And what a better one Thursday will be. For only a moment, Billy's joy was tempered by the provost's message. I don't why the owl needs another day. He'd act a lot quicker with Murdoch or Berlin, you can bet. But it'll still be sweet. So what's another day? Good things do come to those who are patient. Isn't that the kind of thing honest Abe would have embroidered on a pillow. What a jerk.

"Tell me about it."

"Some day, Peter, some day." Billy stood up to remove his shirt and shorts. He was only inches from Peter. Like a burlesque queen, Billy took off his shirt slowly. He let his fingers brush his nipples as he moved the shirt over his head. He had known for some time that Peter was interested in him. And even though Billy had no sexual desire for other men, he loved center stage as he loved manipulating people. Ever since he became sure that Peter swung both ways, he had gone out of his way to tease his younger colleague. He felt Peter's eyes on him and he loved it. Now it was time to take off his white gym shorts and display the crown jewels. But first, he leaned over Peter's shoulder to reach a fresh towel from his locker. The position was exaggerated enough so that his crotch made contact with the other man's shoulder. He kept it there for a moment. "Boy, am I ready for a hot shower," said Billy as his fingers grasped the elastic waistband of his shorts. Slowly, he hoped tantalizingly, he moved his shorts lower and lower. Now he knew his pubic hair was visible. He hesitated. The strip tease shouldn't be too fast. You have to leave something to the imagination. He looked up for a second and was delighted to see Peter's eyes transfixed by the performance. This was not the first time Billy Mann did his bumps and grinds. Now the shorts were off and Billy stood before Peter. His penis, of which he had always been proud, was only a few inches from the still seated Peter. Billy almost hoped he'd try to reach out and touch it. He had rehearsed a response for that eventuality too. Oh, Peter, I do like you, but, blush and hesitation, I'm really not that way. Hand on the other's shoulder. But we can always be good friends. However, Peter simply stared and made no movement. Instead, he stood up, disrobed quickly, grabbed his towel, and headed for the shower room. Billy chuckled and followed.

Each time he showered with Peter, Billy had hoped to see him aroused. But Peter had greater control than he had expected. Or could it be that he didn't find Billy attractive? Impossible. And Billy did try. He soaped himself almost lasciviously. Standing in full sight of Peter, he caressed himself as the shower washed off the soap. But no luck. Peter followed the same routine, but always with his back to Billy. The final act was invariably the shortest. Toweling off his wet body, Billy would offer yet another version of the strip tease. In reverse, he would now dress in a suggestive way, exactly the way that drove Sally crazy. And once again, Peter seemed not to notice. Yet in Billy's richly furnished imagination, Peter saw all and was aroused. Surely, he would masturbate while calling up those scenes of Billy's nude body. Surely he would. He must.

Billy was right about one thing anyway. His performance never went unnoticed. Peter was fully aware of Billy's actions. He is precisely the son of a bitch so many claimed. But he's also going to get tenure and I can't afford to antagonize him. A tenured Billy Mann was not an enemy a young assistant professor wanted. He could be destroyed.

So Peter watched the strip tease, felt Billy's crotch on his shoulder, and said nothing. Not that he had never been tempted. Billy was handsome and his body was beautiful. But Peter understood the game being played at his expense. He had long since abandoned his earlier fantasies of bedding this guy. Thank God he had never made a pass. Peter thought about all this as he watched Billy soap himself. Now instead of wanting to hold him, Peter wanted to punch that handsome face. Beat him bloody. But he only turned his back to Billy.

"Next Tuesday, same time," said Billy as he slipped on his blue blazer. He smiled at Peter. "Give you a chance to redeem yourself." He patted Peter's shoulder. "Gotta run if I'm going to make my class." He left the locker room without waiting for a reply. Might as well give him a few private minutes to play with himself. Billy laughed out loud as he left the building and entered the tree lined path to the humanities building. He walked along, green bag over his shoulder, and nodded pleasantly to all he passed. He felt good. A great squash game, another superb performance, and the Thursday meeting with the provost. Terrific. Billy patted the green bag and felt the two identical packages. One for Dean Donovan, the other for President Maxwell. He whistled a happy song. He had the world on a string. Why not enjoy it. He almost felt like skipping along the path like a small child with nothing at all to worry about.

Peter did not spend any private minutes in the men's locker room. He felt lousy. What he wanted most at that moment was squash lessons from a grand master of the court. He wanted to wipe the court next week with a defeated, mortified Billy Mann. Run the bastard ragged. Beat him so badly that the superior smile would never be seen again in the gym. And if the fantasy could continue, it would be Peter who would perform the strip tease. A desperate Billy would stare longingly at Peter's cock only inches from his face. And it would be an aroused Billy, eyes bulging at Peter caressing himself in the shower. But it would be Peter's performance. Oh Billy, I do like you, but you're just not my type. I like guys with really big cocks. Oh yes, that would be perfect. Make the thing shrivel up to nothing. But that's not even close to reality, Peter thought as he packed his gym bag. His shoulders sagged as he left the building. Fact is the bastard will probably beat the tar out of me again. If only he'd take me up on swimming. I'd leave him in my wake. But Billy's too smart to try anything where he doesn't have an edge. Peter slouched along the path to his building. *How can I get out of these Tuesday games with him? Maybe the bastard will break a leg.* The thought gave Peter a moment's pleasure. *At least I've got a week without him.*

Walter was troubled by the provost's call. He said it was urgent that they meet as soon as possible about a most delicate matter involving a member of the department. A matter he thought it prudent not to discuss over the telephone. *Was all this coded language? Was Lansing really talking about Walter? Was there yet another revelation about his personal life that was now university business? What terrible tales had been brought to the provost? And by whom? Should he call Ben? The provost confided in Ben and often sought his advice. He might know what the urgent call was about. And Ben was safe. One of the few who knew about him and Dennis.*

Walter put the receiver back into its cradle. His face was pale. His hands trembled. *Abraham Smith? It couldn't be. He had hired Abraham. He had befriended him, had Abraham and Eleanor to the house many times. He had gone way out on the limb with the president himself to fight Murdoch and Berlin about tenure for Abraham. Could this man be responsible for the Saturday massacres? I wish Maggie were home. She'd know how to proceed.* He looked out the window at the bright sun. *She was right. You never know when you'll need an umbrella.* It was only then that Walter felt a sense of relief that he was not the object of the urgent meeting. *He was right to call Ben.*

He thought of the last urgent meeting with Oscar Lansing. "So, Walter, tell me about your letter to the campus paper," Oscar had begun.

The chairman examined Oscar's face, looking for any hint of what the provost knew. *Was the question as innocent as it sounded? Just wanting an explanation for Walter's unexpected support of Maxine Jefferson. Or did he know of the reason for the letter, for the literature faculty marching with Maxine's army?* Walter tried to sound coolly professional. "Just a statement of my view of the matter." He did not look away.

"Your view of the matter?" The provost chuckled. "And since when have you been in Maxine Jefferson's camp? You're surely not telling me you agree with that malarkey about a black student union. Come on, Walter, we've known each other too long for that. I'd bet my house on your voting against such a perversity." He stared at his visitor. "You've got to come up with something better than that. And you're not the only one. Ben and Jack marching with her? And young Smith? I was sure he had better sense than that." He waved his hand in a dismissive motion. "The other one, of course, is a viper. I wouldn't even hazard a guess as to what motivated Mann. It's self interest, of course, but the genesis of it I don't know." Oscar leaned back in his heavily padded chair. "So, tell me. Why the letter? Why Ben and Jack joining that woman?"

"Why don't you ask them?"

"I did. But they were so patently elliptical in their responses that I knew something was cooking over in your department. So I'm asking you. You're the chair, for God's sake. Of all people, you must know what they've all been smoking in that fancy Wallace Lounge of yours."

Walter was pleased that Ben and Jack had kept his confidence, but he was unsure about how to proceed at the present moment. "There's really nothing to say other than what I've already told you. I've had a change of heart."

"Baloney," Oscar snapped. He leaned forward. "Look, Walter, I don't want to make a federal case out of this, but I've got to have something to take back to the president. You know by now, of course, that we were all in Maxwell's office when Jefferson's people marched on the administration building. Richard was furious. The way he gets when he's cornered. He didn't have any idea of how to respond to Maxine's taunts. And you don't have to be a fortune teller to divine what Donovan's advice was. It was Patrick who urged Richard to go for the jugular." The provost put his hands to his temples. "My advice was ignored of course. I wanted him to play it by the book, but Richard surely had the next day's press releases in mind. Whenever there's an opportunity for good press, even at the price of bad policy, you know where our illustrious prexy will be." That sly smile again. "Your two colleagues said virtually nothing. Murdoch and Berlin just observed it all. To give them some credit, though, I must say neither of them looked comfortable." The provost stood up and sat on the edge of the desk, directly in front of Walter. "In any event, Richard wants a report from Patrick. I want to ward off the damage that slippery scoundrel might cause. So I've spoken with Ben and Jack, and now with you. What I never expected was the stone wall you three have erected." Oscar touched the chair's arm. "Walter, this will not do. I cannot protect you and your department without cooperation. You can imagine the report Donovan will concoct. With the aid of Mitchell and Beverly, to be sure. Trust me, Walter. They'll use this opportunity to further erode your standing with the president. It'll simply be more ammunition for their assault on your department."

Walter said nothing.

"For God's sake, man, don't you understand what I'm saying? They mean to bring you down and re-create the department in their image. Any damn fool can see the way they've been working Maxwell for weeks." Oscar's voice dropped. "And you and Ben and Jack are not damn fools." He spoke deliberately and slowly. "Don't you men want to save the literature department? Or have you already surrendered?" He pulled a file from a drawer. "And what am I to make now of all these memoranda seeking my intervention? How can I intervene without your aid?"

Walter remained silent. The turmoil in his mind, however, raged. His personal life was not the subject of the provost's call for this meeting. But how could he protect his department from the Murdoch gang and still maintain his privacy? "I don't know what to say, Oscar." Did he dare trust the provost as he had Ben and Jack? He feared Oscar's great moral commitment. Unlike the others, Oscar had administrative responsibilities which he considered sacred. Did he dare?

"So, Walter, I beseech you."

"There are reasons, Oscar."

"Of course there are reasons." The provost was losing his temper. "Of course there are reasons. For heaven's sake, Walter, the reasons are what I must have." He sat back, exasperated. "Do me a favor. Try to frame a couple of simple declarative sentences that even the president will understand. Simple sentences that explain the bizarre behavior you literary types manifested last week. I'm not asking for much, Walter. Not for a great novel or an epic poem. Just a few sentences. That's all. Not much to ask from an English professor, is it?" Oscar's voice betrayed his impatience. There was his reputation on the line too. How he wanted to bury Donovan with a few simple facts that would explain the entire matter. He longed to see Patrick humiliated before the president. A happy bonus, he thought, would be at least a temporary roadblock in Murdoch and Berlin's steam-roller. What I'd give to see all three of them tongue-tied for a change. But it all depended on Walter's simple declarative sentences. He thought of the president preening in front of his wall of honors. Yes, Walter, the simpler the better.

"It's about me, Oscar," Walter said quietly. He averted the provost's eyes. "It's all about me. That's the reason for the letter. Ben and Jack marched to protect me." Walter was tortured as he paused. He wiped his wet palms against the arms of his chair. He finally looked at Oscar. "I've been foolish. No," he hesitated, "that's not right. I've been indiscreet." He colored.

Oscar held up his hand. He reached into his desk drawer and re-moved a folder. "Are you talking about this business?" He pushed the folder across his desk. "These arrived special delivery a few days ago."

The three photographs shocked Walter. His hands shook as he looked at them. He was overcome with nausea. The images blurred as dizziness clouded his vision. "Who sent these to you?" he whispered.

"No note. Just the pictures."

Walter continued to stare at the snap shots. He and Dennis. Sitting close at the bar, hugging each other in the darkness of the pub's parking lot, lying nude on adjacent chaises by Dennis' pool. This last was the most disquieting and the most embarrassing. The chairman was visibly aroused as he lay on his back in the bright sunshine. Walter was speechless, his mind a jumble of colliding thoughts and emotions. "Who could have done this?" His hoarse voice was barely audible. "Who?"

"I think the more important, the more frightening question is did anyone else receive a set of these photos?" Oscar had not taken his eyes from Walter. "If I am the only recipient, the situation is not as grim as you may think." He smiled. Walter thought it the most benign smile he had ever seen. "I couldn't care less about your private life. Trust me, Walter, in my years in this office I've seen and heard many things. My policy is simple. If the university is not damaged by the revelations that cross my desk, they're no one's business but the people involved." He waved down Walter's attempt to speak. "Not to say I wasn't shocked when these nasty things arrived. I was. And disappointed, Walter. Deeply saddened as I thought of your career, Margaret, the boys. But none of this is my business or the university's. Not as long as your private life doesn't affect all this." His hands embraced the campus as he gestured through the window.

He looked directly at Walter. "Does it? Are we on the verge of a scandal? Or are we simply in the presence of a wicked individual's nastiness?" Oscar stood up and placed his hand on Walter's shoulder. "I must have answers to those questions." He smiled again. "You see, Walter, among other things, I'm basically a libertarian at heart. Oh yes, I'm a stickler for procedures and due process. But only to protect the individual. Yes, Walter, the individual must be protected at all times." His voice turned somber. "But the institution must be protected also. That's where I sometimes have to walk a tight rope between protecting both the individual and the institution. When I'm successful, I manage to protect both." He gripped Walter's shoulder again. "As I'm sure we can do in this case. People like Maxwell and Donovan don't care about protecting either the individual or the institution. They care, as do so many of your colleagues, only about themselves. They're smart enough to color their self interest with the appearance of greater concerns, but their actions betray them." He paused. "Enough of my musings about the egomaniacs who surround us. The histrios whom Carlyle skewered so brilliantly." He really wanted to go on, but one look at Walter told him this was not the time to continue the sermon he found so satisfying.

Oscar returned to his desk chair. "Now, the answers, my friend."

Walter had never before appreciated the provost as he now did. Oscar Lansing is really a great man, he thought. Ben was right in his praise of the provost. Praise he had always thought exaggerated. He smiled at Oscar. For the first time that afternoon, Walter's face was neither flushed nor ashen. He actually felt at ease. Must be like confession with a kind, generous priest. "You have nothing to worry about, Oscar. I haven't done anything to embarrass the university. God knows I've humiliated myself. But you must believe me, I've kept my private life off campus. Only with Dennis," he paused, "only with Doctor Collins have I," he paused again, "been involved. Never with a student or colleague," he added quickly.

"And Margaret?"

"She knows. The boys too."

"Good. So blackmail can't be the reason for the photographs."

"Your reputation?"

"Perhaps." Oscar laughed. "Perhaps the photographer believes I am the fuddy duddy, blind, moral stickler that some think." The sermon rose once more to Oscar's mind. "You know, that reputation actually helps at times. But the person who sent these pictures really knows little about me." He stood up. "I think we've had enough soul searching for one day. Go home and have a stiff drink. Let me worry about these." He returned the pictures to their folder. "If no one else got them, there's little to brood about at the moment. It'll be a waiting game now." He walked Walter to the door. 'Let's hope the culprit got his jollies just by sending me the pictures."

"And by waiting for my public disgrace," Walter added.

"And may that never come to pass."

The two men shook hands. Walter wanted to hug Oscar. Never again would the word owl cross his lips.

That was some meeting, but now Walter's thoughts returned to Abraham Smith.

It was a dinner party he dreaded. Not even Maggie's return improved Walter's mood as he dressed for another evening at the Murdochs. Mitchell and Isobel always made sure at least one senior administrator would be at the table. With his luck it would be Dean Donovan pontificating about his brilliance. "Maggie, honey, help me with this tie, will you." A tuxedo no less. Their hand engraved invitation actually called for black tie. The preposterous pretension of those academic social climbers. At least I didn't have to rent a tux. That would have been salt in the wound, spending good money for a lousy evening.

Maggie looked wonderful in her long black dress set off by the pearls he had given her on her last birthday. "You look great," she said. "Very distinguished indeed." She kissed him on the cheek.

Walter was pleased by Maggie's mood since her return two days ago. Was it forgiveness or the horror of spending more time with her parents that caused her affection? Perhaps affection is an overstatement, he thought. At least not apparent anger or hostility. She had hugged him at the airport. She talked all the way home about how good it was to be back. She told him all the grim details of two weeks with the Tafts, especially John who was a terrible patient even when he was sober. I don't know how mother can stand it. All those years. And now to have him around the house all day, to have to nurse him in the bargain. What some women are willing to bear. Walter had thought that the perfect moment for her to bring up the cross she was bearing. But not a syllable about that subject. Nor had there been one since. The boys were, of course, thrilled that their mother was back. Walter knew they were tired of meals with dad, wondering when he would decide it was time for another heart-to-heart talk. James and Jeremy had enough of them. More than once since Maggie's departure, they had pleaded with the gods of teen age sons as they lay in the darkness of their room. Please, no more. May tomorrow be a day without a hale and hearty dad urging them to share more than a meal together. Please, God, no more intimate talks. They longed for the return of their mother.

The Murdoch house looked as if it had been decorated for a special festive occasion. "And it isn't Christmas or Thanksgiving, for heaven's sake," Walter grumbled when he entered the foyer. Fresh flowers and candles everywhere. And a maid in black livery to boot. "Who are they trying to impress anyway?"

"He did get an awful lot of money from the MacArthur people, you know," said Maggie, also appalled by the extravagance.

Before Walter's irritation escalated, their hostess greeted them. Isobel did look smashing in a low cut white gown. Her diamond necklace made Maggie's lovely pearls look like dime store stuff. Probably cut glass, Walter hoped. "Welcome home, Maggie." She offered her cheek to both. Walter always hated the way she kissed, if that gesture could ever be called a kiss. Isobel turned her cheek away and kissed the air. She must think that's very elegant. Walter felt he had made a clumsy maneuver when he returned Isobel's greeting. Sometimes he missed her cheek all together and ended up with his lips on her hair. I wonder which British aristocrat taught her that move. Standing between the Henrys, Isobel placed an arm on each and led them into the living room. More flowers and candles greeted them. Oh, Christ, he is here. An animated Patrick Donovan, drink in hand, stood in the center of a small group, talking and gesturing with his free hand. I can guess the subject of his discourse, Walter thought as he forced a smile and returned the dean's wave.

"Mitchell will join us in a moment," Isobel cooed. "He's in the library with Richard and Barbara."

"Two administrators," Walter whispered to Maggie.

"The library?" she giggled. " Before the grant, it was the study."

Walter was heartened by the arrival of a waiter and his tray of drinks. "Anything besides champagne?" he asked.

"Yes sir, there's a bar in the next room."

"Surprised he didn't call it the grand ballroom," said Walter as he handed a glass to Maggie.

"Oh, lighten up. Get some of your favorite single malt scotch and try to enjoy yourself. You didn't get into your monkey suit for nothing. You might as well try to have a good time. And, trust me, the food will be delicious."

An extension had been added to the dining room table to accommodate the Murdochs and their twelve guests. Walter was not pleased to see his place card between Donovan and Barbara Maxwell. A long standing habit brought Walter to the dining room as soon as possible after arriving at a dinner party. He was always curious about how many there'd be at table. And if there were place cards, which Maggie never used, he got a fix on who would be his dining companions. If the Murdochs had at least arranged the table by the old boy-girl method, he would have escaped the Dean's immediate company. And he was never comfortable talking to the president's wife. He signaled the waiter and held up his empty glass. Scotch neat, he said to him. A few more of these and I won't even hear Patrick. Walter smiled at the thought.

The maid who had greeted them walked through the living room, ringing a tiny crystal bell. Walter rolled his eyes in Maggie's direction. "Dinner is served," she said each time she shook the bell.

If the first course held the promise of the rest of the meal, Maggie was right about the food. Small soft shell crabs on toast were delicious. Walter was sorry he had only two of them. He finished before either Patrick or Barbara. He looked around the table. Everyone seemed more involved with conversation than with the starter. Patrick's crabs were untouched as he spoke to the woman next to him, a distinguished medical researcher. A beautiful black woman. Honey colored. The sort of black woman Walter knew Maxine Jefferson would hate on sight. He'd be sure to mention Maxine to see her response. Her husband, also a physician, sat next to Maggie. No one else from his department was at the table, but there were three empty chairs. Could anyone have stood up the genius and his wife? Walter hoped so. Two new appointments in the sociology department sat between Mitchell and the president. Another instance of nepotism. Walter had not met them before, but he had heard a great deal about the appointments. She was well known, a real star. But to get her, the university also had to hire her husband, at best a starlet. In sociology no less. Not even a real discipline. Walter recalled his anger at the salaries Maxwell agreed to pay them. He wished he could hear their conversation more clearly. None of them speaks English anyway, he thought as he smiled in their direction. Sociologists. But half of my colleagues have abandoned the English language too. Jack's right about the slippery slope we're on. What are their names? German I think. Well, I'm sure the great man will introduce us soon enough. Maggie seems to be enjoying them. She was leaning over, nodding and smiling at what Mr. Kraut was saying. God, she's good. Probably not understanding any of their gobbledygook, but smiling all the way. No wonder everyone says she's a great chairman's wife. What is their name?

"And how are things over in literature?" Barbara Maxwell asked.

Walter assumed such a question comes with being the first lady. Inane question, safe conversation. "Still reading," said Walter with a broad smile. "Yes, we're still reading, even if the students don't or can't. You know their lips tire very quickly."

"And whose lips are you referring to, Walter? Your students or your colleagues."

Walter raised an eyebrow, trying to decipher her meaning.

"I do read the books sent to Richard, you know." She matched his raised eyebrow and touched his arm. "Or should I say I try to read the things some of your people write. Not what I called literary criticism when I was an undergraduate."

How far was she willing to go? Did she include our host, the genius? "You've read Mitchell's latest work?"

She smiled. "Well, I did start it." Barbara leaned closer to Walter's ear. "As with every other thing of his that I've tried to read, this one, too, is, what shall I say? Let me be charitable. It's a crock of crap." She sipped her wine and spoke in a normal tone again. "Wouldn't you agree with my assessment, Walter?" She continued to smile.

Walter decided he liked her. This was the very first time she had spoken to him in an unofficial capacity. Every other time she was clearly the university's first lady, making conversation in the mode of her first question. She now seemed more human. "Oh, yes, Barbara, I agree completely."

She lowered her voice once more. "I've never been able to figure out why Richard is so enamored of him." She waved her hand in a dismissive way. "Oh, I know the reputation he's got. Don't understand it, of course, but I know it's there. I've seen the glowing reviews and testimonials. And the letters. My God, Walter, you should see the letters of praise Mitchell has sent to Richard. And from people at the very best places." She looked into Walter's eyes. "What has happened to your field baffles me. And it seems to be epidemic throughout the humanities. You know, Richard's field was not in humane letters." She laughed out loud. "Isn't that a quaint term." She sipped wine again. "Nothing humane about it these days. Anyway, on occasion, Richard actually does ask my advice about our field," she hesitated and touched Walter's arm, "I hope you don't think I'm being pretentious when I say our field, but I do feel strongly about the humanities."

Before Walter could tell Barbara how much he enjoyed talking to her, the three late arrivals came bustling into the dining room. Walter was astonished to see Maxine Jefferson arm in arm with the Berlins. What strange alliance could the video queen be forging now? He was even more surprised when the president stood to give the black rabble rouser a great hug and a kiss on the cheek. Have I been in some time warp and missed all this kissie-feelie among sworn enemies? He returned Maggie's quizzical look with one of his own.

"So, Maxine, is it a done deal?" asked Richard, smiling at her and the Berlins.

"Signed, sealed, and delivered," boomed Marty Berlin. "A few last minute snags kept the lawyers haggling and kept us from being here on time. But what do you expect from lawyers?" He hoped there were no lawyers at the table. He had promised Beverly he'd be on his best behavior. He knew that meant saying very little and smiling amiably at anyone who looked in his direction.

"Sorry to be so late, Mitchell," said Beverly, ignoring Isobel completely. Beverly always honed in on power players. "And I know Marty is sorry he couldn't get home to change into his tux, but business always seems to call." She touched the president's arm. "And this business was important, wasn't it, Richard?"

Isobel, now on her third glass of wine and accustomed to Beverly's abuse of her hospitality, simply waved them to their chairs. "I assume you academics can read the place cards. I know Marty can read the plain style." He was the only one she smiled at. After all, good old Marty Berlin was probably the only genuine article at her table. She felt a kinship with him. Both long suffering spouses of academic ladder climbers, they knew their roles even if they despised them. In her casual perusal of the national political scene, she believed herself to be the local campus version of Hillary Clinton. Both had the power and prestige their flawed marriages had brought them. Isobel took a long drink of her wine, completely ignoring Mitchell's dirty looks. "I wish you were sitting here next to me, Marty dear, but his highness did the seating arrangement. You know. Power meals and all that high powered stuff." She thought better than use the language she had used that afternoon when complaining to her husband about the place cards. "Mitchell, my dear, would you bring out some more wine, please." She fluttered her eyes in imitation of Professor Berlin. Unfortunately, only her increasingly distressed husband caught her mimicry.

"So, tell us what the big deal is," said Patrick, irritated by his ignorance of what had happened.

"Well," Richard began, "a great day for the university."

Walter was delighted to hear Barbara Maxwell interrupt her husband. "Oh, Richard, this is a dinner party, not some meeting of the regents. Just tell them what Marty arranged."

"'Right, Barbara, right." He winked at the table. "Aren't wives always right?"

"Oh, dear, he's moving into his anecdotal mode," Barbara whispered. Walter liked her even more.

Barbara moved her raised finger, much like a director urging her cast to pick up the pace.

"Yes, yes, I'll get on with it. Just wanted to tell a few stories. All right,

I'll cut right to the quick." He straightened his bow tie and checked the flaps of his well cut jacket pockets. "As you all know, Maxine and I have had a few minor differences about the establishment of a black student union."

Minor differences, thought Walter as he recalled Maxine's march on the administration building and the president's call for the police.

"Anyway, our differences aside, the problem has been solved thanks to Marty Berlin." Richard applauded the real estate man, forgetting that he hadn't yet explained what had transpired. "Through the good offices of our host and Beverly, Marty brought to my attention a remarkable property that had recently come on the market. The Riverdale mansion on University Avenue. I'm sure all of you have long admired the architecture of that residence. And only one block from the main entrance to the campus. A beautiful building in a perfect location. And not on state land. That's the real beauty of the whole thing." He nodded to Mitchell and Beverly. "These two illustrious members of our university family were quick to point it out to me. And they are illustrious colleagues. Always thinking of the best interests of the university."

Walter's heart sank as he heard these flattering words. Score another one for the bad guys. A big time score.

"All that stood between the mansion and a black student union," Richard continued, "were the funds to purchase the place." He moved behind Marty's chair and placed his hands on the beaming realtor's shoulders. "This was our angel. Marty Berlin went to work on his fellow businessmen and in only a week raised two million dollars to buy the mansion." Maxwell waved down the polite hand-clapping. "Before you applaud prematurely, let me say that this good man himself pledged the first five hundred thousand dollars." Richard clapped enthusiastically and urged Marty to stand.

Beverly flushed. Money was one thing, but a speech? Please, she whispered to herself, make it brief and coherent.

"First, let me apologize to our hostess for my attire," Marty nodded to Isobel who blew him a kiss.

"That's a beautiful suit, my dear," she said.

"I was delighted to be of some small service to the university Beverly and I love so dearly," he smiled at his wife, "and to the cause of educational equality for all Americans." He bowed gallantly in the direction of Maxine Jefferson.

Believing Marty was done, Beverly was delighted with his words. But he had more to say. "One of my most fervent hopes is that the black and Jewish communities, allies for so many years in the fight for equal justice, will one day come together again." He paused, as if considering amplification of his remarks. "The hostility against my people that some black demagogues have exhibited must be overcome and defeated by the historical record. By facts rather than vulgar and untrue slurs. It is in that spirit that I was happy to do my small part to further the educational future of black students. They are our best hope for the reconciliation I dream of." Marty sat down, acknowledging the applause of his fellow diners. He looked at Beverly who did not applaud. She bit her lower lip, unsure of how her husband's words had played among the important people around the table.

Isobel stood up, raised glass in hand. "I propose a toast to Marty Berlin," she said, urging everyone to stand up. "I think his thoughtful words well matched his generous gift. Marty, I want you to know how wonderfully refreshing it was to hear straight talk about an important issue at an academic dinner party. You cut to the heart of the matter. And that, my friends, is not a common talent around here." Isobel sat down and nodded to the waiters to serve the entrée. "Now let's enjoy one of the dishes I love to cook." She looked around the table. "Oh yes, I do cook." Smiling at Mitchell, "I really am more than an ornament around here."

Walter continued to marvel at the female uprising he was witnessing this evening. He hoped it would continue, excepting Maggie of course. Wouldn't she have an earful to deliver. He turned to Barbara. "I hope you didn't think I was some male chauvinist before. It's just that I've never really talked with you. That is, beyond the formulaic small talk at receptions and the like. You know what I mean." His look was so sincere that Barbara was touched.

"Of course I understand." She raised her glass to him. "And I never for an instant thought you were a chauvinist."

"Proposing a toast to the literature chairman?" Richard called. "Let us all in on the occasion. Another book on the great bard, Walter? Or is it that swell photograph Barbara was toasting?" The president smiled to the group. "You know, our Professor Henry takes a wonderful picture. The camera really loves him."

For a moment Walter was terrified. Had those awful photographs reached Maxwell's desk? Would even he be so gauche to bring them up at a dinner party? He knew the color had drained from his face. "Pictures?" he asked weakly.

"Oh, I didn't know there was more than one," said the president. "I'll have to look more carefully. I only saw the full page picture on the first page of your new graduate studies brochure. A handsome job. Should attract some terrific students to your program."

Walter recovered quickly. Thank heaven, he thought. "Yes, it is an attractive booklet, isn't it." He didn't dare wipe the perspiration that beaded his forehead.

"And you two took good pictures too," Maxwell continued, nodding to Beverly and Mitchell.

"Do you practice in front of the mirror, Walter?" asked Isobel. "The great one over there," pointing her glass at her husband, "loves to pose."

"I don't think anyone's really interested in my nod to show biz," Mitchell said, trying to unclench his jaws and sound amused. He was glad to see the arrival of the entrée. "Can't you smell Isobel's handiwork?"

"Touche," his wife said. "A good one."

"She wowed some of the best gourmands in New Haven with her beef stroganoff." He waved expansively. "'Bon appetit, folks, bon appeitit."

The guests murmured their approval as they partook of the entrée. For a few moments there were only the sounds of gastronomical enjoyment.

"And what do you think of a black student union?" Patrick asked of the distinguished medical researcher. "My recollection is that you haven't been involved in any of the controversy surrounding that issue."

Susan Tree looked up, surprised by the question. She shot a glance at Maxine whom she had never met before. "I think it's a bad idea. A very bad idea." She returned to her stroganoff.

"That's all you have to say?" Patrick pursued his prey. He detected a weakness and went for it. Conversational parries and thrusts made dinner parties attractive events for him. One's quarry was trapped by the table. There was no possibility of turning one's back on the interrogator.

Maxwell was visibly uncomfortable with his dean's question, and distressed by the new appointment's response.

"No, as a matter of fact, I have a great deal to say about it, but I'm not sure a dinner party is the proper venue for such a discussion." Her voice was rich, deep, and perfectly steady.

Patrick was sorry he didn't hear a quaver of doubt or fear. But he could not yield the ground he had staked out. "On the contrary, Doctor Tree. On this celebratory occasion of the signing of the papers that guarantee such a union, the subject seems unavoidable. Oh yes, a perfectly appropriate subject."

"I agree," said Maxine. "I'd love to hear your opinions on the matter." She delicately wiped the corners of her mouth with the fine linen napkin. "Especially the views of so distinguished a woman of color who's made it in a white man's field." There was only a hint of challenge in her words.

"Me too," said Marty. "I want to hear why I made such an expensive mistake. I really would."

"Oh, Marty, believe me, it was no mistake," cooed Beverly. And don't mention how expensive it was. You could have afforded twice that amount without feeling it. You never complain when you write those fat checks to organizations that keep sending us all that embarrassing junk mail.

Susan Tree carefully placed her fork and knife on her plate. "Well, if you insist, Dean Donovan." She dabbed at the corners of her mouth in a far more delicate way than Maxine had done. "It's really quite simple. I believe in equality. Simple. If a university must have a student union, then there should be a single union for all students. The same as all students should be treated in every other academic endeavor. Equality means precisely that. All students, and I assume all faculty, are equal and, therefore, they must be treated equally." She looked around the table. "I don't think I can be clearer than that."

The dean smiled. "Then, I assume you don't believe in affirmative action programs."

"Your assumption is correct. I do not."

"But where would you be today without affirmative action?" asked Maxine. "You started with two strikes against you. Your gender and your color."

"Probably true," Susan replied icily. "But I am here, am I not? And I am here not because I am a woman or because I am a black woman. I am here because I have demonstrated my abilities. My work and my accomplishments have been color blind. Nor do I check the race or gender of the blood samples I work on. Blood is blood. Equal. The same as the individuals from whom it was drawn. There can be no greater example of equality than we see in my labs every day." She smiled at Maxine. "Or would you prefer the samples be identified by the race, religion, gender, ethnicity, and sexual orientation of the patients?"

Maxine sipped her wine. "A bit extreme, doctor, wouldn't you say?"

"Why? If you want a black student union and black studies programs and, I assume, other separatist measures, why not separate blood? The reason you don't want blood samples separated is because you're intelligent enough to see that proposal as irrational and ridiculous, So why are other separations warranted or wise? What makes them rational?"

Ronald Tree chuckled. "Brava, Susan, brava." He wagged a finger unthreateningly at Maxine. "I think she's got you there, Maxine." He glanced around the table. "This may sound familiar to some of you. You may remember Susan's performance on public television last month. The only woman on a panel discussing affirmative action." He rubbed his hands together. "She laid out one of Farrakhan's ministers, but good. He did everything but call her part of the Zionist plot to take over American higher education." He chuckled again. "It was beautiful."

In a quandary about how to proceed, Maxine tried to gather her resources.

The dean was delighted. His ploy had engendered exactly the sort of dialogue and confrontation he relished.

"But you married a white man, didn't you?" Maxine finally thrust.

"And a Jew too," Ronald added. "Don't forget that. The racists love to mention that little tidbit when they have no real ammunition with which to counter Susan's arguments. Oh, yes, they love to troop out that one." He was not smiling now.

"I'm no racist," Maxine's voice rose. "And I resent your insinuation. I deeply resent it."

"Then why did you mention the subject?" asked Isobel, now feeling little pain. "What was the point of the comment?"

"Only to show how far removed the good medical researcher is from the front lines of discrimination." Maxine felt a tide moving in her direction. "Insulated in her laboratory, she doesn't have the foggiest notion of what's going on in the real world out there." Maxine savored the silence in the room. "You see that, don't you, Susan? You're simply not qualified to make judgments about the state of affairs in the world most of us inhabit."

"That's probably the silliest argument I've heard this evening." Susan's benign smile infuriated Maxine. "You make it sound as if my entire life has been spent in sterile isolation." She sipped her wine. "Give me a little credit. I live in the same world as the rest of you. And I've suffered the slings and arrows of stupid, prejudiced people. Of course I have. But their stupidity doesn't mean I should abandon ideals I believe in. Like equality, for instance."

"It would be nice if the world were ready for your ideals," the male sociologist said. It was the first time he addressed the entire room.

"Oh, yes," said Richard, "let's hear what Professor Schmidt has to say on this matter."

Schmidt, said Walter to himself, that's it. Kurt Schmidt.

"Well, almost every study is on Maxine's side. It was precisely because of deeply ingrained prejudice against people that we now have so many protected groups." He spoke with a slight German accent.

"Indeed," added Becky Schmidt, "we've jointly authored several of the very studies Kurt refers to." She shook her head in Susan's direction. "Whether or nor you want to acknowledge it, my dear, we live in a society fraught with prejudice. Even Kurt's accent. Americans simply don't like others. And others include all those protected groups he mentioned."

"But don't you think affirmative action programs feed prejudice?" asked Ronald Tree. "I mean, if some Americans, and I mean only some, fear or hate what you refer to as the others, why shouldn't they feel even greater anger if they think those others are getting preferential treatment? And at their expense. And with their tax dollars to boot."

"That's just tough," said Maxine. The tide had clearly turned in favor of her position. "It's just too bad if they're unwilling to make up for the sins of their culture. It's high time Americans were required to pay reparations. And I don't mean only to African Americans"

"Reparations?" asked Susan. "Why should Americans at the end of the twentieth-century pay reparations for nineteenth-century slavery?"

"I said not only African Americans."

"Come now, you're being disingenuous. Who else do you have in mind when you talk of reparations? Women, gays, the handicapped? Of course you mean blacks." Susan's voice remained quiet and gentle.

"Well, we did that in Germany," Kurt offered with a wave of his hand. "We knew the right thing to do."

"Oh yes, Germans always know the right thing to do, don't you," said Ronald. "Now you're equating the German treatment of Jews with American treatment of blacks? There's no analogy."

"I don't know about that," Maxine responded. "I think the analogy is a pretty compelling one."

Marty was troubled by Maxine's comment. "You see, this is exactly the kind of argument I hope educational equality will eliminate." He shook his head sadly.

"Facts are facts, Martin," Maxine scolded. "You know, Jews are not the only people who have suffered." She hesitated. "But your economic and political power has made it seem that way. And your control of the media. I'm sorry, Martin, but those are facts. Just as it's true that most of the ship owners who bought and transported slaves were, unfortunately, Jewish."

"Untrue," Ronald cut in, "simply untrue. That's another of the big lies people like Farakhan and Jeffries and their puppets use to poison the dialogue about slavery."

"It's been researched," said Maxine. "And published."

"So have *The Protocols* and *Mein Kampf.* All sorts of rubbish is published. Publication has never been proof of truth. As a historian, you surely know that."

"Enough," said Isobel. "Enough of this subject." She motioned to Mitchell to bring her a bottle of wine. "Goodness, as much as I detest politics and politicians, I do believe we'd be better off talking about them right now. Or even campus politics would be preferable to this," she groped for words, "this deplorable topic." She wrung her hands. "It's just too divisive." She smiled at Marty, then glowered at Maxine. "And it's too revealing of sides of us that are better left in the private shadows of our baser selves."

Mitchell was actually glad to hear his wife's words. "Agreed," the genius said, "this subject is now closed. I suggest we move to a more pleasant and certainly neutral one. Like dessert." He nodded to the waiter. "Wait til you see the show stopper Isobel prepared for the finale of her great meal." He raised his glass in a toast to Isobel.

"Hear, hear," added the president, "a toast to the hostess with the mostest." He stood up and smiled at Isobel. "I haven't had such a superb meal in ages."

Mitchell's praise of his wife did clear the air. Passions were set aside for the moment as the diners applauded the flaming baked alaska the waiters wheeled into the room.

"Like a Jewish wedding," shouted Marty.

Beverly shot him a withering look.

Marty colored and said no more.

Conversation continued in the large, comfortable living room. Mitchell lit a fire even though it was not a cold night. The guests sat in a circle around an enormous glass coffee table that dominated the room. The host's books were arranged in a seemingly casual manner on the table.

Richard gestured toward a thick leather folder in the midst of the several volumes. "Your newest book in progress?" he asked of Mitchell.

"No, that manuscript is already at Princeton University Press. No, these are reviews of my previous work." Mitchell touched the rich leather affectionately. "Feel free to look, if you'd like." He feigned modesty. "If I say so myself, some of these are pretty impressive."

Sure they are, Walter thought. Reviews written by cronies who expect the same glowing remarks from the genius when he reviews their garbage. He smiled at Maggie who was talking with Kurt Schmidt. Not only a German, Walter had decided, but a Nazi too. He wanted to smash his face. He thought of the great old days when so many German social theorists wrote elegant, unscientific books. Now everything in his damn field was quantified. Rubbish is what it is. Another field destroyed by its mania for scientific status. If we weren't so envious of the exalted position of the sciences, if we didn't try so damn hard to emulate them, we'd have remained true to our own callings. A loss of faith set in years ago. He stared at the fire. We want grants too became the mantra. Jack Williams put it right. Fuck students, fuck teaching, just publish crap no one could possibly be interested in . Or should be interested in. And literature? Who cares what books say. Just let your ideologies drive your pens. Grind out your drivel. Make believe you're scientists too.

"A penny for your thoughts, Walter," said Mitchell, thinking the chair was captivated by the leather binder. "Pretty impressive, isn't it? I do think Isobel will have to buy me another one for Christmas." He tapped the folder. "This one's getting too full. Don't want to break the binding, do we?"

"No, Mitchell, I was thinking about other things." Walter did not want to get into a debate about the state of his profession. "Actually, I was thinking of better days," he smiled and waved his hand. "But all things do change, don't they?"

"The old order does pass," Maggie said kindly, intuiting her husband's thoughts.

"And what old order is that?" asked Kurt.

"Oh, nothing. Nothing at all. A private joke, I guess, between Walter and me. Not worth talking about now."

No, thought Walter, not worth talking about here. He felt he was in the den of the barbarians.

"Old orders were meant to pass," said Richard. "Progress must force the old aside. That's the way of the modern world." The president tapped the leather folder. "Mitch's stuff is at the cutting edge. Yes, at the cutting edge of the forward thrust." He smiled, proud of his image. "Can't spend our time replicating the past, the old order, can we?" He directed his words at Walter.

"No, Richard, I guess we can't." He had no stomach for a fight tonight.

"That's the quickest capitulation I've ever heard from you," smirked Patrick. "All those memos extolling the virtues of the past, and now you agree with Richard. What's brought you to your senses, Walter?"

"I guess we've got a new ally in our fight to save the literature department," Beverly cooed. "Isn't that wonderful news, Mitchell? We'll have to remember this evening for more than the black student union," she glanced quickly at Isobel, "and, of course, the great meal."

"I don't think Walter was saying that at all," said Maggie.

"Another great evening at the Murdochs," Walter growled when they got home. "In a tuxedo no less." He pulled off his bow tie and threw it on the couch. "Have a great night in your monkey suit. Weren't those Jeremy's words as we left the house?" Walter dropped his jacket next to the tie. "Indeed. A great night." He walked to the bar. "Nightcap, Maggie?" He hoped she'd agree. Like old times, maybe. Sitting next to each other and performing a post mortem on the evening. Please, Maggie, say yes.

"All right, Walter, but a light one. I had more wine than I really wanted. Didn't you notice how Isobel pushed wine tonight? Like she had stock in the company." Maggie dropped herself onto the couch. "But it was good wine, wasn't it?"

"Do you think they'd serve something less than grand vino to Richard?"

"He wouldn't know the difference." Maggie's smile warmed Walter's expectations. "They could have poured something out of those horrible cardboard wine boxes for all Richard knows."

"But he recognizes labels," said Walter, handing Maggie a weak gin and tonic. "He recognizes labels. Believe me, he made a note of the label. He'll check it out next time he goes to the liquor shop." He sat down close to Maggie. "If it's expensive, he'll be impressed. That's the way he operates." Tentatively, he put his arm on the back of the couch. Like the young teenager at the movies on a first date. Or, at least, the way Walter and his pals did when they were teenagers. Then slowly working the arm to the girl's shoulder. And with luck, by the time the feature was half over, to her breast. Was that called petting or heavy petting? he wondered as he stared into his scotch. Doesn't matter anyway. Today, they probably skip all those fumbling formalities and get right to it. Do his boys do it yet? he wondered. Is it time to have a talk about safe sex? Wouldn't that be some conversation. Be careful when you have sex with little Mary or Jane. Like you do with Dennis, Dad? Yes, a conversation to look forward to. To savor. Dad and the boys trading confidences about their sexual exploits. Better give them a package of condoms and a book.

"What are you thinking about?" Maggie interrupted his reverie. "You seem a million miles away." She moved his arm to her shoulder. "What were you thinking about?" Maggie let her head rest against him.

"Just thinking about the women at dinner tonight. I never would have guessed that Isobel and Barbara were so…"

"Angry?" Maggie finished his sentence.

"Okay, angry. They always seemed so…"

"Dutiful." Maggie held out her glass for a refill. "Remember, we almost always see them when they're on stage. Performing. Playing their roles as loving helpmates. I think you saw them tonight very much as they really are."

"And what's that?"

"Frustrated. Unfulfilled. And, yes, angry at the shitty roles life has given them."

"Well, probably true, but they weren't exactly innocent, unwilling participants in their little plays. They knew what they were getting into."

"Are you sure of that, Walter? Do you really think Barbara knew she was going to end up as a campus first lady to a pompous moron like Richard?" Maggie changed her position so she could face Walter. "And you can bet she knows she's much smarter than he is. I don't envy her. Having to put on her good face every day to greet all those people she doesn't give a damn about. You heard her talk about books tonight. That's what she'd rather be doing. Reading and talking about literature. Instead, she spends her days putting in face time and making small talk about nothing. It must be terrible for her."

"At least Isobel can stay home and drink."

"She's another tragic case." Maggie shook her head. "I know Isobel's one clever lady. But that man has turned her into an appendage of his careerism. She even gave up her own career in science to serve him. Do you think he really feels anything for her? I don't think he feels anything for anyone but Mitchell Murdoch. We heard from the boys how he briefed his own children to respond to their classmates after he got the MacArthur.

Can you imagine that? Even his lovely kids were turned into players in his little farce. All for the greater glory of the master." She laughed. "And isn't that the perfect word? All he does is masturbate. Solitary, solipsistic stroking of his ego. That's the name of his game. And poor Isobel and the children have to bear witness to it every day."

"And never do anything to damage the image."

"Exactly. The same with his female counterpart too. You saw the way Beverly tried to direct Marty tonight. If that man were a poor church mouse, she'd have sent him packing a long time ago. Why in heaven's name he takes it is beyond me. By now Isobel and Barbara may feel trapped. But Marty? He's a nice looking guy. He's loaded. What's he need with the water torture Beverly keeps dripping on him? I tell you, Walter. There's a novel in every household."

Walter looked away, thinking of the book his home would make. Wouldn't they all love to read that one. He shivered as he imagined that book making the rounds of the boys' school.

"So, are we back to something like normal?" Walter brought the conversation to the subject the wanted to raise since Maggie's return. He tried to fathom the look in his wife's eyes. "Are we a couple again?" He took both her hands in his. "I do love you, Maggie. Very much."

"And I love you, too. I really do," she hesitated, "but I still can't get used to the whole thing. God knows, Walter, I had a long time to think about it at the folks' house. I talked to Howard a couple of times. I even called Norma once." She shook her head. "And the boys and I had a good heart to heart yesterday." She touched his arm. "You were really great with them. They told me about your talks." Maggie stood up and paced the large living room. "They're much more at ease with it all than I am. Or at least they seem to be. Only they know what goes through their minds. Or what they talk about upstairs." She stopped by a credenza that held a number of photos. She fixed her gaze on their wedding picture. What a gangling, homely bridegroom he was. And how much she had loved him. "I think I need more time, Walter. More time." She looked at the other photographs. Snap shots, posed studio pictures. "We have a history. That's something precious, isn't it? And irreplaceable." She turned to him. "We are bound by all this."

"Indissolubly bound," Walter whispered. "Let no man put asunder."

"No man?" Maggie smiled ruefully.

"I've got all the time in the world. I'm willing to wait til the conversion of the Jews." He stood up and put his arms around Maggie. "Remember how I'd recite that Marvell poem to you when we were courting?"

"Oh yes. And I knew it was a proposition the first time I heard it."

"Marvell did too."

"So my English prof said. You didn't know we had studied that poem a few days before you got up the courage to read it to me. Never told you that before, did I?"

"You knew?"

"I thought it was wonderful. The way you recited it to me. Imagine what a young girl would do today if her date turned to her and suddenly launched into that poem?"

"Probably in a car at McDonalds."

"With rock music screaming at them from the car radio."

"What do you mean radio? That was in our day. Back in the dark ages. Blaring from the CD player is more like it."

"She'd surely think he was a lunatic."

"Reciting poetry instead of grunting at her. Oh yes, a lunatic at least." Maggie kissed Walter's cheek. "I do love you."

"What do you want me to do? You name it."

Maggie disengaged herself. "Do you really want an honest answer?"

"Yes." Walter feared what it might be.

Maggie stared directly into his eyes. "Stop seeing Dennis."

The answer he feared hearing. "That would make us a family again? Do you really think that would undo the damage I've done to you? To the boys?"

"It'd be the necessary first step."

"But his memory would still haunt us."

"Us?"

"You. Jeremy. James."

"And you. What would the effect be on you, Walter?"

"I don't know."

Maggie sat down on the couch and patted the seat next to her. "You're not like Howard. He's gay. Always has been gay." She took Walter's hand, much like a mother comforting her son. "You're not a homosexual. You had to experiment. And you did. Now you know." She spoke movingly, imploringly. "Now it's out of your system. You now know what's most important in your life. And it's not other men. It's not Dennis Collins. It's what's here in this house." She gestured toward the pictures on the credenza. "It's Jeremy and James. It's me, Walter." Her voice almost broke. "I can't be Norma Collins. I just can't be." She stood up again. "I'm sorry, Walter, but I know I can't live the way she does. She may be a better woman than I, a stronger woman. But I know she can't love her husband more than I love mine." She resumed her place next to him on the couch and hugged him. "How do you think I felt at night, in bed, lying next to you, listening to your breathing, knowing you were suffering as I was suffering, wanting to be held by you, wanting to hold you. And unable to. Walter, I want you to love only me. To be with only me." She wept quietly.

"Oh, Maggie, my love, my dearest love, that's what I want more than you can imagine." Walter gently wiped her eyes with the tips of his fingers. "But how can I undo all of this?"

"Just do it, Walter. Just do it."

"The question is how do we prove it was Billy Mann who doctored the tape." Ben Rosenthal spoke softly, even though there was no possibility of anyone overhearing him. "I'm certain he's framing Abraham."

"Certain?" asked Oscar.

"Of course he did it." Jack ground out a cigarette under the heel of his western boot. "Do you think Abraham could have come up with such a scheme? He's a nice young guy, but he doesn't have the conniving mind or the balls." Jack stood up and stretched. "Come on, men, if we were honest, we'd all admit the guy's a wuss. A decent wuss, but still a wuss." He lit another cigarette. "I like him well enough, but that's what he is." He coughed. "Got to give up these fucking things. Smith's a scholar of the old school. Even older than ours."

"And what exactly does that mean?" asked the provost.

"It means, Oscar, that he might very well fantasize about porno movies and food poisoning, but he'd never have the cojones to pull it off. Oh, he might confide it all to his journal. But do it? Never."

"I think you're misjudging our young colleague," said Ben.

The three old warriors sat on bleacher seats in the deserted football field. The provost's idea of a safe place for their meeting. "You heard the tape," he said.

"Yes, and we heard the clicks, too. Soft as they were, we heard them. You don't have to be a communications expert to know the tape was edited." Jack wrung his hands in exasperation. "Why the hell don't we just take the tape to the police?"

"Yes, I know that was your advice yesterday when we listened to it," said Oscar, "but what if we're wrong?" He smiled condescendingly at Jack. "The point is we're not communication experts."

"And if we're wrong, Abraham is through." Ben shrugged. "And it's Mann we want to be rid of, not Smith."

"You guys are impossible," Jack shouted. "Can't you get it through your brilliant minds that they both might be guilty? Sure, sure. It was the little prick who masterminded the whole thing, but why can't you at least consider the possibility that Abraham was his accomplice? For whatever reason. Only the good Lord knows why, but our sweet Abraham was probably part of Billy's gang." He slapped his hands together. "Case closed. They both go."

"Unless we can convince Maxwell otherwise."

"Are you crazy, Oscar?" Jack laughed out loud. "Convince Richard to drop the whole thing?" He laughed again. "The man's been on a crusade ever since he shit in his pants. You've heard him, for Christ's sake. He loony on the subject. You heard him try to get the FBI involved. And now you think you can convince him to forget about it. Never."

"Don't be too sure," said Ben. "Let's at least think of an argument we might use with him. To save Smith anyway." Ben looked down. "I'd give anything to get rid of Mann before the tenure hearing."

"Sure," said Jack. "Anything to cancel your pact with the devil. Right?" He was sorry immediately for his remark. "Forgive me, Ben. That was wrong of me. An undeserved low blow." He touched Ben's arm as if asking to be forgiven.

"Pact with the devil?" asked Oscar.

"Departmental business," said Jack quickly. "Just departmental business."

"Like your chair's letter to the campus paper?" Oscar raised his hands. "I know much more than you think about your so-called department business. I've spoken with Walter."

Jack raised his eyebrows. "And?"

The provost nodded his head as if words were unnecessary. "I know why you two relics marched with that woman." He reached into his brief case. "And if you ever needed more evidence to hang Mann, take a look at these." He handed over the photographs.

Ben shook his head. "That little bastard."

"At least good old Walter's hung like a horse." Jack handed the pictures back. "Are you saying Billy took these?"

Oscar nodded. "And I don't know who else got them. Or these." He pointed to the tapes.

Jack was convinced. "All right, Ben, so what do we say to the president?"

The draft copy of Walter's article hit the department like a nuclear bomb. Within hours, it had been faxed throughout the campus.

Nowhere was the detonation more shattering than in Billy Mann's office. "That miserable son of a bitch," he hissed, throwing the pages onto his desk. A pre-emptive strike against me, he thought. Why else would he write this thing? Why else? The owl must have shown him the pictures. Another prick. The God damn graybeards sticking together again. Circle their pathetic wagons to keep their enclave to themselves. He punched the air. We'll just see about that. He's not the only one who knows the best defense is an offense. He stood up and moved the poster to reveal the mirror. This is Billy Mann they're dealing with now. Billy fucking Mann. He leaned toward the mirror as if looking for a blemish. He smiled at the reflection. Yes sir, Billy fucking Mann. He raised his fists in the air like a victorious athlete. The owl was not the only one to get the photos and the tapes. Who do they think they're playing with anyway? Some kid on the playground? He thrust his jaw at the mirror. No sir. This is Professor Billy Mann. And I'm going to make mung of them before I'm finished.

Maxine Jefferson stood in the history department office, shaking her head and reading the faxed pages. "Well, I'll be a son of a gun," she said out loud. She smiled broadly. "He's actually got balls. Who would have ever believed it?" Maxine poured a cup of coffee. "Here's to you, Walter." She raised her paper cup in the direction of the humanities building. Still chuckling, she shuffled out of the office in an exaggerated slow step. "Massa's got balls," she drawled to a surprised graduate student who stood in the hall reading a bulletin board. "He really does." She raised her cup to the student and continued down the corridor to her office. Well, there'll be no more letters to the editor from that quarter, she thought. She laughed again. I'll be damned.

Richard Maxwell was dumbfounded as he read the pages. What should the response be from the president to such a document? In all his playing of war games, he had not considered this one. A master at working the press from scripts prepared long in advance for every eventuality a university president might face, he was now forced into uncharted waters. Never mind what to wear, he thought, the question was what the hell to say. He buzzed for his assistant. It was time for advice before the morning papers broke the story.

The same scene was being played out throughout the campus. Patrick Donovan smirked as he drank tea and read the article. A variety of homilies ran through his mind. Oscar Lansing nodded approvingly at the lines he had help craft. He smiled broadly at the ones Jack Williams had penned, wit Walter could never have come up with. In their offices in the green tiled shithouse, Jack and Ben were pleased with their editorial handiwork.

The scene was far different in Wallace Lounge. Almost every chair was occupied as Walter's colleagues read the document they found in their mailboxes only minutes ago. All seemed nervous about speaking out loud. No one looked up from the faxed pages, even after they had completed their reading.

Billy Mann burst into the room, looked around at the quiet men and women, and strutted to the center of the lounge. "So, ladies and germs, how do you like them there pages?" He waved his copy of the article in the air. No one spoke. "Bet you never knew old Walter swung both ways, did you?" Still no response. "Come on, gang, the sky's not falling. So Walter likes guys. Big deal." Billy's strategy began to play itself out. "He needs our support, our understanding now. Not this glum funereal silence." He walked around the room, waving his hands like a cheer leader trying to energize a lackluster crowd. "Come on, gang, wake up and smell the coffee. It's time to plan our support." He smiled broadly as he went from person to person, the very smile he had settled on before his office mirror. He stopped in front of Abraham. "Help me, Abe, help me get the troops in line." He moved to Calvin Willoughby. "Buck up, Cal, he's not going to show you his dick in the men's room," Billy cackled. He leaned close to the old man's face. "Come on, Cal, fess up. You must have wondered what it'd be like with another guy. Sometime there in the distant past when your libido was up and running, you must have thought about it." He patted Willoughby's head and moved on to Helen Abrams. "You've got nothing to worry about. Hell, this time next year you'll be thinking about all this as ancient history while you enjoy all the blandishments of the big apple." He got down on his knees before her. "Help me, Helen. For Christ's sake, help me get these codgers out of their lethargy."

Helen had watched Billy's manic actions and wondered what his game was. There was no love lost between Billy and Walter. But here he was rallying support for their beleaguered chair. If she knew anything, she knew Billy's ploy was in the service of a greater Billy Mann. In the service of himself only. His support of Walter would in some convoluted way benefit Billy. But how?

Jack and Ben entered the room together. They had just finished yet another skull session with Oscar, this time on a conference call from Walter's office. And they knew all their overly hearty congratulations were more false bravado for Walter's benefit than a true objective correlative to the situation. Their chair was not yet out the woods. They also knew the lounge would be as crowded and dangerous as a mine field. They could hear the flapping of the buzzards' wings even before they had opened the door. The turds are already circling, Jack thought. He liked the image of turds, wearing academic regalia, with wings and yellow beaks, flying over the oriental rugs and overstuffed chairs. "Academic turds," he said to Ben. "But I'll give you ten to one they can't even fly." Before the other could inquire about context, the two elder statesmen were witness to the last scenes of Billy's performance. His cajoling of old Willoughby, his urging Abraham for support, now his gallant kneeling before Helen.

Jack took in the entire spectacle. The roomful of nervous academics unwilling to make eye contact with anyone or anything but their own laps. The manic Billy Mann rushing around the lounge like a spin meister urging votes for an underdog candidate. The bemused twinkle in Helen's eyes as she looked in the direction of the new arrivals. He finally spoke to Ben. "With a friend like that one, Walter may be in deeper shit than we thought. So what's dear old Billy's game plan today? It surely isn't meant to help his chairman."

Billy rushed to Ben's side. "Thank God the civil liberties union has arrived." A shiver ran through the older man as Billy embraced him. "Tell them, Ben. Tell them they've got to rally around Walter." Sweat poured down Billy's flushed face as he waved at the room. Ben felt Billy's heat and smelled the now fetid breath. He was overcome by the closeness of the viper. He actually felt faint and leaned against Jack.

"Back off Billy," Jack whispered. He pushed firmly against Billy's chest. "Just back away." He guided Ben to a chair. For a moment, he was at a loss for words. But he knew his words were needed at this moment. They were waiting for him to say something. For the first time since he entered the room, his colleagues had raised their heads. They looked to him for guidance. He bought time by pouring a cup of coffee. He was disquieted by Billy's smirk.

Jack's eyes swept the room, making contact with most of his colleagues. Imagine them looking to me for comfort. Good old Jack Williams, the departmental lush, the butt of their weak thrusts at wit when he wasn't around. Poor Jack Williams. What a promising career drowned by booze. Now they awaited his help. Turds all right. Petty little bastards covering their asses, protecting their miserable fragile egos. Don't expect them to take the lead on this one. Oh no. Risk is not part of their game plans. Never was. So bold when they preen before their graduate students or belittle their undergraduates. So smart when they deliver their papers at scholarly meetings. So loud when the political stakes are without danger to them. Some of them actually call themselves Marxists. Imagine that baloney. A defunct system everywhere in the world except on American university campuses. What a crew. What a fucking crew. Jack continued his perusal of the lounge. That asshole actually wrote an indignant letter filled with arcane and meaningless literary allusions about the latent power of Marxism. Imagine, the putz browbeat some kid columnist for the campus paper who dared suggest communism was bankrupt. Then there's that young clone of Murdoch's who named his fucking dog Marxie. I want to kick that miserable mutt every time I see him in the corridor. With a hammer and sickle on his red bandanna yet. Another genius. His gaze fell on the starlet of the young theorists, a hero among his fawning peers, who constantly argued that the barricades were in his classroom. Imagine that, Jack would often say to anyone who would listen, in his classroom. The barricades are in his classroom. There, the young man declaimed, he joined the battle for world Marxism. Jack couldn't stand looking at the torn jeans and wrinkled plaid shirt the young hero favored. He couldn't yet afford the handsome rags his seniors sported. Or he hadn't yet learned to appreciate all those attractive perks which the hated capitalism could offer a well-paid Marxist member of the academy. And now all of them were speechless as they contemplated their navels. Real revolutionaries. They'd be the first to run if there actually were barricades to attack or defend. Surely the Murdochs would be the first to run to their fancy foreign sports cars and head for their expensive homes in their wealthy gated suburban enclaves. Oh yes, true revolutionaries in tailor made suits and fifty dollar ties. God, I hate them. Fucking fakes who helped ruin the profession. That's the only battle they ever fought with any success. And here they are looking to me for succor. Imploring eyes of troubled children who feared damage to their playroom. Selfish, self-serving pricks. Jack was disgusted. But he had to defend Walter even if it meant lying down with assholes like these.

"Jack," Billy turned his attention away from Ben, "tell these guys we owe Walter our allegiance at a time like this." He touched Jack's shoulder. "Please, help me." He donned his "shucks, I'm just a regular guy trying to do the right thing" demeanor. Billy sighed. "I'm doing my best, Jack." He sat down next to Ben. "You'll never know how glad I was to see you two guys today." He put his arm around Ben's shoulders. The older man recoiled from the touch and immediately stood up. He walked to the opposite side of the room and took a seat next to Helen.

Before Jack could offer comfort to his flock of sheep, Bullock entered the room. One look told Jack that something was up. Mary looked frightened. She went directly to Abraham and whispered in his ear. The young man paled as he stood to follow Bullock out of the room.

Billy's chagrin was obvious. His place in the sun was eclipsed by the secretary's interruption. As he quickly planned a strategy to regain the momentum he believed he had only a few minutes before, Helen rushed from the lounge. She had been close enough to Ab to hear Bullock's words.

She walked briskly to Walter's office, but the door was closed. Bullock sat at her desk. She shook her head sadly when she looked up at Helen. "It's terrible," she said softly. "Just terrible." She continued to shake her head. "The police are in Walter's office." She looked toward the closed door. "State police and campus security officers." Bullock nodded sadly. "They've come to arrest poor Abraham Smith."

Helen sat down in the uncomfortable chair opposite Bullock's desk. "They're arresting Ab?" She didn't have to ask why. But what's Billy Mann still doing in the lounge? Why didn't Bullock summon him too? How did he escape Ab's fate? She wanted to get back to consult with Jack and Ben just as the door to the chair's office opened. Helen didn't know which of her two colleagues looked more pained. Walter was trembling as he held the door open for the four men. Abraham's eyes were filled with tears. He was flanked by the two officers who addressed the department when the investigation had been launched. Helen didn't recognize the last man who sat at the chairman's desk. The best dressed of the group, he was speaking on the telephone. He didn't leave the office when the two policemen led Abraham out of the building. Ab averted Helen's eyes as he passed her.

Walter was still trembling when he finally spoke to Helen. "Are there still many of them in the lounge? I have to talk to the department about this dreadful thing." He took Helen's arm, more to hold on than to give comfort. "Tell him I'll be back soon." Walter nodded in the direction of the man at his desk as he spoke softly to Bullock. "Give the university lawyer whatever help he needs." Walter continued to hold Helen's arm as they walked to the Wallace Lounge. Neither spoke.

The mood at Jack's house was mock somber. After the impromptu meeting with Walter, the Williams house seemed the right place to go, although Jack thought only a few confidantes would show up.

In the kitchen, Jack and Wilma rifled the cabinets and refrigerator to feed their colleagues. "Some of these people have never even seen the inside of our place," Wilma said as she whipped up a southwestern dip. "Pour those chips into the Mexican basket, will you. I'll try to make this thing as appetizing as I can." She emptied a jar of salsa into the mixing bowl. "You think they'll like this?"

"Who cares if they like it." Jack placed glasses on a tray and filled an ice bucket. "Any of that lousy bourbon left? The bottle your aunt said had such a pretty label."

"Better than the rat poison you thought she'd bring you. Try the cabinet you're standing in front of. Way back behind all the other bottles."

"Don't even think of giving these turds my Wild Turkey." Jack was on his knees trying to locate the elusive bottle. "And do we have any of that beer you got such a good buy on when my students were here? The two bucks a case junk."

"It was certainly more expensive than that. I think there's almost a whole case in the garage. But do you really want to serve that to them? Remember, Murdoch considers himself a beer connoisseur."

Jack shook his head. "I should worry about making an impression on him, or the others? Most of them out there in the living room," he nodded his head in their direction, "are the very ones we didn't invite to the wedding."

By the time Jack and Wilma brought in the food and drink, there were about two dozen of their colleagues gathered in the small living room. "Sorry we didn't rent the gym for the occasion," Jack said. He pointed to the low coffee table. "Help yourselves," he offered without much enthusiasm.

"At least try to be hospitable," Wilma whispered. "Like it or not, they're in our home." She smiled as she passed a tray of small quiches she was grateful had been in the freezer.

Jack was suddenly furious. "Let them help themselves, Willie," he said between clenched teeth as he passed her. "You're not their servant girl, for Christ's sake."

"You'd never say that if I were white, would you?"

Chastened, Jack took out his irritation on Billy Mann who stood examining the beer label. "What's the problem with it?" Jack's tone was unmistakable. "Not expensive enough for your taste?" He looked to Ben who was pouring a glass of seltzer water. "Imagine that, will you. Our distinguished assistant professor here wants a designer label brew." Jack almost never invoked academic rank. He bowed in the direction of Billy. "My most humble apology for not having consulted with you before I bought this crap."

"It's not that bad," said Mitchell Murdoch. "As a matter of fact, this is really one of the better cheap beers." He smiled at Jack. It was that superior little smile Jack always wanted to rip off the bastard's self-satisfied face. He knew a put-down was on its way. He smiled again. "As inexpensive brews go, this is, as I said, one of the better ones."

So, where the fuck did you drink this anyway? Jack wanted to ask. "Bought it for my student picnic last month." He was immediately angry at himself for apologizing to Murdoch. Why should I give a damn about anything the genius has to say?

Ben now stood in the center of the room. "We have serious business to discuss." No one paid him any attention. He spoke louder. "Ladies and gentlemen. Please. This is not a social event. Please." A few actually looked in his direction.

Billy Mann rushed to Ben's side. He put two fingers in his mouth and blew a loud whistle. "Hold on, folks. This is important." He whistled again, a loud piercing whistle. "Come on now, people, give your attention to Ben." The room quieted down. Billy took Ben's arm. "My best friend has been arrested. Doesn't that mean anything to you? My best friend. Abraham." He dropped into his sincere mode. "No matter that we're vying against each other for that tenured slot. This is far more important." He loosened his grip on Ben's arm and sat down cross-legged on the floor.

Helen whispered in Wilma's ear. "Best friend? What a bastard." She sipped her beer. "But the creep is good."

Wilma nodded. "A terrific actor."

Ben regained center stage without acknowledging Billy's assistance. The younger man made a mental note of yet another slight from his older colleague. Only a matter of time, old man.

"We're all here because we're concerned about young Smith." He looked toward Walter. "Is there any actual evidence against him?"

The chairman stood up. "I'm afraid there is. Or, at least, the police say there is." He looked at Billy. "Apparently there's a taped confession."

A murmur rippled though the room.

"The police are satisfied that the voice on the tape is Abraham's."

"Did you hear it?"

"Where'd they get the tape?"

"Who made the tape?"

"What exactly does he confess to?"

"Did he work alone?"

"Did he implicate anyone else?"

Walter held up his hand. "A little order, please. These are all reasonable questions. But I really can't answer them with any certainty at this point. I just don't know enough yet."

Jack nodded approvingly at Walter's mendacity. Clinton's got nothing on him, he thought. Only the seriousness of the moment kept him from smiling.

"Well, I for one must say that if he's guilty, I want him punished." Beverly Berlin now joined Walter and Ben in the middle of the cramped living room. No batting of eyes now. "You'll never know the humiliation he caused me. Or the hurt."

"Humiliation? Hurt?" Jack sneered from his spot next to the impromptu bar. He had already drunk too much too quickly. "For Christ's sake, Beverly, that day launched your new career." He laughed a dry bitter laugh. "Punish him? You ought to get on your knees and thank him. Look what he's done for your little institute. If not you, who then is making pornography and smut the stuff of academic discourse?" He stared at Beverly. "At least academic discourse as defined by some people in this room." He glanced in Murdoch's direction. "And, unfortunately, by too many others in our miserable little profession."

"Come on, Jack," Mitchell said in a surprisingly conciliatory tone, "this isn't the time or place for sour grapes." The words clearly contrasted with the speaker's tone. Murdoch waved his hands to the group. "I don't think you really want to start measuring dicks, do you? That's for kids. Or chumps." He smiled broadly. "My dick's bigger than your dick is a game you really wouldn't want to get into with me."

The fact was that Jack was more than willing to mix it up with Murdoch and Berlin. "The question, my friend," said Jack, "is not dicks. Never has been. The question is," he touched his temple with his forefinger, "the mind." He nodded his head. "Always has been. Always will be. Your mind, my mind, the mind of the profession. The mind, Mitchell. Not the ego. Not self promotion. Not faddish bull shit. Not unintelligible, diseased language. In a word, my unworthy colleague, not the garbage you and Beverly and your minions deliver day in and day out to an uncritical, badly educated professorate."

Ben was silently delighted at this unexpected turn in the proceedings. Might as well get it over with. Why not now? Wilma retired to the kitchen, ostensibly to make another bowl of dip. Although she agreed completely with her husband, she was sorry the battle had been joined in her house. And while poor Abraham was in a jail cell downtown.

"Amen." Ben broke his silence. "About time the barbarians were so labeled. I've been around just about longer than anyone here. I know why I once loved teaching and scholarship, why I couldn't imagine doing anything other than being a professor of literature. Now, I can't find it in my heart to recommend that calling. Not to my best students." His voice trembled slightly. "Because of you," he pointed at Murdoch, "and you, Beverly, our calling has become vulgar. It's a terrible thing to say, but it's true."

Walter interrupted. "Not now, gentlemen. Please. Not now. Not here. Not today." He raised both arms. "There's only one subject that has drawn us together today. That subject is the arrest of Abraham Smith. It's not the current state of humane studies."

"But Walter," said Mitchell, "I must have the opportunity to respond to this ambush."

"Not today." Walter shouted. "Do you hear me? Not today."

"Why not today?" Jack shouted back. "There's nothing we can do for Abraham right now anyway." He glared at Mitchell. "And this thing's been festering for too long as is." His voice grew soft and kindly. "You're too much of a gentleman, Walter, to let us have it out at a department meeting. But this isn't a meeting and we're not in our building. We're on neutral turf right now, even if it is my house." He looked around the room. "I say this is a perfect time to air a few differences."

"I think Williams is right." Puffing on his pipe, old Calvin stood up. "You'd be amazed at how intellectually illiterate my graduate students are. All they want to talk about is theory. As if one can discuss theory without having read any primary texts."

"Your seminars?" Beverly joined the fray. "For God's sake, Calvin, all you talk about is the proper form of footnotes and bibliographic entries. Who wouldn't be bored out of her mind in your classes? Like it or not, theory's the name of the game today. Not whether a footnote goes at the bottom of a page or at the end of the text." She shook her head dismissively. "And who needs footnotes anyway?" She waved Calvin away and laughed. "It's the critic's voice we want to hear, not a collection of past writers."

"But my dear Beverly, that's exactly the point." Calvin felt confident. He had rehearsed this speech a hundred times. "If those students were only asked to write a paper that required proper citation methods, they'd know how to proceed." He pointed his pipe at her. "But you never ask them to do any real scholarship. They're ignorant of, even disdainful of, past scholarship. They're interested only in what they think about whatever claptrap you're offering at the time. They don't have the slightest knowledge of real scholarship." He felt empowered. "They don't have any familiarity with literary history and major texts." He sat down, pleased with his performance. He offered one final comment. "You do know, don't you, Beverly, that there was literature written before the second world war." He puffed on his pipe. The tobacco tasted particularly delicious.

"For heaven's sake, let's not go through all this again." Mitchell paced back and forth in the center of the living room, expertly turning so that he faced everyone in the room with each revolution. "We had this debate when we revised the curriculum two years ago." He opened another bottle of beer. "The fact is you guys lost then and haven't ever recovered. The old canon is gone. Dead and buried. Let it be. Let's not disinter a corpse."

"Right," Beverly broke in. "Times have changed, but some of you seem unaware of it. Our students want what interests them, not what a bunch of old men think is good for them."

"So if they want to look at movies of people fucking rather than read Chaucer, that's good?" Wilma asked as she placed a bowl of fresh dip on the table.

"Of course it's good," snapped Mitchell. "Isn't that the hallmark of your beloved capitalistic system? Let the marketplace reign supreme."

"So our students are consumers and we're clerks who sell them what they want?" Wilma laughed out loud.

"Inelegantly put, but yes, you're right."

"You talk about inelegant language?" Jack joined Wilma's laughter.

"Laugh all you want, Jack, but I get published in all the best journals and by the most prestigious university presses. You see, I have something to sell that the consumers out there want to buy." He snapped his fingers. "Simple as that. Create a market and sell your product." He moved to Beverly's side and put his arm around her shoulder. "And we've created markets while the rest of you sit around and whine about the good old days. About an audience that no longer exists. Like it or not, Jack, Ben, we are the future. You guys are hangovers of a past that is no more."

"And good riddance." Beverly batted her eyes at Mitchell. He was the star she had hitched her wagon to. He was the only one in the department who could take her where she wanted to go. Mitchell was the present and future of literary studies and he had the clout to make her career even more lustrous than it already was. "Oh yes, gentlemen," she ignored Wilma and Helen, "your past is gone for good." She squeezed Mitchell's arm which still rested on her shoulder. Beverly's eyes shone. The anticipation of what might still come to pass thrilled her.

"But the future isn't here yet, Beverly," said Ben. "Look at our own department's younger faculty members. I don't see many of them following your lead."

Mitchell offered a bloodless laugh. "Sure, Ben. One's in jail, another's running away to New York, yet another never knows who's in bed with his wife, and Billy here is better at running a minstrel show than turning out a book. Christ, there isn't a decent manuscript among them. That's one illustrious group you're asking us to consider." He drank from his beer bottle. "If the future of this department is in their hands, we're in deep trouble, my man."

Billy looked down. Did he dare support the more powerful side even if his own convictions rested so strongly with the weaker group? And which of the adversaries were more likely to vote for his tenure? He knew Jack and Ben were his implacable enemies. He could always raise his true colors after he gained tenure. "I think Mitchell and Beverly are right," he finally said. "Even if I'm only a junior hired hand around here, I believe I have the right to offer my two cents." Looking at Mitchell, he offered a faux confession. "You're right about me at least. I haven't produced my book yet. But only because I'm revising the entire study to correspond to my new theoretical positions. And I learned those new methodologies from you and Beverly." He was prepared to lay it on as heavily as he thought necessary to earn their favor. "You may not think much of my work right now." He dropped his gaze. "Nor should you. I haven't produced much yet." He looked now directly into Mitchell's eyes. "But, believe me, when my book is published, you'll be proud of it." Now unabashedly pandering to Murdoch and speaking as if they were the only two people in the room, Billy continued. "And with your permission, Mitchell, I want to dedicate the book to you." He dropped his gaze once more. The second edition, and, of course, there'll be more than one edition, will cancel that bit of bull shit. Billy wanted to wave his arms in victory when he saw rosy pleasure overspread Murdoch's face. No one is immune to flattery. Billy had learned that lesson years ago. No one.

"You little shit," Jack shouted. "Get out of my house." He moved toward Billy. "I ought to smack you in the mouth, you self-serving prick." Jack was about to grab Billy's shirt when Ben forced his way between the two men.

"I'd like nothing better than to go a few rounds with you, old man," Billy shouted. "Any time, old man. Any place." Billy jabbed at Jack's chest from behind Ben. "About the only thing you can do better than me is booze it up." Billy was now screaming. "Oh yes, old man, you're good at that. But I can lick your ass whenever I want." He pulled away from Ben and ran his hands through his hair. Calming himself, he sneered at Jack. "And, old man, you better not measure dicks with anyone." Billy smiled at Mitchell. She must be one disappointed new bride you've got there almost escaped from his lips. What he really wanted to do was his minstrel show routine. Black mammy must really hanker for a real cock, doo-dah, doo-dah. But he said no more and left the house.

"Well, that must be the best finale to a departmental discussion I've ever heard," said Mitchell. "On the other hand, we might have just witnessed the best the old guard can offer." He embraced the crowd with open hands. "They can't out-publish us, they can't out-teach us, they can't out-vote us. So what's left to these defunct purveyors of outmoded studies? Why, they resort to violence. Isn't that the route fascists always follow?"

Jack suddenly lunged at Murdoch. He landed a solid punch to the genius' jaw, knocking the younger man to the floor. In an instant he was on him, slapping Mitchell's face with both hands. "You sanctimonious prick," he repeated with each slap. Even after he was pulled off, Jack's arms kept flailing. Flushed and breathing heavily, he still managed to laugh. "God, that felt good." He leaned on Ben and Walter, each of whom held one of his shoulders. "You'll never know how long I've wanted to do that."

Mitchell got up slowly. He rubbed his jaw and glared at Jack. Beverly stood by his side. "You've done it now, Williams. I'm not sure whether I should prefer charges with the police or just write a note to the president." He pushed Beverly's ministering hand away. "I'm all right," he snapped at her. "Just a sucker punch that caught me off guard. I could kill the bastard in a fair fight." His gaze now fell on the chairman. "You see, Walter, you see the department your cowardice has produced. With real leadership we could be something. And the day is coming soon when we will be something to admire." He pointed his finger at the three men standing before him. "And that day's coming soon, my friends. Sooner than you think. The president knows it. The dean knows it. Only you Neanderthals don't get it." He moved to the front door. "A letter to Maxwell should be enough. If he needed a nudge to get him going full steam on our plans, this surely will be it." He nodded to Beverly. "Let's get out of this place." Turning to the rest, Mitchell hurled a challenge. "Choose your sides now. Leave with Beverly and me or stay with them. The choice is clear. Hitch your wagons to the future of this department or sink ever more deeply into the grave of the past." He made eye contact with everyone in the room. "It's now or never."

Walter was unhappy when he saw almost everyone leave with Murdoch. Only Calvin and Helen remained seated after the front door closed.

"The battle has been joined in earnest," said Ben. He put his arm around Wilma's shoulder. "Don't worry, my dear Wilma. It had to happen one day. So, why not today?" He embraced Jack. "Never thought it would lead to a good right cross. But a wallop's better than a whimper." He kissed Jack on the cheek. "A good blow for the good guys."

"How can you make jokes at a time like this?" Walter demanded. "Smith's in jail. The department's on the verge of civil war. Only the good lord knows what Murdoch will report to Maxwell. And what do you think has been delivered to the world about me. No time to make jokes." He shook his head slowly. "I never would have expected this from you, Ben."

"Relax, Walter," Ben said. "Nothing's really changed by anything that's happened here today. What more damage can Mitchell do to us? The president and the dean are already squarely in his corner. What are they going to do now that they haven't already done? If it's going to be an all-out civil war, that's good. A lot better than the subterranean battling we've experienced for so long. Now it's time to marshal your troops, Walter. And now you've got a much clearer picture of who your soldiers are."

"He's right, Walter," Jack said. "Look at the bright side. And there is a bright side."

"I'd love to hear about that," said the chair, now seated next to Helen.

"I did show you a good right hand, didn't I?" Jack threw a punch. "Looked good in there, didn't I? And then there's Billy Shithead. No more worrying about where he stands." He smiled at Ben. "All deals with him are now off."

Helen sat across from Eleanor in the smart white living room. Dinner over, the children were in their rooms preparing lessons for the next school day. The hum of the dishwasher and snatches of rock music from upstairs were the only sounds Helen heard.

"So what did the lawyer say?" Helen asked.

Eleanor shrugged. "He'll know more tomorrow when the police let him see the evidence." She examined her glass of gin as if it might contain some foreign object. She returned it to the large square table before her and lit a cigarette. "Ab always wanted me to quit."

"He's not dead yet, you know," Helen said. "Maybe it won't be as bad as you think. Where'd you get the lawyer anyway?"

"A college friend of Ab's father recommended him."

"How did his parents take the news?"

"How do you think?" Eleanor almost smiled. "Their fair haired darling, the professor, in jail. How do you think they reacted?" Eleanor lit a fresh cigarette from the burned down end of the other. "I thought his mother was going into one her fits of hysteria, but the old dame calmed down enough to actually ask a few intelligent questions. Probably no tenure and now this, she kept repeating. A new mantra for her to chant to the other children. The successful ones, you know."

"And Ab's father?"

"A rock. As laconic as always. You never know what he's really thinking. But I give him credit. No anger. No recriminations. Just got down to business. He got back to me with the lawyer's name within an hour. His voice was as matter of fact as if he were reading from a cue card." Eleanor shook her head. "I've never been able to figure him out. But I do like him. There's real intelligence behind that furrowed brow. And I've never seen him lose his cool. God knows, living with her must drive him crazy."

"What about the kids?" Helen had been concerned about them. She was sure daddy was the favored parent.

Eleanor's eyes filled with tears, the first obvious sign of distress since Helen's arrival. "That was the hardest thing of all," she said. "Telephoning his folks was easy compared to that." She looked over Helen's head at the family portrait on the wall, an oil painted version of a photograph given to them last year by Ab's mother. "That's her contribution to the world of art, you know. She paints from photographs. She thinks she's another Norman Rockwell. Her favorite." Eleanor raised her eyebrows. "But she's really not bad. The children? Well, they had a million questions. I didn't have a single answer. And I didn't have the heart to tell them exactly what Ab's charged with."

"Did his accomplice, the bastard, call?"

"Oh no. You don't really expect him to blow his cover, do you? Probably believes his phone's tapped. He was so careful about everything."

"Sure. Everything except his partner's safety." Helen leaned forward. "Did he make that tape?"

"He must have," Eleanor whispered. "I don't know how or when, but he had to be the one. I asked Ab when they let me talk to him this afternoon, but he shook his head. Later, he said, later. That was all. But I'm sure Billy is responsible."

"How are you going to prove it?"

"Ab's father also hired a private detective." Eleanor shook her head again. "God knows why. All he can find out is that Ab didn't work alone. There's nothing he can uncover to prove his innocence." She sobbed. "He is guilty. Ab and Billy did those things. And if I know my husband, he's already confessed."

Sally had prepared Billy's favorite dessert. Exultant all day, he felt invulnerable. The photos had taken care of Walter. The tapes sealed Abraham's fate. There was nothing that could tie Billy to the crimes. Only the word of a man already arrested and in competition with him for tenure. Who would believe the charges of a jealous, desperate, guilty man? Billy was exuberant. "You should have seen Mitchell's puss when I laid it on him." He took another spoonful of banana tapioca pudding. "I tell you, Sally, he was ready to come. Flushed cheeks, grateful eyes. I half expected to see a creamy white spot ooze through the crotch of his designer pants. What a pushover."

"Will you really dedicate your book to him?"

"For Christ's sake, Sally, of course I'll dedicate the thing to him. You expect me to renege on my word? In front of all those people?" He stuck the spoon into the pudding. "How many times do I have to tell you. Only in the first edition. The first edition. Get it? By the time the second edition comes off the press, I'll have my promotion. Then the bastard can't touch me." Billy was irritated. "You think I really admire the crap he preaches?" He leaned across the table toward his now pale, fidgeting wife. "You should know by now that if this were a perfect world, I'd be shoulder to shoulder with Rosenthal and Williams." He pushed the half-eaten pudding aside. "But those pricks hate my guts." His voice now softened. "And since that's the way the ball bounced, that's the way it is. But they'll see how valuable I really am after I lower Mitchell's flag and run up theirs."

Sally bit her lip. "Can I ask you a question without your getting angry?"

"Why do you always preface your questions that way? For Christ's sake, Sally, I'd have to be a moron not to know that any question following that preamble will make me angry." He moved the tapioca pudding closer to him. "But go ahead. Ask away."

Sally trembled slightly. "How can you talk about a second edition when you're still so far from finishing the book?" She looked down. "What if you can't find a publisher?" Her voice dropped to a whisper. She looked away. "You've worked so hard for so long," her words were now almost inaudible, "what if you never finish the book?"

Even though Billy himself had been tormented by that same terrible prospect in the silence of sleepless nights, he couldn't bear hearing it from anyone else. Especially not his wife. Was her faith in him so shallow? Had he shrunk in her estimation? Didn't he still bring her to such great orgasms that she actually thanked him every time. Tearfully thanked him every fucking time. And now she doubted his scholarly talents. Billy was stunned. The veins on his forehead pulsated with anger. He touched them, expecting to find huge protuberances. Serve her right if I have a stroke right here and now. Then she'll see how far her damn women's dining club will get her in the real world. She'll see how much she needs me, completed manuscript or not. Let her scrub floors for all I care. Then come home to feed her dear drooling hubby. He almost smiled. And no one to fuck her into tearful oblivion. He suddenly stiffened. Unless the bitch finds some other cock to screw her. He fell immediately into a fretful fantasy. There he was locked into his wheelchair, lap robe covering his useless limbs, and her fucking away upstairs with some handsome young stud. Son of a bitch. Probably one of the graduate students who hated him. His imagination scanned the seminar table, trying to discern which of them would be Sally's lover. He glowered at his wife. "That'd make you happy, wouldn't it?"

Sally looked up. Confused, she cocked her head like a dog trying to understand her master's garbled command. "What would make me happy, Billy?" Familiar with his daydream life, Sally was conciliatory. "Honey, what are you thinking about now?" Like the dog, she was always willing to forgive again. In his better moments, Billy knew his wife's love was unconditional.

But at this moment, Billy was not rational. "What do you think I'm talking about? I'm talking about you and Winslow fucking like bunnies while I contemplate my drool." His fantasy had fixed upon Roger Winslow as the culprit. That prick has never liked me or the course. Oh yes, I can always count on that Murdoch clone to toss his smug shit-eating smiles at me whenever he disagrees. The perfect candidate to make a cuckold of me. What better way to prove his superiority. Son a bitch.

"Roger Winslow? That nice looking, polite student in your seminar? He and I?" She laughed. "Billy, what on earth are you talking about?" She put her hand over his. "You know I've never been with anyone else." She squeezed his hand. "I don't ever want to be with anyone else."

He pulled his hand away. "Bullshit. What about Harry Cabot?" He stared at Sally. "So what about hairy Harry Cabot?"

"But that was ages ago. You know that. It was long before I even met you."

"The point is you have slept with other men. So don't give me that dear Billy crap about never having been with anyone else."

Sally sighed. "I should never have told you about Harry. You always throw him up at me when you get into one of your moods. You know perfectly well I meant since we met. Never even thought of another guy since we met." She laughed again. "Roger Winslow. I've met him only once. Here in the house when you had the seminar over for dinner. I'm not sure I'd recognize him if I bumped into him." She shook her head. "Really, Billy. Why would I want anyone else when I've got you? No one fills me like you, Billy." The obscene image, exciting to him at other times, now disgusted him.

"Knock it off. Just knock it off. I'm trying to work out of a lousy nightmare and all you can think of is a roll in the hay."

"And what about all those other women you loved to tell me about?" Sally's patience had run out.

"Different, Sally. It's different for a man. You know that. If I hadn't been so experienced, you'd never have enjoyed it half as much." He offered his most lecherous smile. "You, my dear wife, were the beneficiary of those experiences. Only you. Just think about that for a minute."

Thinking better of pursuing this line, which she had heard often enough, Sally shrugged. "Of course I'm the beneficiary," she said sweetly. She believed none of this, but as always, Sally tried to calm Billy back to the real world. "I've never even thought of another man, and certainly not

Roger Winslow. Let's leave it at that, Billy." She put out her hand. "Can we shake on that, honey?"

Billy had returned to the actual world of the here and now. He smiled warmly, the ingratiating smile he had perfected. He shook Sally's hand. "Of course we can forget it. Let's just chalk it up to the tensions of the past weeks." He took her hand in an exaggerated gesture of gallantry and brought it to his lips. "My dear," he said, trying to sound like Ronald Coleman, "my dear, I do love you very much."

Had the doorbell not rung at that moment, Sally would have been only minutes away from tearfully thanking the great lover for yet another ecstatic orgasm. Billy was not the only superb actor in the Mann household.

"Get the door, will you?" Billy said. He was irritated again. "You expecting someone?"

"You go Billy. I want to start clearing the table."

"I can't get up right now, for Christ's sake. I've got a roaring hard-on, thanks to you." He adjusted his pants and scowled at Sally.

"You're really terrible." She made her patented rehearsed giggle she knew Billy thought cute.

Sally was surprised to see the delegation. Jack, Ben, and Oscar entered the foyer. "We'd like to talk with Billy," Ben said.

She rushed into the kitchen. "Billy," she whispered, "the provost is here. And Ben Rosenthal and Jack Williams."

The color left Billy's face. "Put them in the living room," he whispered back. "I'll be there in a minute. Give me a little time to put on my face." He did not smile. He stood up and ran his fingers through his hair. "Get in there and offer them a drink or something. Show them what you've learned in your dining club."

When Billy joined them, the three men were standing by the bar while Sally made drinks.

"Good evening, Mann," said the provost. "Hope this isn't too inconvenient a time." He nodded to Ben and Jack. "But the matter is important and time is critical." Oscar's look at Sally told her she should leave the room.

"It's all right," said Billy. He poured himself a large scotch and sat down in his wingback chair. He noticed Jack's full glass of bourbon. The other two were drinking club soda. The lush will probably be stinking high before they leave. He was sorry Sally had given him Jack Daniels. Williams was not someone they had to impress. The store label would have been enough. Probably can't taste the difference anyway. She could have given that bastard sterno. "No problem," said Billy. His calm had returned. "So what's so important to bring the brain trust to a mere assistant professor's home." He invoked his title for Jack's benefit. Billy had a long memory for slights.

"We want you to confess your role in the entire Smith matter." The provost was direct.

Give him credit, thought Billy. No pleasantries. Right to the point.

"My role?" Billy looked pained. "And what role might that be?"

"This isn't the time for play-acting," Oscar continued. "We're here with an offer you can't refuse."

Now he's fucking Don Corleone. "But I had nothing to do with Abraham's schemes." He made eye contact with each of the men. "You can't think I'd be party to anything like that."

"Let's cut to the chase," Oscar said. The provost was steely calm. Billy was surprised at how cold his eyes could be. "We know you sent the photographs of Walter to me and the president." He sipped his club soda. Billy noticed that the provost's hand was steady. "We know also that you're responsible for the tape recording of Smith's confession." Oscar pointed a finger at Billy. "And please don't make matters worse by denying any of this. The tape has been examined by the state police forensics lab. It was doctored. They have very sophisticated equipment, you know. Cut and edited expertly to be sure, but it is not an unaltered, pristine tape." Lansing stood up. "Furthermore, the caterer's assistants have positively identified you and Smith. And if more evidence were needed, the police have located the video store where you purchased those vile films. Disguise or not, the clerk identified you."

Billy's smile froze on his handsome face. His hand trembled when he tried to lift his glass. He struggled for the right words in the face of Lansing's stinging information.

Jack was pleased. He had never seen Billy so vulnerable, so trapped, so lost for a facile comment.

Billy's dilemma was heightened by the sound of Sally's quiet sobbing. She had obviously been listening from the next room. He folded his arms over his chest as if to keep his heart beat from becoming audible. His mouth was dry. A half smile separated his parched lips. "What's the offer?" he asked. His voice was hoarse.

Ben and Jack had still not said a word.

"I want a written confession from you. Signed, of course, in the presence of the university lawyers. It will include the events of that notorious Saturday. Both the videos at Professor Berlin's and the poisoning of the food at the banquet. It will also make clear your sole responsibility for the photographs of the chairman and the tape recording that incriminated Abraham Smith. I want you to make clear how you went about making that recording. Finally, I want a clear account of why you did all these things. From the Saturday events to your attempts to destroy the reputations of both Walter and Smith."

"But Abraham is as guilty as I." Billy almost whined.

"I'm perfectly aware of that," said Oscar. "He, too, must answer for his actions."

"And the deal?"

"Clean and simple. I've discussed the entire matter with Richard Maxwell and he approves. In return for full confessions, the university will not press charges against either of you. But you and Smith will tender letters of resignation, effective at the conclusion of this academic year."

"You'll be getting off easy," Ben finally spoke. "I want you to be aware of the role the provost played in convincing Maxwell not to press charges. It could have been much worse for both of you. Believe me, much worse."

"And if I don't agree?" Billy asked.

"Then you'll probably end up in the slammer," Jack said. He couldn't believe Billy would hesitate to accept.

"Perhaps in jail," added Lansing. "Certainly fired from your post. With all the attendant publicity such an action would produce. And a criminal trial." The provost sat down again. He leaned toward Billy. "Your career may be damaged by a resignation. It will most certainly be destroyed by a dismissal and trial."

"Can you guarantee me strong letters of recommendation for my file?" He smiled broadly. "After all, I'll have to look for a new job."

Jack laughed out loud. He shook his head. "Can you believe this? The son of a bitch actually wants letters of recommendation." He stared at Billy. "How about first class air tickets out of here?" He drank from his glass. "You don't get it, do you? The last thing you can do at this moment is make demands of the provost. For Christ's sake, he's busted his ass to keep you out of jail." He stood up and refilled his glass. "If I had my way, you'd be on your way to jail now." He looked at Oscar. "What a piece of work this one is. I told you he'd pull something like this. Give him five fucking minutes to make up his mind before you call the cops."

At this moment Billy wanted to kill Jack. His eyes were filled with hatred. "Why don't you drink your own booze, you lush. Who do you think you are anyway? Coming into my house in the middle of the night, threatening me, helping yourself to my good bourbon. Fuck you, Jack." Now Billy was on his feet. "And fuck you to your mealy mouthed pals too." He was now jaw to jaw with Oscar. "And you can take your offer and shove it up your ass." He went to the front door and held it open. "Now, get out of my house. All of you. Just get the hell out of my house. You guys want to go to court? Terrific. You want a trial? Great." He slammed the door shut and confronted the three men. "You think all I've got are the tape and those porno pictures of dear old Aunt Walter?" Billy laughed. "You want to see the rest of the stuff? Take me to court, you bastards, and we'll see who the embarrassed parties will be." He touched Ben's arm. "I told you, old man, that if I go down, I'll have lots of company."

The three men stared at one another.

"You'd have to be morons to think you've seen all the photos or heard all the tapes." His laugh was almost hysterical. "Believe me, if Billy Mann is sent packing, he'll have lots of company." He pointed at Oscar and Jack. "You two and your beloved Aunt Jemima too." Billy's face was scarlet. Sweat ran down his cheeks. "And Richard Maxwell and his mick dean." He was almost dancing around his guests. "And don't forget those pricks, Mitchell Murdoch and Beverly Berlin. Christ, I can decimate this joint." He threw himself into his chair. "Walter and Abraham were only the obvious ones." His voice was now calm, his eyes clear. "Your darling little Billy has been a busy beaver. Trust me, gentlemen, very busy." His smile was frightening. "You want a fight, you'll get more than you ever bargained for. You want to avoid the blood-letting, then you'll accept my offer." He stared at Oscar. "An offer you can't refuse." He went to the front door again. "Think about it, gentlemen, think about it over night." He held the door open for them. "If I don't hear from you by noon tomorrow, everything goes to my lawyer and the press. Get it? Have I made myself clear enough?" He saluted them. "Even your booze sopped brain should understand what I've said," he shot at Jack's back as the three men walked down Billy's driveway. "Remember, we talk tomorrow morning or the fun begins." The front door slammed shut.

Alone now in the foyer, Billy could not stop trembling. Tears replaced perspiration on his cheeks. He felt faint.

Sally rushed to his side. "What have you done, Billy? What are those other pictures and recordings? I didn't know you had more." She put her arm around Billy's waist and helped him to the couch. She had never before seen her husband cry.

"Of course there's nothing else," Billy whispered. He felt humiliated, trembling and weeping before his wife. Not the way a real man should act. The vision of a confident, robust Roger Winslow raced through his mind. How could she ever again love a weakling like this? He wanted to lash out at Sally, but he lacked the energy. "Of course there aren't other photos or tapes. But Oscar and his cronies didn't know that. This will be the greatest scam of my life," he said, "or my worst disaster." He turned to her. "Don't you see? I had nothing left to fight with except the big bluff. If they're the fucking cowards I think they are, it just might work." He was regaining his confidence. "You can bet Oscar will be on the blower with Maxwell soon enough. And if I read the president right, the last thing he'll want is anything that might blemish his reputation. You know he's been polishing his resume for a more prestigious job ever since he got here." Feeling lightheaded, Billy grinned. He hugged Sally. "It just might work. We may be home free yet."

"Do you know what you're going to ask them to do? I mean, if they fall for it, what's the offer you're going to make?" Sally, too, was feeling more confident. Placing glue in office locks was mere child's play compared to the stakes Billy was playing for now.

"I'll go for broke. Why not? Once I see them on the defensive, I'll ask for the moon."

"And if they call your bluff?"

"Then I accept their offer."

Sally raised her eyebrows.

"Of course they'd repeat the offer. It's to their advantage. And Maxwell's." Billy was close to regaining his earlier ebullience. "Don't you see, the worst that can happen is we look for another job."

"And the best?"

Billy leapt to his feet. "The best, my little lady, is that your husband gets tenure and a promotion."

"But will Walter's task force grant you tenure without your book?"

"Who's talking about the task force? I'm talking about the president's granting me the damned promotion. God, I'd love some more of your tapioca pudding. I can't wait until tomorrow morning."

"What about Abraham?"

"Yes, honest Abe. I think he's got to be part of the deal. Let's make sure he doesn't get fired."

"And the promotion?"

"Are you crazy? He'll be lucky to still have a job. Then he can come up for tenure when the time is right." Billy winked at Sally. "Christ, he hasn't even finished his book yet."

They both laughed as, arm in arm, they went to the kitchen.

"Now for that pudding," said Sally.

The lights burned long in Richard Maxwell's study that night. The president had called this unusual late night meeting as soon as he had finished talking with Oscar Lansing.

The room was quiet as each man pondered Billy Mann's threats. Conversation and eye contact were now at a minimum. Oscar had briefed the group. Maxwell had intoned about the need to protect the university. Patrick Donovan had sermonized about the necessity of high moral standards. Walter had said virtually nothing.

Maxwell decided that only the most vulnerable and the most senior members of the university community should gather at his home that night. Rejecting Donovan's suggestion that all parties to Mann's blackmail threats be present, or at least all parties known to them at that moment,

Maxwell elected to limit the meeting only to men with administrative responsibilities. The last people he wanted to listen to at this critical moment were Murdoch and Berlin.

"So, gentlemen," the president broke the grim silence, "our choices are plain." He cleared his throat an adjusted his ascot. A perfect touch, he thought, to underscore the informality of this late night adventure. Informal but elegant. Yes, surely the hallmarks of his position. And the blue paisley silk robe was perfect. This was his home, after all, and it was late at night. The robe was the right choice. Not the sweat shirt and jeans he was wearing when Lansing's call came through. No, not jeans for the head of state at a time of crisis. "So, my friends, we are now in the damage control mode, are we not?"

"What damage is there to control?" asked Patrick. "We hold all the cards, don't we? Why don't we hang the little bugger and get it over with." He glanced at his watch. "For God's sake, Richard, we've been here for almost two hours already." His clasped hands caressed his lips. "Our credibility cannot be undercut by the likes of Professor Mann. I suggest we move to the final solution to our problem."

"But what if he does have more tapes and photographs?" Maxwell spoke deliberately. He looked at his dean. "What say you to that, Patrick? What if he actually has the materials he claims to have? What then, I ask?"

"It's a gamble we have to take. The alternative, after all, is unconditional surrender to a blackmailer. Is that what you want, Richard?"

The president was flustered. Patrick feared another catatonic seizure might overcome him. Richard shook his head vigorously as if clearing his mind and vision. "I don't like blackmail any more than you, but protection of this institution is more important than Mann's conditions whatever they might be."

Patrick was aware that the president was, in reality, referring to the protection of his own reputation. He was also sure that each of the men in the room was silently brooding over secrets he would rather not have exposed. The great question before them was how much did Billy Mann really have. And it was a question no one could answer.

As if reading the dean's thoughts, Walter spoke. "History is surely on his side."

Maxwell waved Walter to continue.

"That is to say, Mann's pictures and tapes are themselves prima facie evidence of his damnable enterprise." Walter looked imploringly at the president. "How do we know what else he has? Do we dare run the risk of public disclosure of more pictures and tapes? Do we dare that?" Walter wondered what other photos there might be of him and Dennis. He shuddered. The ones he saw were bad enough.

Images of stained clothes flew through Maxwell's mind. What about the episode with Barbara that night in the president's suite? Clad only in towels, rolling on the heavily carpeted floor of his office. Anyone with a powerful camera could have captured those scenes. And more. Richard put his head in his hands. "Imagine pictures of the governor or the chairman of the board rushing to the men's room. A kid with a camcorder could have caught it all."

Oscar's smile interrupted his own thoughts of an edited version of any one of several stories he told his children's bible study group. Little green people cavorting with baby Jesus on the fields of the holy land while a glistening silver space ship hovered over the bucolic scene. He placed his hands to his brow. "A good question, Walter. A very difficult question. Do we dare?" Oscar thought of the many others who might have been captured by Billy's camera and recorder. Jack and Wilma, Ben, Murdoch and Berlin. All those at Beverly's video show gazing and gaping at pornography. Some of the most important people in the state watching handsome young men masturbating. Could they dare bring disgrace to so many? In a quiet voice, the provost offered his fears to the group.

"Nonsense," said Patrick. "The man is bluffing." He pointed his finger at Maxwell. "And it's your duty to call his bluff." He sipped his now cold coffee. "What are we made of? To be cowed by a conniving assistant professor? I for one say off with his head. And there isn't even the question of abrogating tenure in such a case. Not even the damned union would have a leg to stand on. Let's just get rid of Mann." The dean studied the faces of the other men. He was not getting through. "Do not meet with his lawyer. Do not meet with him. Just fire him. Clean, simple, swift. That's what I'd do if I were president."

"But you aren't the president," said Maxwell. "It's my head that rolls if this thing blows up in our faces. My head," his voice rose, "my head. Not yours, Patrick, or Oscar's. Mine, because I am the president." And no little pompous bastard of a dean is going to tell me what he would do if he were running the show. I can see it now. He'd deny any responsibility when the shit hit the fan. Oh, sure, he'd be the voice of reason and moderation when the press came after me. I can hear his lilting Irish cadences now as he destroys me to the reporters. Well, that just isn't going to happen on my watch. I'm not going down because some son of a bitch has been running amok with his baby brownie.

Richard stood up and stretched. "It's been a long night, gentlemen. I think we should sleep on it now." He looked at his watch. "We'll meet again at eight sharp in my office."

"But Richard," Patrick began.

"No, Patrick," the president cut him off. "No more talk tonight. We're done for now. Tomorrow morning I'll have my decision."

Oscar knew what that decision would be. Maxwell would not dare take Billy Mann's challenge. The provost shook his head. He'd do the same thing. The risks were simply too great. And if Billy were not completely mad, his requests would be measured and, Oscar was sure, granted by the president. One viper would win, but the university would be saved. He thought of all those people who would be spared humiliation by simply yielding to Mann. Richard had no choice. He looked at Patrick who was scarlet with anger and disappointment. He had also read the future as Oscar had. Did the man have nothing to hide? Oscar could not believe Donovan was without a buried past.

The morning broke with all the glory of spring. Redbuds and magnolias were starting to bloom as Oscar walked along the central mall to the administration building. The blue sky was cloudless. The green grass still glistened from an early morning watering. The campus was coming to life. He smiled at the thought of freshly scrubbed students filing into dining rooms for breakfast, faculty members gathering their papers for the day's classes, his secretary already arranging a bouquet of flowers in his outer office. This was the world he loved. Even with the terrible decline in standards, the meager backgrounds of his students, the sniping and backstabbing of his faculty, this was still his world, this was still a university. It was now seven forty five and Oscar was happy. He did not want the aliens to come just yet. There was so much for him to do. This was still a world worthy of protection. Billy Mann was nothing in comparison to all of this. Oscar waved to Walter who waited for him by the fountain before the administration building. The sun's rays playing through the running water suggested better things to come. Richard could do nothing else. He had to yield to Billy Mann.

The commencement ceremonies were uneventful. President Maxwell's speech was brief and actually quite good. He was in an expansive mood. After all, he and the university had weathered a tumultuous year. Best of all, he had come through it all unscathed.

As he dressed for his final act of the academic year, he hummed the alma mater, hoping he would remember all the words this year. Knowing so many eyes would be on the head of the entire enterprise, he didn't want anyone thinking he didn't know every word of that dumb unmelodic song. Why in Christ they couldn't have one of the great alma maters he didn't know. He'd have to appoint a committee to come up with something as catchy at the Michigan fight song or that great Cornell tune. But that was a minor problem given the bullets he had dodged in the last few months. Not even the blacks would protest the ceremonies this year. With a promise to break ground for a new wing to the grand Riverdale mansion which would be devoted exclusively to African American studies, Maxine Jefferson had called her troops off the field of battle.

So what if he had to bestow a presidential distinguished teaching award to the newly promoted Billy Mann. Small price indeed. He recalled the trepidation he had felt when he confronted Mann on that day. What would the man ask for in return for his silence? He felt the tension in his colleagues when Billy entered the president's office. Neither Lansing nor Donovan greeted the little toad.

"Pretty nice digs, Richard," said Billy. "You know I've never been in your hallowed office before." He poured a cup of coffee and sat on the corner of the president's large desk. Noticing no ash tray in the room, Billy lit a cigarette. "Don't mind if I smoke, do you, Dickie." He nodded as the president took an ash tray from a desk drawer. Maxwell colored slightly, but said nothing in the face of Billy's Dickie. That he wanted to kill him showed not at all on his closely shaved handsome face.

"Why don't you take a more comfortable seat," Richard said, gesturing to one of the heavily cushioned chairs. The president's voice was steady, his tone amiable.

Billy was impressed. He had expected anger and recrimination from Maxwell. "No thanks," he said, "this won't take long." He blew smoke in the direction of the two silent administrators.

The deal was struck in less than fifteen minutes. Billy was granted immunity from any prosecution. He didn't know that the president had already closed the case. No need to bring in the state police or the governor's people, Richard had told Lansing and Donovan earlier that morning. Maxwell agreed to grant tenure and promotion to Billy and wipe Abraham's slate clean in the process. But, Billy had insisted, no tenure or promotion for honest Abe. Richard recalled how difficult it had been to control his anger when Mann spoke about Smith. "No," he had said, "Abraham will have to get his tenure and promotion the old fashioned way. He'll have to earn it." And it was over, except for Mann's final demand.

"A presidential award for distinguished teaching?" Patrick asked.

"There is no such award at this university," said Oscar.

"Well," Billy smiled, "there sure as hell is one now. And newly promoted Associate Professor William Mann will be its first recipient." He placed his hand on Richard's shoulder. "And I expect a nice little speech from you when you bestow it on me." He thought better about invoking Dickie yet again. Looking at the provost and the dean, Billy said, "aren't you two going to congratulate me? It's not every day a new award is born." Billy's laugh ricocheted through the still office.

Only Billy was aware of his erection. Now, this is one great aphrodisiac, he thought as he left the administration building. Sally doesn't know the ride she's going to have for dessert tonight He touched his crotch.

Richard grimaced at his reflection in the mirror. "Little prick," he said out loud. Standing back, he made a final check of his attire. Looks pretty good if I say so myself. The confident smile returned to his face. His only disappointment at the moment was that his academic gown would conceal the new Armani suit. At least they'll all see it at the reception.

Maxwell's new suit was not the only one in town that day. Sally and Billy had shopped carefully for his graduation clothes. Something understated and sincere, Billy had suggested to the salesman at the town's finest men's store. Something that'll convey stature and grace at the same time. They had settled on a charcoal single breasted with a barely visible fine muted pin stripe. "Perfecto," said Sally as she watched Billy who stood on a raised platform while a tailor made chalk lines and inserted pins into the expensive fabric.

There were no new clothes for Abraham that commencement, but there was palpable relief in the Smith household on the morning of the graduation exercises. No award for him, no tenure or promotion, but his job was secure.

"No thanks to him," said Eleanor as she cleared the breakfast dishes. "I think you better get your priorities straight, Ab. It was disgusting the way you carried on about Billy last night. You'd think he was some kind of saint the way you spoke."

Abraham said nothing. They'd had enough quarreling upon their return home from the Williams' dinner party.

For all his ironic sniping at the academy, Jack Williams loved the pomp and circumstance attendant to it. Another example, Wilma told her guests, of just how old fashioned her husband really was.

Every year on graduation eve, Jack hosted a dinner party for his special friends. "And tomorrow morning," Wilma smiled, "he throws a big breakfast for his students before they head off to the ceremonies." She ruffled his hair. "The only requirement is that they show up in their caps and gowns. I really look forward to it. I've never been to one before, you know. Wouldn't you love to see old Professor Williams flipping pancakes for all those kids?"

The living room offered a far different scene from the last time departmental colleagues had gathered there. No fisticuffs this evening, no quarreling about curriculum revision, no Berlin or Murdoch to contend with. Only good friends and good cheer, and, of course, talk of Billy Mann's coup. "How can we avoid talking about him?" Helen asked in the midst of hoisted glasses and end-of-the year toasts.

"Must we really?" asked Ben. "Bad enough we're losing you. Your leaving our happy little department could have put a damper on Jack and Wilma's party if you weren't going to a new job." He raised his glass to her. "But to even think of that miserable creature raises my blood pressure. Only the good Lord knows what life with him will be like next year. Associate Professor Mann indeed." Ben grimaced.

"Don't forget the teaching award," said Jack.

"But that's a big secret until the graduation ceremonies." Wilma offered a mock scolding.

Jack waved down Wilma's interruption. "I know, I know. It's supposed to be a surprise announcement. But, Wilma, honey, everyone knows about it. I'm surprised Billy didn't put up a billboard."

Abraham colored at the mention of his former accomplice. "Don't forget he saved my hide," he said softly.

"An act of pure goodness." Eleanor's voice dripped venom. "The man certainly should be canonized." Her look at Ab was clear. Don't mention your gratitude again or I'll slug you.

Walter and Maggie had arrived late. Everyone noticed them holding hands when they entered the room. He, too, was strangely in Billy's debt. The young man's bluff had spared Walter from the wider public humiliation he had feared for so long. With Maggie's folks in town for the commencement, Walter had been sure John would have the evidence he had craved for so long. Here would be the proof that Maggie had made a horrible choice when she married the professor. But that crushing scene would not occur.

Newly elected to the alumni board of directors of the upstate rivals, John would be on campus for more occasions than the annual football game. He would surely come to town on each of those trips. Under the best of circumstances, a visit from his in-laws was something to dread. Now the worst of circumstances were to be avoided. Thank God for small favors, he had said to Maggie after Oscar Lansing's phone call. Tenure and promotion were infinitely preferable to what might have happened.

"Welcome," Wilma greeted the Henrys. "Isn't it wonderful to have survived another academic year." She hugged Maggie.

"And I've broken out the good stuff for our distinguished chair," said Jack as he embraced them both. 'None of that lousy bourbon for our real friends. Save that rotgut for . . . " Wilma's look stopped him in mid-sentence. "Anyway," Jack continued, "we're delighted you could make it tonight."

And so the guests moved to the candle-lit dining room where the evening progressed comfortably in a spirit of good fellowship. Laughter greeted pleasant, uncomplicated anecdotes of the past year. More toasts were offered to everyone at the table. The shared feeling was one of a family, which, for the moment, was light years away from the fractious world of their professional department.

Only Abraham's insistent need to defend Billy Mann sporadically brought the group down from its communal high spirits.

"Let's make a deal," said Jack, holding his glass at eye level. "You don't mention him again and I won't read aloud Murdoch's newest article."

"Now, that would be a show stopper, if I ever heard one," said Maggie.

"Or a super soporific," added Ben.

The point was made and Abraham smiled.

"I'm glad you haven't forgotten how to do that, Ab," said Helen. She leaned across the table and kissed him on the cheek. "You know I'm going to really miss you. So lighten up and let me shuffle out of here with a memory of your smiling face."

Abraham was suddenly overcome. His voice shook as he proposed a toast to good friends he wasn't worthy of having.

Moved by the younger man's sincerity and fearing a maudlin speech which he loathed, Jack stood up and led his guests in a raucous rendition of *He's a Jolly Good Fellow.* He moved from the head of the table to a place just behind Abraham's chair. At the final chords of the song, he grasped Ab's shoulders, bent down, and kissed him on the top of his head. "Now, not another word. You have friends because you deserve them. Get it. Because you deserve them. Just the way you deserve that great wife of yours." He moved to Eleanor's place, and planted kisses on her cheeks. He whispered in her ear. "I think he needs to get laid." They both laughed.

She whispered back. "The poor guy hasn't been able to relax since this horrible thing began."

"Don't worry, sweetie. Lifting of burdens can do wonders. Trust me, it'll be clear sailing for him from now on. I can't think of a better aphrodisiac than a life free of entanglements with Billy Mann."

Eleanor returned Jack's kisses. Her eyes were filled with tears of gratitude.

"And what are you two plotting?" asked Joyce Rosenthal. "She's far too young for an old buck like you."

"And what am I?" asked Wilma. "An old crone?" She stood up and hugged Jack. "This guy is younger than most of his students."

Hoots and catcalls greeted Jack's reddening face.

"Well, that's something I never thought I'd see," said Walter. "Jack Williams blushing? An oxymoron if I ever saw one."

Everyone cheered when Jack and Wilma kissed.

Commencement now a memory, the summer of faculty discontent set in. The unrealized hopes and dreams of another year transformed themselves into regretful sighs of disappointment. Books unfinished or unpublished, classes that fell far short of the professors' anticipation during the opening weeks of each semester, the tedium of lives and marriages. Now, the long summer loomed as a challenge to slow flowing creative juices. More than gardens would have to be tended if the fall semester were to be greeted with optimism. Warm weather cocktail parties and barbecues notwithstanding, batteries had to be recharged lest discontent become despair. These were the months to work on manuscripts even if the scholarly ground seemed fallow. A time to create new courses rather than simply rehearse the stuff of former ones. New course descriptions for old courses wouldn't do. Self doubt and recriminations became the bitter cocktails imbibed by solitary scholars sitting alone on their sun-drenched patios.

But, as always, there were exceptions.

Billy Mann enjoyed a splendid summer holiday. His book could now take as long as necessary. And the dedication to Mitchell Murdoch was no longer a consideration. The dedication of the second edition would now be the same as in the first. Billy enjoyed contemplating that dedication, even if he hadn't yet settled on the wording.

Richard Maxwell hadn't received the great offer from a powerful university, but he considered himself more firmly in charge than ever before at his university. He had beaten back barbarians at every encounter. His resume unblemished, he was a man of continuing confidence. The great offer would one day be his. And he was eternally ready. The press conference was scripted, the attire planned, the smile selected.

Some others strengthened marriages, enhanced professional reputations, enjoyed life.

A world within a world, the campus would once again survive the long recess.

The more prudent among the community carried umbrellas on the most blissful of summer days.

For a decade, Richard LevineI was Chair of the English Department at the State University of New York at Stony Brook before moving to Santa Fe. He had previously taught at Miami University and the University of California. Levine is the author and editor of five books on Victorian literature, including a critical study of the novels of Benjamin Disraeli. This is his first novel.

www.ingramcontent.com/pod-product-compliance
Lightning Source LLC
Chambersburg PA
CBHW011737010726
47496CB00010B/2982